D1474182

THE
OBSERVER
EFFECT

BOOKS BY NICK JONES

THE JOSEPH BRIDGEMAN SERIES

And Then She Vanished
Shadows of London
The Observer Effect

THE OBSERVER EFFECT

NICK JONES

BLACK STONE
PUBLISHING

Copyright © 2022 by Nick Jones
Published in 2022 by Blackstone Publishing
Cover design by Bookfly Design
Book design by Blackstone Publishing

Printed in the United States of America

First edition: 2022
ISBN 978-1-6650-4833-0
Fiction / Science Fiction / Time Travel

Version 2

CIP data for this book is available
from the Library of Congress

Blackstone Publishing
31 Mistletoe Rd.
Ashland, OR 97520

www.BlackstonePublishing.com

PROLOGUE

April 12, 1567
MACAU
<small>TRADING HUB BETWEEN CHINA AND THE WEST</small>

The woman takes refuge beneath the branches of a camphor tree, a welcome relief from the searing midday sun. She raises a spyglass to her eye. On the back of her right hand, near the base of the thumb, there's a birthmark in the shape of a star. Adjusting the eyepiece, she focuses on the marketplace in the valley below. The streets are packed with people carrying flagons of wine, rolls of colored silks, and baskets of fruit. Gangs of children tumble and play, acting out sword fights with sticks. Her attention is drawn to a barefoot young man pushing a barrow loaded with wooden boxes. She watches him navigate the labyrinth of winding streets until he reaches the broad harbor where a magnificent galleon, the *Victoria*, is moored, due to set sail at 1 p.m.

There are stacks of boxes and containers on the quay, and tiny figures carry the last of them in carts up the gangplank and down into the *Victoria*'s hold. Farther out to sea, a great Portuguese carrack cuts through the waves like a giant sea monster, heading for Lisbon with its cargo.

Bringing her focus back to the crowded marketplace, the woman methodically sweeps her gaze across the square as tension mounts in her chest. Checking her watch, she tuts impatiently. Where is he? Taking the spyglass away, she squints into the distance, and that's when she finally spots him near the church of Santo Antonio. He stands out, with his tall frame, pale skin, and white-blond hair. Nils Petersen. Lifting the glass to her eye again, she focuses in. He's talking to a sailor, a bald man with dark, weather-beaten skin and arms covered in tattoos. She can't hear their conversation—they must be at least a thousand yards away—but Nils is gesticulating energetically, and the sailor is nodding.

She checks her watch. It's 12:45 p.m. "OK, Nils, time to go," she mutters. Tucking her spyglass into the leather satchel slung across her body, she picks up her skirts and carefully descends the rocky slope toward the town. Everything has gone perfectly so far. She doesn't want any mishaps now.

As she approaches the square, the smell of spice hits her nostrils, tempered by the foul stench of the leather tannery a few streets away. She pauses beneath a row of fig trees, covers her face with a scarf until only her eyes are visible, then waits in the shade, holding the satchel tightly against her side. Nils Petersen appears, working his way through the crowd with a determined expression. He passes her, walks across the bustling square, and slips into a quiet, narrow alleyway that leads to the harbor. She follows him, keeping her distance, the sea breeze a welcome change from the dry heat up in the hills. Ahead, two Jesuit priests dressed in long black robes, heavy crucifixes hanging against their chests, block Nils's path. Their full beards disguise their faces, and it's almost impossible to tell one from the other, although one has a slightly heavier build.

Ducking behind a stack of baskets, the woman watches. She can't hear what's being said, but the voices are stern and angry. The stockier priest grabs Nils's arm and punches him, and his legs give way. The other priest pulls a sack out from under his robe and tugs it over Nils's head. Nils puts up a fierce fight, but he's no match for the two men. He doubles over as one of them knees him viciously in the stomach. The heavyset priest kicks open a low door in the wooden shack just behind him, then he and his companion bundle Nils through it and slam it shut behind them.

The woman waits, her heart beating loudly in her ears. After a couple of minutes, the priests emerge, pull the door roughly shut behind them, and walk off down the street. One of them dabs at his bloody nose with a white kerchief. It seems Nils put up a decent fight—good for him. The church bell strikes 1 p.m., and the woman stands up, brushes dust off her skirts, then makes her way across the square into the alleyway and pushes through the wooden door.

The room is dark and after the harsh midday sun, it takes a few seconds for her sight to adjust. Even through her scarf, she can smell the foul stench of rotten fish. A tumble of old fishing nets is heaped on the floor beside her, and coils of rope hang loosely from rusted hooks along the wall. Shafts of sunlight from holes in the roof cut through the swirling dust and throw patches of light on the scuffed earthen tiles, and she sees Nils slumped on the floor in the far corner, his legs bound and his hands fastened to a metal ring in the wall. His clothes are stained with mud, sand, and patches of blood, and he's been gagged with a dirty piece of cloth. She adjusts her scarf, ensuring that Nils won't be able to distinguish her features, and approaches him. He looks up at her, his face beaded in sweat, hair slick against his forehead.

"Where is your watch?" she asks him.

He tries to speak, but only anxious grunts come out.

"Show me."

He stares at her in mutinous silence. She shakes her head. "You're just slowing things down unnecessarily," she admonishes him. She scans the room, then walks over to a pockmarked wooden bench beneath a small shuttered window. Nils's watch lies faceup on a navy silk cloth. She examines it appreciatively. She hasn't seen one like this before. Its face is nothing special, but its body is fashioned from copper and decorated with engravings of strange, otherworldly creatures and strings of runes, which flicker and gleam as she swings the timepiece this way and that in the half-light.

Nils tries to speak again, this time more urgently. Placing the watch back down on the bench, she walks over to him and removes the gag. He spits pieces of thread, coughing as he speaks.

"Who— Who are you?" he gasps. "What do you want with my watch? Untie me!" He struggles violently to free himself from his bonds. "I must get to the *Victoria* before she sails! What time is it?"

She checks the watch again. "Ten past one."

His face crumples as he leans his head against the wall. "It's too late." He nods at the watch. "Take it if you want. It's a worthless trinket."

"You and I both know that's not true, Nils. And if I did take it, it wouldn't stay with me for long, would it?"

She senses his confusion, as well as his curiosity. "Who the hell are you?" he says again.

She regards him impassively. "I thought like you once, before I saw the truth, then I realized there was another way."

"What are you talking about?"

"Things are rarely what they seem." She leans in, and even though her face is covered, her eyes betray a hidden smile. "You've failed your mission, but I'm here to give you a second chance."

PART 1

1

To call it "running" would be a stretch. I'm lurching and weaving past shoppers, haring down Montpellier hill like a maniac. Lack of sleep and my current fitness level leave my head feeling as though someone's buried an ax in the top of my skull, and the pain is making it hard to see. As I reach the Promenade, a wide tree-lined pedestrian street through the center of Cheltenham, my phone starts playing "Should I Stay or Should I Go" by the Clash.

I answer the call, trying not to lose momentum. "Vinny!"

"Yo, Cash," he says. "You there yet?"

"Nearly. I'm running a bit late."

"Considering . . . everything, your timekeeping is rubbish," he chuckles.

"It would help if I could sleep," I say, panting as I cross the street.

"That viewing again?"

"Same one. Three nights in a row now. It stopped in exactly the same place, with Scarlett telling the other traveler that she's giving him *another chance.*"

Scarlett's a time traveler. I caught her planting a radio in my shop, a focus object that bonded me to a dangerous mission in 1960s London. Vinny came with me on one of the jumps. Although he got badly injured, it hasn't dampened his enthusiasm for time travel, and he's one of the only people who knows about my travels.

Vinny harrumphs. "If you ask me, after what Scarlett did to you, I doubt she's trying to help that other guy."

"I'm sure you're right," I say, dodging a lamppost and crossing the street at a jog. "I just wish I knew why I'm seeing this."

"Have you heard from Iris yet?"

"Nothing."

Right after I completed the London mission, my sister, Amy, sent me a letter from the future, telling me that a woman called Iris Mendell would be in touch to explain what had happened and why. It's been two months and there's been no contact. Nothing. I've been wondering if this Iris person has forgotten about me, and maybe my time traveling days are over. I'm not sure how I feel about that.

"Maybe Amy was wrong," Vinny says.

"Maybe." I don't even have conclusive proof that the letter from Amy was genuine, and I haven't asked her about it because the letter told me not to, which is a bit of a catch-22 and drives me mad when I think about it too much.

"So what are you going to do?" Vinny asks.

"There's not much I can do but wait. It seems odd though, nothing for ages and then this viewing . . . I've had it every night for a few days now. It feels like the world has shifted a bit, like something is about to happen."

Turning into Ambrose Street, I see the Different Corner bookshop just a few doors away. In the window is a poster, which reads: "Book Launch Today—11 a.m." Below the text is a photo of a book and two grinning people. One of them is Alexia Finch.

Alexia is a hypnotherapist who helped me travel back in time to save Amy, and we started to fall in love. When I got back, though, everything had changed, and Alexia didn't remember our relationship anymore. What she actually remembered was a doomed fling with my alter ego, Other Joe, the version of me who was making his way very successfully through life until I saved Amy and replaced him. (I still get flashes of guilt.) I discovered through a viewing that Other Joe had behaved like an idiot and hurt Alexia, and now I'm having to deal with the fallout.

I sent Alexia a heart-on-my-sleeve message a couple of months ago, trying to explain that I've changed, but I haven't heard back. Then, Vinny spotted the poster for this book launch last week and told me about it. So now, I just want to say my piece to her face. If it doesn't work, I'll let it go.

"I'm here now, Vin. Better go."

"Good luck. Tell her how you feel. Be honest and vulnerable. Maybe even cry. Women love that, apparently. I read it in a magazine. Right; time for my celery juice."

I'm not sure I heard that right. "Celery juice?"

"As if." He's still laughing when he hangs up.

The shop window is thronging with people. I wonder briefly if this is a bad idea and nearly turn on my heel, but a young couple coming out of the shop holds the door for me. It's the nudge I need. "Thank you," I say and push my way through into the cozy interior.

I like the place immediately. Someone with obvious taste designed it to feel friendly and welcoming. The external walls are stacked with books on simple white shelves, and small tables here and there are loaded with piles of paperbacks. To the right of the front door is a small café, responsible for the enticing aroma of good coffee and homemade cakes.

At the back of the shop, a podium is surrounded by people, and a very tall, robust man speaks into a microphone. I recognize him as Alexia's coauthor from the poster. Pushing a little nearer to the crowd, I accept a glass of sparkling wine from a jovial man in red trousers and tune in to the speaker. He keeps pulling back from the microphone because his voice is so powerful, a deep basso softened only slightly by a friendly Canadian twang.

"Oftentimes, people think that when they love someone, the other person makes them feel that way," he says. "Am I right?" There's a murmur of confirmation from the crowd, and a few helpful people exchange thoughtful glances. "Actually, I'm wrong," he says, beaming his lighthouse smile. "Love is not a *choice*. Passion is not a *choice*. Our feelings of love and passion come from in here." He thuds his fist against his chest, and it sounds like a barrel. "The trick is to find someone who enables you to feel love, to find something you're passionate about. And there is no limit to how much love you can feel. If you stay open to it, your heart just gets bigger and bigger. Circumstances change, people change, but love just grows."

The audience breaks into an appreciative round of applause, and the huge man steps down from the podium. I crane my neck to spot Alexia, wondering if she's up next, but there's no sign of her. I scan the room but get distracted by a red-haired woman sitting in the café. She's dressed entirely in black—that deep black you only get from really expensive gear—and her long, wavy copper hair lies loosely over her shoulders. She's wearing huge sunglasses, despite the fact that we're indoors on a gray March day. They suit her, though. I realize I'm staring, but before I can turn away, Rock Chick pushes her buggy glasses down her nose and eyeballs me, flashing me a bold grin and neon-bright teeth.

I have to say, I'm getting used to this. It's been three months since I landed back into Other Joe's life, but I didn't inherit any of his memories. So to cover for this, Amy and I decided to tell everyone I'd hit my head in a bike accident and developed amnesia. Other Joe was a big part of Cheltenham's social scene, with his fingers in lots of pies, so I've had plenty of practice at deciding in a split second whether someone knew him, and whether they liked him or not. He was also a bit of a player and left a trail of broken hearts across town, so I've had more than my fair share of women shooting daggers at me too.

I wave hesitantly at Rock Chick, disinclined to initiate a conversation but also not wanting to appear rude. I decide she's not likely to be an old squeeze of Other Joe's because she looks too happy. A work contact? She winks, then pushes her glasses back onto her nose and begins to scroll through her phone. I'm relieved.

I'm just heading back toward my red-trousered friend for another glass of courage when a loud voice from behind startles me.

"What are you doing here, Bridgeman?" I'm assaulted by the sickly smell of oversweet citrus and turn to see Gordon, Alexia's boyfriend, regarding me with distaste. He's taller than me and good-looking—I suppose, if you like that sort of thing—but his too-tight curls and expressionless face are unsettling. He looks like an android. "Shouldn't you be at work?"

"Shouldn't you be at charm school?" I reply, without thinking.

He sneers at me. "Seriously, what are you doing here?"

He steps forward and stands way too close for comfort. It feels as though tiny bitter lemons are invading my nostrils. I stifle a sneeze. "Seems you're struggling to find an answer," he says. "Let me tell you why *I'm* here. I'm here to support my girlfriend's book launch." He waits for a response. I say nothing. "By the way, did you hear? She's got an office in the building where I work now, right next to mine. Obviously makes it easier to manage our lives; now we can share the commute. She's so much happier, you know?"

Silently, I curse Other Joe again for messing things up. When I landed back in his life and discovered his relationship with Alexia, I also found out that he had been her landlord, but he'd sold her office building to a hotel company and served notice to all the residents. Desperate for Alexia not to leave Cheltenham, I canceled the hotel deal at substantial cost and embarrassment to Bridgeman Commercial Properties, but she moved out anyway. Gordon saw his chance and moved in on her. I curl my lip and shake my head. I can't help it.

Gordon flexes his jaw and puffs out his chest. "Today's a big deal for Alexia. Let's all be grown-ups about this, OK?"

"You can try."

"Don't spoil this for her, Bridgeman," he says condescendingly, as though I'm a naughty child.

Fury starts to build inside my chest, but before I can formulate a suitable put-down, Gordon's attention flicks to someone in the crowd. "Ah, there's Alexia's father," he says smugly. I follow his gaze, but I can't tell who he's looking at. "I don't suppose you've met him. He's an excellent chess player. I must go and say hello. Will you excuse me?" He straightens his tie, then saunters off into the crowd.

"Smarmy arsehole," I mutter under my breath. I spot the time on a large retro orange clock on the wall and note with a jolt that I have to leave in twenty minutes. It's Dad's birthday party tomorrow—we're having a big bash at a posh restaurant in town—and I'm meeting Mum and Amy there at 1 p.m. for the rehearsal. When I told Vinny about it, he was incredulous: "Whoever has a rehearsal for a *birthday party*?" Well, that's my mother for you. Nothing left to chance.

First, though, I need to find Alexia. I notice a line of people snaking around the side of the shop and disappearing behind a tall bank of shelving crowded with plants. Peering around the edge of the shelving unit, I see her sitting at a low table stacked with copies of her book, looking tired but happy. She's wearing a dark-green silky jumpsuit, silver hoop earrings, and her hair in a ponytail. She has a pen in her hand, and she's making small talk with the customers. I decide my best course of action is to wait in line, so I join the back of the queue, watching people proudly walk past me, signed books in their hands.

Finally, it's my turn. The shop disappears, and it's just me and the love of my life.

"Hi, Alexia."

She shows a flicker of surprise as she recognizes me, then recovers her composure. "Hello, Joe," she says. "I didn't expect to see you here."

"I saw the poster in the window the other day. I think it's brilliant you've written a book. Congratulations."

She flicks a glance across the store toward Gordon. "Thanks."

"It's OK. He knows I'm here. We've . . . chatted." I pause, almost losing my nerve, but then decide just to go for it. "Do you have a couple of minutes?"

"People are waiting in line to see me. Does it have to be now?"

Back in January, I had a viewing of Other Joe and Alexia in conversation at a friend's wedding. They'd been seeing each other for a while, but things had become awkward. It seemed clear that Other Joe was playing away from home, and Alexia, visibly upset, finished things with him. After the viewing, I sent Alexia a message, saying how sorry I was for being an idiot, asking if we could talk, but she never replied.

"I won't take up much of your time. I just need to know, did you ever get my message? About what I said at the wedding?"

Her face falls. "I did. But I don't think this is the time or the place, Joe."

"I was hoping to hear back from you."

"What did you expect me to say?"

Now that she asks me, I don't really know. Was I really expecting Alexia to throw herself into my arms with a simple, "I forgive you, you're the love of my life, and can we pick up where we left off please?" I fix my gaze on her left shoulder, face flaming with embarrassment.

She says, "Anyway, I thought you couldn't remember anything?"

"I'm getting treatment," I lie. "Some of my memories are coming back now."

"That's convenient."

"I just hoped you'd give me a chance to explain. I messed up at that wedding. I acted like an imbecile. I want to tell you now what I should have told you then."

"Joe, it doesn't matter anymore. I'm with Gordon now."

"Are you though? Really?"

She looks affronted. "What does that mean?"

"Just hear me out, please?" I remind myself that I must play the part of Other Joe here and remember the history he shared with Alexia. I channel him and apologize on his behalf. "You and I had something good going on. So good, I couldn't handle it. I didn't appreciate how unbelievably lucky I was to be with you. I acted like a child, messing around with other people. Pointless, stupid behavior." I draw in a breath. "I've learned a lot since then."

She leans toward me and lowers her voice. "Don't pretend to be the man you think I want. You won't be able to keep it up. I'm not interested in a relationship with anybody who can't be honest with himself." She sits back up and scans the line behind me. "Anyway, thanks for coming!" She dismisses me loudly with fake brightness. "I think you'd better go. Looks like your friend is trying to get your attention."

"What friend?"

"Over by the door."

I turn around and see the red-haired Rock Chick waving at me from the front of the shop. Oh God, has she decided she wants to speak to me now? "She's not my friend. I have no idea who she is."

"Really? She certainly seems to know who *you* are. Perhaps you've conveniently forgotten?"

I can feel Alexia slipping away. I play my last card. "I wanted to give this back to you." I pull her butterfly earring, the one that triggered the viewing of the wedding, out of my pocket and place it on the table between us. "You dropped it at Andy's wedding," I say. "I kept it for you."

"Thanks, but I don't want it anymore. I threw the other one out."

I was hoping she might be more pleased. "I probably should've given it back to you sooner. Sorry."

"It's fine. They weren't expensive, just costume jewelry." She looks at me, her smoky blue eyes steady. "Worthless, really. See you around, Joe." She pastes on a smile and beckons forward the couple behind me.

That's that, then.

As I weave my way through the crowd, someone taps me gently on the shoulder. I turn, expecting to see the red-haired woman who just ruined my conversation with Alexia, but instead, I come face-to-face with a man's chest. I tip my head back to see his face. It's Alexia's coauthor.

"Colin John," he says, his voice even deeper than it was through the amplifier. He holds out his hand, and it completely dwarfs mine.

As a rule, I don't trust anyone with two first names, but he is a huge bundle of kindness, I can feel it. "Joseph Bridgeman," I say. "Good to meet you."

He beams down from his great height. "I saw you with Alexia."

"Right," I say. "I . . . er . . . used to be her landlord."

"Uh-huh. I know."

This guy is a relationship guru, so I steel myself for some not-too-subtle coaching, but he doesn't say anything else. He just watches me. I feel uncomfortably hyperobserved. My need to fill the void becomes overwhelming.

"So . . . you guys wrote a book. That's impressive."

"It had to be done," he says confidently.

"Why?"

"I kept coming across people who were stuck, and then I met Alexia at a conference, and we got talking about how we might be able to help. We both wanted to do something bigger. Reach more people."

I want to take part in this conversation in a meaningful way. "I thought it was interesting what you said about love, that we don't get it from other people."

"It's true, Joe, isn't it?" He leans forward, really eyeballing me. It doesn't feel intrusive, though; it feels like connection. "The trick is finding someone who enables *you* to feel love. It comes from within you, do you understand?" he asks kindly, checking that he's explained properly. I sense empathy, like he really wants to help me see another angle.

The feeling of love comes from inside.

"I think I do know what you mean, actually."

Colin John winks, smacks me on the shoulder, and laughs like a mountain. "Good luck, Joseph Bridgeman," he says. "I hope to see you again sometime."

"Likewise. Thanks."

He holds open the door, and I step out into the brisk spring air.

I walk back along Ambrose Street, and as I turn the corner, I nearly walk straight into the red-haired woman. She's leaning against the wall, smoking.

"Jesus, Bridgeman, you sure took your time." Her American accent is strong, unexpected. "This country! I'm freakin' frozen!" She throws her cigarette to the ground, stubs it out with a black stiletto boot, and holds out her hand. "Gabrielle Green, temporarily at your service. I'm here to take you to meet Iris Mendell."

2

I *knew* something was going to happen today, but I wasn't expecting this. Amy's letter said Iris would be getting in touch with me, but she didn't mention anyone called Gabrielle. Still, I take the woman's hand and am shocked by the power of her grip. She shakes my hand once, hard, then sort of flings my arm back toward me, like she's accidentally picked up something unpleasant. I look her up and down. "Why didn't Iris come herself?"

"She's a busy woman, and you're hardly top of the list. Let's go." She walks off down the street.

I think about what Scarlett did to me—planting that radio in my shop—and my gut contracts. I call after Gabrielle. "Have you got any ID, anything to prove that you are who you say you are?"

She stops and spins around, hands on her hips. "No, I don't have any ID! Listen, Bridgeman, if you wanna see Iris, now's your chance. Come, don't come, it's no skin off my nose." My head spins. I don't know if I can trust this woman, but at least she's not creeping around like Scarlett did—she's yelling at me in a street full of shoppers. Gabrielle Green lifts her sunglasses onto the top of her head and checks her pocket watch. It's a similar timepiece to mine, except hers is a gold-plated half hunter stitched into a thick rawhide leather strap on her wrist, steampunk-style. It suits her. "You have ten seconds to make up your mind."

What do I do? I've been waiting for someone to explain what happened in London. I want to know why Scarlett planted the radio in my shop and I want to know why I'm getting viewings of her again all of a sudden, with this new time-traveler guy. Plus I need to understand why W. P. Brown—Bill, the man who blackmailed me into a potentially lethal time-travel mission—gave his life to save mine. This might be my only chance to find out. Mum and Amy are going to be upset if I miss the party rehearsal, but I'll be back for the main event tomorrow. Hopefully.

"I'll come," I say, pulling out my phone. "I just need to send a text."

Gabrielle lights up a cigarette and sucks in a lungful of smoke. "Make it quick."

I send Mum and Amy the same message, telling them something urgent has come up, apologizing and promising to be at the party on time tomorrow. The second I press send, Gabrielle stalks off down the street again. People instinctively get out of her way.

"Where are we going?" I ask, trying to keep up with her. She ignores me. My mobile phone vibrates and Amy's grinning face appears on the screen. I don't pick up.

"One of your little friends wondering where you are?" Gabrielle scoffs.

I don't take the bait. There's so much I want to know, but the idea of opening up the conversation with her makes me nervous, like shoving my hand into a bag of snakes. I venture a question anyway. "Can I just ask—"

"Let me stop you there." She holds up her left hand like she's swearing on the Bible.

"I haven't really started."

"No, but you're about to. You're gonna have a ton of super annoying questions about everything that's happened recently in your lonely little life. So let's get a couple of things straight. First of all, there's some stuff that Iris wants to tell you herself. And that includes the Romano mission. It's off the table. Got it?"

"Er . . ."

"Second of all, I'm not here to answer your dumb questions. I'm just here to take you to see Iris. End of story."

"Have I upset you in some way?" I ask. She doesn't respond. I decide to give up and hope Iris is more forthcoming. We route march our way up

Montpellier Street, past Imperial Gardens, and it's only when we finally get to the top of the road and Gabrielle heads for the entrance to the Broadway Hotel that I realize where we're going.

"We're meeting Iris *here*?" I ask, astounded. "In this hotel? She's in *Cheltenham*?"

"What did you expect? A private jet?" Gabrielle greets the doorman, winking at him lasciviously. "Yo, Brian. How's it hangin'?"

"It's hanging beautifully, thank you, madam," he replies with a straight face. "I hope your meeting goes well."

Gabrielle leads the way into the foyer. A crystal chandelier is suspended in the center, modern artwork in minimalist frames hang at judicious intervals around the walls, and the air smells of money. I follow her meekly across the black-and-white tiled marble floor to the ornate wooden reception desk. I've never actually been inside this place. I've always felt too lowly.

"Afternoon, Ms. Green," the receptionist says. "Your meeting room is all set up."

"Thank you so much," Gabrielle says sweetly. "Appreciate it." She graciously accepts a key card, then leads me back across the foyer, through a seating area with a display of Victorian tea plates on the wall, and into a long wide hallway laid with navy-blue carpet.

I'm finally going to meet Iris Mendell, and it's going to be in a meeting room in Cheltenham? Is she going to show me a PowerPoint about time travel?

At the end of the corridor, we reach a set of cream-colored double doors. Gabrielle slides the key into the lock and pushes the doors ajar. The lights click on. I follow her into a sizable meeting room with a high ceiling and a row of arched windows looking out onto the street. The doors click shut behind us. Gabrielle flicks a switch, and the blinds on the far windows lower themselves, buzzing quietly.

The tables have all been pushed to the sides of the room. Gabrielle unfastens the leather strap from her wrist, and I get a better look at her watch. I was right. The timepiece itself is similar to mine, an antique pocket watch, but Gabrielle's is a jarring mix of contemporary and classical, especially worn like this on her wrist. The fascia is mid-gray with rose-gold numerals. Beneath that, the skeleton mechanism is visible through a central aperture, its numerous jewels glinting beneath the overhead lights.

She turns the watch over and places it facedown on the floor in the center of the room, positions three chairs in a triangle around it, then takes a seat on one of them, facing away from me. I notice the rear casing of the watch, accessible via a stitched circular flap in the watch strap, is engraved with wording, but I can't make out the details.

For a second, nothing happens. Then, the back of the watch rises up and blooms like an orchid, delicate metallic-silver petals unfurling, and a flurry of small green lights fly out of it. They hover a foot or so above the floor as though finding their bearings, then drift out like fireflies before attaching themselves to the corners of the room. They flash, slowly at first, getting gradually faster, until they're going so fast the light is solid again. Then, the silver orchid whirs into a spin, its petals glowing softly, transmitting lambent cones of turquoise light that travel across the room and over our bodies with a vibrating hum.

After a moment of absolute silence and stillness, a faint red glow appears in the center of the room, pulsating like a ghostly heart. With each beat, the light gets stronger, and within a few seconds, it takes the shape of a human being. Steadily, the figure becomes brighter and more solid, until a woman is standing in front of me. Tall and elegant, she has pale skin, high cheekbones, and a defined jawline. Her bottle-green dress hangs loosely over her slender frame, and a simple string of pearls adorns her throat. I've seen her before, when I had the viewing of Bill by a loch. She was wrapped in furs, but I know it's her. I never forget a face.

"Hello, Joseph," she says. "I'm Iris Mendell."

"Hello, Iris," I say. I know she's only a hologram because I've just witnessed her likeness being generated right in front of me, but my goodness, the clarity! I feel like I could reach out and touch her.

"Hey, boss," Gabrielle says cheerfully, leaning back and crossing her arms.

"Gabrielle. It's good to see you. Thank you for coming all this way and bringing Joseph to see me." Iris's voice is low and measured, with a hint of an accent—German maybe?

"No problem. It was my pleasure," Gabrielle says.

Iris focuses her attention back on me. "Forgive me for not shaking your hand. As I am sure Gabrielle explained, I am not actually in the room with you, so I cannot interact physically."

I glance at Gabrielle, annoyed that she didn't prepare me better. She winks at me, seemingly enjoying herself. I turn back to Iris and can't help staring. Her subtle luminescence gives away the fact that she's a projection, yet she looks so real, totally solid. Her feet are positioned perfectly on the floor, and the way the shadows fall across her face is consistent with the light sources around us. She may not physically be here, but in all the ways that matter, she's in the room.

A cascade of questions tumbles around my head, but I begin with the simplest one. "If you're not really here, then where are you, exactly?"

"I'm in Scotland. And compared to you, I'm in the future. The date here is June 17, 2131."

I stifle a laugh. "I'm sorry, did you say 2131?"

"Correct, 2131."

"And we're having a conversation across time, live?"

"Indeed," Iris says. "I know it's a lot to take in."

I do some very rough mental calculations. In her time, I am well and truly dead. My brain teeters on the edge of a mind-blowing realization. If Iris is in the future, doesn't that mean the present that I thought was happening right now, defining itself second by second as I breathe in and out, is actually the *past*? Suddenly, the handrails I've been holding onto my whole life seem to slip away.

Iris smiles kindly. "It takes a while to adjust to the idea of communicating across time. You'll come to terms with it in due course. In the meantime, you should know that you yourself are partly responsible for making this conversation possible."

Gabrielle sniffs.

"Me? How?"

"Through the great work you did on your mission in London. As an indirect result of your actions, Gus Romano fulfilled his destiny, becoming one of the world's great theoretical physicists. The protocol we're using right now, to communicate across time, is just one of many advances made possible by his work: Instant Communication Across Relative Universal Space-time. We call it ICARUS for short."

In a droll tone, Gabrielle says, "It's an acronym."

"Indeed it is," Iris says calmly. "On behalf of the entire Continuum, thank you, Joseph. You did an outstanding job on the mission, under very difficult circumstances. And please thank your friend Vincent for his help too."

"I will," I say, imagining how thrilled Vinny will be to hear that Iris knows his name.

"Now," Iris says, "please feel free to ask your questions. It's why I came to see you. I imagine your experience on the Romano mission left you with many things you don't yet understand. I believe you'll take things in more efficiently if you lead the conversation." She pauses. "Before we begin, however, I must tell you that your experience so far is not how we usually induct new travelers, and for that, I apologize. Bill was always the one who took new recruits under his wing and taught them what they needed to know. Historically, my colleagues and I just played a supporting role, and I'm not used to taking the lead. Still, I will do my best to explain. Where would you like to start?"

I draw in a long, steadying breath and tell my head to forget that I'm talking to a woman who hasn't been born yet.

"I want to know about The Continuum," I say. "Who you are, and what you do."

"Of course," Iris says. "The Continuum is a privately funded organization of time travelers and technologists. We monitor the past for change events and, where we can, we alter time for the better."

"Change events," I say, the terminology familiar. "Like saving Lucy Romano."

"Yes. Change events are specific, defined opportunities to alter the past."

"But how do you pick them? How do you decide what to change?"

"Good question. Actually, we don't decide anything. Change events occur naturally. We didn't create any of this—focus objects and change events and so on—we just gave them a name and built a system around them."

I try to calculate the implications. "So if change events occur naturally, are you suggesting that . . . that *time* decides what needs to change?"

"That's right." Iris nods kindly. "I know that this can be difficult. It may help if you think of time travel as nature's immune system. If you think of change events as pathogens, as things that need to be corrected, then time travelers are like antibodies, seeking out the damaged parts of time and healing them. It can be complicated, of course, but we work for the greater good. All we've really done at The Continuum is leverage the unique opportunity that time has given us to connect lone travelers, like you, to their purpose."

Amy's letter described The Continuum as "healing time," but still, whenever anyone says they are working "for the greater good," a huge warning flag flutters inside my brain. That phrase presupposes a complex set of goals and values that I'm just not going to unpack right now. I'll worry about how they decide what's right and wrong another day.

"How many of you are there?" I ask.

"Just over fifty at our headquarters in Scotland, but across time, we collaborate with hundreds of travelers."

"Hundreds?" And to think that when I discovered I could travel, I genuinely thought I was the only one. That is, until I discovered that Amy was a time traveler too. "Is Amy there now?" I ask cautiously. "In your time, I mean?"

"Not just now. She visits us here, and she has done so for many years. Perhaps one day you will meet her. For now, we all felt it best to keep a little separation. This is something we can discuss, of course, whenever you want to."

In many ways, it's a relief. I'm worried about my sister's mental state, but if an older version of her suddenly materialized, I think I might lose it altogether. I relax a tiny bit, only realizing now how tense I've been since Gabrielle barged her way into my day, and a more pressing concern bubbles up to the surface.

Scarlett.

I decide not to talk about my new viewing yet because I want to hear what Iris has to say about what happened to me in London first. I'm particularly keen to see if what she says lines up with what Bill told me.

"I was wondering . . ."

"Go ahead," Iris encourages me.

"I want to know who Scarlett is, the girl who planted the radio in my shop."

Gabrielle all but growls, but Iris ignores her. "Scarlett is a former time-travel student. She studied with us for a while, with a view to becoming a member of The Continuum. Unfortunately, it didn't work out."

"Why not?"

"She didn't agree with the constraints under which we work. We tried to persuade her to stay, but being part of The Continuum is an individual choice. In the end, she left. We didn't think we would hear from her again."

So far, this is consistent with my conversation with Bill. "But why did she plant the radio in my shop? Why did she attack me?"

"We're not certain, but we have a theory. We had already assigned the mission to a more experienced time traveler, so we believe that bonding you to such a critical mission was a calculated attempt to stop The Continuum from getting ahold of the Romano theorem."

Gabrielle jumps in. "She chose you because you're a rookie, and it was a tough mission. She must've thought you'd screw up." I glare at her. She glares back.

"We were very concerned when we saw that you'd traveled to London," Iris says. "Once a mission is triggered, things move fast. Your life was in danger, and we risked losing the Romano theorem for good."

"Is that why Bill blackmailed me?" I interject.

"Yes. However, he would have wanted you to know that he found it very painful."

I recall my viewing of Bill at the loch with Iris, and I remember his resistance to the blackmail plan. Still, I find it hard to believe that there was no other way. Keep your friends close and your enemies closer, they say. I just need to work out who's who.

"Why didn't he tell me what was actually going on, like you have? Why all the secrecy?"

Iris pauses, studying me, clearly trying to decide if I'm ready to hear more. "We ran many simulations to see if we could achieve a successful outcome in another way, but there was no viable alternative."

"You're saying you knew that if he hadn't blackmailed me, I would have failed the mission?"

"Yes, but more importantly, Bill knew that you would lose your life. He saw it."

"But why sacrifice himself to save me? I hardly knew him. And Lucy was safe."

"But *you* weren't," Iris says. "Saving your life became Bill's final mission."

She lets this sink in. I recall him appearing at the last moment, taking the full blast of Frankie Shaw's shotgun. "But I still don't understand. Why did Bill give his life to save mine? What's so special about me?"

"Your potential," Iris says. "All time travelers have psychometric viewings when they connect with objects, but your abilities go beyond anything we've seen before. Bill told me that you saw our conversation at the loch, and Scarlett planting the radio. You are unique. You see things we can't. And that could change everything."

"He died to save me because of my *viewings*?"

"Bill knew how vital your gifts could be to us. He was prepared to risk everything to save you." Iris leans forward a little. "I can imagine how you might feel about the blackmail, Joseph, but our work at The Continuum can be complex. Sometimes we have to make difficult decisions."

"Ain't that the truth." Gabrielle stands up and stretches her arms to the ceiling. "Let's get back on track here, shall we? Scarlett is a terrorist. No doubt she's already planning her next attack. For all we know, she could be watching us right now."

My hands go clammy. I could still be in danger. What's to stop Scarlett from taking another pop at me? I study Iris, her cool blue eyes calculating, and watch Gabrielle pace the room. If Bill sacrificed his life because of the things I can see, then it's only right I share my latest viewing with Iris. It might help.

"I need to tell you something," I say. "I've had another viewing. I've seen Scarlett again."

Iris and Gabrielle listen in silence as I describe the viewing in detail: the traveler failing his mission, Scarlett's promise to give him another chance.

When I finish, Iris moves her fingers just in front of her. Ten images hover in the air beside her. Headshots, all men, all different. "By chance, are any of these the traveler you saw?"

I guess she's testing me, but she doesn't need to worry. "That's him," I say, pointing to the man I saw with Scarlett.

"The little bitch!" Gabrielle exclaims. "I knew she'd be involved!"

"Who is he?" I ask.

"His name is Nils Petersen," Iris says. "He's one of our most experienced travelers. He failed his latest mission in Macau, the one you saw in your viewing, and it was the first time he'd ever failed. We waited to debrief him and find out what had happened, but he never made it home."

"Where is he then?" I ask.

"We don't know," Gabrielle says, "but at least his watch didn't return to The Continuum, so we know he's still alive."

"Actually, we've had an update on Nils's whereabouts, Gabrielle," Iris says. "Felix picked up a new signal last night. It's faint and intermittent, but it's definitely Nils's travel signature."

"Why didn't you say so before? Where is he?" Gabrielle asks.

"Paris, 1873."

"What?" Gabrielle blinks in confusion. "That's my next mission. How the hell did Nils end up in Paris without touching the focus object? It's in my safe upstairs . . . at least it was last time I looked." I can almost see her mind whirring. She turns on me. "Did you see a metronome in your viewing?"

"A what?"

"A little wooden thing with a ticking arm that musicians use to pace themselves."

"I know what a metronome is."

"So did you see one?" she snarls.

"Gabrielle," Iris says, "the focus object hasn't been activated. Nevertheless, somehow, instead of returning to 1920, Nils has become bonded to the change event of your next mission."

"How could that even *happen*?"

"Felix has the whole team working on it. Felix is our technical lead,"

Iris explains to me. "Apparently, Nils is in a kind of limbo, slipping between states, flashing in and out of existence."

"But that's impossible!" Gabrielle exclaims. "Is he in Paris or not?"

"Felix says yes, but the timing of his appearances is, so far, impossible to predict. And time is short. If we don't get Nils home before your mission is complete, Felix believes we'll lose him for good."

"We can't lose anyone else." Gabrielle's voice cracks. "Not after Bill."

"I know," Iris says. "And that is why we must do everything within our power to bring him safely home."

Gabrielle clears her throat and lifts her chin. "Listen, Iris, it's not long until I go. I'll bring Nils back when I do the Paris mission."

"I appreciate your enthusiasm, Gabrielle, but we need more data before we start making rescue plans. At least, thanks to Joseph's viewing, we now know that Scarlett is involved in Nils's disappearance. After the Romano mission, we suspected her, of course, but we had no evidence."

"Why do I feel like we're waiting for her move, though?" Gabrielle says, frustrated. "Why don't we take the initiative, go after Scarlett?"

"If we knew how to find her, we would."

"Hasn't Felix found a way to track her yet?"

"He's working on it." Iris turns to me. "Scarlett doesn't travel in the same way that we do. She can only travel on the back of other time travelers, so to speak, which means we can't see where she is. She's essentially a ghost."

"She's a damn parasite, is what she is," Gabrielle retorts. "She was a complete pain in the ass from day one. We never should have trusted her." Gabrielle pulls out a cigarette, spots the smoke alarm in the corner of the room, and grumpily puts it away again. "Bridgeman, can't you lock onto her with one of your dream sequence things?"

I shake my head. "They're not dreams, they're viewings, and it doesn't work like that. I told you, I don't have any control over them."

She arches an eyebrow. "Wow. I can see why everyone's so excited, that really is a *super* useful skill." She turns to Iris. "Why has she done this, boss? What the hell is she trying to achieve?"

"We don't yet understand Scarlett's motivations," Iris replies. "She's made no contact and placed no demands on us."

Gabrielle's jaw sets. "She can't be working alone," she says. "She's way too dumb."

"We don't know that," Iris says. "We should avoid speculation and stick to the facts."

For a moment, there is silence. Gabrielle festers, and Iris regards me thoughtfully. "I wonder," she says. "You said you can't control what you see. So how do your viewings of other people work?"

How do I answer that? How does any of this stuff work? I've had a psychometric ability with objects for as long as I can remember, but these people-focused viewings only began on the Romano mission a couple of months ago.

Iris tries again. "For example, what triggers them?"

"I'm not sure. I never know when they're going to come."

"But there must be a reason why you see viewings of certain people, and not of others?"

"I only get viewings of people I've seen in the flesh, eye-to-eye, if that's what you mean. I think I need to have established some kind of emotional connection with them." I can feel Gabrielle glaring at me, probably itching to make some snarky comment. I keep my eyes firmly fixed on Iris.

"I see," Iris muses. "So the viewing of Nils and Scarlett is only available to you because you have met Scarlett?"

"I think so. I saw it all from her perspective."

"Interesting. So then we shouldn't expect you to see a viewing from Nils's point of view, because you've never met him." She considers this. "What if you were to see Nils—connect with him eye-to-eye, as you put it—might you get a viewing then?"

"Maybe," I answer. "There are plenty of people I've met face-to-face that I haven't had viewings of. In theory, though, it's possible."

"Iris, no," Gabrielle growls. "Absolutely not."

Iris seems undeterred. "We don't know what happened to Nils, but if we can find out, it might help us to get him home. We're doing everything we can from here, but in the meantime, I would like to know if you would be willing to join Gabrielle on her first jump to Paris."

Gabrielle jumps in. "With all due respect, Iris, Bridgeman's a rookie!

He doesn't know anything. Look what happened to him in London, for God's sake! I don't need someone to babysit. This mission is gonna be hard enough. Let *me* find Nils while I'm on the mission. I can do both. Nils knows me. He trusts me."

"Gabrielle . . ." Iris's voice has a subtle note of warning.

"Please, boss. You know I work better alone, I always have." Gabrielle seems less angry now, more raw. I wonder about her life, the things she's seen. I know as well as anyone that saying you work better alone doesn't necessarily mean it's true.

Iris gives Gabrielle an almost imperceptible frown, and Gabrielle lowers her head in deference. Iris turns to me. "Joseph, the viewing you've shared with us today was helpful, but it's only part of the story. We need to know more. If you accompanied Gabrielle to Paris, you might connect with Nils and trigger another one of your viewings."

"Even if I find him, which sounds unlikely," I say, "the chances of triggering a viewing are pretty small."

"There, he said it," Gabrielle enthuses. "And what if we run into Scarlett while we're there? This is too dangerous. We can't put Bridgeman at risk." I raise my eyebrows at her, seeing straight through her paper-thin concern.

"It's a small risk, and a balanced one," Iris replies. "We should remember that Scarlett attacked Joseph in his own home last time." She turns to me. "In all time travel, there is inherent risk, but we will not put you in any unnecessary danger. You would be joining Gabrielle on her mission as an observer only. It is your choice."

"Can you tell me about this Paris mission?" I ask, curious to know what I may be letting myself in for.

"Of course. Gabrielle, would you like to give Joseph the rundown . . . ?"

"No, you go ahead," Gabrielle mutters.

"In October of 1873, there was a huge fire," Iris explains. "The Salle Le Peletier opera house, home to the Paris Opera, burned to the ground. No one knows what caused the fire, but it destroyed the life of this man." The fingers of her left hand move, and then an oil painting appears in the air, a few feet away from me and about five feet from the floor. It's a portrait of a handsome man in his midtwenties, wearing a peach jacket and frilly white cravat. His hair is a shock of dark curls, his smooth cocoa skin marked only by a single beauty spot on his right cheek. "His name is Philippe Chevalier. He was conductor of the opera."

"He died in the fire?" I ask.

"No, but he was badly hurt. His injuries were significant enough to alter the course of his professional and personal life. We cannot change the fire, as too many people witnessed it, but we need to change what happened to Philippe, so that he can reach his potential."

Both women watch me, one hoping I'll say yes and the other hoping I'll say no.

Iris seems to care about Nils, and so does Gabrielle. Listening to them reminds me how precious it is to feel part of a team or an organization or a family. If I say no, I get to walk out of here. I can go back to my family, my life, my shop . . . and wait for Scarlett to have another go at picking me off. But if I go to Paris, am I just being used as bait to lure Scarlett out of the shadows? And if they actually think I can help, they're likely to be disappointed. I can't guarantee I'll find Nils, let alone get a viewing, and even if I do, it might well be useless.

At least going to Paris feels active. And there's strength in numbers. If Scarlett follows me and Gabrielle, at least there'll be two of us to deal with her. And Gabrielle appears to hate Scarlett slightly more than she hates me.

It comes down to trust. I can't think my way out of this one, I've got to feel it, listen to my instincts. Scarlett is causing harm. She put me in a dangerous position in London, and it looks like she's endangered Nils's life too. I don't need to trust anyone on that, I saw her do it. Iris and her people do seem to be—what was it Amy's letter said?—"healing time."

"You know that the chances of me having a viewing that's actually useful, in time to help Nils, are very slim, don't you?"

"We do," Iris reassures me. "But I believe it's worth trying."

I wonder what Vinny will say. He would never forgive me if he heard I had the chance to go back more than a hundred years, to an opera fire, and didn't take it . . . It sounds shocking, but if I'm only there to observe, then hopefully it'll be a lot safer than London was. The thought of Vinny is the last push I need.

"I can't promise I'll find Nils or be able to connect with him, but I'm willing to give it a try. I'll go with Gabrielle to Paris. If I can help, I want to." I'm a little surprised to discover that I mean it. I do want to help. I'm still working out what I really feel about Bill, but if he came back to save my life, then I owe a debt to him and to his friends.

"Thank you, Joseph," Iris says. "We are most grateful. I believe that if you follow your instincts and use your gift, you might help us find a way to bring Nils home. What you decide to tell your sister is up to you, of course, but please remember her letter. Don't discuss her future with her. Everything needs to happen naturally, in its own time, without intervention."

"But I can tell her about The Continuum, right? That I'm going back to Paris?"

"If you feel that's the right thing to do." Iris turns to Gabrielle. "Please ensure that Joseph gets the relevant translation tech and upgrades." She pauses, unblinking. "And I know you will give him a full briefing and support him throughout."

"Absolutely," Gabrielle says, flashing me a beaming smile.

It's mostly teeth.

3

"Whiskey, no ice." Gabrielle barks her order at the young lad behind the bar. I trailed her along the hotel corridors like a docile puppy, assuming that she was trying to find somewhere to brief me on the Paris trip, but she's giving nothing away.

"Single malt, madam?" the bartender asks, indicating a selection of five bottles on the shelf behind him.

"Gimme the most expensive one. Make it a double." I'm about to explain that it's still a bit early for me and ask for a coffee, but she gets in first. "Don't you have someplace to go?"

I'm taken aback. "I thought we were going to plan the trip back to Paris. Iris said you were going to brief me."

"Cheers." She takes the glass of whiskey from the bartender and downs it. "Another double. Charge them to room twenty-two." She wipes her mouth on the sleeve of her jacket. "I'll call you when it's time to leave. Anything you need to know, I can tell you when we get there." She says it like we're going to be taking a train to Paris.

"Wouldn't it be better if you filled me in on some of the basics now? What if we don't get much warning before we leave?"

Gabrielle downs the second whiskey, fishes in her handbag for her room key, then stalks across the bar toward a door marked "Bedrooms." She stops halfway across the room and turns back to me. "Listen, Golden Balls," she says loudly. Out of the corner of my eye, I see the bartender stifle a smile. Gabrielle notices this too and beckons me over. Obediently, I approach. She lowers her voice. "I want to find Nils as much as anyone else, and if your fantasterrific superhero skills can help us track him down, all good. But you don't need to know anything about my mission, OK? It's mine."

I wonder, not for the first time, if Gabrielle was an only child. "I know it's your mission, but can we just take five minutes, please? Could you at least tell me a bit about Nils?"

She deflates a fraction of an inch. "Nils Petersen is a good man. He's been attacked, he's lost, and I'm going to find him." She pulls open the door to the bedrooms, releasing a rush of cool air from the corridor beyond. "Now, I need to prepare. Later, Bridgeman."

"But how do I contact you?"

"You don't. I'll call when the time comes. Just be ready."

"What does that mean?"

She releases the door and strides off down the corridor. I don't know how she moves so fast in those boots. Her voice, still loud even from thirty yards away, filters back to me. "You've traveled before. Figure it out, Sherlock."

Back out in the fresh spring air, walking along the busy street, it's hard to believe I just talked with a woman who won't be born for at least another, what, fifty years? It's all catching up with me and I'm starting to feel mildly freaked out. There's only one thing for it. I need to get me some ballast.

Vinny picks up on the third ring.

"I've been waiting to hear from you! How'd it go, Casanova?"

Emotionally, I've rubber-banded between 2131 and 1873 over the past couple of hours, and it takes me a minute to recall Alexia's book launch— was it really earlier *today*? "Not good," I tell him. "Gordon was there."

Vinny tuts. "You thought he might be."

"It's confirmed. They're seeing each other. He told me Alexia's hired an office next to his."

"Moron," Vinny says.

I chuckle softly. "That's not why I'm calling, though—to whine about my broken heart. I've got news. I met Iris."

"No way!" Vinny says. "You actually met her?"

"This woman called Gabrielle met me at the book launch and took me to meet Iris at the Broadway Hotel, but Iris wasn't actually there. She was projected into the room like a kind of hologram."

"Like Princess Leia?"

"Sort of, except a million times better. I could only just tell that she wasn't physically present in the room. But the most amazing thing was that she was calling me from the future."

"The future?" Vinny whistles through his teeth. "How far are we talking?"

"You won't believe me."

"Try me."

"It was 2131."

"Sheesh madeesh! Do they have flying cars?"

I laugh. "I knew you'd ask that! I dunno, mate. I didn't travel to the future, Iris projected herself to me. I think they were trying *not* to blow my mind."

"Did you see Amy?"

"No. Iris said they know Amy, but I didn't see her. That might have been a step too far. My brain might've exploded."

"Maybe she was there watching you from behind one of those two-way police mirrors!"

"Maybe. The coolest thing, though, was the tech they were using to project Iris . . . we made it possible, Vin, you and me!"

"What do you mean?"

"We saved Lucy Romano, and that meant that Gus could go on to invent all kinds of incredible stuff, and his thinking eventually leads to live holographic calls across time. ICARUS, they call it."

"Wowzers. Communicating across time," Vinny says, his voice wistful. "Gus Romano. I told you he was a genius."

"You did, and you know what else? That viewing I keep having, of Scarlett and that blond bloke? He's a missing time traveler. They want me to help find him—"

"Hang on, Cash." I hear some muffled sounds at the other end of the line, then a woman's voice: *Vincent? Our food's here.* Vinny comes back on the line. "Best convo ever mate, seriously, but I'm going to have to go."

"Sorry, Vin, I didn't realize you had company! You should've said."

"It was a surprise to me too," he says, sotto voce. "Anyway, we probably shouldn't be discussing this over a public line. We could be bugged. Anybody could be listening. Come and see me in the shop when you can; we can talk properly there."

"Will do. Have fun."

"Looking at these portion sizes, that is highly unlikely. Catch ya later."

He hangs up, and I scratch my head. I can't remember ever calling Vinny and interrupting a . . . a what, a date? "You dark horse," I chuckle to myself, hoping it goes well for him. I've never understood how such a warm, genuine guy could stay single for so long, when other men I've known, some of whom behave like misogynistic boneheads, churn their way through endless lines of women.

On Montpellier Road, Bridgeman Antiques shines like a welcome beacon. Its name is picked out in gold lettering on a dark-gray painted sign above the door, and the sparklingly clean dual bay windows are packed with interesting artifacts and quality pieces of antique furniture. As I enter the shop, the little brass doorbell tinkles, and Molly looks over. She's with a customer, a thirtysomething man in dreadlocks and a leather jacket, and she's showing him an art deco cocktail cabinet. Molly is an absolute godsend. She's wonderful with the customers, looks after the shop efficiently, and sometimes looks after me too, like when Vinny and I arrived back from 1963, injured and accompanied by a vintage ambulance bed. She whisked us straight to hospital, and no one was any the wiser. She's very discreet.

"Afternoon, Mr. Bridgeman," Molly says. She doesn't smile, but there's warmth in her expression. She's dressed immaculately as ever, in a gray wool dress with golden buttons, and caramel shoes.

"Hi, Molly," I say, and to the customer, "Good afternoon. Are you finding everything OK?"

"I am indeed," the man says. "This your place?"

"It is." Each time I say it out loud, I take just a little more ownership of the shop that my predecessor, Other Joe, created and left for me.

"It's really cool, man. I own Dialogue, a little eatery down in Pittville. Maybe you know it? Anyway, your stuff really suits my vibe."

"I'll have to book a table sometime," I tell him, imagining a date with Alexia.

"Do it. And listen, I know how tough it is to find good staff, and it's even harder to keep them. You struck gold with Molly here."

"I know," I agree. "She's amazing."

"Oh, Mr. Bridgeman!" Molly protests. "You're the one who chooses all the pieces."

"Maybe so, but I couldn't do it without you," I say, and she blushes. "Anyhow, good to meet you," I tell the man. "I'll leave you in Molly's capable hands." I make my way through the shop, past rows of glass cabinets filled with antique goods and curios, as Molly picks up the sales conversation again.

"As you can see, the woodwork is in exceptionally good condition, and the grain is rather attractive," she says. "It's rare to find a specimen in such a perfect state."

Gold is right. I feel incredibly fortunate. I had never dared to dream of a life like this.

I go through the door at the back of the shop and up the stairs to my flat. Overcome with weariness, I prepare a three-shot latte with the automated bean-to-cup coffee machine in my fancy kitchen. As the machine does its thing, I look at my phone, remembering that Amy left me a voice message earlier. I hit the mailbox button and hear Amy's breathless voice. "Seriously, Joe, you promised you'd be here! I can't believe I have to do this on my own! This whole 'leave of absence' thing doesn't mean you can do as you please, you know. They've given you time off to get better, not to disappear. You know what Mum's going to be like. She's going to ask for my opinion but not really want it . . . She doesn't really want me there; she wants you." There's a pause. "God, Joe! Just meet me at the restaurant at eleven a.m. tomorrow. Don't be late. And the dress code is smart." She hangs up. I feel bad, but I'll make it up to her tomorrow at the party.

I climb the sparkling stairway to heaven that leads to the loft room and sink gratefully into one of the old leather sofas. Grabbing the iPad, I set the lighting to a warm yellow that wraps around me like a blanket and sip my coffee.

I cast my mind back to the first day I time traveled. I'd been to see Alexia for my first hypnotherapy session, and she'd shown me some breathing exercises to help me relax. I had a hot bath and a cup of herbal tea, tried the exercises, and then—*bam!*—I traveled back five minutes. I remember struggling to come to terms with what had happened and the deeply terrorizing but strangely captivating experience of watching another version of myself in my bedroom, hoping he wouldn't see me, wondering if things would ever be the same again. I could never have imagined that that first trip would lead me here.

I look through the bifold doors that lead onto the terrace, watching the gray clouds scud across the sky. I told Iris I wanted to help find Nils, and when I said it, I meant it, but now that I'm safe at home, I wonder if I really do. I don't know these people, and I'm just going on gut feel. Gabrielle is a hypertouchy live wire, but Iris seems genuine enough, and it seems as though even Bill was a good guy in the end.

Wandering across to the wall near the bar, I peruse the photos of Other Joe. He comes across as focused, organized, his life just how he wanted it. That life is now mine, but just like his clothes, it doesn't fit, not quite. Judging by other people's reactions to me, Other Joe must have been more business-focused, more of a ladies' man, a bit more into his appearance, a touch less emotionally available. This life feels a little empty to me, and without Alexia, somewhat pointless too. Am I trying to find a purpose by offering to help find Nils? Is that it?

I drain my coffee and decide to go back downstairs for another. No such thing as over-beaned in my world. Then, I pause. Iris called me from 2131. An instant connection between my present and the future. I'm still trying to figure out how that works. When I woke up this morning, I thought my day was a blank page, but it turns out it's already been written. And if that's the case, Iris knows whether or not I'm going to brew another coffee. She knows if things are going to pan out with Vinny's new woman. She knows whether Alexia and I are ever going to end up together. And she knows when I'm going to shuffle off this mortal coil and meet my maker too. I get an intense crush of claustrophobia and wonder how I can live my whole life knowing the entire thing is predetermined, that I'm living in the past like some dusty old fossil. How can that be true? Are my choices nothing but an illusion?

It's a bloody good thing the world at large doesn't know about time travel. It would be like knowing there's an afterlife. It would fundamentally change how we view our existence. The reassuring belief that we can only move through time in one direction enabled our primitive brains to function in reality. Mine's feeling a little floaty right now.

Am I just playing at creating a future that's already been written?

PART 2

4

Blowing warm air into my hands, I stamp my feet to try to get the blood flowing.

After missing the rehearsal yesterday, I didn't want to be late for Dad's surprise party, but I got to the restaurant too early, so I've been standing in the cold waiting for Amy for twenty minutes. Inside, I can see people in posh clothes, chatting and laughing, the sorts who always arrive early for parties. They drift around, holding glasses of wine, "mingling." It's one of my most hated words. I find socializing difficult at the best of times.

I breathe deeply into the icy air, hoping it will wake me up a bit. I had a terrible night. I didn't have any more viewings, but I kept replaying yesterday's conversation with Gabrielle and Iris. I woke up exhausted. If today hadn't been so important, I would have stayed in bed and tried to get more sleep. Instead, I got up, had the mother of all showers, and put on the smartest non-black suit I could find in my closet. So much is whirling around my head: the future, my trip to Paris, the missing time traveler, and the fact that my life may be in danger again . . . But I need to try and compartmentalize all of that. For the next few hours, I need to play the successful—if forgetful—son. I need to be here for my family. Not so long ago, I would have given anything to be celebrating Dad's birthday. I hope I can hold it together. I don't want to embarrass myself. I'm sure Other Joe wouldn't have given in to tears.

I hear footsteps and turn to see Amy jogging toward me. "Is Mum here yet?" she puffs. She's wearing a long green velvet dress, a leather jacket, and a beret. As she reaches me, she leans on my shoulder and holds one of her feet a few inches off the ground. "These bloody shoes. I'm in agony!" I don't think I've ever seen her in stilettos before. She notices me staring. "Mum threatened me on pain of death not to wear my Converse."

"You look lovely," I say. "I'm sorry I couldn't be here yesterday."

"I can't believe you dumped me in it like that. Mum was so stressed! I'm worried she's going to make herself ill. You promised you'd be there, Joe. What happened?"

Over the past couple of months, I've been putting a lot of time into my relationship with Amy, and it's paying off. We chat often, we've been meeting for breakfast regularly, and I've even started going to the pub with her and her friends most weeks. I don't want to jeopardize that, but I know I can't tell her the truth. "It was a delayed delivery to the shop. A load of heavy furniture. Molly couldn't handle it on her own." Amy scans my face, wanting to believe me. I'm not proud, but I've become quite an accomplished liar lately, and she buys it. "Anyway, I'm here now. What do I need to know?"

She pulls a wry face. "Just try to stay cool. Mum will be rushing around herding people, and Dad will be his usual charming, laid-back self. Our job is not to rock the boat, do everything we can to make sure Mum's plans come good, and get out the other side of this horrible day in one piece."

"Horrible?"

She drops her head. "I try, I really do, but I hate family stuff. I hardly slept. I'm planning to drink through it. Should've had a shot before I left home. Shall we?" She adjusts her beret, plasters on a smile, and leads the way through the heavy doors into the noise of the restaurant.

Inside, I get my first look at my father's guests. I scan the room, and there's the occasional flicker of recognition. A cheerful man in a Hawaiian shirt waves at me from across the room. I don't know who he is, but I wave back. Amy and I pick our way up the side of the dining room to avoid the growing crowd, navigating past tables of canapés and yucca plants in huge pots. Mum's behind the bar, holding a clipboard. Her reading glasses are balanced on her nose, and she's talking to a harassed-looking young man in a white shirt, who I presume is the maître d'. She's wearing a bright-red dress and matching lipstick, and her hair is up in a chignon. She looks fantastic. I'm about to tell her how proud I am, but when she looks up, she ignores me. "Amy, love, would you help Luca here with the seating plan?" she says. "Your cousins have arrived unexpectedly and messed up the entire thing."

"All right," Amy says, obviously grateful to have a job to do. She sidles through the gap and takes the clipboard from Mum.

"Mum, I'm sorry about yesterday," I say hurriedly. "I had to help Molly move some heavy furniture."

"I see," she says dryly. "Lucky Molly." She turns to go, and then turns back to me. "Oh, and Joe, I hope you've got your speech ready. It's a terrible shame you couldn't rehearse. We're doing them at two p.m., after the meal."

I had totally forgotten. "I don't think I should speak, really," I say. "I'm still blanking out from time to time. I'd hate for it to happen in front of everyone." Mum blinks at me like an owl. "It would spoil things for Dad, don't you think?"

"Have you been to see Dr. Sharma again?" she says. "Your head is taking rather a long time to heal."

Dr. Sharma is my parents' tame neurosurgeon. Unlike the family doctor, who was mildly concerned by my sudden weight gain and bewildered that my appendix seems to have grown back, Dr. Sharma couldn't find any evidence of trauma to my head—not physically, anyway. So he prescribed a three month career break along with "plenty of fresh air," which Dad interpreted as a prescription for weekly golf sessions.

"I haven't seen him since he signed me off work."

Amy taps Mum on the shoulder, saving me from further interrogation. "Mum, I've sorted the seating out. Anything else you'd like me to do?"

"Could you take that tray of champagne around?" Mum says. "The Jensons have just arrived . . ." She flicks a glance at the front door, where a pink-cheeked family of five is battling to remove their coats without elbowing other guests.

"Do you trust me with it?" Amy replies, winking at me and handing me a glass. "I jest! Don't worry, I'll make sure everyone has a drink." She wanders off, lifting a glass from the tray and taking a long sip.

"Anything I can do, Mum?" I ask.

"No, I don't think so," she says, taking off her reading glasses and sliding them into her handbag. "Although I need to tell you, I'm afraid there was a bit of a mix-up with the plus-ones."

"What kind of a mix-up?" I ask, trying to sound interested.

"One of your father's golf friends . . . I don't really know any of them, so I just suggested they all bring a guest, whoever they liked."

"Right," I say. "Seems fair enough."

"Well, I'm afraid Gordon Fuller brought along someone you know."

"Gordon Fuller?"

Cogs turn slowly in my head, and then, in a sudden rush of understanding, I realize why Mum has been beating around the bush. Oh God. This can't be happening.

Mum says, "That's him over there, at the end of the bar." I follow her gaze to the far corner of the room. Near the door to the kitchen is Alexia, and beside her is Gordon, looking like the cat who got the cream. Alexia hasn't taken her coat off yet, and she's checking her phone. "I hear you two stepped out together for a while. I hope this isn't going to make things awkward." Mum says this like it's an instruction. "Right, your father will be here soon. Go and mingle, Joe. Now, where's Luca gone? I hope he's remembered the cake . . ." She walks off, talking to herself.

I glance over at Alexia again. Perhaps sensing my attention, she lifts her head, and our eyes meet for a second before she looks away. She made it very clear yesterday that she and Gordon are an item. I wasn't prepared to see them here, but I'm not going to make a spectacle of myself. Behaving like a panting puppy is the last thing I need to do, and anyway, I won't give Gordon the pleasure.

I down the flute of champagne in my hand, dump the glass on the nearest table, and decide to try and make the best of things.

A couple I don't recognize approaches. "Cheer up, Joe, it might never happen!" says the man, a fortysomething in a mustard suit and a navy bow tie. When I explain that I don't remember who they are, the woman, Sheena, tells me that her husband, Geoff, used to work for Dad. After some embarrassing small talk, I'm massively relieved when Geoff and Sheena wander off in search of more champagne.

Next up is a woman I vaguely recognize. "Do you remember me, Joe?" she grins. "I'm about thirty years older than the last time we met. I'm Diana, your cousin. From Norfolk." It turns out I haven't seen Diana for so long that we're actually able to talk about camping holidays when we were kids, shared memories that I still have.

Trying to channel my social whiz of a mother, I introduce Diana to Sheena and Geoff, then scan the room for Amy. I spot her across the restaurant, hunkered down beside a giant fern with a glass and a bottle of champagne, staring into space. The tray is empty beside her. I wave to attract her attention. Seeing me, she raises the bottle as if to offer some, but I shake my head. Then, she lifts her glass and points to her right, toward the middle of the room. Following her gaze, I spot Alexia making her way toward me. She's wearing a navy Jackie Onassis–style shift dress and black suede heels—simple but elegant.

As Alexia approaches, she blushes, but her face remains impassive. "Hi, Joe," she says quickly. "I was going to call you, but I didn't want you to think . . . I just wanted to say sorry."

I ignore my beating heart. "For what?"

"You know, it's a bit awkward, isn't it, me being here? I wouldn't have come, it's just, well, Gordon was invited, and . . ."

"It's fine, it's not your fault. Anyway, it's not as awkward as being in a room full of people you can't remember, who think you ought to know who they are."

Alexia half-smiles. I half-smile back. She looks like she wants to say something, then stops herself.

"Can I get you a drink?" I say.

"I've got one, thanks. Over there, at the bar." At the back of the room, Gordon is standing guard over Alexia's glass of wine, watching us like a hawk.

I decide that the best thing I can do is act as though I'm moving on—I can cry into my pillow later. And anyway, I have the feeling Amy needs me. "OK, well, it's good to see you, and thanks for coming over and saying that. I hope you enjoy the party." I give Alexia a brief smile, then turn and walk with purpose toward my sister.

I'm only halfway to Amy when Mum starts banging a fork against a water glass. "Everyone, everyone! Thomas is on his way! We need to move to the dining room. Quiet! Luca, music off, please!"

We follow one another obediently through an archway into a private dining area. The spacious room has a high ceiling with decorative plaster work. Tall sash windows span the width of one entire wall. Around the edges of the room, narrow tables are laid with spotless white cloths and loaded with food. Streamers are strung across the room and two red helium balloons in the shape of numbers—a six and a five—bob about at head height next to a big noticeboard covered in photos from Dad's life. "Gather round, facing the door!" Mum tells everyone, indicating the center of the room. "And then keep quiet! He'll be here any minute now." A hush descends. There's a rustle of whispering and an odd cough.

"On my signal," instructs my mother in a loud whisper. "Three . . . two . . . one . . . go!"

The door on the far side of the room opens, and in walks my father.

The room erupts in ragged unison: "SURPRISE!"

Dad's face is a picture of delight. The clapping and whooping make me jump, but my father takes it all in stride. In his polo shirt and red-framed designer spectacles, he appears younger than his sixty-five years. He laughs and begins to clap. People stand and greet him warmly. Hobbling a bit, still waiting for his new knees, he claps people on the back, hugs them, thanks them for coming. Mum joins him, and he pretends to be cross, then he kisses her, and they hold hands.

I feel the watery heat of tears welling in my eyes, and I wipe them away. Dad is sixty-five today. He's surrounded by people who love him, at a party organized by my incredible, pin-sharp mother. This is a scene I imagined so many times during my lost years, alone and hopeless. It may be complicated, but it's family. It's love. It's something to celebrate. A tear threatens to spill onto my cheek, and I scan the ceiling for a few seconds to discourage its progress. Alexia catches my eye, her expression warm.

"Speech. Speech! SPEECH!"

Dad pretends to resist, then practically wrenches the microphone from my mother's hand. "Well, hello everybody!" he says, his amplified voice reverberating. "What a complete surprise! I don't know how some of you kept this secret, looking at no one in particular . . . Sheena!" Standing just a few feet from me, Sheena giggles and sticks both thumbs up. Dad continues. "As I'm apparently sixty-five years young today"—he pauses, and people whoop and whistle—"I thought I'd tell you a little story about when I met this gorgeous woman here." He squeezes Mum around the waist. She flushes and half-heartedly tries to push him off. He launches into a story about how, as a teenager, he got a friend to steal Mum's purse at the dance hall one night, so that he could give it back and have a reason to talk to her. He's a natural speaker, confident and funny as a stand-up comedian.

This is how I remember him before we lost Amy—larger than life, always in control, always one step ahead—and it's wonderful to see. But this is bittersweet too. I feel the missing years. I never had them in my timeline, where Dad had given up. I'm happy I gave those years back to him, but I can't help feeling envious of the time Other Joe had with him.

But I can feel there's a lot of love in this room today. When I spot my wealthy Uncle Danny, his arm proudly around the waist of his latest trophy wife, I'm haunted by different days. When we lost Amy, I remember Danny coming around and being a great support. "I'll always be there for your family," he said. Lines like that cease to have meaning, though, when you've lived in a parallel universe where those values are tested. When our family finally fell to pieces and Dad took his own life, Danny faded away. Some people step up in a tragedy, but others disappear. Danny strokes the back of his wife's neck, whispering in her ear. She giggles. I feel ill.

"Still, I couldn't have done any of this," Dad says, his cheeks flushed with champagne, "without my wonderful family."

He talks about when "the kids were little," memories of happy holidays. Then, he talks about me. A lot about me. He talks about my days at university, my sports prowess, how rewarding it is when people get serious about their careers, and how brilliantly I've done in my work for the family business. And as the minutes go by, Dad goes on and on about how proud he is of me and all the things I've accomplished, how he always knew I'd take his place on the board one day. I feel the heat rising in my face, just embarrassment at first, but then I get confused. He doesn't mention Amy at all, not once. I look around to see if anyone else has noticed, but all I see are enrapt faces soaking in Dad's oratory.

"So, ladies and gents, let's all raise a glass. Here's to my son, Joseph—I couldn't be more proud of you and everything you've achieved, despite your recent health challenges. And here's to my beautiful wife, for arranging such a fantastic event. And finally, here's to family!"

"To family," everyone intones obediently, clinking glasses.

"I'm booked to play golf in about half an hour, so drink up!" Dad teases, and he's rewarded with a ripple of laughter.

I don't see Amy anywhere. I work my way through the crowd, who all want to talk and ask questions, but I make my excuses, determined to find Amy.

"Joe?" Someone taps me on the shoulder. Turning around, I see concern on Alexia's face. "If you're looking for Amy, she just left. She seemed really upset."

"She left?"

"Yes. I saw her talking to your dad over there, by the door where he came in. Actually, it seemed more like an argument, to be honest. Then, I saw her grab her coat."

"Should I give her some space?" I ask, unsure whether Amy would want my company if she's distressed. "I want to help, but I don't know what to do."

Alexia considers this. "I don't know Amy, but she's clearly upset. I think you should go after her. You don't need to try and fix anything. Just listen."

5

After a short walk, I pass through the gate to the community garden and spot Amy immediately. Her plot is the one I would have chosen for myself: tucked right in the corner, surrounded on two sides by a thick laurel hedge and partly hidden from the path by a small shed decorated with paintings of huge, hyperreal flowers in vivid yellows and blues. I follow the grassy path between scabby patches of bare earth and tired cabbages. Amy is digging ferociously, still wearing her leather jacket, her long green dress flapping about her legs. Her party shoes have been replaced with shabby black Wellington boots with heavy treads that look a couple of sizes too big for her.

"I was worried you were gardening in your stilettos," I call out.

She stops digging and looks up, frowning. "What are you doing here? You should still be at the party." She pushes her hair out of her face and unwittingly streaks her forehead with mud.

Before I left the party, I asked Mum where she thought Amy had gone. Mum said she'd probably be here at the garden, but advised me to leave her alone. "You know she won't thank you for butting in," she said. "Remember New Year's Eve?" Of course, I don't remember, but maybe that's no bad thing. Clean slate and all that.

"I was worried about you," I tell Amy. "Mum said you'd be here."

Amy snorts and starts attacking the ground again. Breaking up clumps of earth with the spade, she pulls out spindly weeds and thick white roots, throwing them into a big green plastic bin.

"She said I should leave you alone, but Alexia thought I should come after you, so . . ."

Amy rubs her nose roughly on the back of her hand. "Right," she says. She isn't making this easy.

"I came to check you were OK. But if you'd rather I left, I will. I don't want to be in your face. I just want you to know I care."

She shoves the spade deep into the soil, then folds her arms. "Do you know why I left the party?"

"Dad's speech?"

She kicks at a clod of soil. "That was definitely the icing."

"For what it's worth, I was really embarrassed," I say. "He didn't mention you at all. Does he always go on about me like that?"

"Always. Other Joe never minded. He was quite happy soaking up the limelight."

"Have you tried talking to him about it?"

"He doesn't listen to me. Mum's tried, but he says he doesn't know what she's talking about, which makes it even worse." Amy disappears into the shed and comes back out carrying an armload of beanpoles. She lays them on the ground, pushes four of them into the soil in a square shape, and ties the tops together with a length of string.

"Can I help?" I venture.

"You can follow me with the seedlings if you like, plant them at the base of each pole. They're over there." She points to a tray of little leafy plants in small pots.

"I've never planted anything in my life. How do you do it?"

"Take the plant out of its pot, but don't disturb its roots. Poke a hole in the ground that's a bit bigger than the root ball. Put the plant in the hole. Fill it in and press down. Repeat."

I try to stand on the grassy path as I work. I've got posh shoes on, but connecting with Amy feels more important than keeping Other Joe's gear in perfect condition. "So what's the deal with Dad then?" I ask. "I remember you told me things were difficult when you were a teenager."

Fiercely, Amy stabs another pole into the ground. "When I was young, I remember things being really happy. The four of us were your normal family, if there is such a thing—the usual ups and downs, but we were a unit—and I felt like I really belonged. I felt like a Bridgeman."

Gingerly, I push a seedling into the earth. "So what went wrong?"

Her mouth hardens. "I don't think Dad ever forgave me for all the seemingly random disappearances. He just couldn't cope with a troubled daughter. Did I tell you I left home for a while? He was really angry about that. And when I eventually came back, even though I learned to control my traveling, it was too late, the shutters had come down. Nothing I could do or say got through to him. It broke something. He didn't actually disown me, but I think if Mum hadn't stepped in, he would have." She stares at the ground, remembering. "Mealtimes were the worst. Stuck at that table, eating together like a family, but with this silent chasm between Dad and me. I felt invisible to him."

"How did you stop traveling? I don't think you ever told me."

"Meditation. I just kept practicing. Do you remember Aunt Silvia?"

"The name doesn't ring a bell, but I'm a lot better with faces."

"She looks a bit like Cher. Long dark hair, amazing cheekbones. Anyway, I went to live with her in Cornwall for about eighteen months. She helped me figure out how to recognize an impending travel wave before it got big enough to knock me over. I'd be flat out for a few days afterward, but I learned not to time travel. In some ways, she saved my life."

"She sounds amazing. Is she still . . . with us?"

"Very much so. Still living in the same place, a little white farmhouse near the top of a hill, along with a herd of pygmy goats."

"I'd like to meet her sometime."

"She and Other Joe didn't have a lot to say to each other, but I think you two would have more in common." Amy lets go of the beanpoles in her hands. "I've run out of string. Can you grab me another roll from Martha? It'll be in the glove box." She indicates an old orange-and-cream splitscreen Volkswagen camper van parked beyond the shed. It's a bit shabby, with patches of rust on the wheel arches, but it's got a friendly face.

Inside the van, I find the string spilling out of the glove compartment, along with a packet of travel mints. I also find a thick woolen scarf in black and yellow stripes laid across one of the back seats, and I wrap it around my neck. It's getting chilly again, and I'm not dressed for gardening in March weather.

"Nice van," I say when I get back, handing Amy the string. "I didn't know you had a camper."

"It's not mine, it's Miles's. I'm driving it while he's in Mallorca." Miles is Amy's boyfriend. I use the term loosely. Miles is a passionate free climber, one of those mad people who scale rock faces without any ropes. He lives half the time in England, earning a bit of cash doing temping and odd jobs, and half the time climbing in Spain, so they have a rather on-off relationship, which seems to suit them both.

"How are things with Miles at the moment?"

"What do you mean, 'at the moment'?" Wow. She is *so* spiky.

"OK, just generally then."

"Fine." I've met Miles a few times. Most Thursday nights I go to the pub with Amy and her friends, and he often turns up. He's friendly enough, but he never hears anything you say the first time you say it, and he wears this slightly vacant expression, as though his body is present, but his mind is off conquering imaginary peaks.

"Just 'fine'?"

"OK, great then! He's been away for a couple of weeks. I think he's due back sometime next week. Depends on the weather. I guess I'll see him when I see him. At least he doesn't pressurize me."

"Is that enough for you? Is that what you want?"

"Why wouldn't it be?" She says it lightly, but the message is clear. She garrotes another bundle of beanpole tops. "Anyway, this isn't just about Dad."

"OK," I say, remembering Alexia's advice and waiting.

"I've got this really weird feeling, Joe. It started just after you came back into this timeline. Don't get me wrong, I'm not blaming you, but I can't shake it."

"What kind of feeling?"

"Familiar. At first, I thought I might travel again, but it's been years since that happened." She shakes her head. "That's not it. I don't know; it's like a sense that something's about to happen."

Against the far hedge, there's a galvanized water trough, fitted with a primitive ball cock valve like an old-fashioned toilet. A small rivulet of water pours out of a fissure in the metal, and the valve hisses quietly as the tank constantly refills. Amy ferries watering cans back and forth, drenching the beans I've just planted, and for a few minutes, I watch her in silence. Then, I decide it's time to come clean.

"Amy, I need to talk to you about why I couldn't get to the rehearsal yesterday. It might be related to how you're feeling."

She stops watering. "The second you didn't pick up, I knew something was going on. It wasn't anything to do with Molly, was it?"

"No," I admit. "Actually, I went to meet The Continuum, the people that blackmailed me to complete the Romano mission."

She puts down the watering can. "Joe! Why didn't you tell me?"

"I didn't know how to tell you over the phone, and anyway, I didn't know where I was going or how long for. You would have just been worried."

"But I could have come with you! Why am I always the last to know about everything?" She looks on the verge of tears, angry ones. "I've accepted the fact that I'm not welcome in the Bridgeman family, but I feel like I'm always on the outside of everything else too!"

"Don't say that." I try to put my arm around her, but she shrugs me off. "I know things aren't straightforward, but Mum and Dad love you so much. When we lost you, the family fell to pieces. It destroyed us. I was there, remember?"

"I'm not belittling what you went through, but the life you remember is just a fairy tale now. It might as well be, anyway. I sometimes wonder— in my darker moments—if I'm living a stolen life, that even though you saved me, the universe knows I should be dead."

"I can understand why you might feel that way, but—"

"Listen, Joe! It keeps grabbing at my heels, trying to pull me under. It's left me with this feeling like I've never quite surfaced from the water. Like a piece of me is still at the bottom of that lake." She picks up the spade and plunges it roughly into the ground. "I was being naive, you know."

I'm confused. "What do you mean?"

"I was so excited when you came back from saving me. It felt like a second chance. I actually believed that with this version of you here, things might change for the better. I started to look forward to waking up each day, to see what it would bring. But I was kidding myself. If anything, things are worse."

"Amy, no!" I protest, upset and frustrated. "They can't be! I've done everything I can to make things better for you. I just want you to be happy." She looks at me. Sometimes it's what people don't say that speaks the loudest. I can tell she's choosing not to remind me of all the times I lied to her about traveling back to London, how my traveling caused her visions to flare up again. "I didn't ask to get involved in the Romano mission. We've talked about this. You know I didn't. And at this meeting yesterday, they just wanted to explain what happened, and now I want to tell you."

Amy stands the spade against the shed wall, picks up a bag of compost, and pours the fine brown silt into the bottom of the trench she's just dug. I wish I could have taken her with me to meet Iris. She could have asked her own questions, drawn her own conclusions, instead of hearing it all through me. But Iris was very clear: Amy can't meet The Continuum yet, and she mustn't find out about her future role with them. It's too soon.

"Can I tell you about it? I want you to know, Amy. Please. This matters to me."

"If you like," she mutters, crouching and smoothing out little heaps of compost with her fingers.

"They wanted to explain everything, which was good, because you know I wanted some answers. Amy, the weird thing is, they're in the future. I mean, a long way into the future. Over a hundred years."

"Jesus." She stands up. Shivering, she pulls her jacket tighter around her torso. "Thank God I never traveled that far into the future." I take off the black-and-yellow scarf and lay it gently around her shoulders. "Thanks," she says, wrapping it snugly around her neck. "So did you get your answers?"

"Mostly, yes."

"And is it properly over now? The traveling, I mean?"

I wish I could tell her it was, but that's the old Joe. Amy is affected by things no matter what I say, and if I deny them, all it does is drive a wedge between us. "Not quite. They need my help. One of their time travelers has gone missing. They think he was attacked by the same woman who planted the radio that sent me to London. I told them I had a viewing of him, so they want me to help find him."

"Why did you tell them about the viewing? You don't owe them anything! You could have just kept quiet and gone home, and they'd have been none the wiser."

"But it was haunting me, driving me mad. I hadn't slept in days."

"I know what that feels like," she murmurs.

"And I didn't know what it meant, but when they said one of their guys was missing, I just knew that was what I've been seeing. A man's missing, Amy, maybe in serious danger."

She picks at her fingernail. "Are you going to help them?"

"I think so. I said I would."

"But why do you trust these people? You don't know anything about them, not really. Look at how badly they treated you, blackmailing you and threatening to put everything back to how it was . . . It's pure evil, Joe."

Amy's still angry with The Continuum, and who can blame her? "I can't explain it, Amy, but I trust them. I just do. They've promised me I'm just going along as an observer on this trip to Paris—"

"You're traveling to Paris now? How far back are you going?"

"To 1873. The missing traveler is there, they think."

Her hands clasp into tight fists. "I know that if you hadn't been brave enough to travel I wouldn't be standing here," she says, "but I can't believe, after everything I've just said, that you're going back to Paris with these people. And apart from anything else, who gave them the right to change things? How do you know you're not going to make things worse? It's like they're playing God."

"They don't see it that way. Iris told me that The Continuum is like a kind of immune system. They don't decide what to change. They just fix the things that time tells them to."

"That's what they're telling you, is it?" Amy pulls the clip out of her bun, shakes out her hair, then fastens it back in place. "At least this explains the constant unease I'm waking up with every morning."

I don't want to dismiss Amy's feelings, but I think she's wrong. "What can I do to reassure you?"

"I can see that helping The Continuum might give you a sense of purpose, but Joe, all this time travel is making *my* life difficult. I know the last time wasn't your fault, but this time you've chosen it."

"I wish I could prove to you that it's all going to be OK."

"Well, you can't, can you? Just do what you want. You will anyway."

"Please don't be like that."

"It's true though. I've told you that it's affecting me, but you won't stop." She picks up the wheelbarrow, lays the spade inside it, and pushes it toward a large brown heap on one of the nearby plots. "I've got a lot to do."

"Can I help?"

"I think it's best if I just get on with it. On my own."

She strides away purposefully, the spade tumbling noisily in the wheelbarrow, disturbing a group of crows that flies off, cawing in disapproval, toward the setting sun.

6

You've failed your mission, but I'm here to give you a second chance.

I wake up to the sound of my own voice, replaying Scarlett's words to Nils in Macau. The viewing again. I hold my breath, waiting for Scarlett to say more, willing the reel to keep rolling, but every time it stops at precisely the same place, as though the vinyl is scratched and the needle keeps jumping back around to the beginning.

It's still only 6:30 a.m., but I'm shot through with adrenaline and wide awake, so I roll out of bed and through the shower, throw on a shirt and some black jeans, then settle on one of the barstools in the kitchen. As my supersonic coffee machine brews my latte, I wonder how Amy is this morning. I can see why Mum said to leave her be, but I'm determined to do the reaching out this time. I've done a lot since my travels to London to repair the trust between us, but after yesterday we're back on a precarious tightrope over an abyss of mistrust. Amy and Dad clearly have some problems to work out, but I'm more worried about the deep-rooted sense of unease Amy talked about. That kind of talk reminds me of my old life. It smacks of depression. I'm going to stay close, even if she pushes me away.

I decide I'm going to see Vinny today. Talking things through with him makes me feel like I can deal with whatever life throws at me. I head downstairs into the shop, wind the clocks, walk the floor, and am busy checking yesterday's sales log when Molly arrives.

"Morning, Mr. Bridgeman," she says.

"Morning, Molly. You're early today."

"A few things to catch up on, and Bob is popping in later."

I have an inkling Molly holds a torch for Bob, one of my suppliers. She claims she doesn't approve of his scallywag ways, but she gives herself away with a faint blush whenever he's around. She removes her camel leather gloves and folds them neatly inside her handbag, then hangs her woolen coat on the rack. "Rather a good day yesterday. I rehomed the Queen Anne dressing table."

"I saw that! Who took it?" Molly and I have joked about this particular piece ever since I took over from Other Joe. It had been in the shop for as long as she could remember.

"A couple passing through on their way down to Weymouth. They run a bed-and-breakfast down there, thought it would suit one of their bedrooms."

"Brilliant," I say. "Glad it's found its new owners." Molly told me recently she sometimes likens the shop to an animal shelter. To her, the objects we sell have all been abandoned, and it's our job to care for them until they find their "forever homes."

We busy ourselves, Molly doing her daily round of dusting and stock-checking as I peruse the latest magazines to see what's hot, savoring the simple pleasures of a quiet morning and the chance to calm my busy mind. A couple of customers pop in to browse, and Molly sells an egg cup decorated with ducklings to a little girl who comes in to spend her birthday money.

Once the child and her father have left, I stand up and stretch. "I'm going to pop over and see Vinny."

Molly inclines her head in implicit approval. "Send him my regards," she says.

I walk through the chilly streets and across the park, scattering a crowd of pigeons who are busily picking at last night's discarded kebabs. Replaying my recent phone conversation with Vinny, I try to work out who the woman was. I didn't recognize her voice, and Vinny sounded unusually distracted. I also wonder how I'm going to break it to him that he can't come to Paris with me. He was upset he couldn't travel back to London with me the last time, but as his knee was in pieces, it was out of the question. This time it's not up to me. Gabrielle Green is only taking me under duress. I can't imagine her face if I turned up for the trip with Vinny in tow. Actually, I can, and it's not pretty.

When I get to Vinny's Vinyl, the door's shut, and the glass is so misted up I can't see inside. As I walk down the steps, I hear the muffled sound of music, a track with a heavy beat, and above that, raised voices. It sounds like an argument. I hesitate for a second, then go through the door.

Vinny glances up as I enter, raises a quick eyebrow at me, then focuses back on his customer, who hasn't even taken a breath. It's Dave. Dave is originally from Cardiff, still sounds as Welsh as the day he left, and he's one of Vinny's regulars. Dave can talk nonstop about every intricate detail of a record you've never even heard of, and it doesn't occur to him that you might not want to know. He's short—can't be more than five foot four—but what he lacks in stature, he makes up for in volume.

I tune out Vinny and Dave and take the opportunity to soak in the reassuringly familiar atmosphere of this place. The smell never changes, a combination of sour carpet, damp stone, and secondhand record sleeves. It's hard to explain why that smell is comforting, but it is. You get the occasional top note of stale sweat or carbolic soap, depending on the customers, but today it's the original scent. I leaf through racks of old vinyl, drawn as ever to Vinny's Beatles collection. I smile as I flick through the discs, wondering who will end up buying these and discovering the gems that are dotted between the hits.

"Cash!" Vinny calls to me. "You might know this. One of Dave's Dastardly Conundrums."

Dave sniggers. "I bet he won't."

"I bet I will," I say, walking over to the desk. Dave doesn't seem to like me very much, and for some reason, although I usually avoid conflict, I enjoy winding him up.

He folds his arms and stares up at me belligerently through bushy black eyebrows. "All right then, smart arse," he says. "What sophomore album was originally going to be called *Sheep*?"

"Is it well known?" I ask suspiciously. Dave is famous for asking us to guess the impossibly obscure.

"You could say that. Sold about twenty-four million copies."

"Right . . . I think I know this one." I try to sound confident, but I'm playing for time, racking my brain for the answer.

"See?" Dave turns triumphantly to Vinny. "Told you 'e wouldn't know."

Vinny deflates a little. "Oh well, never mind. Dave, you're going to have to—"

"That's it!" I cry.

"What?" says Vinny, confused.

"*Nevermind*. Nirvana, 1991. If I remember right, they double tracked Cobain's vocals because that's what John Lennon did."

Dave grunts in disgust.

Vinny chuckles. "Good one, Cash! I remember now . . . *Sheep* was an inside joke about how the masses would all flock to the album, and they got that right. *Nevermind* was added to the National Recording Registry a few years back, you know."

"The *what*?" I love Vinny's inside knowledge of music, but his facts are a bit obscure at times.

"National Recording Registry. It's the US government's collection of the most culturally significant sound recordings. They've got all kinds of cool stuff. Martin Luther King's 'I Have a Dream' speech is in there somewhere, and the soundtrack of *Star Wars*. If there was an asteroid strike and that was all that was left of us, just imagine what a future civilization might think. Apparently 'Footloose' is in there too."

Dave guffaws. "Kenny Loggins? Culturally significant? You're 'aving a laugh, aren't you?"

"Never been more serious," Vinny says. "Right, Dave, are you going to buy that lot?" He indicates a pile of vinyl stacked up at the end of the cash desk.

"As it 'appens, Fatcheeks, I'm not."

"Right. Bugger off then. Cash and I have some business to attend to."

"Roger that." He saunters off toward the door. "See you tomorrow."

"I'm closed Mondays," Vinny counters.

Dave seems baffled for a moment, then grins. "You're a card, Mr. Fry. Ta-ta." He yanks open the door and stomps up the steps to street level. The door bangs shut behind him.

"What did he call you?" I ask Vinny.

"What do you mean?"

"*Fatcheeks?*"

"Oh that. Means *hamster* in Welsh, apparently. 'Term of endearment,' so he says." He saunters over to the door and turns the sign to Shut. "Right then, Cash, follow me to the fat cave. We've got things to discuss." He leads me back through the shop to his office, standing back so I can enter ahead of him. "Lean before mean."

"You're not mean, Vinny."

"You've never tried to take food off me."

Vinny's office is more like a graveyard for crockery than a place of work. There's a desk in here somewhere, I know there is, but it's hidden beneath a motley collection of stained coffee mugs, stacks of old magazines, hundreds of photos, and several empty cookie packets.

"Been sifting through old memories?" I ask, grinning at a faded photo of a much thinner Vinny standing proudly outside Vinny's Vinyl. "I remember him."

"Oh yeah, that was the day I opened," he says. He closes the office door behind him. "Happy days."

I pick my way around the desk, crunching bits of cookie underfoot. I move a curry-stained dinner plate onto the floor and lower myself into the battered leather chair sulking in the corner.

Vinny balances himself precariously on a machinist's stool opposite me. "Right, Cash, don't leave me in suspenders. Uncle Vincent is sitting comfortably. Tell me everything."

"You don't look very comfortable," I say.

He shifts a bit. "S'OK. It'll keep me focused. So you met Iris? And she's in the future? You said she was some kind of hologram?"

"It was incredible, Vin," I say. "You'd have wet your pants. Gabrielle put her watch down on the floor—"

"Who's Gabrielle again?"

"American woman. Came to meet me at the book launch and took me to meet Iris at the Broadway. She's a time traveler too."

"Does she have a watch like yours?"

"Sort of. Except she wears hers on her wrist with this leather strap—grunge style. Anyway, she took it off and laid it on the floor, and these things flew out of the back of it into the corners of the room, like bright green fireflies, and they scanned the room, then they started to behave like mini projectors, and this woman—Iris—just sort of appeared in front of me."

"A three-dimensional hologram. Incredible." Vinny rubs his tummy and searches for a fresh packet of cookies. "Was she solid? Materially, I mean?"

"She looked solid, but she said she wasn't really there, and so she couldn't interact with anything."

"Did you try and touch her, though?"

"Of course not! I wasn't about to start poking around!"

"I need to read up on hologram etiquette," Vinny says pensively, as he chews a piece of shortbread. "I'm more familiar with android protocols. Anyway, when we talked on the phone, you were just about to tell me about this missing time traveler."

"Right. His name is Nils Petersen. He's the one I've been seeing in my viewing."

"What happened to him?"

"They don't know, but Scarlett was there, Nils disappeared, and then he unexpectedly turned up in Paris in 1873. And they think my viewings might be the key to finding out what happened to him."

Vinny's eyes light up like beacons. "So cool. Heading back into the past, a mystery that needs solving, and you might have the answer!"

My heart sinks. He looks so excited. How am I going to tell him he can't come with me? "I don't have the answer, not yet anyway. What I've seen so far doesn't help much, except it confirms that Scarlett was involved. The viewing keeps stopping at the same place every time, but I know there's more. I've just got to find a way to access it."

"What did Scarlett do to him, Cash? First, she sends us off to London; now, she's disappeared this Nils bloke. What does she want?"

"They don't know. She used to be one of their students, and all they know is that she doesn't agree with the way they do things. But she hasn't made any demands or threats, hasn't made any contact with The Continuum at all."

"Weird." He scratches his head. "So how come you saw a viewing of Nils? I thought you had to connect with people?"

"It was from Scarlett's viewpoint, so I think it's because I have a connection to her."

"And they think you going to Paris might trigger more of your viewing to come through?"

"That's what Iris is hoping, anyway."

"Paris, though! In 1873!" He giggles like a schoolboy.

"I know. When they were asking me to go on the mission, I thought you'd never forgive me if I said no."

"Too right! So why did Nils end up there?"

"It's a change event—a mission, apparently—and somehow he's become attached to it. There was a huge opera house fire, completely destroyed the entire building."

"Holy cashmolee! What do you have to do?"

"I wish I knew. It's Gabrielle's mission, and she isn't exactly forthcoming with information."

"But you're on the same team!"

"I don't think she sees it that way."

"Maybe she's threatened by you."

I consider this, trying unsuccessfully to recall a single instance of Gabrielle showing any vulnerability. "It's tough, Vinny. I want to be useful. I want to help them find Nils, but I don't know enough about what's going on. Gabrielle said she would brief me on the way, but you know how it is when you travel: you go from here to there in a blink of an eye." I pick grumpily at a loose thread on the arm of the chair. "I think Bill would've briefed me properly if he'd been here."

"Yeah. Poor bloke, cut down just as you were beginning to learn from him. How about Iris, can she fill you in?"

"For some reason, she trusts Gabrielle to brief me. She didn't tell me much more than I've told you." I lean in, grab one of the cookies, and take a bite. Its sweet, buttery, crumbly mouthfeel is reassuring. "I feel better talking to you about it, though. What would I do without you?"

Vinny's face falls, and his shoulders slump. "Cash, I can't stand it. I can't put it off any longer. I've got to tell you something."

"What is it?"

"I don't think I'm going to be able to come to Paris with you."

My initial rush of relief fades to concern. "Why not? Are you OK?"

"Healthwise? Fit as a fiddle," he says. "Nothing like that. I've had some . . ." He raises his hands in air quotes, ". . . news."

"What news?"

"You're not the only one who's been contacted out of the blue."

I put two and two together. "The woman you were with yesterday?" He nods. "Who is she?"

"An old flame of mine. Kassandra." He tilts his head wistfully, like a puppy denied a bone. "She always reminded me of Kim Wilde, back in the day. Gorgeous, she was. Filled out a bit now, but haven't we all. Still lush, though."

"Why did she get back in touch?"

"You're not going to believe this," he says. "I can barely believe it myself. Turns out"—he swallows hard—"I'm a dad."

"Oh my God, Vinny, that's amazing!"

"I've got a daughter, Cash. She's fifteen." His eyes shine a little brighter than usual as he clears his throat. "She's called Charlotte."

"Congratulations, Vinny." I stand up and give him an awkward hug, trying not to topple him off his stool. "Have you got a photo?"

"No. I mean, I saw one yesterday, but I haven't got one to show you."

"Wow. You're a dad." I shake my head in disbelief. "And you had no idea?"

"None. Kassandra was always the one that got away. You know?"

My heart contracts as I recall Alexia handing me her Saint Christopher necklace. *Just promise me you'll bring him back.* "How do you feel about it all?"

"Honestly, it's a dream come true. Me and Kassandra were good together. I know it didn't work out at the time—she ended up marrying someone else—but turns out we created a life! An actual human being. Charlotte's half me! Poor kid." He chuckles softly.

Vinny is a hopeless romantic. It's good to see him so happy, but I can't help worrying. He seems to be taking all of this at face value. Call me cynical, but I can't help wondering what Kassandra's motives are. Why turn up now? What does she want? Vinny is my friend, and he's such a natural optimist that I don't want him to walk blindly into a situation that isn't what it seems.

"Is Kassandra still married?" I ask carefully.

"Nope. They got divorced last year. She said they grew apart. She's moved back to the area, which is why she thought she'd get in touch."

"Did you ask why she didn't tell you about Charlotte before?"

Vinny looks surprised. "Er, no, I didn't think to. I'm sure she had her reasons." He really is smitten.

"And does Charlotte know about you?"

"Kassandra told her about me last year. Apparently, she's been hassling her mum ever since. Wants to meet me. Wants to meet her . . . dad." His chest puffs out and he looks, if it's possible, a little bigger than usual. He waves his hand toward the desk. "I've been putting together a photo album for her, making up for lost time. I should probably pull together a list of my top albums, TV shows, and films too . . . Maybe you could help me, Cash? She's got fifteen years of her old dad's life to catch up on! Imagine, all that time passed and neither of us knew the other one was there." His face clouds over. "Wish I'd known when she was a baby. I love little ones, bouncing them on me knee, making 'em giggle. I feel bad though, Cash."

"You mustn't, Vin. You didn't even know she existed."

"I'm not talking about Charlotte. I'm talking about you. I feel bad leaving you to time travel on your own."

"Mate, you mustn't. To be honest, I don't even know if you could have come. I'm being dragged along with Gabrielle, and she's made it very clear she'd rather I wasn't involved."

"But why?" Vinny scratches his head. "I still don't get it. Doesn't she want you to help find this Nils bloke?"

"I've no idea," I say. "She seems to care a lot about him, and she's very angry with Scarlett, but she's also being a complete trout with me. She point-blank refused to tell me anything about the Paris mission."

Vinny spins slowly around on his stool. When he's turned full circle, his expression has shifted. "OK, so I was thinking . . . I could be the Norman to your Jesse, if you like?"

Somewhere in the back of my brain, some rusty teenage TV connections spark into life. "*Street Hawk?*"

"Yeah," he says, as though it's obvious. "Even though I can't come with you, wherever you go, I'll be back at base, helping out."

"Until you're ready to get back in the field."

"That's right." He taps his temple. "Let me take care of things in the background."

"Nothing would make me happier," I say.

I think of my friends in terms of a circle. Some are fair-weather friends. They float around the edges, and they're a blast when the sun's shining. Nothing wrong with that. Some are inside the circle. We have a laugh, but they'll give me the time of day when things aren't perfect and occasionally share some of their vulnerabilities. But some friends, like Vinny, are at the center of everything. They listen, advise, and tell me the truth even when it hurts. They take interest in my hopes and dreams. They celebrate with me when I triumph, and they cry with me when I fall. If you have friends like that, treasure them.

I stand up and reach out my arms. "Get over here, you big old dad you." Vinny climbs off the stool, and we have a proper bear hug.

When it's over, Vinny pats me on the back, and we sit again. "How did the party go, by the way?" he asks.

"I think Dad really enjoyed himself, and most people seemed to have a great time, but Amy got upset and left early."

"What happened?" he asks, popping a whole cookie into his mouth.

"She and Dad don't get on, so she doesn't enjoy family stuff at the best of times, and Dad's speech was a bit . . . wrong. I went after her, and we had a chat. I tried to help, but I don't know . . . I told her about this Paris stuff, because I don't want to hide things from her anymore, but I'd say she was just as bad when I left her. Maybe worse."

Vinny swallows his cookie. "It'll be OK, Cash. Give her some time. She's just going through a sticky patch, but with you looking out for her, she'll come out the other side. Nothing stays the same for long. Look at me! Last week, I was Cheltenham's most eligible bachelor. Now, I'm Charlotte's dad!"

I chuckle. "You never know what's around the corner."

"Best that way." Vinny's face falls. "Cash! I've just had a terrible thought. When are you off to Paris?"

"I don't know. Why?"

"You might miss quiz night!"

7

The following day Gabrielle Green calls at 4 p.m. She loudly informs me that we're leaving in an hour and to get my ass to the Broadway Hotel pronto, then she hangs up. I do as I'm told, and as I run across Cheltenham, I wonder what one should pack for a trip to 1873, apart from antibiotics. So far, my trips back in time have been little jaunts in comparison to my impending journey. My nerves are jagged with anticipation, but also singing with excitement. The past is waiting, and I think I'm about to experience what real time travel is all about.

I knock. Gabrielle opens the door and glares at me. I follow her inside.

Her suite is grand, palatial even, but she's done her best to bring it down a level. Clothes are scattered across the floor, and in the gaps are cans and bottles and empty pizza boxes. In comparison, my place is positively tidy. In the center of the room is a small leather suitcase next to a coffee table, and in the far corner there's a tall cardboard container, the kind they store your clothing in when you move. Inside are racks of extravagant clothing, fit for the most authentic TV period drama.

"Did you bring your pocket watch?" she asks.

"Yes." I instinctively tap my chest, feeling my silver hunter beneath my jacket. Gabrielle seems annoyed, which makes me wonder if she was hoping I might forget it. Although, based on past experience, that might not have mattered. Bill gave it to me, to help with the Romano mission.

When he told me I couldn't lose it, he meant that literally. It has the ability to ping back around my neck if we are separated too long. In some ways that's reassuring; it's also a little unsettling.

Gabrielle explains that we're leaving at 5 p.m. and gives me strict instructions on what to wear. As I get dressed, I realize this is the first time I've known in advance exactly what year I'm going to. Hopefully, in these clothes, I will blend in. I study myself in the mirror: white shirt, cream-colored trousers, pointy shoes, and a long black jacket buttoned up over my chest. The finishing touch is a top hat and blue silk scarf. Initially, I was uncertain, but now that the outfit is complete, I reckon I've scrubbed up rather well.

"Christ," Gabrielle sniggers. "You look like Ebenezer Scrooge."

I turn to face her, thinking up a decent retort, but when I see her, I'm completely disarmed by her breathtaking outfit. It's hard to believe, but she has become elegance personified, in a dark-red bodice that puffs out into a long velvet skirt. Creamy-white frills of fabric explode from her neck and cascade down her chest. The rear of her dress stretches up and back in gravity-defying fashion. If she wanted to, she could smuggle me into the past under there and no one would know.

Facing the mirror, she starts jabbing pins into her hair. I've never seen such a complicated stack of reinforced twists and rolls. On top, she places a tiny silk hat in matching red.

"Seven minutes to go, Golden Boy," she says, through a mouth full of hair grips. "Just enough time to go through the three most important rules: don't try and change anything, don't slow me down, and don't get in my way."

I sigh, tugging at the upstanding collar of my shirt, which is so stiff it's already chafing my neck. "Is there anything I need to know that doesn't begin with *don't*?"

She spins and glares at me. "You need facial hair."

"I'm sorry, what?"

"Your baby skin is gonna stick out like a spanked ass."

She rummages around in her suitcase of surprises and hands me a couple of warm, sticky brown things, a bit like flattened slugs.

"What are these?"

"Sideburns," she says, matter-of-factly. "Put them on."

"They look fake."

"Five minutes, Bridgeman!"

"All right." I peel them gingerly apart and press them to my jaw, just below my ears. They immediately grip my skin like leeches, which is deeply unnerving, and then sprout into bushy, realistic-looking facial hair. I tug at this new growth, fighting the urge to panic. What if these are permanent?

A sharp stabbing pain at the top of my left arm snaps me back into focus. I'm horrified to see Gabrielle holding a fat, now-empty syringe. "What the hell are you doing?" I gasp.

"Oh sorry, did you want the plague?" she snarls.

"Of course not," I retort, feeling light-headed and rubbing at my arm. "But it's polite to ask before you inject someone."

"I'm going to do me too," she says defensively. She picks up an identical syringe and jabs it into her arm, wincing briefly. "It's a two-way inoculation. We don't want to pick anything up or bring anything back, and we certainly don't want to infect Paris with your gross naïveté."

"Ha bloody ha," I say. This is going to be a long mission.

"I have a clean record," she says. "Eleven successful missions. I've never failed, and I'm not going to start now."

"And I'm not an idiot."

"That's questionable."

"I did OK on the Romano mission. Just cut me some slack, will you?"

She huffs irritably. "Find Nils, then I'll cut you some slack. Until then, just do as I say and don't try anything stupid."

Another *don't* rule. She's testing my patience, but we're about to head back a couple of centuries together, so I keep my mouth shut and play along for now.

Gabrielle checks her watch, which is concealed beneath a layer of lace, and glides to the door with uncharacteristic poise. There's a horseshoe hanging from a hook, which she spins until it's the right way up. She moves to the desk and pulls out a rabbit's foot on a silver chain from one of the drawers. She kisses that, places it back down, and then knocks three times on the wooden top.

My nerves are already buzzing. Watching her weird superstitions is not helping.

She focuses her attention on the small travel case by the coffee table. I've been aware of it since I arrived, and I can feel the psychometric energy pouring from it in invisible waves. Its power has been building and is tangible now—as though it knows we're here and wants us to unlock its secrets, similar to the radio that sent me back to the 1960s. It's a focus object, our ticket to ride. I'm sure of it.

Gabrielle snaps open two metal latches, lifts the lid, and pauses. Inside the box is an object wrapped in a cloth. I hear distant music, and for just a moment I think it might be in the hotel, but I'm hearing echoes of the past: classical violins, pianos, haunting melodies, and faint voices calling over each other.

"You hear that too, right?" I ask.

Gabrielle shushes me. "Unless you want me to go without you, I need to concentrate." She gently extricates the focus object from its housing, as though trying not to leave fingerprints, and places it on the coffee table. She exhales loudly and then unwraps it.

It's an antique metronome, a neat pyramid of faded walnut, chipped and well-used. On its side is a tarnished bronze winding ring. Its timing rod—currently set to the central position—begins to move, left and then right.

Click . . . Clack . . . Click . . . Clack . . .

The weight that controls the tempo slides down a little each time it passes the center, increasing the speed with every movement. My mind keeps pace, anticipating the huge jump we're about to make. Nervous energy swirls in my stomach and then ripples over me in a wave of cautious excitement.

"Are you ready?" Gabrielle beams delightedly at me like a sister who knows I'm in big trouble, and her constant disdain actually fuels my determination. I lift my chin. "I'm ready."

She takes my hand, her skin hot and clammy. "Don't get any ideas. It's just on the way out." A chorus of harmonized voices rises in a crescendo that sends shivers over my entire body. A glowing mist cascades down the sides of the metronome like a slow-motion waterfall in moonlight. It's utterly mesmerizing. As though sensing my admiration, a deep, resonant hum joins the orchestra like a bow drawn across the lowest string of a hundred cellos.

Gabrielle is practically vibrating, and her face is glowing with excitement. "I freakin' love this part!" she yells, and I find myself grinning back at her. Madness appears to be catching.

The metronome is now revving like a piston engine. A symphony fills my head. The hotel room dims, the present fades. Gabrielle grips my hand tightly and, with the other hand, reaches out and touches the metronome.

Traveling is instantaneous. I've learned it's much better to close my eyes.

In a searing rush the metronome releases its pent-up energy, a story it's been waiting to tell for nearly a hundred and fifty years. The hotel room, the deafening orchestra, the present, they all disappear in a disorientating rush. Gravity shifts suddenly; my ears pop and my stomach flips.

I open my eyes to total darkness. I can't even see my hand in front of my face, but I can tell I'm lying on my back next to Gabrielle, and I can smell saw dust and fruit and vegetables. We're moving, jolting roughly back and forth, and there's a rumbling beneath us, the sound of hooves and muffled voices. Gabrielle's hand tugs away from mine. Reaching up, I feel the rough surface of a tarpaulin a foot or so above my face. Seems like we've landed in the back of a horse-drawn cart. It lurches and then comes to a stop.

"Right, here we are," Gabrielle says nonchalantly, as though we've just shared a three-hour bus journey. She scrabbles around in the darkness next to me, lifts the tarpaulin, and peers out. "Come on, let's go."

I work myself upright, struggling over sacks of vegetables, and clamber cautiously down from the cart onto a broad street packed full of carriages. It's dark, and the air is cool. Stone buildings tower above us on each side. I'm expecting the driver to ask us what we're doing, but his focus is on a uniformed man standing in the road, gesticulating wildly. I think he's talking to the driver about his horses. It's hard to tell; my French is more than a little rusty. In fact, it's pretty much nonexistent. As I adjust to the new light, temperature, and culture shock, I wonder if the arrival experience will ever become familiar.

I follow Gabrielle to the edge of the road. She grabs the silver hunter from around my neck and holds it to her wristwatch for a couple of seconds until it bleeps. "OK, we're synchronized," she says. "October 28, 1873."

I admire my surroundings. Paris, 1873: the boulevards ablaze with ornate iron gaslights that extend forever in all directions, the sidewalks crammed full of exceptionally well-dressed people.

"Local time is 9:35 p.m.," Gabrielle continues. "That means the fire is in full flow already."

"We've landed on the night of the fire?"

"Of course, you always land at the end first."

I think about how I watched Lucy Romano gunned down and then went back to stop it from ever happening. It reminds me of how Vinny likes to read novels. He always skips to the end first, to see if it's worth bothering with. Perhaps time is the same.

"What do we do now?" I ask.

She checks her watch again. "Still calibrating. Just remember: you're here to find Nils, to observe only . . . Do not slow me down."

She strides off, darting and weaving between the brightly colored throngs of people, like a professional figure skater navigating a crowd of amateurs. The wide sidewalks are thrumming with couples, smiling and happy, in no hurry at all. The men are dressed in dark suits, and it's impossible to spot one who isn't wearing a top hat. The women are trounced up like French fancies in pristine pastel dresses. Gabrielle looks right at home, or at least she would if she weren't rushing. These people, long gone, stroll through Paris as if they have all the time in the world. I follow her past enticingly lit shops, most of them selling coffee and ice cream. Seats are set up outside; people chat and laugh and pass the time. I catch a whiff of coffee and cognac, warm and bittersweet. I'm embarrassed to say I was expecting Paris to stink, to be one massive open sewer, but the truth is it's way cleaner than I imagined—cleaner than twenty-first-century Paris anyway. It's glossy and confident, and everyone is beautifully turned out.

A waft of creamy vanilla makes my stomach growl, right as Gabrielle turns to me and growls herself, "This is taking way too long. We're miles from the opera house." She darts into the entrance of a brightly lit jewelry shop where an elegant middle-aged couple browses through the window, admiring sparkling diamonds and precious stones.

The boulevard, crammed with carriages, has become blocked by a long cart stacked high with barrels. People are shouting things I can't understand, but I do recognize the universal hand gesture for "Get the hell out of the way." The couple turns to see what the fuss is all about. The man talks at me. I can't understand a word. I look to Gabrielle for help, but she's facing the other way, scanning the street, so I swallow, flush red, and point at my mouth. The woman leans toward her husband and, behind her hand, whispers in his ear. He tilts his hat at me, and they walk off down the street. They obviously feel sorry for the poor, mute man.

Gabrielle tuts. "We need to get ourselves a ride. We're losing time."

"Iris mentioned some translation technology so I can understand the lingo. Can you give it to me, please?"

"You don't need to understand," she replies curtly.

I stand my ground. "Gabrielle, I know it's a long shot that I can track Nils down, if he's even here. But if I'm supposed to find him, I need to connect with this place, with the people. How can I do that if I don't understand what they're saying?"

Gabrielle reaches into her capacious carpetbag and pulls out a small black box. "Fine. Hold out your hand." She tips what looks like a grain of rice into my palm.

"What is it?"

"Put it in your ear."

I do as I'm told, fumbling a bit, worried I'm going to drop it. As the tiny device touches the skin of my ear canal, it disappears. I imagine myself on my hands and knees searching for it, but then I feel it burrow under my skin. No pain, just the worrying sensation of a foreign body inviting itself in.

"What the hell is it?" I say, mild panic building.

She glowers back at me. "Please stop drawing attention to us."

I would probably continue to panic if it weren't for the loud ringing in my ears and sudden fireworks exploding in my brain, like pyrotechnics of understanding. I'm worried my head might pop, but then the pressure subsides. Glancing up, I see that the sound I heard was a real bell. A red omnibus, packed full of firemen and drawn by two magnificent white horses, comes to a stop in the street. One of the firemen—a broad man wearing a black suit and boots, an impressive brass helmet, and matching buttons—jumps down to try and clear the traffic jam. "The opera house is on fire!" he booms, his mustache so long it twitches to its own rhythm as he talks. "Clear the streets immediately. Make way, make way!"

His voice is deep and rich with a strong French accent, the words flowing with a smooth nasal quality, and yet he's speaking perfectly understandable English—at least that's what I hear. I scan the street and, with childlike wonder, discover that I can read all the shop names and signage. It seems this clever little device isn't just about translation; it's fundamentally altering my understanding of everything around me. The world feels like mine again. All it took was a minuscule piece of the future to bury itself in my ear. This might be difficult to surrender.

The fireman organizes his men, and people begin to cooperate, opening up gaps in the road. In all the excitement, I lose track of Gabrielle. I should have known she would ditch me. I swear out loud. "God damn it. Why the hell would she do that? What a bitch!"

"I can hear you, you know," she says, her voice inside my head like a ghost. I spin around. No sign of her. "Look to your left, dummy."

And there is Gabrielle, about fifteen feet from me, middle finger raised. She's seated among four firemen who are hanging onto the side of the omnibus. "I got us a ride," she says, her voice as clear as if she were standing right next to me. "You've got about five seconds to hop on."

8

I dart across the street toward the omnibus, but before I can climb on, my path is blocked by the fireman who cleared the traffic jam. He towers over me. "Where do you think you're going?"

One of his men steps in and gestures at Gabrielle. "Colonel, they are reporters for the *New York Times*. They need to get to the opera house. I said we would take them."

He considers this for a fleeting moment, but it's evident his concern is elsewhere. "It's your choice," he says to us authoritatively. "But I can't guarantee your safety. Just hang on tight."

I squeeze myself onto a bench next to Gabrielle and grip the metal rail that runs the length of the omnibus. The horses whinny and take off, the vehicle lurching forward. We gain speed, the bell clanging loudly as we pass through a narrow gap in the traffic. People dart out of the way. Others watch with interest, probably wondering what's on fire. I guess some of them will read about it in the paper tomorrow, marveling at how they were only a few miles from the scene.

Through the streets we charge, illuminated by gaslights, bright as day. The bell warns those ahead to move aside. I'm surprised by how smooth the ride is. I was expecting cobblestone, but the road is covered with something more akin to tightly packed gravel. Our carriage makes almost no sound, just the squeak of the wheels and the steady beat of the horses' hooves.

My head still buzzes with my sudden knowledge of the French language. "What the hell has this thing done to me?" I ask Gabrielle, massaging my ear.

She smirks. "Just a bit of temporary rewiring. Don't worry, you won't be permanently clever."

"So I can speak French if I want to?"

"You're speaking it right now."

"No, I'm not."

"Yes, you are. Try it out on someone."

I turn to the fireman next to me. "Excuse me, how much farther is it?"

He turns back to me and, speaking English with a very authentic French accent, he says, "Just a few minutes, we're nearly there."

Astonished, I turn back to Gabrielle.

"See?" she says smugly. It's hard not to be impressed. Fortunately, I don't have time to consider the damage that the implant might also be doing to me. We screech around a corner and cross a bridge over the river Seine. Glowing boats bob in the darkness on either side of us. We pass through a thin swirling mist, and I smell the first tinge of bitter smoke. The air thickens, transforming the brilliant globes of gaslight into a runway. The streets are emptying, and the smooth surface gives way to a bone-rattling cobblestone street.

The sky glows orange, flames reflected on the nearby buildings. Screams soar above an omnipresent, groaning rumble. We rush past a stampede of bewildered-looking people, their faces blackened by smoke. A horse gallops past us without a rider. I see a young girl dressed for the cancan run by on bare feet, sobbing. Two men are fighting, another trying to pull them apart. A pack of dogs scampers along the road, barking excitedly. Hot wind carries the acrid smell of wood smoke, along with a sense of madness in the air. The light intensifies around us, and the crackling, popping, and low roar of the fire are clearer now. We turn a corner and are plunged into a scene from hell itself.

The opera house is being consumed by a ravenous inferno, adjacent buildings shining gold in its menacing glow. It still stands defiant, but it's obvious that it's going to lose, and soon. Half of the auditorium roof is already gone, revealing a lattice of smoldering red beams. The front of the building remains eerily intact, a row of tall archways framing and accentuating the fire within.

Thousands of people surround the doomed building, dressed in their finest evening wear. They shout and gasp as bright orange flame spews into the night sky, followed by swirling clouds of thick gray smoke. Their expressions match my own: shock, pity, fear, panic. Of course, I checked this out on Google before we left. A few news articles, some illustrations of the fire—all with that reassuring long-ago distance. History on a screen, flat and unmoving. Soundless. Safe. Nothing could have prepared me for this shocking display of fire's raw and uncontrollable power.

The firemen seated around us jump down from the carriage, moving in an organized fashion, focused and seemingly without fear. A couple of them head toward a steam-powered pump, bright-red and gleaming, like something from a toy train set. They draw hoses from reels at its base, dragging them toward the battle. Men have already formed lines, creating a fast and effective relay of water buckets. Bravely, defiantly, they work together like ants trying to save a nest. The fire growls, crackles and hisses like an angry beast. People shout back as though proving they aren't afraid. The heat is oppressive, stealing oxygen from the air. My eyeballs are completely dry, my lungs already burning.

Instincts take over at times like these, when faced with the madness of such an explosive force. My entire being just wants to run, to back away, so I watch in awe as the firemen run *toward* the fire, dragging hoses under their arms like the tentacles of a huge sea monster, alive and pulsing with cold water. They are trying to save lives, knowing they could lose their own. I spot some of them clambering up ladders propped against the side of the building. They shoot jets of water down onto the fire, creating boiling clouds of steam.

Gabrielle says, "Are you OK?"

I turn and stare at her, uncertain what to say. I thought I knew what I was getting into, but now that we're here, I'm close to slipping into shock. My stomach cramps; I can't get enough air. I try to focus. I'm supposed to be searching for Nils. But what does that mean? Did I really think I was going to spot him in the crowd? What was my plan? Wander over and calmly explain that I'm here to save him?

"Can you hear me?" Gabrielle looks as though she's winding up a hard get-a-grip-Bridgeman slap.

"I'm all right," I force myself to say. "It's just, the fire . . . it's so out of control . . . I can't believe they didn't lose the whole of Paris!"

Gabrielle checks her watch. I do the same; 10:03 p.m. She regards the fiery glow with a grim expression, then turns her attention back to me. "Listen. This is my chance to get clues, to figure out what I need to do when I come back. I need to get closer. Why don't you stay here, get yourself together, keep your eyes open for Nils, just tune in . . . do whatever it is you need to do."

"But what happens if we get split up?"

"It doesn't matter. When I return to the present, you will come with me whether we're touching or not. Got it?"

It's so tempting to back away from all this, to do as I'm told. It's what Gabrielle wants anyway, for me to just fade away, but the honest truth is that I don't want her to leave me here on my own. "I'm OK. I'll come with you."

"Suit yourself, but I'm not slowing down."

She pushes her way through the crowd. I follow, trying not to stare at the people, some being carried, faces cut and burned and smudged black with soot. The opera house groans, a terrible, sorrowful sound. People cry out as a section of the roof collapses in on itself, sending a rushing gout of brilliant flame high into the air. It's followed by a thundering crash that briefly silences the crowd.

On we go, pushing toward the opera house through a wall of oppressive heat. It hurts to blink. One of the tall arched windows explodes, sending a lashing tongue of flame into the narrow street and forcing the crowd to scramble away. Glass and glowing embers shower down, horses rear, people shout. There's a surging stampede, and some people fall. I lift a woman back onto her feet, but she's gone before I even see her face. Gabrielle helps another, asking everyone we pass if they have seen Philippe Chevalier. She's shouting it at an elderly couple when a young man, face contorted with fear, grabs hold of her arm. "Philippe saved us," he says, voice trembling, "but he went back inside."

"Why?" Gabrielle asks him.

The man shakes his head, his sorrowful expression reflected in the incandescent glow. "I don't know. He got us out. We were all safe, but he went back inside." He pushes his way back through the crowd. We keep moving, but it's slow going. We help people who have fallen as we work our way around stacked furniture and other belongings rescued from the fire.

I keep checking my watch, mentally cataloging events as best I can. It helps to focus on something. It's 10:26 p.m. Another crash, this one so loud it sounds like the world itself was made of glass and just exploded. The crowd is stunned into a haunting silence as Parisians watch their beloved opera house burn. There is a shocking inevitability to this.

At 10:40 p.m. someone cries, "Look, it's the Phantom!" People point to what remains of the entrance to the opera house. Emerging through the flame is a ghostly figure wrapped in steaming rags, who staggers forward and collapses.

People immediately rush to the figure. Someone kneels, turns, and shouts, "It's Philippe! He's alive!"

A fireman douses him with a bucket of water, which hisses angrily upon contact. A couple of men in uniform pick him up and place him on a makeshift stretcher. There is no protocol, no checking his vital signs, no precautions in case of spinal injuries. This is hurried, rough and brutal. With a man at either end of the stretcher, they lift Philippe and shout, "Make way! Clear a path!" Gabrielle and I try to follow, but the mass of people lifts and surges like an angry sea. Philippe's head lolls to the side, eyes pinched shut. The charred rags he must have soaked and wrapped around himself are seared to his skin. His face is partially burned, but that will heal. His arms are a different story, the skin blackened among flashes of angry red. Horrified, I look away and notice a man pushing people aside to reach the stretcher—a tall imposing figure with a long beard, red cravat, and determined expression. When he reaches Philippe, he leans over and whispers into his ear.

Philippe gazes up at him, but my view is impaired. One of the firemen pushes the man out of the way: "Give us room! Let the man breathe!"

Gabrielle tugs at my arm, her expression grim. "This is going to be tough, but if we're going to help Philippe, we must get involved. We need to try and talk to him." I nod and follow her through the mass of people.

A woman next to me screams, sending my heart rate into an even higher gear. "There are people on the roof! Up there! Somebody, help them!" She points, her expression abject horror. I follow her outstretched finger and see a man and a woman perched high on a ledge, surrounded by angry, roiling clouds of smoke. They are dressed for the opera, cowering beneath a stone statue. Tendrils of fire lash around them, working up and around the side of the building. In a few seconds, they will be faced with a terrible choice.

People on the streets below hastily gather hay bales and smashed-up tables and chairs that I presume were dragged from the building. It's understandable, they have to do something, but if the people on the roof jump, they won't survive the fall.

"Can we help them?" I ask Gabrielle.

"It's OK," she says. "No one dies tonight, remember?"

"But are you sure?" I watch helplessly as the couple presses their backs against the statue, fire licking at their feet. Smoke plumes around them in a blue haze. There is no way they're going to escape. Gabrielle must be wrong.

Then, unbelievably, a wall of cool wind passes over Paris. It clears the smoke around the trapped couple and sends the fire in the opposite direction, back toward the center of the building. The crowd collectively gasps in surprise and relief, and I join them, my heart pounding.

I spot the fireman from earlier, the colonel with the huge mustache who cleared the street and brought us here. His brass helmet gleams, and he reminds me of a gladiator going into battle. He positions a ladder against the wall and scales it at speed. Others join him, shouting defiantly against the fire that dares to devour their history. As I watch a fireman guide the couple down the ladder, onlookers call out encouragement, and a few of them applaud as the last of the group reaches solid ground.

The stonework where they had taken shelter moments before collapses in on itself, sending a deluge of sparks into the night sky and a cloud of gray dust over those near to the building. Parisians on the street appear lost, bemused, or consumed by a morbid fascination, uncertain whether they should stay and watch.

We head toward a designated area for the injured, separated by carts, barrels, broken chairs, and tables. Stretchers, some no more than planks of wood, are organized in rows. Survivors hold rags to their faces, coughing and moaning. A row of horses and carts are loaded with the injured.

There's no sign of Philippe. In the distance, I spot the distinctive outline of a tall man, the one I saw whispering in Philippe's ear. He is walking slowly away from the fire, accompanied by a small group, some holding instruments, others dressed in full operatic garb.

I clear my throat, which is gravelly from the smoke. "Who is he?"

"You don't need to know."

"Listen," I say, forcing myself to sound calm, "I get the whole lone-wolf thing you have going on, but it might help if you explain the basics."

Gabrielle sighs. "That's Dominic Monier; he's the opera house manager."

"OK, thank you. So, what do we do now?" I ask.

She checks her watch. I do the same, pulling my silver hunter from around my neck. It reads 11:15 p.m. The word *Waypoint* lights up the upper section of the fascia, along with a needle that acts like a compass. I rotate the watch slightly to line up the needle.

Gabrielle straightens her hat and pulls her gloves more firmly onto her hands. "Now, we investigate."

PART 3

9

Gabrielle and I follow the opera house manager and members of his company through the busy Parisian streets. She walks a few feet ahead, like she's embarrassed by me. The men tip their hats to each other, and couples talk, sharing details of the fire with expressions of shock and concern. Questions circulate about how the fire started and the expected death toll. This is social media by word of mouth, slow and meaningful. I realize that the power of the present is relative. This isn't ancient history. It's tangible. Important. Now.

A horse-drawn carriage passes by, injured people lying helpless in the back. I feel dazed, my adrenaline spike dropping as fast as my body temperature, aided by the chill night air. My stupidly pointy shoes have rubbed the back of my ankles raw, but I'm not going to complain. How could I, after what I've just witnessed?

Gradually, the crowd thins. I'm watching for Nils of course but can't get rid of the feeling that my presence has so far been pointless. Gabrielle said it herself: she could complete this mission and probably find Nils without me. What can I do that she can't?

We arrive outside a restaurant that wouldn't look out of place in the present. The glass-fronted ground floor is covered with a striped canopy. The facade comprises decorative plasterwork and cornices, and an intricate gaslight bathes a cobbled area where numerous tables are set up. It's packed and alive with news of the terrible fire, people spilling out onto the street. A rakish man with an air of ownership works his way around the tables, pouring wine, his bald head shining beneath the streetlights. His staff hand out bowls of water so people can clean the ash and soot from their faces. I'm struck by the camaraderie, the sense of coming together in the face of tragedy. The opera manager's group is about to enter the restaurant, but they pause as a haunting sound echoes through the narrow streets—a lone violin.

The vibrant chatter fades and everyone turns their focus to a young girl, barely into her teens. Her dark hair is unkempt, her red dress torn at the edges. She stands in the middle of the street, violin pinched beneath her neck, and plays a moving sonata that captures the mood perfectly, with a command over the instrument that is way beyond her years. Her body sways, lifts, and flows with the music, as though in conversation. People listen respectfully, the sorrow of Paris channeled through the girl's fingers, a balm for their loss.

A man next to me wipes tears from his cheeks. I ask him if he knows the girl. He looks confused. "Why would I? She is one of the invisible."

"The invisible?"

"A street kid. Where she learned to play like that, we will never know." He waves a hand toward the restaurant. "The owner lets her play, gives her food occasionally. Some of the regulars give her tips too. She uses her talent, makes her way in life, and tonight she has captured what we all feel." The years flash over his face, and for a moment he's lost in deep thought. "A terrible loss," he sighs, shaking his head. "Hasn't Paris suffered enough?"

I nod in agreement, uncertain what to say.

The girl's bow glides, finding impossible harmonies as she loses herself in the soaring flight of her song. I'm transfixed. She reaches a captivating crescendo and sends a final note drifting away on the cool air. A few moments of silence are broken by a warm round of applause. The owner raises a glass and toasts the opera house. His customers do the same. The girl takes a bow.

Gabrielle murmurs. "Bach, Sonata no. 2."

"Never heard it, but it was beautiful."

"You've seriously never heard it before?" She snorts in derision. "Baroque music is not top of my list either, but at least it's put some color back in your cheeks."

"Seeing the fire was a shock, but I'm feeling a bit better now."

"Oh good," Gabrielle says with so much sarcasm that it almost feels genuine. "I'm *so* happy to hear that. Now tell me, Chosen One, are you getting any of your visions? Any magic clues to Nils's whereabouts?"

"Nothing so far," I reply reluctantly.

"Shame," she says, sounding pleased. "Never mind. Why don't you follow your instincts somewhere else, and we can touch base when we get home?"

I consider this. And although the restaurant looks warm and inviting, and the smells coming from inside are divine, I do wonder if leaving her to it might be for the best. That said, though, what would I do on my own? "I still think we should stick together."

"Whatever," Gabrielle shoots back. "We have less than an hour. I need to find out as much as I can about why Philippe Chevalier went back into that building."

I think back to what we just witnessed, the memory still glowing like the skin on my face. "Someone outside the opera house said he saved them and then went back inside. Philippe wasn't trapped, he *chose* to go back in when he knew the danger. Why would he do that? He must have been trying to save other people, right?"

She scowls at me. "Let me do the talking. Don't draw attention to us, and don't do or say anything stupid." I smile at her with as much fake love as I can muster and follow her inside.

The restaurant is buzzing. An old-fashioned till rings, and the chatter almost drowns out an accordion player propped up in the corner, happily lost. The heat of the kitchen and the hundred or so people crammed around circular tables keep the October chill outside. The majority of the walls and the ceiling are paneled wood, painted an unusual matte black and adorned with mirrors that reflect the yellow glow of numerous chandeliers and wall lights. The smell is an intoxicating mix of roasting meat, tobacco smoke, sweet alcohol, and bitter coffee.

A portly waiter with an impressively manicured mustache offers us a cramped table for two. "Food choices are on the menu," he says, "although as you can probably tell, there may be a little wait." We sit, and he pours wine without asking. "The house Bordeaux is free of charge this evening."

Gabrielle smiles graciously. "Why thank you, that's very generous."

He nods, as though free-flowing wine is to be expected. "I adored the opera, mademoiselle. Like all of us here tonight, I am devastated about the fire, and this is a small gesture to help salve the broken hearts of Paris. *Santé.*"

I take a sip of my wine, my mind still trying to process the fact that our English conversations are actually happening in French. These brief exchanges with other people matter. I have an unusual, unexpected sense of belonging. I turn to Gabrielle. "When we were outside, a man said he thought Paris had suffered enough. What did he mean?"

Gabrielle drinks her wine down in one gulp and tuts in disapproval. "Did you even go to school?"

"I attended, but some of the lessons were a bit of a blur."

"You really are an uneducated heathen." She shakes her head, then lowers her voice. "In the space of about ten months, they had a siege, the Prussian bombardment, and the Commune of Paris. You've heard of these events, right?"

"Not really, no," I admit.

Gabrielle leans back, exasperated. "OK, well it was bad, and it's only a couple of years ago. Paris has suffered a lot, and the opera house fire feels like another wound. Hard to believe right now, but in the grand scheme of things, what happened tonight is a minor setback." She looks around the room, soaking in the atmosphere. "Paris is on the up. They relocate to a new opera house; things get better. You need to remember that."

I'm hoping the waiter might refill Gabrielle's glass. The wine seems to be improving her mood. She gestures to the corner of the room. I follow her eye line and spot the group of people we followed from the fire. The musicians have stacked their instruments in the corner and taken up three tables. In the center of the restaurant, the opera house manager shares a table with a man and woman who have the appearance, heft, and haughty gravitas of opera singers. The man is a huge presence, with luxurious black hair and a beard of the same color. His forehead is beaded with sweat, which he dabs at dramatically with a white handkerchief. The woman wears a bright-yellow dress, and her blond hair is a burst of flamboyant curls. She looks like a massive, walking cake.

The opera manager stands and taps his glass. He waits while the chatter dies down. Now I can see him up close, I notice how well-groomed he is, his neatly trimmed beard sharpened to a point, his buttons gleaming, shoes polished to a shine. As he strokes his beard, a large signet ring on his right hand winks in the light. He frowns deeply, a man with the weight of the world on his shoulders.

"Ladies and gentlemen," he announces, his voice powerful but laced with pain, "I would like to say a few words if I may." He pauses, waiting for the chatter to die down a little more. "Some of you know me, but for those who don't, my name is Dominic Monier. I am . . . or perhaps I should say, I *was* the manager of the Salle Le Peletier. My beloved opera house was lost tonight in a truly terrible fire. A tragedy. The death toll is unknown, but as some of you may know, Philippe Chevalier was injured. I ask that you raise a glass with me to toast the loss of our house and to pray for Philippe and any unfortunate souls who may be missing or perished on this most awful of nights."

People stand in silent unison and raise their glasses. The manager wipes away tears and is about to continue when another man shouts, "It's the curse of the Phantom! He burned the opera house down."

Others join in. "The curse! I told you so! The Phantom has taken his revenge!" The cries get louder but are interrupted by a woman's voice that commands respect and immediate attention. "Enough!" she roars.

The restaurant plunges into silence. The accordion player is nudged to stop by one of the waiters.

An elderly woman I hadn't noticed until now shuffles slowly into view, supported by an ivory cane that taps on the floor as she walks. People move aside as she approaches Dominic Monier's table. She's wearing a dark-purple dress with white cuffs, and pearl stud earrings. Her long white hair is scraped back over her head and rises up into a fierce crown. Her skin is pale and wrinkled like old paper, but her sharp eyes work their way around the gathering.

She studies the manager, waits until he squirms a little, and then addresses the room. "I have been saying for some time now that the opera house was a box of tinder just waiting to go up in flames. Yet, no one would listen to me. I see only two possible explanations for what happened tonight. The fire was either an accident . . . or it was deliberately started." This sends the crowd into a murmuring frenzy. The old woman's expression remains stoic as she surveys the impact of her words.

The flamboyant prima donna, almost vibrating with frustration, does her best to interject. "With all due respect, Madame Delacroix, the curse is real. We have all seen the Phantom." She looks around the room, but no one else speaks up. "Oh, come along, you can't all deny it," she pleads.

Madame Delacroix bangs her cane to the floor. "There is no Phantom! And there is certainly no curse. I believe it was an accident caused by gross incompetence." She growls the word *incompetence*, glaring at the manager, who she clearly blames. He hangs his head. "Nothing can bring the opera house back, but the people whose job it was to avoid such a thing must focus on the cause and ensure that it never happens again."

Monier bobs his head as an awkward silence consumes him. The maître d' implores the accordion player to resume and instructs his waiters to refill everyone's glasses. The restaurant returns to some semblance of normality, buzzing with this latest drama.

I turn to Gabrielle. "Do you think this phantom could be Nils?"

I expect her to scoff, but she seems to genuinely consider this. "We shouldn't rule out any possibilities, but I doubt it. Sounds more like a sales gimmick to me."

She's probably right. I feel like a spare part again.

Gabrielle folds her arms and leans back. "So you haven't felt anything, any clue as to where Nils might be?"

"Nothing," I tell her honestly. "I don't know what Iris thinks I can do to help find Nils. We haven't seen him. How am I supposed to connect to him?"

"I'm usually right."

"How do you mean?"

"You coming along was pointless."

I want to protest, stand up for myself, but part of me agrees with her. I sense we're being watched and turn to see Madame Delacroix studying us, like a judge presiding over our fates. She stares at me unblinking, as if waiting for me to give myself away. I do my best to nod back at her with confidence.

Gabrielle unfolds her arms and leans in. "Look, I care about Nils. I want to find him too."

"Then what do *you* think I should do?"

When she finally speaks, her tone is unfamiliar, almost helpful. "Felix said Nils was attached to the change event in some way, so . . . following Philippe's story is probably the best chance of getting a lead on Nils, right?"

"Makes sense." I feel a fleeting sense of teamwork, which I know will evaporate any second, so I seize the momentum. "So if we focus on your mission, what would you normally do now, in situations like this? Are you trying to figure out how to stop the fire?"

"No, that's not why I'm here. The observer effect means the fire can't be avoided."

"The what? I remember Iris said something about the amount of people who witnessed the event, but I still don't understand. Why does that mean we can't stop the fire from happening?"

Gabrielle tuts impatiently. "When Madame Delacroix over there was staring at you, you felt uncomfortable; you knew you were being watched, right?"

"OK, but—"

"Observation has energy, it carries weight. The fire was witnessed by thousands and impacted many more. Observation is a multiplier. It solidifies events so they can't be changed."

I'm craving clarity, but I imagine this is a subject that could run for hours, and that's time we don't have. I decide to leave it for now and focus on her mission. "Well, if you're not going to stop the fire, what are you planning?"

Gabrielle seems pleased that I've asked. "Jump one is usually the end, the change event, but I'm thinking beyond this. I'm focusing on jump two because chances are I'll arrive before the fire. How long before is anyone's guess, but if I end up going inside that building, I want to know everything. I want to know why Philippe went back inside, how the fire started, all of it. And that isn't going to happen sitting on my ass, talking to you. To get information, you have to get involved. Watch and learn."

She strides to the center of the room, pulls out a chair, and, lifting her skirts, climbs up onto it. She claps her hands together, gaining some attention, but not enough. It seems the crowd has heard enough speeches for one night. Gabrielle waves her hands in the air and bellows at the top of her lungs. "Ladies and gentlemen. Can I have your attention?" That works; the chatter dies down. "My name is Gabrielle Green from the *Boston Globe*." She pauses, letting that sink in. "This evening, we have witnessed a terrible tragedy. The people of the world will want to know what happened. Who better to tell them than the people who were there? I implore all of you to talk to me, tell me your story, share it with the world. Publicly mourn your loss."

The prima donna clicks open a fan and cools her face. "Will our names be printed?"

"Unless you tell me otherwise, yes, your names will be published. The article will lead on the front page." Gabrielle hops down. The restaurant is quiet for a moment, a collective inhalation that explodes into a frenzy of activity as various members of the opera company line up to spill their stories.

Gabrielle organizes them into a line, then winks at me. She knew exactly which levers to pull for this particular bunch, the ones labeled "Ego" and "Publicity." I watch her work, wondering if I'm finally seeing how a professional time traveler goes about her business.

My attention is drawn to a young woman in her midtwenties, seated in the corner, studying the room. I can sense she has something she wants to share, but she seems uncertain, scared even. She watches Gabrielle for a minute or two, then lowers her head and starts gathering her belongings.

Bill told me to tune in and use my intuition more. Well, I feel a strong urge to talk to this woman if I can. In fact, she might just be the reason I came here tonight.

10

The young woman has high cheekbones, pale skin, and glossy black hair tied behind her head in a fancy updo, creating sweeping locks that cover her ears. She's wearing a simple black dress, with a pearl necklace that accentuates her slender neck. Unlike most of the women in here, she wears very little makeup. Her wide brown eyes assess me nervously as I approach, pupils dark like a wild animal. I stop a little way from her, leaving some space between us.

"Can I help you?" she asks, flicking anxious glances toward the door.

"I would like to talk to you for a minute, if you don't mind." I notice a bowl of water, gray with ash, and a dirty cloth beside it. "Did you see the fire tonight?"

She gazes at the tablecloth, picking at a stain with her finger. "It was awful."

"Yes, it was."

She studies me, expression now calm and determined. Her inner strength is obvious. She's tough enough to walk out if I push her too hard. "I don't want to be in the newspaper."

"You won't be," I assure her.

"Then why do you want to talk to me?"

"I'm feeling pretty shocked about the whole thing, and you looked like you might be feeling the same." I study her and risk a smile. "After such a horrific event, it's good to talk. And sometimes the best person to share your feelings with is a complete stranger."

She considers this. "I saw you with that woman. You're a reporter. How can I trust you?"

I respect her healthy pessimism for the press and wonder if that makes her progressive in this era, in contrast to the line of fame-hungry people spilling their guts to Gabrielle. "I'm not with the newspaper. I'm here because a friend of mine is missing. My name is Joseph."

After a few seconds, she says, "I'm Marguerite."

"May I sit with you for a while, Marguerite?" She bobs her head, and I sit opposite her. "Did you work at the opera house?"

"Yes. I'm a seamstress." She looks down at her hands, which are blackened and scratched. "I was good at my job."

"I'm sure you still are."

Thankfully, she continues to talk. "The fire came so fast, it was horrible. I dread to think how many people lost their lives."

"Everyone escaped," I tell her. "No one died."

"How do you know?"

"It's just . . . what I heard, and I think it's true."

"Still," she says, lowering her voice, "someone told me what happened to Monsieur Chevalier. Poor man. He loved that place. It was such a handsome building." She lets out a burdened breath. "It's so hard to believe it's gone."

"I know it's hard to imagine now, but the opera house will find a new home. Life will carry on."

Her face is full of doubt. "Do you really think so?"

"I know so."

My confidence seems to comfort her a little. "You said you were looking for your friend," she says. "Was he in the opera house when the fire started?"

"Yes. Maybe."

"I hope he's safe," she says. "But I'm afraid I don't know how the fire started, if that's what you're planning to ask me."

She's opening up. I can see her processing, calculating her words. I decide to steer the course of our conversation, see if I can find out what's on her mind. "Actually, I'm more interested in what people here are calling 'the Phantom.'"

She exhales a short, exasperated laugh. "People *claim* they have seen a ghost, a man in a cape, haunting the opera house." She searches the room for the opera manager, who is in deep conversation with Gabrielle. "It is good for ticket sales, that's all."

I lean in slightly, lowering my voice. "Have you ever seen the Phantom?"

"No." She looks away from me, like a guilty child.

"It's OK, Marguerite, you can talk to me."

She seems relieved that I'm pushing her, giving her an excuse to open up. "I don't know if it was your friend, and I don't know if he was inside the opera house when the fire started."

"Why don't you tell me what you saw?"

She finishes her wine and thoughtfully sets the glass back down on the table. "I have lived in Paris my whole life. I have seen many wonderful things, and some terrible things, some of them unimaginable, but what I saw . . . it defies explanation. I was alone backstage, working on a dress for the finale, and I saw someone—a man."

"When was this?"

"A few days ago. It was late. There was no one backstage but me, and yet suddenly, I knew I wasn't alone. I *felt* it. And then, I saw him. Reflected in the mirror. At first, I thought he was one of the mannequins, but then he moved. A man standing behind me. I screamed."

"I bet you did."

"I almost ran, but I saw his expression. It was clear to me then that he did not intend to scare me. He looked just as surprised as I was, and scared too."

"Can you describe him?"

She blinks rapidly, in thought. "He was tall, blond hair, a strong jawline. I remember his blue eyes particularly. They were very bright but full of fear."

Yes! I don't want to count my chickens, but this sounds very promising. "I think you saw my friend," I tell her. "His name is Nils Petersen."

"Nils," she repeats. "What happened to him? Is he dead? Is he a ghost?"

"A ghost? Why would you say that?" She swallows and stares at her hands, wringing them nervously in her lap. "It's all right, Marguerite, you're doing well. What happened next? Did you talk to him?"

"I called out to him, asked him what he wanted from me. He looked surprised. He began to talk, but I couldn't hear him. That's when he began to . . . change."

"Change? How do you mean?"

"He flickered, like sunlight on a lake." She avoids my gaze as she talks, her expression pained, her voice distant. "His outline was multicolored, and he became transparent, like a spirit. He was walking toward me. I was still looking into the mirror; I wondered if perhaps this was a trick of the light. I turned, fearful that he had come to kill me, but he had disappeared. I checked the mirror again, half expecting him to be standing there still, but he was gone. You must think I am mad, monsieur."

"Not at all. I'm just relieved that you've seen him."

"You mean, you believe me?" Her face is full of concern. "This has been gnawing away at me. I didn't know what it meant. Was it a sign? A vision? Was I supposed to take action? And then, the fire came. I've been sitting here tonight convincing myself that I saw the devil, that he had come to wreak havoc, and I didn't warn anyone, and now you tell me he's your friend? I don't understand. You need to tell me what's going on. Please?"

I look at her, unsure what to say. I would struggle to explain this to someone in the present, let alone in a time such as this. "First of all, there is nothing you could have done to prevent the fire," I assure her. "Nils is a traveler who got lost. He's scared, but he means you no harm. I don't know exactly what's happened to him, but I think he's kind of stuck between worlds, if you can imagine that?"

"He's in limbo?" she suggests.

"Yes, something like that."

She regards me, deep concern etched on her face. "Can you help him?"

"I hope so."

"But the fire. If he was stuck like you say, then surely . . . it's too late, no?"

"The opera house is gone, but I don't think it's too late to save Nils." I hope it's true. Gabrielle and I have arrived at the end of this particular story, but if my experience is anything to go by, we will come back and get a chance to alter things. "I just need to find him and bring him home."

"Where is home?"

"A long way from here. The fact that you've seen him, though, it's confirmation that he's here, in some form at least."

"What should I do if I see him again?" she asks.

"I don't think you will, but if you do, tell him The Continuum is coming to help him."

"The Continuum? What is that?"

"If he can hear you, he will understand."

She smiles but looks tired, as though the last few days have finally caught up with her. "I feel better for telling someone. I think you are a good man, Joseph. In this world, that is a rare thing." She glances over my shoulder. "I believe your colleague is trying to get your attention."

I turn to see Gabrielle glowering at me, tapping her wrist.

"It's time for me to go," I tell Marguerite.

"And you promise to let me know if you find your friend?"

"I promise," I tell her, knowing that if I do see her again, it might be before we've had this conversation. "How will I contact you?"

"The owner of this restaurant knows me. You can leave a message with him. I must know the outcome. It's going to play on my mind."

"I understand. Thank you, Marguerite."

As I make my way toward Gabrielle, I glance back at the young woman, her life, in my past, stretching out ahead of her. Dead and yet living. Now and then.

"Sorry to drag you away, lover boy," Gabrielle says, "but this is hardly the best place for us to go pop."

We head back outside, the cold air a shock.

"The girl said she saw Nils," I tell Gabrielle excitedly.

"Seriously?"

"Yes."

"Are you sure you weren't leading the witness?"

"She described what he looked like, said he was flickering, like a ghost."

"And you believed her?"

"Why wouldn't I?" I indicate the busy Parisian boulevards with a wave of my hand. "I mean, this whole being in 1873 thing is unbelievable, but I think she's telling the truth, yeah. What did you find out?"

"Usual stuff. Interesting leads. I'll debrief The Continuum when we get back."

We both react as I feel the familiar nip of brain freeze in the base of my skull, an indication that we're going to travel soon. I don't know if I've become accustomed to the feeling, but it's nowhere near as bad as it used to be. I check my silver hunter. It's nearly midnight, and the countdown shows there are just ten minutes until we leave. Gabrielle rubs the back of her neck as she contemplates the roofline of a nearby building. "We need to find somewhere quiet."

"What? Up there?"

"Yeah, it will be a nice view. Follow me."

We scale an iron staircase attached to the exterior of a hotel. There's no guardrail, and the stairs wobble disconcertingly as we make our way up. We reach the top, and my fear of heights kicks in with a vengeance. Gabrielle strides across a flat section of the roof and sits down, dangling her feet over the edge. It's cold, feels like it might rain soon. There is no light pollution, and from here we have an amazing view of the opera house, a glowing ball of orange ejecting a steady stream of oily smoke over the Seine. I'm physically unable to stand any closer than ten feet from the edge. My knees want to buckle. On the horizon, the faintest smudge of sunlight illuminates the underside of a thick gray cloud. A new day approaches, the first without the Salle Le Peletier opera house.

Gabrielle sighs loudly. "Jeez, Bridgeman."

"What?"

"Your face," she complains. "Cheer up, no one died."

"I still find that really hard to believe."

"Trust me, it's a lot harder when people do, and you can't stop it."

"Christ," I murmur, "how do you cope with that?"

"You just do." She folds her arms. "Now, shut up and enjoy the view."

Gabrielle's skin shimmers, like shards of silver rainbows, becoming translucent and luminous. I see the blood pumping beneath the surface, her life force, her mortality. She's phasing in and out, and I'm doing the same. One by one, my senses fall away. Smell goes first—the bitter smoke, the cool air, the damp, earthy tinge of wet roof tiles. The distant sound of the fire, people and horses below, the whistle of the wind, all gently fade. I admire the star-filled night sky above me, my final view of Paris, and watch the smoke drifting across a full moon.

11

We're back in the silence of Gabrielle's hotel room. It feels like a long time since we were here, but in reality, we only spent about two and a half hours in the past. When traveling, the time passes at the same rate in the present, which means the local time is now 7:35 p.m., and it's getting dark outside.

Gabrielle flicks a switch on the wall, and the room is instantly bathed in brilliant electric light. We were only in the past for a few hours, but the immediacy and convenience of the lights sideswipe me. It isn't just the LED bulbs; everything seems different. The air smells artificially clean, the surfaces of the walls are a little too perfect, the furniture manufactured and angular. There are strange sounds too: ticking pipes, whirring fans. And in the distance, the hiss of traffic. It's amazing how quickly I adapted to Paris. I know I will adjust again, that this sensation will fade, but for now, my brain appears to think this is all new information.

Gabrielle strides across the room and picks up the phone. "I'm ordering room service, you want anything?"

Feeling dizzy and nauseous, I decline.

"You need to eat," she says. "I'll order enough for two."

I fight a surge of bitter acid in my stomach and surrender to the absurdity of it all. "All right, why not?"

Gabrielle kicks off her shoes and cradles the handset in her ear. As she orders, I follow her lead, easing my painful, blistered feet out of my stupid, pointy shoes. I remove my socks and walk barefoot on the smooth, soft carpet.

"Right, that's the most important call done," Gabrielle announces. "Now, we'd better contact Iris."

She removes her watch from its leather strap and places it on the coffee table. She twists the winder and then presses it with her thumb, as though starting a stopwatch. I witness the same futuristic light show as I did when I first met Iris. Tiny fluttering green lights attach themselves to the corners of the room, ready to project the future in real time.

Iris's outline appears, initially just a faint impression, but then she joins us in the hotel room, fully dimensional, albeit across a universe of time. She wears a long dress and laced ankle boots, the style more casual and retro than futuristic. Her mid-length gray hair is pulled into a short pony-tail. She turns to Gabrielle and says, "It's good to see you. Welcome back." Then, she looks at me, and I recognize compassion in her face. "How are you, Joseph?"

"I'm OK." But the hesitation in my voice says otherwise. For me, events in 1873 feel like they are still happening. But I know that's not true. All of it is ancient history. Now we're back in the present, talking to the future. I'm beginning to understand why they call themselves The Continuum.

"It can be quite a shock, going back as far as you've just been," Iris says. "Before we debrief, I wanted to bring Felix in on this."

"Felix?" I ask.

"Along with myself and Bill, he's one of the founders of The Contin-uum. He designed and built Downstream." She pauses a beat. "It's a kind of computer that allows us to observe space and time and discover oppor-tunities for change. Felix hopes to show it to you one day. For now, he would like to meet you, if that would be all right?"

Meeting more people from the future after traveling over a hundred years into the past threatens to fry my poor little brain, but I tell her it's fine. A glassy silhouette, like a complex honeycomb made of the finest blue crystal, appears in the room and solidifies into the form of a man. I know you shouldn't judge a book by its cover, but considering that Felix has been described as the techy one, his appearance is unexpected.

He wears a gray linen shirt, faded blue trousers, and leather sandals. His dark hair reaches his shoulders, wavy and unkempt, and his skin is midsummer brown. He's middle-aged, of average height, but his build is muscular and lean. If someone asked me to guess his job, I'd say he was a professional surfer, not a programmer.

The man takes in the room, acknowledges Gabrielle, and then turns his attention to me. He smiles warmly, revealing deep dimples in his freckled cheeks. "I'm Felix Greystone. It's so good to finally meet you, Joseph." His voice is deep and calm, the gentle warmth of West Coast America, which only reinforces the surfer vibe. He walks forward a couple of steps, one of his projected feet now cutting through a suitcase on the floor, a reminder that this incredible illusion has its limits. "After everything you went through in London, I speak on behalf of all of us at The Continuum when I say how much we appreciate you helping us again. We put you through hell."

"You did."

He frowns. "I'm sorry about that."

I study him, allowing our words some room to breathe. The nightmare of London suddenly seems to pale in comparison to the inferno we just left, but it doesn't change the facts. Now that I've been to Paris and felt useless for most of the trip, my plan is to tell these people what I know and then step away. I'm done.

Iris breaks the slightly awkward silence. "Gabrielle, why don't you give us an update on the mission?"

Gabrielle switches modes and becomes a super-efficient data-dumping machine. She outlines each stage of our jump, adding time checks, locations, and details of the people we met, including the opera house manager and the old spinster I had already begun to forget.

Iris asks, "Any idea why Philippe might have gone back inside?"

Gabrielle considers this. "Not so far, but for a first jump, it was a good one. I followed the staff and picked up lots of stories, narrow escapes— things you would expect from survivors. If I had to guess right now, I think he went back inside because he was either looking for someone or retrieving a personal item, something that mattered to him. I have leads, ideas I want to research before the next jump."

"Sounds good," Felix says. "We're already analyzing the jump data. I will see what I can find out." He turns to me. "Now, tell me about Nils."

Before I can answer, Gabrielle speaks in a flurry. "Lots of people were talking about a phantom, but it's not Nils. There were plenty of preexisting news stories and witness accounts before we got involved. The rumors of this phantom were instrumental in the rising popularity of the opera house before it was destroyed, but all of that said, there was one unusual sighting." She glares at me, rolling her right hand and nodding, as though I'm slow on the uptake.

I clear my throat. "Right, yes. I talked to a woman called Marguerite, a seamstress at the opera house. She told me she was working late one night and saw a man fitting Nils's description."

"That's good news," Iris says. "How sure are you that it was Nils?"

"Her description was very specific," I reply. "She was convinced she'd seen a ghost."

"A ghost?" Iris asks.

"She saw Nils in the mirror, standing behind her. She described him as translucent, but when she turned around, he had vanished."

"Very interesting." Felix blinks rapidly, lost in his thoughts. "Did she talk to him?"

"She said she tried but couldn't hear him," I say. "It sounded like it was all over very quickly."

"That ties in with our data," Felix says. "It seems Nils hasn't fully manifested in Paris. His signal is weak. It's in and out and never reaches full capacity. This sighting gives us dimensional data, though, a time and a place, potentially a way to triangulate his location. Kyoko and I will get to work, see if we can create a way of tracking him on your next jump."

"How is Kyoko coping with this?" Iris asks.

The corner of Felix's mouth curls up into a wry grin. "You know her, she's saying we need more time to analyze the data, that she can't work under these conditions, but she'll be OK. Leave it with me."

The three of them are quiet for the first time since the conversation began. It gives me a chance to consider my next move. The whole time I was in 1873, I kept telling myself that all I had to do was try my best, get home, and stop time traveling. That way, I would have shown some willingness, maybe paid back some kind of debt, and I could just bid farewell to The Continuum and get on with my life. Now that I'm back, I'm wondering if that's true. Are they about to ask me to join Gabrielle on the next jump? If so, am I going to say yes?

"I don't feel like I was any use at all," I say honestly.

Before Gabrielle can agree, Felix cuts in. "Observation has power, and each time a traveler ventures into the past, the interactions and observations cause a disturbance. That energy gives us a huge amount of data. Just being there has helped, Joe. Your conversation with Marguerite, it all matters. It's all part of the picture."

He may just be trying to make me feel better, but it's working. It's good to know that my efforts—even if they haven't really led to much— are appreciated by two out of three in this virtual room. Also, Felix's words resonate with what I've just seen and experienced. Gabrielle was determined to squeeze every last drop of juice out of our time in 1873. She wanted to see as much as possible, talk to people, interact. *Ripples*, Bill called them.

"So what happens now?" I ask.

Iris says, "We can't ask any more of you, Joseph." I glance at Gabrielle. She looks relieved, and I wonder if she was also waiting for me to be asked to go on the next jump. Iris continues, "I know you've made it clear that you can't control your viewings, but I'm hopeful that your experience in Paris might trigger one. If you do get anything, or if you have any thoughts or ideas or questions, please contact me."

"I will," I assure her, "but how do I contact you?"

"Using ICARUS," she says, as though it's obvious.

"Can you tell me how to do that?"

"Did Gabrielle not explain this to you already?"

"I was going to, but we ran out of time," Gabrielle replies.

Iris glares at Gabrielle and then purses her lips, resetting her stone-like expression. "Very well. As Gabrielle did not have time, I shall explain it to you now. Ensure you are in a secure location. A locked room is ideal. Place your watch facedown in a central position in the room, press the winder twice, rotate it clockwise, and then press again. The watch is bonded to you, so there is no danger of anyone else accidentally activating the connection."

I consider this, and although Iris has already explained that the ICARUS technology only exists because of Gus Romano, I can't help but require clarification. "And my watch can definitely do this?"

"Yes," Iris says. "When you were on the Romano mission, ICARUS hadn't been invented, but when you saved Lucy Romano, you changed your own timeline as well as ours."

My brain does a little clench, and I decide to just go with it. *My watch is clever. Twist and press. Talk to the future. Got it.*

"Do you have any further questions, Joe?" Iris asks.

"Probably," I say, "but I can't think of them now."

She smiles. "Get some rest. Please feel free to contact me at any time."

"OK," I tell her. "Thanks."

"Thank you again for helping, Joe," Felix says.

Iris addresses Gabrielle. "Shall we talk again tomorrow?"

"Sounds good, boss."

And that's how my second conference call with the future comes to a close. No one waves or presses any buttons. Iris and Felix simply fade away, and my reality is back.

Gabrielle says, "You did your best, we know a bit more, and now . . . well, you're done."

"Yeah," I say, already feeling the earlier adrenaline spike paying off its debts. My stomach growls. I hear a tap at the door and a man's voice call, "Room service!" and I have to admit that Gabrielle was right. I'm starving.

A young man, dressed smartly in hotel attire, wheels in a trolley with various plates and dishes and a huge silver dome. Seeing our attire, he hesitates, his eyebrows raised. We're still dressed for the late nineteenth century, so I can't really blame him. He sniffs the air and studies the room. We must reek of wood smoke, wine, and tobacco. I smile at him innocently, and he grins back with mischief in his expression. He probably thinks that we're doing a bit of fancy role-play, but I'm too tired to care.

He leaves, and Gabrielle lifts the lid on enough food for four people: club sandwiches, coleslaw, French fries, and a bucket of beers on ice. Room service is the most sensible suggestion Gabrielle has made so far. We position ourselves on either side of the trolley and dig in. We don't talk for a while. The sandwiches are delicious, and the buzz of the beer hits my brain, a fast track to feeling grounded.

Gabrielle seems totally relaxed, as though popping back to 1873 to see a colossal fire and a poor guy badly burned is just a normal day. As I down the remains of my first beer, I consider that for her, perhaps it is. We stick a decent dent in the food but can't finish it all.

Gabrielle taps the side of her cheek. "Give them a good pull, like you mean it, and they'll come right off."

"Huh?"

"Your sideburns."

"Right," I say, rubbing my fingers over them. "I kind of forgot they were there." After a little persuasion, I peel them away from my skin, and they flatten quickly into their original form, like a sea anemone contracting in on itself when sensing a predator. I study them with curiosity and then place them on a nearby table.

Gabrielle begins pulling long metal pins from her hair. There must be a hundred of them. She sniffs her armpits, wincing. "Man, I need a shower."

I walk to the window and look down from the third floor onto the present. We've been gone about three hours. The sky has turned gray. Car lights cut through the night. People chat on their phones. Modern life. The internet. A connected world. Time in the past and time in the present might pass at the same speed, but my mind is going to take a while to readjust.

Gabrielle interrupts my thoughts. "Don't forget to leave your Paris clothes here."

I turn around and am shocked to see that she's down to her underwear. Of course, I look away immediately, but I can't help noticing how surprisingly toned she is despite her healthy appetite and unhealthy food choices. Some people are just lucky, I suppose.

"So I guess this is goodbye?" she says, her tone filled with sarcastic sorrow. She winks and pads off to the bathroom, leaving the door ajar. I hear the shower and see steam.

Quickly, I get changed, keen to be fully dressed before Gabrielle appears from the bathroom again. It's a relief to be back in normal clothes, but I'm still hyperaware of the residual odor from my trip to Paris. The first wave of exhaustion hits me, and the idea of a shower and my bed suddenly feels essential. I open the door to leave.

"Joe!" Gabrielle shouts.

"Yeah."

"In here."

I gingerly poke my head around the bathroom door. Thankfully, it's full of steam now. Gabrielle's soaked head appears from behind a shower curtain. "Pass me that shampoo."

I hand her one of the little bottles, keeping my eyes averted.

"Oh, and try to get one of your funny dreams going, will you?"

"Viewings."

"Whatever. Just do what you can. I want to save Philippe and Nils."

"I'll do my best."

She starts whistling, and I hear her clattering bottles of shower products. I wonder if I will ever see her again and can't help feeling that there are things left to say, but I'm too tired to bother.

I leave the hotel, and that's when it really hits me.

Cheltenham.

The present.

It's filled with technology, traffic, electrical lighting, an onslaught of differences. Everyone is dressed in casual clothing. Compared to the amazing outfits I've just seen, it's as though people now just can't be bothered. Most of them are staring at their phones, serious and sullen. There's the odd one who seems present in the present, but that's rare.

I think Blur might have been right when they said, "Modern life is rubbish."

The sound of a siren builds. An ambulance screeches past, blue light bathing the street, and I suddenly see the era in which I live through a new lens. Antibiotics. Painkillers. Super Glue. Smoke alarms. I realize this could be a long list. Maybe modern life has some saving graces too.

My shower, for example. It should have come with its own e-learning course, but I've finally mastered this chrome wonder of modern plumbing and engineering. The main showerhead thunders a waterfall of warm water over my head and back. My skin glows as though I've spent a full day sunbathing. My eyes sting, and my lips are dry. I guzzled half a liter of water when I got home, and I'm still thirsty. The inside of my nose is black and sticky. I wash my hair twice and it still stinks of bitter smoke, although the smell might just be baked into my memory like a stain. I feel drained. Closing my eyes, I let the water cascade over my face and let my mind wander. Bright images reside there, animated snippets of time. The black-and-white images of the past, now painted in vibrant color. It's a hell of a thing, time travel. Scary. Dangerous. But also exciting.

It makes you feel alive.

12

There's a lot I still don't know about The Continuum, but one thing they have right is giving travelers enough time to decompress after each trip. It's important. You need time for the emotional impact to settle down. Being an antique dealer might give me an advantage, I suppose, because I'm already familiar with some of the styles and fashions of late nineteenth-century France, but actually visiting has sideswiped me. Witnessing a beautiful building being consumed by a vicious inferno is harrowing, and unlike Gabrielle, I can't just snap my fingers and step back into ordinary life. It's a week since I got back, and I keep getting flashbacks: how loud it was, how crowded, how my eyes wouldn't stop watering. I keep remembering the thousands of people—those living, breathing souls—and realizing that the moment I traveled home, they were all dead again. I'm working hard to ensure that none of this affects my interactions with Molly, my customers, or my friends and family, but it's a huge strain. I'm like a swan, serene on top, but pedaling like mad below the surface.

It's enough to drive a man to drink, which is partly why I'm standing at the bar of the Duck and Grouse, ordering myself a pint of ale and getting ready to take part in the fortnightly pub quiz. I look over to the corner and spot Amy at the round oak table where we usually sit, with Miles, Sue, Greg, and Jess. Together, we are the "Sherlock Homies," an enthusiastic amateur pub-quiz team. For the last couple of years, the others have been coming down here every other Thursday night to take part in "The Great British Quiz-Off," and when Amy invited me to join them, I jumped at the chance. The first time I came, I was tickled pink when I found out the quiz night was run by Vinny. Amy hadn't mentioned it because she didn't think I knew him that well, and Vinny hadn't mentioned it because apparently, Other Joe hated pub quizzes. It's just supposed to be a bit of fun, but some of the teams take it all very seriously, which just encourages us to mess around all the more.

I wave at my team, tipping my hand toward my mouth in the international sign language for "Would you like a drink?" Amy shakes her head, but Sue, Amy's best friend, waves energetically back. "White wine spritzer," she mouths. "Large!" I give her the thumbs-up and pass her order to Quinn, the sexy barman. For the record, he's not my cup of tea, but the girls all insist he's gorgeous, and at halftime, there's usually a scramble between them to get the next round in.

On my way to our table, Amy's boyfriend, Miles, intercepts me. "Hey, Joe, good to see you, man. I just wanted to let you know, I've got a ton of competitions coming up, so it's going to be . . . well, it could be a bit difficult."

"What could?"

"Running Amy's business. I can't do it this time."

I'm baffled. "Why would you need to?"

"If Amy needs some time out, it's going to have to be somebody else. Last time it was out of season, so it wasn't a problem, but this time I've got a load of trips planned, you know?"

"OK. Thanks."

Miles takes the peanuts from under my arm. "Let me give you a hand with those." When we get to the table, he gives the nuts to Amy, sits, and loses himself in his phone.

"Hi, Homies," I say, handing Sue her spritzer. "Are we feeling like losers tonight?"

Greg puts down his pint and wipes beery foam from his ginger beard. "Absolutely. The Quizzicles are in. By the window." I glance over and see them, four men and one woman, all gray-haired, bespectacled, and looking like they're preparing to take an exam. They're sipping tiny goblets of sherry, nibbling snacks like church mice, and reading reference books. Sideburn Sid, as we've nicknamed their leader, leafs through what looks from here like an atlas. "I expect they'll leave everyone miles behind, like they did last time."

"What?" Miles looks up from his phone and flicks hanks of long blond hair out of his face. He wears his hair in a topknot when he's climbing; I've seen the pictures. "Did somebody ask me something?"

"Nope," Amy says, ripping open the peanuts. "All right, Joe?" She gives me a beaming grin and stuffs a handful of nuts into her mouth, chewing manically.

"Hi, Amy," I say, taking the last spot at the table between Miles and Jess. I wasn't sure she would be here after our chat at the community garden the other day, but I'm glad she is. "Could you leave some of those peanuts for the rest of us?"

She yawns. "Sorry. I'm so tired I've got the munchies." She pushes the packet toward me across the table.

"How's tricks, Jess?" I say to the woman beside me.

"Fine, thanks. All good." Jess is six foot one, a police trainee, and a semiprofessional basketball player. She doesn't offer her thoughts on the questions unless she is one hundred percent certain she knows the answer, but whenever Vinny gives us a sports round, she comes alive. Her specialties are basketball and equestrian stuff—she has her own horse—but she knows about most sports. Even if she didn't, we like having her on the team, in case things ever kick off in the pub.

A voice booms from the loudspeaker above Amy's head. "Ladies and gents, get your drinks in and line up your snacks. Fifteen minutes till kickoff." I look over my shoulder and see Vinny at his quizmaster table, microphone in hand, shiny purple bomber jacket zipped up to the neck. It's truly hideous, but it has the word *MAD* emblazoned across the back in gold sequins, and he loves it. I salute him and he winks, waving a sheet of paper. From this far away, I can't see the detail, but I'm guessing it might have logos on it. I stick double thumbs up and grin. My general knowledge is patchy—I'm OK at films and music—but logos are my niche. Last time we had a logo round, we got twenty-four points out of twenty-five.

"Why are you looking like the cat who got the cream, Jojo?" Amy asks, downing the last of her energy drink.

"I think there's going to be a logo round."

"Logos," she says disparagingly. "Capitalist guff. I hope there's one on science and nature this week. Or geography. Miles got us a full house with the name of that lake in Russia last time, didn't you?"

"What?" he says, tearing his eyes away from his phone.

"Lake Taymyr," Greg says affably. Greg is Sue's husband, and he's head-master of one of the local primary schools. His special subject is geography, but he doesn't just know about the stuff they teach the kids; he knows all of it. Sue takes care of current affairs, so they make a good team. In fact, from the look on his face whenever the rest of us mess up, I suspect he actually knows the answers to all the questions, but he lets us answer. I imagine he's a brilliant teacher. "You did well last time, Miles. Got us a winning round."

"Yeah, I did, didn't I," Miles says. "Bit of a fluke, I think, but if the right questions come up, you know . . ." He reaches for his gin and tonic and grasps it in his clawlike hand, all muscles and sinew. Amy sometimes calls him Popeye, because of the cartoon proportions of his arms and shoulders. He has an instrument of torture called a fingerboard installed above one of the doorframes in Amy's flat. It's a long flat wooden plank with shallow indentations that climbers use to maintain upper body fitness, and I've watched him hang from it for several minutes by just one of his little fingers. He was assisted by half a bottle of rum at the time, but still, he's no featherweight.

"Could Mr. Joseph Bridgeman please report to the quizmaster?" Vinny's voice reverberates across the room. He beckons me over with the jerk of his head. I don't usually like to disturb him while he's setting up, but I'm keen to fill him in on what happened in Paris.

I make my way across the room, which is filling up rapidly, and sit on the stool at his table, separated from the main bar area by a carved wooden screen.

"Cash! I've been dying to know how you got on!"

"I don't think this is the best place to talk about it, Vin."

He glances over his shoulder like an amateur sleuth. "There's no one close enough to hear," he says, "and anyway, they're all gearing up for the quiz." He's right, no one is paying us the slightest bit of attention. "So what was Paris like? How was the grub?"

I chuckle. "We didn't have time to eat anything, but Paris was amazing."

"Did you see the fire?"

I fill him in on all the details: our rough landing in the back of the cart, the journey to the opera house with the firemen, and the unexpected horror of watching such a culturally significant building succumbing to the flames. He winces when I tell him about Philippe's injuries.

"That must have been tough."

"It was, but I hope there's a chance to change it."

As expected, Vinny wants to know everything, so I talk him through meeting Marguerite and her sighting of Nils.

"A ghost?" Vinny says this so loudly that the barmaid looks over in surprise. He stage-whispers, "Sorry. Do you think Nils is dead?"

"No, but what Marguerite saw ties in with this idea that he's only half in Paris—he's there and he's not, if you see what I mean."

"Interesting. And what about Gabrielle? Did you learn loads? Did she help you out?"

I snort into my beer. "She kept telling me not to slow her down. She's not exactly a natural teacher—in fact, she was a pain in the arse. I had to practically beg for the lingo implant."

"The what now?"

"Oh yeah, they have this mad biotech, like a microchip that buries itself inside your ear, and then everything you hear is in English, and everything you speak is in French." I lean a little closer. "I've still got the implant in now. Seems like it's permanent."

"Wowzers!" Vinny exclaims. "D'you reckon it would work on Klingon too, y'know, if they came to take over the planet?"

"Probably."

"So cool," he says dreamily. He lays a giant bear paw on my shoulder. "Sounds like Gabrielle has been a bit of a rascal, but don't worry about her. I've been doing some research. You need to come over sometime. I'll take you through it all."

"That's really good of you, mate, but I spoke to The Continuum, and they said they didn't need me to go on the next jump."

"What? They said that?"

"Well, technically, Iris said that she didn't feel they could ask more of me."

"Ahhh." Vinny grins as though he's one step ahead of me. "You'll go on the next jump. They're just giving you some space."

"D'you think? I might offer to do it anyway, just to wind Gabrielle up."

He laughs. "That's the spirit. Anyway, I believe in being prepared. So let's move forward, presuming you'll be heading back."

"OK, thanks, mate." I chew absentmindedly at a fingernail.

He studies my face. "That's not all, though, is it? Tell your Uncle Vincent."

"It's Amy. She seems a bit better tonight, but I'm worried about her."

We both glance over at the Homies table, where Amy's chatting with Sue. She looks happy enough, but I'm not buying it. "Have you told her what's going on?" Vinny asks.

"Sort of. I told her I was going to Paris to try and find this missing traveler, because I didn't want to lie to her again, after the Romano mission. I thought I was doing the right thing, but she didn't take it too well."

"Don't you worry about your sis. She'll get there, I know it."

"I hope so." Vinny's support makes it easy for me to forget he's going through his own emotional turmoil. "How are things going with Kassandra, by the way?"

"I'm meeting up with her again next week. Pretty exciting, but I'd better crack on, Cash. Nearly time for kickoff!"

The first half of the quiz flies by. With a bit of help from the others, I fill in all the logos, and we trip our way through a food-and-drink round, a history round, and a '70s music round.

"Right, ladles and jellybeans, you've got a twenty-minute break now to wet your whistles and limber up for the second half! Back in a jiffy." Vinny gives a little bow and slips through the staff door to the kitchen. He told the pub he didn't want money for his quizmaster services, so they give him free plates of French fries with curry sauce instead. We won't see him again until twenty seconds before the quiz resumes, when he'll spill out of the kitchen wiping smears off his face and pick up two pints of Guinness from the bar on his way back to his microphone.

"Drinks, lads?" Sue flicks her eyes around the table. Everyone else puts in an order, and she turns to me. "Come and give me a hand, Joe, will you?" She collects our empty glasses and heads across the room, and I grab my pint glass and follow. I've had to piece things together, but I've learned that Sue is Amy's oldest friend: they've known each other since they were nine years old. They've had some crazy times together, did a bit of traveling back in the day, and stayed close even though their lives have taken very different paths.

When we get to the bar, Sue squeezes between two hefty rugby types and waves a twenty-pound note at Quinn, who comes straight over. She puts in the order and hands him the money. "I'm just nipping out for a smoke. Back in ten for the drinks, OK?"

Quinn winks. "Your wish is my command, Princess."

Sue giggles. I can't believe this slimy guff works on anyone, let alone Sue. I thought she was smarter than that.

She turns to me. "Come and grab some fresh air with me, yeah?"

"Me?" I don't know Sue that well, and although she and Amy are close, she and I haven't really spoken much.

"Yes, you! You never used to come out with us. It's nice to get to know Amy's big bro a bit. I reckon that fall off your bike did you some good!" She nudges me and winks.

"You're probably right," I say. She leads me through the pub and out the back door into the courtyard. There are a few people smoking, and two women are chatting beneath one of those vile, planet-burning patio heaters.

Sue offers me a cigarette, but I decline. She lights up. "I hope you don't mind, but I wanted to have a word with you about Amy. I haven't seen her like this for a long time."

My nerves are immediately on edge. "Seen her like what?"

"Come on, Joe, you must have noticed. She's up one minute and down the next. And she's not sleeping properly. Have you not noticed the bags under her eyes?"

"She doesn't seem quite herself," I admit, throwing a nervous glance back at the door. It's firmly shut, but I keep an eye out in case any of the gang decides to come and see where we've gone. "She was so miserable after the party the other day, but she seems like she's on a high tonight. Do you think it's got anything to do with me?"

"I don't, actually. Just after you had your accident, she had a bit of a wobble, but then she was OK again for a while. This is something else. I think she might be painting again." Sue says this with portent, as though she's expecting me to cower in terror.

"Painting? That's just one of her hobbies, isn't it?"

"Hardly." Sue breathes a plume of smoke up into the night sky. "When I say painting, I'm not talking pretty pastel watercolors. I'm talking mad stuff, really nightmarish. There's a fine line between expression and obsession, and she's crossed it before. Even Miles has noticed. I can tell something is worrying her, but God knows what it is. Don't you remember the other times? The signs are all there."

"Other times?"

Sue frowns at me, her face full of concern. "I'm worried sick we're heading for another Denmark. Poor love, it took a couple of years for her to properly get her equilibrium back. I'd do anything to stop that from happening again, but I need her to talk to me first. Until she acknowledges something's wrong, I can't help."

"What do you mean, another Denmark?"

Sue looks shocked. "Have you forgotten that too?"

"Sorry. There are still big chunks I can't remember . . ." I tail off.

"It's all right. Amy went backpacking on her own for a while when we were in our early twenties. She promised she'd stay in touch, but she dropped off the radar. I wasn't too worried, but then she missed three check-ins in a row, and I panicked. Luckily, she had me down as next of kin, so when it all went tits up, the hospital in Copenhagen called me and not your parents. She'd taken an overdose."

"An overdose?" My throat constricts, and I have to swallow before I can speak. "You're kidding."

"She said it was an accident. I think it was a cry for help. She acts like she doesn't need people, but she does. Don't let her push you away."

"I've been hearing that a lot recently."

"That's because it's good advice."

I think about Amy on her own in Denmark, feeling so desperate that she wanted to sink into oblivion. "What about Miles? Is he good for her, generally? I can't work him out. He seems a bit . . . switched off."

Sue gives a wry smile. "Miles is OK. He isn't a bad person, but I think Amy's just spinning her wheels."

"Why do you think she's with him, then?"

"It's an avoidance tactic. One way to get through life is to kill time with someone, even if they're not right for you. It's just another kind of drug. An anesthetic. She's stuck. They both are."

"So she doesn't love him?"

"If you'd asked me when they first got together, I'd have said she didn't, that it was more of an arrangement. He's away so much, and she's so independent. Now, though? Maybe she does. I don't know. She certainly cares a lot about him." Sue shrugs and takes a long drag from her cigarette. "I wouldn't trust him as far as I can throw him, but we're not talking about me, are we? He's a lot better than some of the guys she's been out with."

"Like who?"

Sue shakes her head. "You wouldn't want to know. You came to blows with a few of them over the years! I was always jealous that Amy had you to stand up for her. Good job she did, though. She was one hell of a wild child back in the day. Drove your poor parents up the wall."

I seize the opportunity to find out more about Amy's time in Cornwall. "Amy told me she left home for a while when she was a teenager, went to stay with an aunt down south."

"Silvia," Sue says. "Yeah, that was a difficult time. She and I lost touch for a while, but when she moved back to Cheltenham, we picked up where we'd left off."

"Why did she leave home?"

"Lots of reasons. Your usual teenage angst, I suppose, with the benefit of hindsight. Amy was particularly hard work, as some teenagers are, and your dad found her impossible to handle. I think your mum decided that some time apart was the best way to avoid total breakdown, take some of the pressure off." Sue has two kids, both still at primary school, so she's well placed to give a parent's perspective.

"Do you think that was when things started to go wrong with Dad? Things between them still aren't that great, and here we are—what—more than a decade later."

"I'm not sure that was the beginning, but it was definitely a turning point. I know things are still rocky. She told me about your Dad's party, but there's something else going on with that girl—I know there is."

A young lad sticks his head out of the pub door to check on his arguing teammates, and we hear Vinny's deep voice ricocheting around the pub, announcing the imminent kickoff.

Sue grimaces at her half-smoked cigarette and stubs it out viciously underfoot. "Disgusting habit," she says, grinning at me. "And the bloody babysitter always sniffs the air when I get in, like my mum used to do."

"Thanks for filling me in," I say. "I'll see if I can get Amy to talk to me. We're a bit closer since my accident knocked a bit of sense into me."

Sue holds the door for me, and I follow her back into the heat of the pub. "Keep me posted, all right? Sometimes I'm so busy with the kids that days go by and I haven't got around to giving her a call. She might seem OK right now, but things can go south pretty fast, so let's both keep an eye on her. If I know one thing about your sister, it's that she's really good at covering things up. She might seem OK on the surface, but there's a lot going on underneath."

13

I drift off to sleep and almost immediately into the middle of a dream where things are in full flow, as though it's been rolling along without me.

Alexia and I are holding hands outside a church as people shower us with petals and good wishes. A rhythmical chant starts to build from somewhere behind us: "Throw the bouquet! Throw it! Throw it!"

Alexia laughs. "OK, OK!" She pulls me forward until we're about ten feet in front of the crowd, then she turns her back to them, and everyone counts down. "Three, two, one, go!"

She flings the bouquet over her head, and as she turns to see who's going to catch it, I witness Gabrielle lurch from the crowd and launch herself into the air, roughly snatching the flowers from the hands of one of Amy's friends. "Yeah!" she whoops with abandon, and I note with horror that she's lost all her teeth.

"I don't recognize her. Is she on your side?" Alexia asks me.

"I *think* so . . ." Out of nowhere, I hear pinging, a bit like sonar, a soft but insistent sound that reverberates through the air at three-second intervals.

"What's that horrible noise?" Alexia asks me. "It's giving me a headache. Can't you get them to turn it off?"

"I'll ask, honey. Hang on." I go back into the church to look for the vicar, but the sounds get louder and louder until I realize, groggily, that I'm dreaming. The sound is in the real world, and I need to wake up.

Squinting, I turn on the bedside light and pick up my silver hunter, which is vibrating gently with each ping. The screen is streaming text— *Incoming call from THE CONTINUUM*—and indicating the buttons to either accept or reject the call. I sit straight up in bed. Why are they calling me? Worried that the call will disconnect if I sit here thinking for much longer, I click the Accept button.

"Joseph, it's Felix."

His voice fills my brain, as though through top-quality earbuds. I waggle my head a couple of times, and that's when I remember the implant. This is just like when Gabrielle and I were speaking to each other in Paris.

"Hi, Felix," I say, like it's no big deal talking to someone over a hundred years away.

"I'm sorry it's so late," he says. "I'd have called earlier, but everyone always wants a piece of me—you can imagine how it is running a place like this—and I wanted to find some time for us to connect one-to-one."

I'm not sure how to take this, but I can't deny I'm intrigued. "It's fine," I say, hoping there's not a tiny futuristic camera somewhere on my watch and he can't see my pajamas. "I was still up."

"Excellent. Listen, I prefer to see people's faces when I'm talking to them. Are you up for meeting here, at Greystone House? Virtually, I mean. I thought I could show you around a bit."

My heart leaps with excitement. "That sounds good." *Beam me up, Felix. Let's have a glimpse of the future.* I jump out of bed and rummage around in the drawers for clean clothes. "Can you give me a couple of minutes?"

"Take your time. Let me know when you're ready."

I hop to the bathroom, pulling on my socks, and splash cold water over my face. I look at myself in the mirror. "Keep calm," I tell myself silently, "take this in stride, soak everything in, and remember to concentrate." A few minutes later, I'm dressed in jeans and sweater, I've tamed my pillow-crumpled hair, and I'm standing upstairs in the loft room, the blinds pulled down and the coffee table pushed to the side to maximize the space I have.

"Felix? Are you still there? I'm ready."

"Excellent. Have you set up your watch?"

Damn, I left it downstairs. "No. What do I need to do?" I ask as I run back downstairs toward the bedroom.

"Hasn't Gabrielle shown you how to do it?"

"I've seen her use hers," I say, rummaging around in my bedside drawers and pulling out my silver hunter, "but she didn't show me how to activate mine. Iris told me how to do it, but I can't quite remember." I run back up the stairs two at a time.

"All right. Set it facedown on the floor in front of you, then press down and click. Rotate the backplate seven hundred and twenty degrees to the left, then click again."

"Seven hundred and twenty . . . ?"

"Rotate it twice, all the way around. Then click again."

I follow the instructions, and the backplate, hinged on one side, springs open, revealing a small chamber beneath. "OK, I've done that."

"Great, you're all done. Leave the watch on the floor."

I step back and watch the tiny green projectors stream out like neon flying ants on a summer's day. They find their spots around the room and then flicker to life, strobing rapidly, and the words *PLEASE WAIT* appear, hovering in the middle of the space before me. I'm praying the future has finally ditched the concept of hold Muzak.

"I can see you now. Bringing you in."

My loft falls away, as though it were merely projected onto a thin sheet of silk and some omnipresent God just switched the slide. The sudden transition makes me feel queasy. I am now standing in a grand hallway, projected into my eyes using technology that I can't really comprehend. Felix grins a welcome. I needn't have worried about my pajamas. He's wearing sandals, baggy track pants and a shabby polo shirt both in the same unbecoming shade of gray, and a leather strap around his neck with some kind of carved wooden talisman hanging from it. He smooths a long strand of wavy brown hair behind his ear, and I hear the soft rustle of fabric as he sticks his hands in his pockets. The illusion of sharing the same space and time is all-encompassing.

"Welcome to Greystone House," he says.

Some of the furniture in my loft would be invisible if it weren't for the faintly glowing red lines surrounding it. I presume this is to avoid me crashing into it. As a test, I take my first, awkward holographic step. "Am I moving at home too?" I ask, my voice as unsteady as I feel.

"Yes. We would ideally use matching rooms, but just don't move too much and you'll be OK. Full immersion can feel strange to start with. It takes a while to adjust, but you get used to it."

Remaining still, I take in my new surroundings and force myself to breathe normally. The effect is powerful, but he's right about the adjustment, and my poor scrambled brain does a pretty good job of assembling and accepting this new reality. We're standing in what appears to be the entrance to a stately home, its floor laid with huge off-white marble tiles. Immediately in front of me, a grand oak staircase rises straight up to a mezzanine split into two graceful curves. On either side of me, wood-paneled walls are hung with oversized oil paintings and pierced with giant leaded glass windows which twinkle as I move my head, each ancient pane set at a slightly different angle. The windows give out onto the darkness outside, and through one of them, I can just make out the crescent moon shining bright in the evening sky. To my left, just behind Felix, there's a huge metallic globe. It's nestled near the side of the hall like a dark pearl, about six feet top to bottom, apparently floating a couple of feet off the ground. Some kind of modern art, maybe? "This place is very cool."

Felix nods. "When we were designing the new space, I wanted people to feel the power and the significance of the work we do, and I think we achieved that."

"You were involved in building this place?"

"Yes." Felix folds his arms and looks around the concourse, like a monarch surveying his kingdom. "Greystone House was in my family for several generations before I inherited it. It was built even before your time, so it was a bit dilapidated when I took it on, but it was on a good plot of land, so when the time was right, we developed this place. This house is just a small part of the property now. It's where I have my office." He pauses. "But I guess you'll have seen all of this anyway, with that gift of yours, right? Hey, I should warn you, I was involved in some very shady stuff in my student days. I hope you're not easily offended."

He throws back his head and laughs freely, the echo reverberating around the atrium, and it's infectious. I laugh with him. "It doesn't seem to work that way," I say. "I think we have to meet physically, in the flesh, before there's any possibility of me seeing anything, and even then, I don't get viewings from most people. Even if I did see something, I wouldn't embarrass you by sharing it."

"Good to know I won't be making headline news anytime soon. You know, once I figured out who I was, I invested everything I had in The Continuum, though what drives me has changed over the years. In my twenties, I was a hundred percent focused on money. Then, I got into technology, learned how to code, and got hooked on the power the tech industries had to change the world. I thought that would never change, but it's crept up on me, what we do here, and these days I'm hooked on the immense power we have to help others."

"I'm only just getting my head around what you guys are all about," I admit, "but I've been very impressed so far." For some reason, I find myself wanting his approval. "What kind of technology were you in?"

"Data analysis. I started out as a trader, poring over financial charts, but I ended up working on historical data." He laughs at my expression. "I thought someone might have told you—I'm not actually a time traveler myself."

"Really? I'd assumed everyone at The Continuum is a time traveler."

"You gotta watch those assumptions, Joseph," he says, eyes twinkling. "I watched all the time-travel movies as a kid, played all the games, and it became a kind of obsession, so when I jumped out of trading in my early thirties, I decided to try and create a machine that would transport me back through time, to visit the past and make better sense of the future. It wasn't straightforward—I nearly drove myself mad. I was a lost soul for a while, tying myself in loops, but then someone set me on the right path. And one of the best things I ever did was surround myself with brilliant people like Bill and Iris. We all brought something different to the table. I've never wanted to be surrounded by yes-men, I want to be challenged. It's how you get the best results. It's how you outdo the competition." He shrugs. "Life doesn't always turn out how you planned, does it? My destiny was not to travel in a time machine, but instead to join the dots, and I ended up creating Downstream."

"Iris told me about it, said it was some kind of supercomputer?"

"That's right. And this is part of what it tells us." Felix steps to the side and waves his hand at the globe before us, and it begins to glow. I recognize the shapes of Europe and Africa and realize this is a replica of the Earth, displaying live day and night cycles. And by live, I mean *live*. I imagine it's like looking down on the planet from the International Space Station. The continents are dappled with the shadows of miniature clouds that scud across the surface. The oceans are a shifting mass of emerald and cyan hues. On the dark side of the globe, cities glow amber. I walk around the sphere and notice pinpricks of blue light here and there.

"What are those blue things?" I ask.

"Those are our people," Felix says, "our travelers. Their positions are layered, like electron shells around an atom, and the layers correspond to the times they're currently in." He wanders slowly around the globe with me. "I wanted to display this in the atrium because it reminds us that we're part of a network of travelers across time and space. We all get tied up in the intricacies of individual missions, but I don't want anyone to forget the big picture."

"It's breathtaking," I say. "I had no idea there were so many travelers. How many are there?"

"Currently, across all time, three hundred and eighty-seven."

"Currently?"

"Now and then, someone changes their own timeline, like you did with your sister, and they become visible to us. If we end up recruiting them successfully, we add them to the list."

I marvel again at how wrong I'd been when I thought I was the only one. "You said that this was a part of what Downstream shows you. What else does it do?"

"It shows us change events and identifies focus objects. I'll show you sometime. It'll blow your mind."

I've been wondering why he's brought me here, at this time of night, with no one else around. "What else did you want to talk about?"

"Iris knows I've brought you in," he says, "but she doesn't know why. I need to talk to you about Bill." This takes me by surprise. "We all miss him, you know. I don't want you to think that we don't. He was a good friend and brilliant sparring partner. He brought balance to the leadership team, and his loss has left us in pieces."

If Felix is trying to make me feel even more guilty than I did already, it's working. "I'm sorry to hear that. I'm sorry about all of it. If I could have saved him, I would have, but I've played it through in my head a thousand times, and there was nothing I could have done."

"We know that." Felix rubs his chin thoughtfully. "But it's more complicated than it might seem. Iris and Bill were together at one time, romantically, and they always stayed close. She told me she feels like she's lost a part of herself."

I recall the viewing I had of the two of them by the loch. Poor Iris. I can't believe how well she's holding it together. "She must hate me," I say. "I feel horrible."

"Don't. I'm not trying to guilt-trip you here; I'm trying to explain. Because Iris is such a professional, she's putting all her efforts into supporting you, tracking down Scarlett, and trying to get Nils back, so she doesn't have time to mourn. I actually think it's providing her with a welcome distraction. But all that means is that it's down to me to pick through what happened in London, when Bill came back to save you." He folds his arms behind his head and stretches his chest. "Not my favorite job, detective work," he says, "but I've been working through the data, analyzing what happened on your last jump in London, and things don't quite stack up."

I feel inexplicably anxious all of a sudden, like I'm on trial. I try to swallow the feeling, force it back down my throat. "How do you mean?"

"There are a few anomalies in the data from Bill's jump to London. There's a standard pattern to the jump data we receive from people's watches and usually, it corresponds exactly with what Downstream predicts, complementing its data to give us a full picture of what happened and what's been changed. Bill's is different, though. Did you notice anything strange in his behavior during your last jump to London? Anything that seemed unusual?"

I cast my mind back. "I remember thinking he moved extremely fast, but to be honest, I was being shot at and my adrenaline was off the charts. It was all a bit of a blur."

"Of course." Felix tips his head thoughtfully. "I know it's difficult, but do you remember how many versions of Bill you saw? The data seems odd . . . It could be nothing, just a transmission issue, but I'm trying to finish the report, and I hoped you might be able to help . . ." He leaves the question hanging.

"I think I saw two versions of him."

"Just two?"

"Yes. I remember presuming he'd been there before, and that he was on his second jump to the same point in time."

"Right," Felix says. "He was very upset about blackmailing you, and when he saw you die, he didn't hesitate to travel back again to save you." He stares into space for a moment, thinking. "There's something else I need to know, but it might be difficult for you to talk about."

"It's OK. Go ahead."

"Sorry to ask you this, Joe, but after Bill was shot . . . did he die immediately?"

I flinch at Felix's directness. "No, it . . . it took a little while."

"And you were with him?"

I nod, swallowing the lump in my throat as I relive the scene.

"I'm glad he didn't die alone. Did he say anything to you?"

I clear my throat. "He said he hadn't wanted to blackmail me and told me that I was his final mission."

"But nothing about how he saved you?"

"No."

"And you didn't ask him?"

"It didn't even occur to me," I say. "I guess I presumed it was like any other jump, that Bill had seen an alternative version of events and come back to change the way things played out."

"That's all right," Felix says. "There are a few things that don't quite add up, but I have to be honest, I'm reaching here. I'm not even sure what I'm looking for. I just wanted to be certain that we weren't missing anything. I'll keep crunching the data, and Iris can focus on finding Scarlett."

"What's the deal with Scarlett, by the way?" I venture. "Both Bill and Iris told me she used to be a student here."

"Good question." Felix lets out a long, heavy sigh. "To explain that, first I need to talk about how things work—the rules, if you will. The most crucial thing to understand, if you ever decide to join us on a more permanent basis, is that time is in charge. It has the power to give and take. We just move in the space that it provides." Felix's eyes flicker, as though scanning through his memories, some of them clearly painful. "The majority of the past can't be changed, and Scarlett didn't like that. She believed we should figure out a way to stop wars, disasters, atrocities. Life is full of loss and injustice, and she wanted to put that right."

I digest this. "I can sympathize with her point of view, to some degree."

"As can I. She's young and idealistic, but there's the way we wish things were, and then there's how they actually are. I tried to explain to her that I don't make the rules, I just reveal them." He shakes his head. "Bill always saw the best in people. He insisted she had potential, even after she'd gone. I liked her too. She was a nonconformist, much like me. A healthy dose of cynicism is a good thing, but she just couldn't get behind what we do here. It's a journey, and some people don't make it."

I think this through. "I get why she left, but I still don't understand why she attacked me, and then Nils."

"Exactly what she's up to is a mystery to us as well," Felix admits. "But we'll figure it out eventually."

"Gabrielle said you were building a tracker to try and find her. Why can't you just use the globe here?"

"Unfortunately, Scarlett doesn't travel the same way you do. She can't connect with focus objects herself. She has to follow other time travelers on their missions, traveling in their wake. She's unique, the only one who's ever traveled like this. And it means that for now, we can't see where she is or where she's been. But I'll crack it in the end. I always do. And then we'll find her."

It suddenly makes a lot more sense why The Continuum was so interested in my viewings of Scarlett, and why they've asked me to go to Paris with Gabrielle.

"For now," Felix continues, "we need to keep you safe and do what we can to get Nils home." He glances down at his watch. "My team needs me. It's never-ending. I mean, what was that? Fifteen minutes of peace? Sometimes I miss the early days when it was just a handful of us, but it's nice to be wanted, I suppose. Joseph, I could chat all night, but I had better let you go." He offers a warm smile, then his expression becomes more serious again. "You know, Bill told me once that he felt you were the most exciting discovery since we started The Continuum. He may be gone, but I'm still here. I know Iris told you the same, but if you ever have any questions, you come and talk to me, and I'll set you straight. OK?"

"Thanks. I do have a question, actually. I've just remembered something Bill said to me. I wanted to ask you what it meant."

"Go ahead," Felix says.

"Just before he died, Bill said he and I were going to have adventures together, and he wanted me to remember them for him. What did he mean?"

"Ah yes, complex chronology." Felix's tone alters, and he slips into teacher mode. "It happens to most time travelers at some point in their careers. You bump into someone you know, who doesn't know you yet. Depending on the circumstances, you may have to play along and act as though it's the first time you've met, so as not to impact the future."

I think about this. "Are you saying that when Bill first arrived in my shop, he and I had already spent time together? But it hasn't happened for me yet?"

Felix nods. "As with everything in physics, time is relative. Here, in 2131, Bill's life may be over, but your relationship with him is still ahead of you. I'm envious. Time is precious—it gives us so much—but like I said, in the end, it's always in charge. Enjoy your time with him when it comes. He was one of the good ones."

"I will," I say, and it feels like a promise.

14

Once Felix has left me back in the present, I sit out on the terrace for a while and watch the moon, full and round and more than one hundred years younger than the one I saw through the window of Greystone House, and when I eventually get to bed, I dream of a younger Bill and a fresh-faced Iris wandering arm in arm through grand, paneled corridors, making plans for the future. Upon waking, my mind returns fully to the present. Morning sun floods the room, and along with it, my recent conversation with Sue at the quiz night. I need to drop in on Amy, see if I can get her to tell me more about her past.

I go over to her flat in the late afternoon and ring the bell a couple of times, but there's no answer. I let myself in to have a scout around, see if I can get any insights into how Amy's feeling. She gave me a key a few weeks ago—she's got a key for my place too—"just in case," to use her words. Well, this is a case in point.

I put the key in the lock and push my way into the flat. I have to shove the door a couple of times to get through because there's a pile of leaflets and envelopes on the floor behind it. Leaning down, I gather up the mail and put it on the table by the door.

The living room is dark, the curtains drawn, but as I reach for the light switch, I see Amy asleep on the sofa. She looks so peaceful, her face smooth and rested, her belly moving gently up and down as she breathes.

I decide to brew some tea and hope that she wakes up while I'm pottering about in the kitchen.

Amy's not the tidiest of people. Her flat always feels lived-in, but the kitchen's clearly taken a hammering for the past few days. Piles of dirty dishes are balanced on the counter, empty milk cartons are lined up on the draining board, and there's a cluster of dirty mugs around the kettle. Rolling up my sleeves, I fill the sink with hot, soapy water and set about tidying up while the tea brews. I'm just sweeping the floor when Amy wanders into the kitchen, yawning. "I thought it was you," she says, stretching her arms above her head.

"I wanted to see if you were OK, but when you didn't answer the door, I let myself in."

She rubs her eyes. "Sorry I was asleep when you got here."

"Don't worry, you looked like you needed a nap." I hand her a cup of strong tea. "There's no milk left, but I've put a spoonful of honey in, for energy."

"Cheers." She sips the tea and peers up at the kitchen clock. It's just after 4 p.m. "Do you want to come and sit down for a bit?" I follow her into the living room, and she flops back down on the sofa while I raise the window blinds. She squints as the subdued afternoon light pervades the room. "I must've been asleep for hours," she says. "I hate that, waking up halfway through the day. Makes me feel jet-lagged. Do you know what I mean?"

"I do," I say. It's scarily reminiscent of my old life. "Have you not been sleeping again?"

She lifts her mug to her mouth and blows on her tea. I notice her fingernails are black, and there are blobs of paint all over her hands and forearms. "Not for a few weeks. I tried those herbal sleeping tablets Mum gave me, but they just gave me an itchy throat. I probably ought to go to the doctor, but I hate being prodded and poked."

"I'm worried about you," I say gently.

"Don't be daft! A little bit of sleep deprivation never did anyone any harm. Ask any new mother. Sue didn't sleep through the night for two years after she had Nathan, and she's one of the healthiest people I know."

"It's not just the sleep though. You've been quite up and down recently. You were miserable after Dad's party, but you seemed pretty high at the pub."

"I guess, but so what?"

"I had a chat with Sue. Actually, Sue had a chat with me, I should say."

"When? At the pub quiz? I wondered where you two had gone. I thought you'd just popped out for a sneaky cigarette, but you were plotting, were you?"

"We weren't plotting. She's worried about you too. She said this is a pattern." I waver for a second, then decide to go all in. "She told me about Denmark."

Amy's face falls. "I wish she hadn't. I didn't want you to know. I don't want you to worry, Joe. It's all in the past, water under the bridge."

"Sue doesn't think so. She's concerned you're . . . becoming unwell. She said she thought you were painting again."

"I am painting," she says, "but I'm fine. I don't take any of that stuff any more, haven't for years." She takes a sip of tea. "Remember those visions I had of London, of the church and the stained glass window? The feelings and the visions were stronger this time, more powerful, and when they get like that, I have to paint them."

"So you're painting the future?"

"Yes. Sometimes that future's mine, sometimes it's other people's, but this time I think it's yours again. You told me you were going to travel to Paris. Was there a fire?"

"You've seen that?"

"I've painted that and more," she says. "You'd better come and see."

I follow her into the cramped, dingy space where she keeps all her art gear. It's packed with cardboard boxes, stacks of canvases, and old curtains draped over unidentifiable boxy shapes. The walls are spattered in places with splashes of paint. My eye is immediately drawn to one of the larger canvases: an oil painting about three feet square, a riot of flaming red, tangerine orange, and vibrant yellow depicting the burning of the Salle Le Peletier. The earthy tones of the building and the street are set against bright, expressive flames that rage through the opera house, sending plumes of smoke into the night sky. Amy has perfectly captured the monumental scale of this terrible event with an accomplished and confident hand.

In places, I can see the frenzied movement in her brushstrokes, and in others, a graceful elegance captures the evocative scene in exceptional detail. The shadows are thin layers of inky black oil, but the paint in the highlights, such as the flames, has been applied in multiple layers. Some areas are so thick that the paint sits proud on the canvas, the textured brush marks clearly visible, giving the painting a three-dimensional, almost sculpted, feel.

"My God," I breathe. "Amy, it's incredible."

She picks up the painting. "This looks familiar then?"

"It's the opera house fire in Paris. I saw it myself, and you've captured it perfectly."

I marvel again at the scene Amy's created, in awe of my sister's undeniable talent. Where the main doors would have been is a gaping hole, and standing in front of it is a white ghostly figure, its form dripping into a steaming pool of shimmering silver-blue.

"The figure in the doorway," I say, "that's Philippe, the man I told you about."

Amy seems relieved. "I thought it was a ghost, haunting me through my art. I was properly spooked."

"No, it's definitely a person," I assure her. "I saw him briefly. He was a brilliant musician, apparently, and he was badly hurt in the fire. I can see why you thought he might be a ghost, but I think he was just wrapped in wet sheets while escaping from the building." I study the picture in wonder. "When did you paint this?"

"Three weeks ago."

"Three weeks?" I stare at Amy in confusion. "But I hadn't even met up with The Continuum at that point."

She shrugs. "Like I said, I'm painting your future."

I feel like I'm on the brink of understanding the impossible. The strangest feeling consumes me, surrounds me in fact, as though my thoughts decouple from my body for a split second, as though time is a sphere and I am standing in the center and, if I were to reach out my hand, could touch both the past and the future.

The thought is fleeting, gone as fast as it came.

Amy is talking to me. I turn to her. "I'm sorry, what did you say?"

"I said I've done a couple of other paintings since this one. I thought you might want to take a look." She moves to a stack of canvases beneath the window and pulls one out. "I painted it four or five days ago. I have no bloody idea what it's supposed to be."

The change of style is so jarring that it takes me a while to tune in. It's as though a completely different artist created this one, a subtle blend of dark blues and deep grays in thick acrylics and some sort of metallic paint, dreamlike and semiabstract. Amy has depicted a strange, alien desert, with malformed rocks and ledges connected by smooth dry channels. Towering over all of this twisted landscape is an angular metal structure, an industrial-style lighthouse, built with metal girders that give it the look of an electricity pylon. Its cone-shaped searchlight streaks acid-yellow across the canvas. In the center of this atmospheric scene is a melting pocket watch, draped like liquid over a kind of stone altar, spilling over the sides and pooling into a glistening sea of mercury that takes up the entire bottom half of the canvas. There is a lot to take in, but the watch is the clear focal point, and though it's grossly distorted, I recognize some of the details. It's Nils's pocket watch, the one I saw in my viewing of him and Scarlett in Macau.

"Weird, isn't it?" Amy says. "I painted it in about an hour. It raced through me so fast I could barely keep up with the paintbrush. Does it mean anything to you?"

"Maybe, yes," I tell her. "I think the watch might belong to the missing time traveler, Nils. The way you've painted it, I'm wondering if it's going to be melted in the fire or damaged somehow. That might be why he's unable to land properly."

"So it helps you, seeing this?"

"I'm not sure yet, but it might, yeah."

"What about the lighthouse? Is it symbolic, do you think?"

I study the lighthouse again: the sharp geometric lines of its structure, the warm glowing bulb at its peak. I cast my mind back to the viewing, the port, the ships in the harbor, but I don't recall a lighthouse, or anything like it. "I don't know what this means," I say. "I don't recognize it."

"I wish I could tell you more." Amy puts the painting back down on the floor. "But I have to say, it's a massive relief to get this out of me."

"A relief?"

"You know that sense of unease I told you about? It's gone, for now anyway. It builds until I can't stand it, but then an image comes through, almost as if it has a soul of its own. The images whisper and cry and wrap themselves around me like lost spirits. It's suffocating. I have to get them out of me before they drag me under, and painting's the only way I know how." She gazes out the window. The flat late-afternoon light deepens the shadows beneath her eyes and around her mouth, and I recognize the exhaustion on her face.

"Thanks for showing these to me," I say. "It means a lot."

"I know you're going to travel again, so if my paintings help you in some way, then that's good." Amy leans the painting with the shimmering silver sea against the wall and turns back to me. "You know, I've been blaming your traveling for this awful sense of dread, but I think it might be me. I've been suppressing my visions because they overwhelm and frighten me, but the harder I push them down, the more powerful they become. I let go, just give in and paint. And then, I feel a hell of a lot better."

15

Vinny pushes the pizza box across the kitchen table. "I love you enough to give you my last slice," he says. We've eaten our way through two mega-grande pizzas from the takeaway joint around the corner, and we're finally slowing down. "Go on, you know you want to."

"You have it, Vin," I protest. "It's a full house too. Look—a piece of mushroom, a bit of anchovy, and"—I lift a piece of red pepper—"there's even some ham under there."

"Very tempting indeed," he agrees, "but I need to be thinking about my waistline."

"Why? What's up?"

"You know, if I'm going to be a father to Charlotte, I've got to think about the messages I'm giving her. We are what we eat." He pats his tummy thoughtfully.

"One wafer-thin slice isn't going to make a difference, is it?" I cajole him.

"It might." He lifts up the pizza slice and hands it to me. Beaten, I take it from him. "There's a good chap. Waste not, want not."

The rest of Vinny's house looks like the aftermath of a student party, but the kitchen is pristine, a hub of seriously creative chefery. Vinny keeps it spotless, and everything has its place. It's like an altar to nourishment.

"So how are things going with Kassandra?" I ask.

"We're going out for dinner on Friday night, to a country pub near Cirencester."

"Sounds posh. Is your daughter coming too?"

"No, Kassandra doesn't want me to meet her yet. She wants to spend some time 'connecting' with me first so that Charlotte's 'comfortable' with me when we meet. I think she wants to brief me, in case I put my foot in it."

I flinch at this. It sounds manipulative, as if Kassandra's approaching Vinny's reunion with his daughter as a military operation. "And are you OK with that?"

"Absolutely. I know I can be a bit loud sometimes. The last thing I want to do is scare Charlotte."

"You won't scare her!" I say indignantly. "She's going to love you."

"I hope she does," Vinny says, "but if Kassandra can coach me a bit, then that's great, isn't it?" He sighs dreamily. "I can't wait for you to meet her. Kassandra, I mean. She's amazing—so sorted, so sure of herself, you know? She's a brilliant mum to Charlotte. She's also a total goddess. I bet when people see us out together, they think 'Blimey, that bloke's punching above his weight.'"

He's clearly besotted, at the mercy of a million molecules shooting around his nervous system with just one thing on their tiny minds.

"Anyway," Vinny says, downing the last of his beer, popping the caps off two fresh bottles, and pushing one over to me, "enough of yours truly. What's new, Cash? Spill the beans."

I lean forward, getting ready to blow Vinny away. "Felix called me, and took me to Greystone House, the Continuum headquarters."

"Sheesh madeesh!" he exclaims. "No way! When? How?"

"Last night. He spoke into my ear, through my implant. I nearly jumped out of my skin! We used the technology I told you about, but this time they projected me there, and it felt real."

"Wow," Vinny says breathlessly. "My best mate, combobulating with the future. So how was it?" He fidgets in anticipation, and an image flashes into my head of Vinny as a little boy on his birthday, surrounded by piles of new toys and plastered in birthday cake. "Tell me you saw flying cars?"

I laugh. "I wish I could, but I was inside Greystone House, so I didn't see anything outside at all, apart from the moon. I guess we might be mining it by 2131, but either way, it's still there. He also showed me a globe with dots all over it that represented all the time travelers."

"So cool. Did you see any of the others?"

"No, just Felix."

"What's he like?" Vinny asks, peeling the label on his beer bottle.

"He's cool, actually—for a data guy. Looks a bit like a surfer. He's got this laid-back vibe, like he's got nothing to prove. He's one of the founders of The Continuum, and he built Downstream, which is some kind of supercomputer that they use to track change events."

"He sounds like Tony Stark and Elon Musk had a love child."

I chuckle. "That's about right."

"What did he want?" Vinny presses.

"He wanted to talk to me about Bill. Apparently, there's something strange in the data from when Bill came to London to save me, and Felix wanted to know what I could remember."

Vinny thinks this over. "Why didn't Iris ask you about it when she debriefed you after London?"

"Turns out Iris and Bill had a thing going on, and she's too cut up over losing him to talk about it much. That's what Felix implied, anyway."

"Blimey O'Reilly. Poor Iris." He swirls the beer around in his bottle. "I can imagine how gutted she must feel."

"I know." I bat away the sadness that flashes up in my chest. "Anyway. I told him everything I could remember, for what it's worth."

Vinny guzzles down most of his beer and wipes his mouth. "It's so cool, Cash. Traveling into the past, chatting to the future. You're the real deal." His brow furrows suddenly. "Gosh. Sorry, I meant to ask, how's Amy doing? She seemed tired-but-wired at the quiz, you know?"

"Yeah, she's been a bit manic lately." I take a long draft of beer. "Actually, I saw her this afternoon. You know Sue, Amy's best friend? She cornered me at the pub, told me Amy took an overdose when she was younger, and she's worried Amy's heading in the same direction again."

"Holy cashmolee," Vinny says, sitting back. "An overdose? That's serious, Cash."

"I know. I was shocked, so I went to see her earlier this afternoon. She was fast asleep when I got there, didn't know what day it was when I woke her up. She was disappointed Sue had told me, said she didn't want me to know. It's obvious she thinks we're all making a fuss for no good reason. Here's the thing though, Vin. She's been having visions of Paris, of Gabrielle's mission, and she's been painting them."

"Really? Did she show you?"

"Yeah. She wanted to see if they would help me with the mission. One was in a traditional style, of the opera house fire, with Philippe standing at the entrance. It's almost exactly what I saw when I first got to Paris with Gabrielle, except that—get this—she painted it three weeks ago, even before Gabrielle met me at the book launch. The other one was weird, a sort of abstract coastal scene, with a lighthouse and Nils's watch melting into a sea of what looked like mercury."

"Jeez. What do you think it means?" Vinny asks.

"I don't know yet. I guess it's linked to my future somehow, but I'm trying to keep an open mind for the time being."

"Fair enough." He chews a fingernail absentmindedly. "Just thinking . . . Amy didn't paint the London stuff, so why's she painting Paris?"

"She said her visions and feelings are stronger. She feels like she has to get them down, out of her head."

"Did this used to happen with Other Joe? Did Amy see his future too?"

"I don't know. Why?"

"Because you two have obviously got a special connection. Like gin and tonic. When you're heading off somewhere, Amy feels it coming, and when Amy's feeling down, you're tuned in to that too. It's precious, Cash. Go with it."

"You could be right." Vinny's words make me wonder if I should talk to Iris about Amy again, see if I can find out more about what her future holds, and how I can help her through this.

"Dessert?" Vinny goes to his huge, American-style refrigerator and pulls out a packet of frozen chocolate ice cream bars.

"I'm stuffed, mate."

"All the more for yours truly." He pulls out a couple of the bars, unwraps one, and packs the entire thing into his mouth like a hamster, and I realize that Dave's nickname for Vinny, "Fatcheeks," is spot on. "Now then," he says through a mouthful of ice cream, "I know you said you weren't going on the next jump, but you and I both know you are."

"I'm really not sure about that," I say firmly.

"I told you at the quiz, Cash, you'll be going on the next jump. They'll want you to. They need you."

"Right, so you can see the future now too, can you?" I say, a little brusquely.

"No," Vinny says, looking hurt. "But I know you, Cash. If they ask, you'll want to help. In the meantime, I'm going to be a good little sidekick and do all I can to prepare you, just in case. Walk this way." He pushes back his chair and leads me into the living room. Just like the war room he set up for the Romano mission, the usually chaotic space has been turned into a hyperorganized information zone, with whiteboards and pinboards covering every inch of wall. In the middle of the room, just in front of the sofa, is a small dining table piled high with books, and beside them is Vinny's laptop. "I've been doing my homework, Cash," he says proudly. "You said my research on the London mission was helpful, so I thought I'd get stuck in again, especially as your American bird's an information-hoarding harridan."

"Wow, Vinny, this is amazing," I say, acknowledging to myself that if The Continuum asks me to travel again, all of this data could really come in handy.

"You've got your hands full, and I've got plenty of time to kill. Plus, you know how much I like my factoids. Bloody interesting, actually. Now, sit yourself down here." He moves a pile of paper off an armchair. "I'll take you through what I've found out. Hold on, though, one thing missing." He nips out of the room and returns carrying two glasses. "Little shot of brandy? It's vintage. French, as it happens."

"Nice touch. Cheers."

Vinny clinks his glass against mine. "Buenos días," he says.

I sip the amber liquid and feel it swirl gently into my belly, like a warm, internal hug. "That's just the job," I sigh.

"Hey, hold up! What did I say when we toasted our glasses just then?"

"Er, you said buenos días. Why?"

He looks disappointed. "Did it sound Spanish?"

"Yes! Obviously. It is Spanish."

"But what about that tech in your ear? I thought it would translate it for you."

"Oh, I see! No mate, it doesn't seem to work unless I'm time traveling."

"You're kidding!" Vinny says, crestfallen. "I was thinking we could listen in on what the waiters are saying next time we go for a curry. Which side's it in again?" I point at my right ear. He approaches me and leans in close. "That's a bloody waste of perfectly good biotech," he says loudly into my ear.

"I don't think they can hear you," I say, "but I agree. I'll have a chat with Iris next time I see her."

"You do that, Cash." Vinny drains his brandy and sets his glass on the table. "Right, where was I?" He rubs his chin pensively as he reviews his whiteboards. "First things first. In case you were wondering, I haven't lost the plot. I know Iris and the gang have only roped you in to help them find Nils, and this opera house mission isn't yours to solve. But if Nils has landed smack in the middle of the change event, then I figured the more you know about the mission, the better, right? As we know, everything is connected."

"Sounds brilliant. Fire away. No pun intended." I don't know if it's the brandy or Vinny's bullish enthusiasm, but I'm feeling more positive. If I do end up going to Paris again, at least I'll be prepared.

Vinny walks over to the left-hand pinboard. "These are a couple of newspaper reports from the time," he says solemnly. "Fire at the Paris Opera," reads the first headline. "Paris Theater Consumed," reads another, beneath a detailed illustration of the fire. I shudder at the sight of the impressive opera house ablaze, surrounded by hundreds of people, many running from the scene. Tiny figures extend ladders toward desperate people on the roof. Firefighters on the ground attempt to tackle the inferno but look woefully outgunned. It's all in black and white, just a sketch, but the artist has skillfully managed to capture the heat, the desperation, and the panic of that night.

"I always used to see drawings like this and feel disconnected, as though they were pictures from storybooks," I say. "Not anymore though. I was there, and this is exactly how it was. Did you find out what caused the fire?"

"No one knows," Vinny says. "Some people said it was faulty gas light-ing, but that's unconfirmed. At least no one died."

On the next board, I notice a print of a portrait of Philippe, the same picture Iris showed me. "That's Philippe Chevalier," I say, pointing at the portrait. "He's the guy who got hurt in the fire."

"Lush-looking, isn't he?" Vinny muses. "I read he was rather popular with the ladies."

"I can imagine." Philippe's eyes are alive with possibility, and his lips are upturned in a pout that suggests he has a flirtatious secret to share. "When I saw him, he was a mess, but I recognize him."

"You and your memory for faces. I thought you would," Vinny says. "Poor bloke. He was destined for the glittering heights of fame and fortune—the talk of the town—but the fire put an end to all of that. I couldn't find any trace of him after that night."

"It's horrendous. Watching that building going up in flames, seeing people injured like that . . . It was really hard to watch."

Vinny turns to me as if he's just had a brilliant idea. "Cash! Why don't you just stop the fire then, when you go back? You'll have more time to find Nils, and Philippe won't get hurt. It's win-win, isn't it?"

If only life were as simple as Vinny makes it seem. "I wish we could, mate, but it doesn't work like that. The Continuum told me that observation carries a kind of weight, that when people witness events, it fixes things in time, sort of bakes them solid. And that means we can't undo the big stuff."

"Right." He rubs his nose. "So we couldn't go back and unsink the *Titanic*?"

"Apparently not."

"Or unshoot JFK?"

"Nope, nothing like that. I don't fully understand why not, but I've been told those are the rules."

Vinny considers this with a serious expression. "So what are you supposed to be doing in Paris, if you can't stop the fire?"

"Helping Philippe. We think we need to stop him from getting burned, from going back into the building."

Vinny scratches his bald head in consternation. "Nothing I've read about the night of the fire even mentions him."

"It's OK. If the internet knew why he'd gone back into the opera house, The Continuum would know, and they don't. It's what we're going to try and find out on our next jump."

"What does your gut say?" Vinny asks.

"That Philippe is a decent man. I think he might have been trying to save someone."

"But no one died."

"Which could mean he succeeded."

Vinny ponders this. "You might need to be careful. If you stop him from going back in, then whoever he saved might die."

"It's a good point. Hopefully, that won't happen. I don't think time will let us change something that doesn't fix the problem."

"OK," Vinny says dubiously. "There's another thing though, Cash—in my research I found a suspicious number of articles about ghosts." He points at the third board, with printouts related to the opera house and thumbtacks in various locations, each connected with a piece of thread to a separate label. "Some people, like that woman you interviewed in the café, were saying the opera house was haunted. There are other eyewitness accounts of people seeing a ghostly man in various places throughout the building. I've marked each of the spots with a tack, and I've printed out the report of each sighting. Of course, the opera house could have genuinely been haunted, so some of the sightings could have been actual ghosts, but I wondered if some of them might be Nils." He rubs his hands together in excitement. "What do you think?"

I don't pick on Vinny about his belief in ghosts, even though I think it's poppycock. I don't want to burst his bubble. "You could be onto something," I say. "I met a seamstress who said she'd seen a ghost in the costume store, and I thought the same thing—it could be Nils. The Continuum is going to build a kind of tracking beacon to help locate him."

"Cool. Anything else I should know?" Vinny asks.

In my mind's eye, I scan through the trip to Paris again, and one face stands out above all the others. "I did meet this one older lady, a patron of the opera. She's called Madame Delacroix. I feel like she might be relevant to the mission, although I've no idea why."

"Excellent! I'll do a bit of digging. If you still want me to, that is."

"Honestly, Vin, I don't know what I'd do without you. I want to help them to find Nils, but I'm not making much headway."

"Cash, those guys need you because of your superpower. They can't see the things you can, you told me that."

"But I didn't see anything when I was in Paris, and I haven't seen anything since I got back either. What use is a superpower if I don't know how to use it?"

"You just need to reconnect with Scarlett. She started all of this."

"But how?"

"You've got to find a way to trigger the viewing . . . deepen it maybe." He thinks for a minute. "How about the CCTV system in your shop?"

"Molly takes care of all that. What are you thinking?"

"When I was installing your sound system, I had to work around the cabling for the security system. Like spaghetti, it was. You have cameras all over the joint. So, I was thinking, you've probably still got footage somewhere of the night Scarlett broke into your shop. Seeing that again might trigger a viewing."

"Vinny, you're a genius! If I've got the footage, I can take a screenshot of her face and use it as a focus object. It's got to be worth a try."

"Good stuff." Vinny checks his watch. "Right Cash, I'm going to have to oust you. I'm gonna be late for my spin class."

"Your what?"

He bursts out laughing. "Your face, Cash! As if."

On the way back through the kitchen, Vinny pauses at the fridge. "My gut's telling me I'm feeling peckish. My belt says lettuce, but my heart says cheese." He pulls out a generous triangle of brie, unwraps it, and bites the end off. "Got a lot of things right, those French dudes," he says, chomping appreciatively. "No stress, but once you finally realize you're going on this jump, if you can bring me some snacks from Paris and some vintage champagne, that would be all good."

16

Half an hour later, back in my flat, I find the security manual neatly filed on one of the shelves in the study, silently thanking Other Joe for being so organized. As I hoped, all the recorded footage is archived to a local drive. I fire up my laptop, log in, and familiarize myself with the interface. After searching through the FAQs for a while, I confirm that if the alarm goes off, the camera starts recording. Excellent.

I click on a tab titled *History* and find a list of entries for every day. Most of them say *No security alerts*, but I keep scrolling back until I get to the night of the break-in.

And then, I see it:

12:17 a.m. Alarm Triggered

I brace myself, click on the video file, and press play.

The shop is dark, so the footage is shot in infrared and looks a bit like a photo negative. A slim, hooded figure enters Bridgeman Antiques, glowing white like a ghost, and walks quickly toward the back of the shop. Scarlett's face is partially covered, but as she walks past the security camera, she looks up, straight into the lens. She turns away, puts her backpack on the floor, lifts Tommy Shaw's radio out of the bag, and places it carefully in cabinet twenty-two before disappearing out of shot.

Grabbing the cursor, I scrub back, rewinding frame by frame. I pause just at the instant Scarlett looks into the camera. She stares straight at me, a self-satisfied smirk on her face, dilated pupils bright white in the infrared. My pulse quickens, and already I can feel the stirrings of a renewed connection with her. I save the still and send it to the printer, brew myself a chamomile tea, and head upstairs to the loft, where I sink into the sofa and try to focus. It's quiet in here, just the faint sound of the wind outside, and I try to release the stress and anticipation that have taken hold of my body.

"Close your eyes, Joe," an imaginary Alexia whispers in my ear, "and remember your breathing: four seconds in, hold, seven seconds out." Recalling the mellifluous tone of her voice is reassuring, and it grounds me.

In . . . two . . . three . . . four . . .

Hold . . .

Out . . . two . . . three . . . four . . . five . . . six . . . seven . . .

I recall my viewing of Scarlett and Nils in the hut, her promise to give him a second chance. *I need a second chance too*, I implore Scarlett. *If you were really trying to help him, then let me in, let me see how this plays out.*

I hear a truck go past outside, and it breaks my concentration. Man! Come on, Bridgeman, focus!

In . . . two . . . three . . . four . . .

Hold . . .

Out . . . two . . . three . . . four . . . five . . . six . . . seven . . .

I return to my breathing, quieting my conscious mind. Gradually, my heart rate slows and my mind clears. The trick now is not to fight it. When I feel myself drifting back up into consciousness, I concentrate on breathing again, filling my mind with thoughts of Scarlett, and sink deeper.

Now. It's happening.

I feel at one with the universe as a warm tide washes through me. I let go, slipping willingly into the dark. The comforting blackness starts to fade as I enter a viewing. *Stay relaxed, keep breathing, here we go . . .*

I'm floating on warm thermals, high above a coastal town. Rocky slopes lead to a port of some kind. I drift down through a baking-hot market square, the intoxicating smells of leather and spices mix with fruits and vegetables, deepened by the heat of a midday sun. I pass a church and slip through a wooden door into a stone building, the stench of old fishing nets overwhelming. Shafts of sunlight cut across two figures. One is Nils, seated and bound. The other is Scarlett, Nils's watch glinting in her hand.

Nils glares up at Scarlett with contempt. "A second chance? You're out of your mind! You have no idea what you're talking about." The hut is hot and stuffy, and he sweats as he struggles against his bonds. He tries to pull the metal ring out of the wall, but it's firmly attached. "Untie me, for God's sake! Those men could return any minute. We need to get out of here."

"I will untie you," Scarlett says, "but there's something I need to do first." She lays Nils's watch on the bench and pulls a small leather pouch from her satchel. Unrolling it carefully, she selects a narrow steel rod, about three inches long, with thin gold tubing at one end. She flicks open the case of Nils's watch and deftly inserts the gold end into a tiny socket just beneath the three-hour marker.

"What are you doing to my watch?" Nils says. Scarlett ignores him, concentrating as the watch face goes blank. It bleeps three times and the word *Settings* appears across the middle of the screen. "Talk to me!" A vein bulges in his forehead, and the color has returned to his cheeks.

"I am a time traveler," she says. "I'm with The Continuum, and I'm here to help you."

"If you're here to help me, then why won't you let me go? Are you on a mission too? I don't understand."

"We don't have much time." Scarlett flips the watch onto its back, revealing its intricate skeleton mechanism, studded with tiny jewels of red, blue, and green.

"Why are you doing this?" Nils says.

She doesn't answer, but a thought bleeds through:

Because I have to know how he did it.

She examines the watch and focuses on a circular chamber, golden in color, about the size of a child's fingernail. Using a minuscule soldering iron, she traces a tiny circle the size of a pinhead and lifts it gingerly with a small pair of pliers. Burn marks scar the outer edges of the incision, a small aperture that peers up at her like a bruised eye. Wiping sweat from her forehead, she picks up a glass pipette and inserts it into a small bottle filled with a pearlescent silvery fluid. Holding her breath, she draws a few millimeters of the liquid into the glass tube. The molecules of the elixir shift and stir, its surface glowing softly. Clenching her jaw, she squeezes three precise droplets into the chamber. The watch fizzes, and the jewels inside it glow hot for a second, then fade. Lifting another tool from the workbench, its tip crackling with a fierce blue energy, she seals the fractured chamber shut, leaving almost no trace of her handiwork.

Flipping the watch back over, she checks the screen.

Triterbium: 77%
Oscillation: 3 Hz

Relief and the joy of a job well done sweep through Scarlett's body. She can't remember the last time she felt this elated.

She uses the steel rod to reset the watch to its normal running mode, and the screen obediently displays its standard face. The time is 1:14 p.m. Laying the watch down on the bench, she approaches Nils and unties first his legs, then his hands. He rushes over to the bench, picks up his timepiece, and examines the display.

"What the devil have you done to it?" he growls. His body is taut with anger.

"Can you see? The final jump indicator has gone out."

He grunts. "That doesn't mean anything. It's just a light. Maybe you disabled the display."

Men shout in the distance. Nils flicks a nervous glance toward the door.

"I haven't touched the display," she says. "You need to listen to me because we don't have much time. If you check your watch now, you'll see the countdown. It will say there's just over a minute until you jump again."

Nils frowns and looks at the watch. When he looks up again, she can see in his eyes that she was right. He's listening now.

"When you leave here," she tells him, "you won't be going home."

"Who the hell are you?"

"It doesn't matter who I am. What matters is that I know who you are and why you're here."

"You don't know me," he scoffs. "You're bluffing."

"You are Nils Erik Petersen. You live in Oslo, Norway. You've never failed a mission. You've successfully completed seventeen, some in just a couple of jumps, and this is your eighteenth. You've been here three days. Your insertion point was inside the church of São Lourenço, and you arrived just after six a.m., during morning mass. The data indicates that nobody saw you land. This is your final jump, and you were about to complete your mission before you were attacked by those men. How am I doing so far?"

Nils is silent.

"When you travel, you'll come back around to this waypoint again. You'll land in São Lourenço church just after six a.m. on Sunday. I'm giving you another shot at this waypoint, Nils. You can still complete this mission."

He flinches, and his skin takes on the semitranslucence that precedes a travel event. The pressure in the room increases, and the air feels thicker, like before a storm.

"You cannot invent your own rules!" Nils insists. "Everyone knows there's no such thing as a second chance. Time opens waypoints for us, but once our time is up, they're permanently shut. That is how things are."

She sighs. "Open your mind, traveler," she says. "Nothing is forever. New evidence is always coming to light. That's how science works." He has almost gone now, his body phasing in and out like a lightbulb about to blow. "Good luck, Nils."

A split second later, he's gone.

Scarlett wonders for a moment where Nils is, but she has no doubt that the changes she made to the watch were perfectly executed. She packs away her tools. She will be drawn to him in time, and then she will know.

Before the priests can return, she slips out of the cabin and hurries back toward the hills.

PART 4

17

Waking from a viewing is utterly disorientating. The emotional journey is akin to waking up in a recovery room after an operation, hearing the disembodied voice of someone calling your name, asking if you're OK. It takes me a while to shed Scarlett's skin, my consciousness scrambling to reclaim ownership of my awareness. I'm slumped on the sofa. Scarlett's printed image stares up at me from the floor. I snap upright, run to my desk drawer, grab a pen and notepad, and write furiously, capturing everything I can remember. I close my eyes and focus on the moment she tampered with Nils's watch, the words and numbers burned into my memory.

Triterbium: 77%
Oscillation: 3 Hz

I slump back, relieved. I sit for a while, steadying my erratic breathing. Iris was right, I did see more, and it confirms that Scarlett tampered with Nils's watch. It's time to fire up my futuristic bat signal.

After locking the doors and drawing the blinds, I place my silver hunter facedown on a small table in the center of the room and circle it like a shark. Was it twist twice and then click? Or was it click twice, then twist? I try a few variations and eventually hit on the right one: click, rotate the winder twice, click again.

The green light show kicks in. Iris appears a few moments later, dressed in a light-blue pantsuit, her white hair swept up and to the side in a sharp wave, her pale skin contrasting burgundy lips. She smiles.

"Hello, Joseph, good to see you." Her voice is flinty. "How are you?"

"I'm good, Iris. I've had another viewing. I've seen what Scarlett did to Nils's watch."

"His watch? Sorry, please bear with me." Iris glances to her right and shakes her head at an unseen person in the room. "Joseph, I'm at Greystone House, and I have Felix with me. Currently, this connection is between you and me only, and our location is set to your present. Rather than bring Felix to you, may I invite you into the room here, so you can tell us both what you saw?"

"OK," I tell her, excited to see another glimpse of the future. "Sure."

"Good. I will send a message to Gabrielle as well, see if she can join us." Iris takes a step toward me, and when she speaks, her voice is soft. "Are you ready?"

"Ready." Without a sound, my loft slides away as smooth white walls build up around me. The ceiling lowers, and I find myself in a small minimalist meeting room with a tall circular table in the middle. There are no chairs. It resembles the kind of stand-up pod you might find in a trendy Soho office.

Iris stands in front of me, exactly where she was before. The familiar red outlines of my furniture remind me not to move around, that I am not truly in the future. It's tough to remember, though; the illusion envelops me completely.

Felix stands next to a large rectangular window, a silhouette fringed in cool blue light. He wears a loose-fitted flannel shirt, long shorts, and sandals, and today his hair is tied back in a ponytail. "Hello again, Joseph," he grins. Through the window I can see the inside of a huge dome-like structure, made up of massive hexagonal panels the size of cars. People are working on sections of it; sparks of neon explode from handheld tools.

"Where are you, I mean . . . we?" I ask.

"We're in a meeting room adjacent to the Observatorium," Felix says, clearly proud of his creation. "I hope to give you a proper tour soon, once this is all over."

"That would be good," I say, possibly the understatement of my life.

Another figure appears, sparkling like a golden glass of champagne. The fascinating spectacle resolves into the rather disappointing shape of Gabrielle. I was already feeling queasy; her arrival does not help. She's standing in the corner of the room, legs slightly apart, arms crossed. She looks shabby in her usual black rock-chick gear and shiny yellow patent leather boots. She's wearing sunglasses, and her face is impassive.

"Yo," she says, chewing gum, her lackluster delivery conveying an obvious hangover.

Iris says, "Hello, Gabrielle. Apologies for the short notice."

Gabrielle clears her throat, which rattles like a tired old engine. "Sorry, took me a while, been letting off some steam."

Felix grins. "Attagirl!"

"Any data on the insertion point for the next jump?" Gabrielle asks.

"Downstream is showing that it might be a little earlier," Felix says, "maybe as much as a week before the fire."

"Bingo." Gabrielle tips her head forward and peers over her glasses, her bloodshot eyes on me. "Now then, Bridgeman," she says, with a hammy attempt at a British accent, "what's so urgent that it simply couldn't wait?"

"I've seen Scarlett again," I tell her, not hiding my annoyance. "She did something to Nils's watch. I saw the whole thing."

Gabrielle does her best impression of a statue. Felix studies me as though I am the most fascinating new toy in his box. "Well this is incredible!" he says. "Tell us exactly what you saw, from the very beginning. Take your time. Tell us everything."

I recap the recurring portion of my viewing. Gabrielle tuts, as though she's already seen this movie. Then, I focus on the latest chapter, how Scarlett used tools to tamper with the watch, and the readout I saw just before Nils traveled.

When I'm done, the room falls silent. Felix and Iris exchange a glance, then Felix looks at me. "Bill was right, your gift is astounding. This level of detail, this isn't psychometry, this is something else. This is unique." His eyes sparkle. "You saw this from Scarlett's point of view?"

"Yes. As if I was her."

"The whole thing's freakin' creepy," Gabrielle shivers.

"And you're certain of the numbers you saw?" Felix asks, ignoring Gabrielle.

"Yes, I wrote it down as soon as my viewing ended. Scarlett dialed it in very precisely."

"Right." Felix paces the room.

Gabrielle pushes her shades up onto her head. She looks tired; her eyes are puffy. "What Scarlett did requires a deep understanding of our systems, intricate tools, and not to mention knowledge about the whereabouts of our travelers." She turns to Iris. "I told you, she isn't working alone. She can't be; she's not smart enough. You believe me now, right?"

Iris sighs deeply. "I didn't want you to be right, Gabrielle, but it appears to be the case. We need to increase our security."

"What did she do to Nils's watch?" I ask Felix. "The silver liquid in the syringe—that's triterbium?" A connection sparks in my mind: Amy's abstract painting, the watch and the silver sea. She had already connected these dots, albeit in a cryptic way.

"Based on what you saw," Felix replies, "it appears Scarlett may have deliberately destabilized Nils's return trip, forced him into a quantum super-position of states."

"Keep things in English, Felix," Iris says gently.

"Sorry." He winces and clears his throat. "Triterbium is a rare element, which we refine and convert into a radioactive isotope." He pauses with a grimace.

Iris takes over. "There is a small amount of triterbium in all of our watches. It powers them, helps with stability. We don't need it to travel, but when used in combination with the time crystals, it guides us to change events and helps us to remain in the past for longer. It's a grounding force."

Felix paces the room. "It seems that Scarlett altered the settings on Nils's watch and reduced the triterbium. It's destabilized him. That could—in theory—disrupt his ability to ground himself on the return trip. He didn't go back home to Oslo after his mission in Macau. It's like he was climbing a mountain, slipped, fell through time, and then grabbed hold of the only thing he could, the change event in Paris. Perhaps it had a kind of gravitational pull, enough to attract him out of the void."

Gabrielle cracks her knuckles. "Two travelers bonded to the same change event? Is that even possible?"

"We didn't think any of this was possible," Felix says abruptly, "and yet it seems to be happening. That could be why his signal is weak and sporadic."

Gabrielle walks to the window, stares out, and in an uncharacteristically quiet voice says, "She deliberately sent him into the void."

"The void?" I ask.

Iris looks uncomfortable but composes herself quickly. "Before we had triterbium, before we balanced our trips using our watches, the return could be a little . . . treacherous. You will have seen the carousel of reentry points when you saved your sister."

"Zoetropes," I murmur.

Gabrielle turns, her irritation obvious. "Quantum corridors, windows, doorways, zoetropes. Call them what you like, they're just different names for the same experience. It's what's beyond them we need to worry about." She pauses. "If you miss those doorways, if you run out of options or slip outside of them, there's nothing. Just the void—space without time."

I shudder, remembering my journey to save Amy, the spinning windows, a seemingly endless dark sea.

"Is there anything else you can tell us, Joseph?" Iris asks. "Anything else you saw?"

"Nothing I saw, but when I have a viewing, it's like walking in someone else's shoes. I see what they see and occasionally, some of their thoughts bleed through as well. I get a sense of their emotions, their motivations."

Felix studies me. "And what did you feel this time?"

Carefully, with Gabrielle's eyes burrowing into me, I say, "That Scarlett didn't mean to harm Nils, and she certainly doesn't want to kill him."

Gabrielle snorts. "Oh, so now you read minds too?"

I glare at her. "No, I'm saying I picked up some of her deeper emotions. I'm sorry if it's not what you want to hear."

"So, based on what Joseph has told us, what are you thinking?" Iris asks Felix.

"I think we need to ground him."

"Touch?" Gabrielle suggests. "You mean I can locate him and drag him back with me?"

"I'm not sure that will work," Felix replies. "I don't think Nils has fully landed in 1873. He's like a ghost, half-there, half-not. Before we can think about dragging him anywhere, we're going to need to ground him." Felix's mind seems to drift, and then his attention snaps back to Iris. "I need to talk this through with Kyoko."

"That sounds like a good idea," Iris agrees.

Felix turns to me. "Thank you for this information, Joe. Without you, we would still have been completely in the dark."

I shrug. "I just hope it helps."

Gabrielle exhales loudly. "I still don't understand why she would do that to him."

Iris considers this. "If we lose a traveler, it weakens us. And while she has us all busily running around, we risk failing another mission."

"That's not going to happen," Gabrielle growls. "I'm going to complete the Philippe mission and save Nils."

"About that," Felix says. "That conversation Joe had with the seamstress who saw Nils? We were able to use the sighting data to create a tracker. If Nils appears, Gabrielle, you will be alerted. I've updated your watch. You can switch between Philippe and Nils by rotating the dial."

"Sound good, thanks."

"What about my watch?" I ask him.

"What about it?" Gabrielle snaps.

She's angry and I can understand that. I'm angry too, and the more this conversation goes on, the more that fire builds. It would be easy to think of the Paris mission, and the missing time traveler, as none of my business. I've told The Continuum all I know. I could easily walk away, but then what? What's to stop Scarlett from coming after me again?

In a clear voice, I say, "I want to go on the next jump."

"Absolutely not," Gabrielle shoots back.

Felix holds up a hand. "Let's hear him out, Gabi."

She folds her arms. "You won't persuade me this is a good idea."

I say, "Scarlett came after me first. She started this. She was determined

I would fail the Romano mission, put me in serious danger. I've been trying to ignore the facts, but you told me what happened. I died. Bill had to save me. He's dead because of Scarlett. What do you expect me to do now? Sit back and hope for the best?"

"Let me handle it," Gabrielle says, but the venom has gone out of her voice. I think that deep down, she understands my reasoning. And Gabrielle is tough, but Iris is the boss, and she's going to say yes.

Iris bows her head for a moment. "It's dangerous, Joseph, more so than usual. You're right, Scarlett could attack again. She may turn up on the mission, try and stop us, finish the job with Nils. Who knows, maybe even scupper our chances with Philippe too. We can't ask you to do this."

"You aren't," I say. "I'm offering."

Gabrielle laughs. "Listen, I know your gift is *amazing* and everything, but you aren't much of a traveler. You slow me down."

I glare at her, my blood simmering. "I'm involved now. I saw what Scarlett did to Nils. Firsthand. I've seen what happens to Philippe too. I accept that I'm not very experienced, but surely two is better than one. We can track Nils now. I might see him. And if I do, then that could trigger another viewing, give us more clues."

Gabrielle draws her sunglasses back down over her tired eyes. "Your call, boss."

Iris says, "If you are willing to join Gabrielle on the second jump, Joseph, we would be fools to say no."

"Excellent," Felix says. "It's decided then. I will update your watch remotely."

"Thank you," I say. "It feels better to be doing something, rather than just waiting." I can feel Gabrielle's eyes burrowing into me through her shades. Oh yes. It's going to be fun.

Felix says, "I'm going to find Kyoko. If we're going to figure out how to ground Nils, we have a lot of work to do. Good luck, both of you. See you when you get back." His expression shifts, a determined plan forming as he vanishes from the room.

"Right then, if you'll excuse me," Gabrielle says a little too politely, "I have an appointment with another bottle of wine."

"Of course," Iris says, her tone professional. "Goodbye, Gabrielle."

Gabrielle performs a sardonic bow and pops out of existence.

Iris and I enjoy the silence for a moment.

Eventually, I say, "I have more questions. Can we talk?"

"I'm happy to. Why don't we get you home first?"

The illusion of the cold, empty pod collapses, as though made of white sand, and we are back in my loft, the familiar warmth of what feels like the past easing me back into my present. Home. It's a relief, but I'm more determined than ever to help Nils.

Iris walks around the room, taking in some of the details. She seems more relaxed now.

"How are you moving around so easily?" I ask. "The meeting room we were in was small."

"I wasn't in the meeting room," she explains. "I'm in my office. I have plenty of room here."

"That makes sense." I'm constantly reassessing my definition of time and space, here and there. "It feels strange not offering you a drink, though."

She laughs, maybe the first time I've heard her do this. "I know what you mean. Sometimes we plan ahead and share a drink. Some things don't change with time."

I decide to go straight in with a question that's been gnawing at me since first meeting her. "I need to know—how does The Continuum decide what to change? How do you know what you're doing is right?"

"That is indeed the question you should be asking," she says. "Thankfully, we don't decide what needs to be changed. The immune system analogy is helpful here. We work without agenda. We simply do time's bidding. Repairing, healing, reconnecting. The fact we don't choose the missions makes things much easier."

"In what way?"

"So many terrible things have happened over the course of history. How would you even begin to choose who to help first?"

I think about Amy, Lucy, and now Philippe. "Do you ever get involved in big events, like major disasters or terrorist attacks?"

Iris shakes her head. "The majority of the past cannot be changed. It's protected by the sheer number of witnesses, of lives affected. The fact that millions of people see and hear of those events means they're off-limits. The observer effect creates an impenetrable barrier, complete resistance to change. But in the shadows, there are small human stories, wrongs that can be put right. Rare opportunities to do good, unburdened by the pressure of observation. This is where we work, and these seemingly small interactions, when corrected, can lead to amazing, positive outcomes that grow over time to have massive impact."

My mind races to absorb this, but with each flicker of understanding, new questions jostle to the surface. "How did you discover all of this?"

"That's where Felix comes in. He discovered a way to study time, unearthed its secrets. He will want to show you Downstream himself. When you see it, it's actually quite simple, elegant even. It identifies focus objects, which charge up with the emotional energy of a moment in history that can be changed."

This conjures images of the Roberts radio that threw me back to London and the metronome we used to reach Philippe. "I know it's Gabrielle's mission, but can you tell me about Philippe, what he's going to do with his life if he isn't injured?"

"In terms of specific details, no. Initially, all we see is the opportunity. The change event is like a beacon, it signals the potential. With each successive jump back in time, we gain more insight. It's another reason why the traveler is so essential."

"How do you mean?"

"The human element. Choosing the right interactions with the past gives us valuable data. After each jump, we can analyze and fill in the details, connecting the dots back to the change event, the inception. Each mission is a story, one we don't fully understand until we are near the end. At this stage we can see that Philippe's story is about human potential, self-expression, and inspiring others. We will know more after your next jump."

"Thank you for telling me," I say, assimilating this new information.

"You will have many questions, and I hope that when this mission is over, you might consider learning more about The Continuum by accepting a proper induction into what we do."

"When we're done, I'll think about it," I say, honestly. "But right now, we need to talk about Amy."

"Of course. How is she?"

"She's struggling. My traveling is affecting her. She's painting Paris, the opera fire. I need you to reassure me that it's going to be OK, that she gets through this."

"She will be fine. This is how it happens."

I frown. "So you know all this? My life is just a script to you?"

"Not at all. We only analyze time that is connected to a mission or directly threatens The Continuum. It's one of our rules. Your life, your choices, they happen day to day, and I know nothing of these. However, I do know and want to assure you that Amy is going to be OK. What's happening to her in your time is part of her story, a natural process that, in the end, will be good for her."

"I don't know how long I can carry on like this without seeing her," I say. "The version you're referring to, I mean."

Iris nods, silently. She doesn't speak for a while, but when she does, her tone is reluctant. "I am wary because I don't want to influence the natural flow, but I am going to tell you something that I hope will ease your mind." She holds my gaze. "Amy begins her journey to us soon."

"She's going to travel?"

"Yes, and all you have to do is be there for her. All will be well."

I sigh, my heart heavy and relieved at the same time. The idea of Amy traveling scares me, but I decide my brain may have taken in enough new information for one day. I need to park this train of thought and focus on my immediate concern: traveling to 1873 with a woman who hates my guts.

"There's something else. I want to help find Nils. I want to be useful, but . . ." How do I say this? "Gabrielle isn't the easiest person to get along with."

"I understand," Iris says. "I know that Gabrielle can be difficult to work with, but she is an exceptional time traveler."

"Why does she hate me so much?"

"She doesn't hate you. She just cares, perhaps too much sometimes, but it comes from a good place." Iris purses her lip. When she speaks, her voice is soft and reflective. "You need to talk to her about the Romano mission."

"The Romano mission? Why?"

"It's not for me to say," she says. "Just talk to her. Trust me. Clear the air if you can."

18

"Repeat after me: Vinny is awesome. He knows everything. I should always trust him." I laugh into my phone and do as I'm told.

"Good," he says. "Now that's out of the way, I don't get it. Why is Gabrielle being so annoying? Aren't you trying to help?"

"I am, but you wouldn't think so. From the minute I met her, she's been nothing but rude and obstructive. I wish you and I were going to Paris together instead."

"Me too, Cash. I'm starving. I keep thinking of all that antique food we could be eating."

"Seriously, it's no fun getting hauled around by a surly old trout."

"She's probably testing you, you know, with the old good cop, bad cop routine. I'm sure it's all part of her character arc."

"Her what?"

"You've seen *Lethal Weapon*, right?"

"I have, but it's been a while. Why?"

Vinny's tone becomes serious. "It's your classic buddy movie. Initially, you don't get along, but then you end up being forced to work together, and you earn each other's respect."

I curl my lip. "I don't care enough about her to want her respect. She's not much of a team player."

"Neither were you." His tone is thoughtful and considerate. "You told me you were practically a hermit in your old life."

"I was. But that's different. I had my reasons."

"How do you know she doesn't have reasons too? Give the woman a chance. Sometimes people surprise you if you let them."

"I don't know," I say dubiously. "The thing is, there's so much to learn. I feel like I'm missing a teacher in all this. I need training. I know I've changed my tune, but I keep wishing Bill was still here."

"I can imagine, mate. But we don't always need new lessons."

"How do you mean?"

"You know, like with music. I was listening to a Carole King track the other day, the lyrics, the composition . . . I swear, I experienced a completely new song, even though I must've heard it a thousand times. Sometimes, *we* change, and then the lessons we've already been given suddenly make sense."

I ponder this. "I see what you mean. Thanks, mate."

"No problem. I'm probably talking rubbish, but that's my job. Call me when you get back, yeah? I want a full update."

"Of course. Cheers, Vin."

"*Adiós, monsieur.*"

I turn my phone over and over in my hand, thinking about what Vinny said about Gabrielle. Iris had already sowed the seed, but he's made my mind up—next time I see her, I'm going to have it out with her. We don't need to be best friends to work together, but her behavior has been shockingly bad. She might have her reasons, but I don't care. Most people would have told her to take a long walk off a short plank by now.

Monday and Tuesday are quiet in the shop, as they often are. Molly and I reorganize the stock, and by the time Wednesday rolls around, I'm beginning to relax a bit.

"Tea, Molly?" I ask, just after 3 p.m.

"Yes, please. I'll have a lapsang souchong."

In the kitchenette, I hear the shop bell ring, and a woman comes in. She and Molly have a conversation about the window display, then it's quiet for a bit. There's a bit more conversation, this time in lowered voices, so I can't hear what's being said.

I'm just squeezing Molly's tea bag against the side of her mug when she pops her head around the door. "There's a customer wondering if you'd have a look at something for her," Molly says. "An item she's brought in."

"Does she want a valuation?" I ask hopefully.

"No, she'd like you to . . . see what you can tell her about it," Molly says. She lowers her voice. "She's heard through the grapevine about your gift for tuning into the history of certain items . . ." She tails off a little awkwardly. She knows I feel ambivalent about sharing what I see when objects trigger a viewing. I've done it two or three times over the last few weeks, and the first time it seemed to give the person some real peace of mind, but it doesn't always work that way. Sometimes it freaks people out. I need to be careful. I don't want to turn my gift into some kind of circus act, with me as some kind of sideshow freak.

I follow Molly out into the shop. The woman, who's holding a pink glass soap dish in her hand, looks up. She's stylishly dressed in a short camel trench coat and slim black trousers, a dark gray scarf knotted at her throat. She wouldn't look out of place in *Vogue* magazine, apart from the outsized handbag. It's enormous. I imagine she could pull anything you need right out of it—sticking plasters, antacid tablets, a map of Edinburgh.

"This is Mr. Bridgeman," Molly tells the woman.

"Hello," I say. She looks vaguely familiar, but I don't think we've met. "How can I help you?"

"It's a pleasure to meet you, Mr. Bridgeman," the woman says. "You have a wonderful shop. Such a range of items. I'm visiting my daughter here in Cheltenham, and I'm looking for a gift for her."

"I hope you find something you like," I say. "We try to have a range of goods in-store that will appeal to all tastes."

"Where do you get your stock?"

"We go to auctions and house clearances, and sometimes people bring things in. Some items are always popular, like jewelry and collectible porcelain, but others are less obvious, and you have to go with your gut. I tend to pick something out if it speaks to me."

The woman places the soap dish she's been holding on a shelf just beside her, then rummages in her handbag. "Actually, Mr. Bridgeman, would you have time to look at something for me? A friend of mine told me . . . I thought you might get one of your feelings? I hope you don't mind my asking."

"I don't mind, but I'm not sure I can," I say, hoping to put her off. "Most of the time, an object doesn't have anything to say to me. It only happens very occasionally."

The woman pulls out a colorful Hermès scarf and unwraps it to reveal a small silver fountain pen, engraved with the letters *SJF*. "Would you see if this tells you anything?" She hands the pen to me. "It's been in the family a long time. It would mean a lot to me."

Reluctantly, I take it from her. "There are no guarantees," I say. "It's a one in ten chance at best."

"I understand. Thank you for trying." She clasps the scarf to her chest, waiting expectantly.

I play my part, holding the pen in my right hand and closing my eyes. There's nothing. I'm sort of relieved, and I'm about to open my eyes and return the pen when I'm suddenly transported to a freezing, muddy field scattered with tarpaulin tents. I am pulled with a powerful downdraft toward one of the tents and pass through to the interior, where a young soldier is writing a letter. Love and fear are fighting for control of his heart, and his face is wet with tears. The anguish is so strong that I nearly drop the pen. The shock breaks the connection and catapults me back to the present.

The woman looks at me, concerned. "What did you see?"

I take a deep breath, knowing that I can't tell her what I saw. The emotions at play are powerful, and I have a responsibility to be prudent with the knowledge I glean. What if I tell this woman something that ruins the memory of someone dear? I can't take that risk. "Nothing. I'm sorry."

"You must have seen something!" she presses me. "You're white as a sheet!"

The shop bell rings, and a couple enters. They eye us uncertainly, and Molly goes to welcome them. The moment has passed. I hand the woman her pen, excuse myself, and slip away upstairs.

Twenty minutes later, after a restorative latte and a bit of reflection out on the balcony, I go back downstairs. The shop's empty. Molly turns to me as I enter. "Is everything all right? I've been worried."

"Yes," I say. "I just don't want people getting the wrong idea about my ability. It's not something I want to publicize too much."

"Quite," Molly says. "Shall we have that cup of tea now?"

She's still in the kitchenette when my mobile phone rings.

"We're on," Gabrielle rasps down the line. "We leave in thirty minutes."

"Thirty minutes?" I splutter.

Molly sticks her head out of the kitchenette. "I beg your pardon?" she says.

I shake my head, point to my phone, then lower my voice. Molly disappears again. "Could you not have given me a bit more notice?" I tell Gabrielle. "I do have a life, you know."

"I'll be there in twenty."

"You're coming here?"

"I'm on my way to your little store now."

"Don't come through the shop!" I say. "Come around the side, to the fire escape. I'll let you into the flat."

"Be ready, Bridgeman." The line goes dead.

"No need to be so bloody rude," I mutter.

"Is everything all right?" Molly asks me calmly. She's the most unflappable person I know. If a comet were due to hit the earth and cause an extinction-level event, she'd probably just mention it in passing while the tea brewed.

"I have an unexpected appointment. Molly, would you be able to watch the shop for the rest of the day?"

"Of course," she says. "Shall I come in tomorrow as normal? Eight thirty?"

"Yes, please," I say, crossing my fingers behind my back and hoping I'll live to see another dawn. "See you tomorrow."

I rush upstairs to grab my silver hunter and do a quick scan of the flat to check that I haven't left anything electrical turned on. I've just got back down from the loft when Gabrielle arrives. Despite the chill outside, she's just wearing a leopard print blouse hanging loosely over black jeans, and big sunglasses.

She hauls a big solid-looking suitcase up the last couple of steps into my flat, rejecting my offer of help. "Jeez, it's hot as an old people's home in here," she grumbles, fanning her face and lifting her sunglasses onto her head. She looks dreadful, like she only got a few hours' sleep, and she smells of old beer. "Can't you turn the heat down?"

"How long till we go?" I ask.

She checks her wristwatch. "Ten minutes. We need to get changed. Where can we go?"

"Up here," I say, leading her back up the wide underlit staircase to the loft. "Let me take that." I try to take the suitcase from her, but she yanks it back out of my hand.

At the top of the stairs, she eyes the loft appreciatively and whistles. "You sure landed on your feet here, dintcha?" She pushes the suitcase onto its side, unzips it, and pulls out a black frock coat, white shirt, cream silk cravat, and a pair of square-toed shoes. "Here's your kit," she says, carelessly tossing the clothing at me. I'm already halfway down the stairs to my bedroom when she calls me back. "Hey! Don't forget your lid." Impatiently, she hands me a gleaming black top hat.

I get changed and clatter back up the stairs to the loft. Gabrielle has metamorphosed into an elegant and refined Parisian socialite, her dark-blue dress clinging to her torso then spilling into full skirts gathered into a bustle at the back. She's piled her hair into a tower of curls—or she's wearing a very convincing wig—and she's adorned it with a small blue bonnet at an impossibly steep angle, which she's tied around her chin. To complete the outfit she's wearing white gloves, and a fringed parasol hangs over her arm.

She regards me with a critical eye as I arrive at the top of the stairs, and hands me my self-attaching sideburns. I place them below my ears. They grip, and then burst into life like time-lapsed spring flowers.

"Thirty seconds," she says, checking her watch.

The room shifts beneath my feet, time tugging at us like the tide. Gabrielle takes my arm. She might look the part, but she still smells musty.

"When are we going to land?" I ask, not expecting an answer.

"A week before the fire," she says, smiling sweetly.

I have no idea if she's telling me the truth. Suddenly, all the fight leaves me, and I surrender to the situation. I'm heading back to 1873 Paris with a traveler who hates my guts, trusting an organization that—let's be honest here—I know very little about, not to mention the ongoing threat of a manipulative parasite called Scarlett, who's probably going to coast in on our coattails and send us spinning into infinity, given half a chance. I'll just have to deal with what happens as it happens.

The moment arrives. I close my eyes. For a split second, I feel the warmth of the sun streaming in through the loft windows, the reassuring solidity of the floorboards beneath my feet. Then, the fresh, tangy odor of ozone fills my nostrils, and Gabrielle and I leave Cheltenham behind.

19

Bright, dappled light dances over my eyelids. The air is cool and fresh with the scent of wet grass. In the distance I hear birdsong.

"Bridgeman!" Gabrielle barks.

I cautiously open my eyes. We're standing beneath a weeping willow in a large park, near the edge of a deep blue pond. Paris is bathed in sunshine, the sky a crisp, pure cyan blue. Nearby, a group of little boys in sailor suits jostle and argue, playing with model boats. Their mothers, dressed like birds of paradise, watch them, chatting and admiring one another's outfits.

My watch buzzes soundlessly against my chest. I pull it out of my jacket pocket, remembering the terror of surrendering it to Frankie Shaw when he heard it buzzing, and sending silent thanks to The Continuum for what I assume must be an upgrade. The fascia reflects the sky, and I notice a faint honeycomb texture, a hint of the magnificently detailed display. The word *Calibrating* appears, along with local time and date.

12:31 p.m. 22 October, 1873.

"You were right, an entire week until the fire," I say.

"Wow. He can count too," Gabrielle says, walking ahead.

A sudden splash and alarmed quacking draw our attention. One of the little boys throws a stone into the lake. The ripples spread, rocking the ducks up and down. One of the mothers calls over. "Jules, stop tormenting those poor creatures! Play nicely. Look at Michel, see how good he is." Michel beams like a cherub at the lady, but from where I'm standing, I can see he's holding a pebble the size of a peach behind his back. Boys. I suspect they would be the same no matter what year we ended up in. The mother spoke in French, yet I understood every word, and I realize now why people say you can feel at home anywhere if you learn the lingo.

I catch up to Gabrielle. "So what do we do?"

"Until we get a waypoint, we may as well head toward the opera house."

I follow Gabrielle through ornate wrought iron gates, out of the park, and onto the street. Horse-drawn carriages fill the boulevards, which are lined with people, all dressed beautifully, politely acknowledging each other as they stroll. Some shade their eyes with parasols. Thanks to Gabrielle's magic wardrobe, we fit right in.

A nearby wall is covered with posters, their typefaces and illustrations wonderfully sharp and new. I'm so used to seeing these in arty frames, old and torn. I'm drawn to one poster in particular, which reads:

Le Prophète at La Salle Peletier
OPENING NIGHT!
29 October

Again, I'm struck by the fact I am not only able to understand the language but read it too. At school, French was always a total mystery to me. I could never rationalize why phallic carrots are feminine and girly curtains and cushions are masculine, let alone why inanimate objects need a gender at all. "If my French teacher could see me now," I say, "she'd eat her hat."

Gabrielle ignores me and peels back the decorative lace covering her wrist-mounted watch. I see it update. The top half forms a compass heading. The waypoint alert appears, along with the distance and time left to reach it: 450 meters, 9 minutes.

"Interesting," she says. "It's the opposite direction of the opera house."

She heads off, and I run behind her. In the distance I hear what I think is the rumble of thunder. We jog past family groups, past a pair of gentlemen deep in conversation, around women carrying little dogs in their arms and hurrying their children along. We make our way between wooden buildings and emerge onto a wide boulevard, which is one of the busiest roads I've ever seen. The sound wasn't thunder, it was the drumming of hundreds of trotting hooves against the earth. The carriages pass scarily close to each other, drivers cracking whips, horses whinnying.

I thought the roads in the present were dangerous. There are no clearly marked lanes, but there must be six or seven streams of carriages speeding past us.

"We need to get across," Gabrielle shouts above the din. "See you on the other side."

"Wait, what?"

She looks both ways, dives between two black carriages, and disappears into the chaos. Gabrielle is not only extremely annoying, she's also a lunatic.

I scan the street, trying to pick the best time to cross. Plenty of people are doing it, waiting and then whipping through the mayhem. It's like the world's biggest game of chicken. I take a moment to steady myself and tune in to the rhythm and speed of the passing traffic. Attempting to channel the timing I honed while jumping through zoetropes, I look to the right and spot a gap just after a cart loaded with sacks. I lean slightly forward, rocking back and forth on the balls of my feet. "Three, two, one, go!"

I launch myself into the fray, senses on high alert as I run. A man on what I seem to remember from school is called a velocipede hurtles toward me. Wheels screech, people shout, horses buck and kick. The air is filled with dust and heat and sweat. It's madness.

I narrowly avoid getting steamrollered. The driver of a smart little polished wooden carriage yells, "Watch where you're going, you imbecile!" I wave apologetically and knock my hat off in the process. I grab it off the ground and hold it tight to my chest as I weave my way through the last few streams of traffic.

When I finally reach the other side of the street, I lean over to catch my breath and my composure. I will never take road crossings for granted again. I search for Gabrielle and spot her walking ahead. She hasn't even turned around to see if I'm following her. I nearly died, and she doesn't seem bothered at all. My fear flips to anger and I jog to catch up with her. "Gabrielle, what the hell is your problem?"

She stops and turns on me, her dark uncaring eyes simmering. "You. You are my problem, and as expected you're slowing me down."

People glance furtively at us as they walk by, shocked by this public outburst. I draw in a breath and face Gabrielle. "You want to help Philippe, you want to succeed on this mission, and you said you want to find Nils too. So why won't you work with me? We're on the same team, dammit!"

"Oh yeah!" Gabrielle says, shaking her head in disbelief. "You're a real team player."

"Hey! What does that mean? What the hell is wrong with you?"

"I work alone. How many times do I have to say it? I don't need you."

"I get it, but isn't this all a bit cliché? I'm a rookie, and you're a professional time traveler, therefore you hate me. You were a rookie too once, remember?"

"You don't know anything."

It's not just anger in her words. I try to second guess what's eating her.

"I know you probably blame me for what happened to Bill."

"Don't you *dare* talk about Bill," she glowers.

"I knew it. That's why you're pissed off with me. Why don't you get it out? Scream and shout if you need to, but it wasn't my fault he died. If someone had told me what was going on, maybe trusted me, then it might have been different."

"Jesus, Bridgeman," she says. "You're even more stupid than I thought. I'm upset about Bill, yeah, but this isn't just about him. This is about what you did to me."

"What on earth are you talking about?"

Her jaw flexes, she pierces me with her gaze. "You stole my mission."

"I haven't stolen it, I'm here to help find Nils. This wasn't even my idea!"

"No, genius," she snaps. "The Romano mission . . . It was mine."

I stare at her, my mind connecting multiple dots into a clear and now obvious picture. I recall Iris and Bill both telling me that a more experienced traveler had been allocated to the mission before the radio was planted in my shop and I was bonded instead. Turns out that traveler was Gabrielle.

"I didn't know that," I tell her.

"Well, you do now." Her expression is flat. "I spent months researching that mission. I was all set. There wasn't a single fact that I didn't know about Frankie Shaw, London, the 1960s. And then, with just hours to go, it was taken from me. Just like that."

"Gabrielle, I—"

"Shut up a minute, will you?" she snaps. "I know it wasn't your fault. I know that bitch stole the focus object and planted it in your shop. But it doesn't change the fact it was *my* mission. Romano was important. I'm glad it got done . . . but Bill shouldn't have died." Her voice catches a little. "It didn't need to happen."

No wonder Gabrielle's been so sharp with me. She knows I didn't take the Romano mission from her, but she's still angry about missing out. And on top of that, it's clear that Bill was more than just a teacher to her. He was a mentor, perhaps even a friend. I consider my next move. The fact she's told me is cathartic for her—it might even clear the air—but what I really need is to get her working with me, showing me the ropes, explaining how this whole pro-time-traveler gig works. I need to build a bridge.

Carefully, I say, "I'm sorry you didn't get the chance to finish the job, after all that preparation. I really am. But don't you see? There's a common enemy here. All of this is happening because of Scarlett. If you and I fight like this, we're just playing into her hands. She's the one we need to focus on."

"She's a ghost. We'll never find her."

"We might," I assure her, "because we have one advantage."

"Oh yeah, what's that?"

"Scarlett doesn't know that I can see her, that I've been viewing her. She'll slip up and give herself away sooner or later."

Gabrielle pulls a wry face. "I hope you're right. I hate being on the back foot like this."

It's a rare and refreshing display of vulnerability. An honest reaction. I decide to offer one of my own. "You know, I really am sorry about what happened to Bill. I didn't get to know him as much as I would have liked."

"We all miss him, but if I have to go, I wanna go out like he did," says Gabrielle, her eyes misting over, the lines around them softening. "He was the best. He guided us all, always seemed to know what to do. He'd have laughed us out of town if we'd tried to tell him he was a hero, but he was, every day."

"I wish I had known him better."

"He was one hell of a teacher," she says, sighing heavily. "He's the one who should be teaching you, not me . . . I can't do it."

"I don't expect you to, but if you can just include me a bit more, give me a few tips, show me the ropes, then I think we might have a chance to find Nils and complete your mission."

She studies me, and I can't tell if she's going to punch me or hug me. "Right, well that's enough of all this touchy-feely crap. We have work to do." She checks her watch and heads off. The sky has clouded over, but the air between Gabrielle and me feels a little clearer.

We follow our waypoint, walking along immaculate boulevards with the ladies and gentlemen of Paris. At every street corner stands a policeman, replete with sword and watchful eye. The atmosphere is bustling but orderly.

At the end of the street, we arrive at a wide bridge. It's built from pale stone and dotted with streetlamps. Curved stone balconies line both sides of the carriageway. Ladies with parasols admire the view, and ubiquitous carts rumble over the cobbled surface.

Gabrielle stops. "Behold the New Bridge," she says loftily.

"What happened to the old one?"

She rolls her eyes. "It's actually the oldest bridge over the Seine. It used to be covered in stalls, but the last emperor took 'em all off, wanted to smarten it up."

A spark of familiarity flickers into my consciousness. "Wait a minute. I've seen this in a painting, I think. Renoir."

"Yep. He painted it in the summer of 1872, about nine months ago."

My brain judders as I struggle to adjust my frame of reference. Pierre-Auguste Renoir is alive. I imagine him sitting at this very spot, painting the view I'm seeing right now.

Gabrielle checks her watch. "Well, we're in the right place."

"This is the waypoint?"

"Yeah. They can update sometimes, but right now this is where we need to be. There's a kind of attraction. Can you feel it?"

I try, but I don't sense much. I nod enthusiastically, though, because as far as I remember, it's the first piece of time-travel advice Gabrielle has ever offered me.

Sunlight cuts through clouds, highlighting a section of the bridge with vibrant color. One man stands out. I recognize him immediately: it's Philippe Chevalier, conductor of the opera house, a man who in one week's time will be horribly burned, unless we figure out a way to stop that happening. He's dressed in a smart black coat and walking with purpose. Women eye him approvingly as he passes. He smiles, touching his hat in greeting.

He passes us, and we follow him. After a few minutes, he quickly checks the street and then ducks into an alleyway. Keeping our distance, we walk narrow lanes, winding our way through cloistered side streets and dark alleyways that smell of damp stone, rotting vegetables, and urine. It's a relief when we emerge into a small square.

Philippe has stopped outside a magnificent three-story mansion. It's predominantly redbrick, with a dark slate roof that stretches halfway down its facade, framing the top-floor dormer windows. There's a small yard in front, enclosed by iron railings painted gloss black. A gate leads to a huge front door, adorned with frosted glass and a shiny brass knocker. He scans the street, as though checking if he's being followed. We turn our backs.

"What's he doing here?" I murmur.

"I'm not sure," admits Gabrielle. "This property didn't feature in my research."

Satisfied he hasn't been seen, Philippe quickly climbs the wide steps to the front door of the mansion. He doesn't knock, just pushes the door and disappears inside.

"Does he live here?" I ask.

Gabrielle surveys the house. "All the information we have on him shows that, at this stage in his life, he is given lodgings by the opera house manager. There is no way he could afford anything this grand on his own."

"Do we follow him?"

"Maybe," Gabrielle says. "Let's take a closer look."

She casually crosses the street, and I follow. When she reaches the gate in front of the mansion, she stops abruptly, and I narrowly avoid a mouthful of bustle.

"What's up?" I ask.

Gabrielle tilts her head, as though listening. "Can't you feel that?"

Again, I send my senses out into the world, but I don't feel anything but the cool air. Indicating the door, I ask, "Should we go inside?"

Gabrielle steps back and gestures toward the iron gate. "Knock yourself out. Give it a shot."

I reach out to unlock the gate, but my legs don't want to go any farther. I lift my left foot to take a step but feel a push back, like when two magnets repel each other.

"That's weird," I say. The sensation is unusual. I *could* walk forward, and I'm in no doubt that I could open the gate and climb the steps, but it would be much harder than normal. I would go so far as to say it feels wrong, like stepping out into traffic or leaning out of an upstairs window. My intuition is telling me all of this without words.

"It's resistance," Gabrielle says. "You might get the odd subtle clue in the present, but these feelings are extremely heightened when you travel."

"So this is a warning?"

"I think of it more as guidance."

"But I thought we were supposed to be here?"

She pauses, again as though listening. "Oh, we're supposed to be *here*." She studies her watch, then surveys our immediate surroundings. "But we aren't supposed to go in . . . we might need to wait for Philippe to come back out. Let's see if we can find our way to the rear of the house, get a good look at the place." To the left, the mansion butts right up against the house next door, but to the right, there's a narrow lane, which follows a high garden wall. "This way, Bridgeman," says Gabrielle, setting off down the lane. "I've got a feeling about this."

We make our way down the track, following the wall until we come out at the other end. We carry on following the wall around the corner to a huge wrought iron gate with a picturesque walled garden beyond it. There's a small round lawn in the middle, surrounded by low hedges and fruit trees heavy with ripe apples and plums. The tended beds beneath the walls are packed with plants and flowers, none of which I can name. The garden is manicured and orderly, not a leaf out of place, like something you'd see in a posh lifestyle magazine. I try the latch on the gate, but it's locked.

"Do we need to get closer?" I ask.

"When's the last time you climbed a tree?" Gabrielle asks, glancing up at a nearby chestnut tree.

"That is not going to happen."

She seems to genuinely consider it, but then capitulates. "To be honest, in this cream puff of a dress, you're probably right." She lays one hand flat on the wall and closes her eyes, concentrating.

"What are you doing?" I ask.

"Tuning into my surroundings."

"The wall?"

Her eyes remain closed. "Psychometry doesn't just work with objects. It works with buildings too."

"Can I do that?"

"Doubtful."

"I mean in theory?"

"All time travelers can. History has a pulse. You just have to learn how to feel it." After a few seconds of perfect stillness, her eyes flash open. "This way."

We walk the perimeter and push our way through brambles until we reach a shaded section of wall that has collapsed, due to the growth of an aggressive apple tree. Repairs are underway, but there is a gap big enough to climb through.

"You saw this?" I ask.

She grins and clambers into the garden. "Time helps those who listen."

I follow her into the courtyard. She yanks my jacket hard, pulling me down. Her eyes are laser-focused on a hedge in front of us. On the other side, a gardener is snipping aggressively at an unruly shrub with a pair of shears. We crouch motionless, barely breathing, until the gardener heads back across the lawn with an armful of cuttings. I check my watch; the sensitivity on the waypoint needle is high, the time and distance down to single figures. We stay low and follow the hedge toward the house, hiding behind a shrub just a few feet from a set of grand French windows.

A flash of movement catches my eye. Philippe stands in front of a marble fireplace beside a music stand. Four small children face him in a semicircle, listening intently. On the mantelpiece I notice a metronome, *the* metronome. Philippe pushes the thin metal pendulum to the left, and it begins to swing. He grins and waves his arms, conducting, but we can't hear any music, just the distant bubbling of children's laughter. He reaches down into a large leather bag and hands out a selection of wooden sticks. The children take them reverently. The little boy farthest from us, the tallest and thinnest, wears a thin cheesecloth smock and loose brown trousers held up with a thin leather belt that's far too long. Next to him are a boy and a girl, both with hair like candy floss and bright pink cherub lips. I guess they're brother and sister, twins maybe. They stand very close together, giggling.

Nearest the window, with her back to us, is a dark-haired girl in a shabby red dress; one sleeve is ripped at the elbow. Her arm pokes through as she practices her bowing technique. We watch Philippe instruct the children, crouching low to gently correct the position of their arms and then prancing around the room to the rhythm they create as they clack their sticks together. These kids have no idea how lucky they are. This is not how I remember school. My teachers were all grumpy dropouts with bad breath and appalling fashion sense. Philippe appears to be an inspired teacher who also knows how to have fun.

Time is watching. It knows about him, and his untapped potential.

The little girl in the red dress turns, and I get my first proper view of her face and her serious dark eyes. I realize I've seen her before. When she turns away again, I whisper to Gabrielle. "That little girl in red was playing violin outside the restaurant on our last jump."

"I remember," she says. "She was amazing."

I watch the group, enthralled by such talent. "He's brilliant, the kids adore him, but he clearly didn't want to be seen here. Why would he want to hide this?"

Gabrielle muses, "The house may be grand, but the kids are obviously poor, probably orphans. If people knew that Philippe, a hugely successful conductor, was hanging around with these little scruff merchants, I guess it could do serious damage to his reputation." She checks her watch. "OK. The waypoint has updated again. We're done. Let's go."

"Hang on," I say, frowning. "We went to all this trouble just to see Philippe teaching some kids?"

"Yes."

"But we didn't do anything. We didn't interact with anyone."

"Observation *is* interaction," Gabrielle explains. "Time wanted us to see this. It might help us when we come to the final jump."

"How do you know?"

"I don't for sure, but it often plays out this way. I know it seems inconsequential, but think of it like time giving us clues. We just don't know the whole story yet. And anyway, if time showed us exactly what to do, what would the fun be in that?"

She checks that the coast is clear. I stay low and follow her back across the garden, through the gap in the wall, and out onto the street.

My silver hunter buzzes silently against my chest. It says *Waypoint* in big black letters against a bright-white background. Above it is an arrow that swings smoothly around as I move, like the needle of a compass. Gabrielle checks her watch too.

"The waypoint looks like it's toward the opera house. You ready, Bridgeman?"

"Lead the way."

The vibe has shifted between us. I doubt Gabrielle will ever be warm, helpful, or gentle, but I don't need her to be. That isn't who she is, and I'm not trying to change her. This is simply about finding a way to work together. We walk quickly now, the ever-present sound of hooves and a hint of fresh manure in the air.

"I thought it would smell a lot worse," I admit.

"They've built sewers all over Paris," Gabrielle explains. "You should be glad we didn't arrive a hundred years ago."

I'm only just getting used to 1873. "How far back have you time traveled?"

She doesn't look at me, just shrugs. "Don't remember exactly, but I've seen dinosaurs . . ."

"You're *kidding*!"

Gabrielle turns, breaking into a widemouthed grin, and winks. "Sucker."

20

The opera house is a magnificent two-story building. Its arched windows and decorative stonework add a touch of serene elegance to its solid grandeur. I peer up at the roofline, the bluish hues of lead tiles bathed in warm sunlight. On the first floor is a row of tall columns, each with life-sized statues that seem to be guarding the building.

Seeing the opera house like this, resplendent and unknowing, brings a deep, aching sadness. This poor, doomed building. It's hard to believe it will be consumed in a week. Gabrielle stands beside me, also taking in the view. She lets out an annoying laugh.

"You're so predictable."

"What do you mean?" I ask.

"I know what you're thinking, but it's not why we're here. We can't save the opera house."

"There must be something we can do."

"Like what?"

"I don't know," I mutter, "maybe contact the fire service?"

Gabrielle tuts. "You're such a pussy. I'd stop thinking about changing things if I were you."

I study the opera house, so regal and calm today, as though impervious to harm. At the front of the building, I spot a man busily cleaning the windows, and another wave of sadness breaks over me. I've seen those windows explode in a shower of hungry embers. All of this, gone in a week. I think about the time it took to build, the vision of the architect, the discernible passion of the entire team. Knowledge of future events can be incredibly painful, and my throat tightens with a form of pregrief I wasn't expecting. My eyes start to water, probably from all the dust on the streets. "Surely while we're here, we have to try, don't we?"

Gabrielle rolls her eyes. "Oh, here we go. Turn on the waterworks."

"I'm not crying, it's just . . . we really should try and . . ." My throat dries up and I begin to cough, loudly.

"Listen to me," she says. "Take a long, deep breath."

I notice how tight my chest feels. I try to draw breath, but it feels as though an invisible force is squeezing my lungs, constricting my airway. Considering what else I've been through recently, it would be odd to have a panic attack now, but that's exactly what this feels like.

I tug at my collar. "What's happening to me? I can't breathe!"

"Resistance," she says, without a trace of concern. "You need to put all thoughts of stopping the fire out of your mind."

"What are you saying?" I croak, my hands slipping to my knees. A group of men nearby turn, concern etched on their faces. One of them calls out to ask if we need help.

Gabrielle waves them away. "Seriously, Bridgeman, you're going to blow a fuse. Just stop!"

More people take an interest, stopping in the street, and a policeman on the other side of the road looks as though he's about to come over. Close to passing out now, I decide to do exactly as Gabrielle says, and force myself to focus on finding Nils. The relief is instant. My lungs expand as though a dam has just broken. I soak in the oxygen, gasping. "What the hell is going on? How did you do that?"

"Me?" She laughs. "You're giving me way too much credit. That was all your fault, you and your stupid, fanciful ideas of beating time at its own game."

I rub at my throat, vision pulsing, and take a minute to compose myself. "So . . . I was making that happen?"

"Yep. You were planning to stop the fire."

"Are you saying that time is aware of my intentions, and it wants the fire to happen?"

"No," she replies, "time isn't sentient, but there are rules. Trust me, it's a blessing that we can't just change whatever we want. The possibilities would eat you alive. This fire is going to happen, we can't stop it. It's the observer effect." Gabrielle gazes over the busy street, the immaculately dressed people, smart horse-drawn carriages, and raucous street vendors plying their wares. "There are thousands of witnesses on the night of the fire, not to mention the newspaper reports that follow. News of the fire eventually spreads around the globe and reaches millions. If it helps, try and think of the fate of this place as being baked into history."

I straighten up, my panic slowly fading. "But I was only *thinking* about trying to stop the fire. How does time know what I'm thinking? That's nuts!"

"It's not nuts," she snaps. "Ideas have power." She taps the side of her head. "But resistance always wins. So if you enjoy breathing, let's focus on why time has brought us here and get back on track, shall we?" Her tone is the epitome of passive aggression. "The change event is Philippe and his injury, and not the fire. Got it?"

I nod in resignation. "Got it."

"And Nils is somehow attached to this change event. So we have work to do. We need to get inside the opera house and see if we can find Philippe. We need to talk to him. I want to know why he goes back inside a burning opera house when, as far as we know, everyone was already out. If we understand that, we might be able to change Philippe's outcome just enough."

The sun cuts through the clouds, warming my skin. I think back on how the heat poured from the building, so strong it pushed everyone back. I shudder. The idea of going back inside the inferno is about as appealing as jumping into a deep fryer.

"Could we just tell Philippe to stay away?"

"Maybe. It's hard to know at this point. It really depends on what drives him. That's what I want to find out."

"But what if we just grabbed him and tied him up somewhere?"

"I've tried that kind of thing," she says, "and it rarely works. If Philippe is determined, he will find a way."

"But I thought you said time wanted us to help him, to save him?"

She tuts at me, clearly irritated. "Time is offering us a chance to nudge Philippe's life in the right direction, but it also wants as much of the story to remain the same as possible." She holds out her hands, palms up, as though weighing something. "Assistance versus resistance. We exist somewhere in the middle. It's a balance. In the end, the best results come if it seems like we were never here. We leave things almost the same but . . . tweaked." She shakes her head. "Christ, Bridgeman, I can't spend all day teaching you the basics. We need to get on with this. Keep your eyes peeled for Nils—if he's attached to the change event, then being close to Philippe is probably our best bet. Let's go."

We cross the street, "the basics" thrumming through my addled brain. Does all this tie in with what's happened to me since I learned I could travel through time? Was I working within these parameters with Amy and Lucy? Maybe. In fact, I think I may have felt resistance a few times, certainly at the fairground. Now that it has a name, it's easier to acknowledge. And I've definitely felt time guiding me, choosing the right street in London, for example, finding a police box in dense smog on instinct alone. Bill called it *subtle serendipity*, time's way of giving us a hand when we need it.

Gabrielle nudges me in the ribs. "Heads up. Follow my lead. And remember, as far as he's concerned, we haven't met him yet."

A tall man in a striking purple suit and cravat approaches us. I recognize him immediately as the opera house manager. His green eyes glow in the sunlight, and his brown hair is oiled and swept back over his head, devilish beard trimmed neatly into a point. He acknowledges me and then bows to Gabrielle. "Dominic Monier, manager of the Salle Le Peletier, at your service. Do you require assistance? You, sir, looked as though you had been taken ill."

"You're very kind, but we're well, thank you." Gabrielle steps forward and offers her hand. "Gabrielle Green."

Monier kisses it. "A pleasure, madame."

She waves a hand daintily in my direction. "And allow me to introduce Mr. Charles Henry Taylor, publisher of the *Boston Globe*."

He raises an eyebrow and tips his hat. I do the same. "Very good to meet you, monsieur," he says, "although I'm afraid if you're here for the

preview, you will have to forgive me. Today is an exclusive event for benefactors of the opera house."

"What event are you running?" I ask.

"A tour of the opera house, and an exclusive performance of one of the
scenes from our latest opera, *Le Prophète*."

Gabrielle shifts her persona and immediately becomes overtly feminine
and shockingly charming. "Why, that is *such* a shame," she wheedles. "The
opera house would make such a *fascinating* article."

"Article?" he says, twirling the point of his beard with his forefinger.

"That's right," Gabrielle blushes. "Although I am merely an assistant
and don't wish to speak out of turn." She flings a sidelong glance at me,
cheeks glowing, eyelids fluttering.

"No, I mean yes, I mean—please go ahead, Miss Green." I just manage
to remain in character.

"Thank you, sir. Monsieur Monier, Mr. Taylor was just telling me that
a piece focused on such a well-run opera company would be very popular
with our readership."

The manager studies me suspiciously and then settles back on Gabrielle. "You are his assistant?"

"Yes, and I would be thrilled to . . . how can I put this? See behind the
curtain." Gabrielle's voice is now a deep, throaty purr. It's astonishing how
persuasive she can be. "I would love to see all the . . . ins and outs, if you
will, to really see how you run this place." She twirls a lock of hair in her
fingers and actually licks her lips. It turns my stomach.

The opera manager swallows, tugs at his collar, and considers her with
hungry eyes. "I am certain that we can make an exception on this occasion,
especially for a woman as charming as you, mademoiselle. You will be my
guests, and once the official tour is complete, I will grant you a personal
interview. How does that sound?"

"Absolute perfection," Gabrielle says.

He offers her his arm, and they walk toward the opera house. I follow,
already feeling like a spare part. Gabrielle turns her head and winks at me.
I can't help breaking into a smile. Like her or loathe her, she gets stuff done.
And now, it seems, we are getting the full tour.

A row of ornate streetlamps leads to the entrance, which is shaded beneath a striped awning. We pass through a foyer where members of staff take hats, coats, shawls, and canes. I count at least twenty people here for the event. The men are all wearing black suits with long tails, white shirts, and cravats, and the women are all wearing pretty dresses in bright shades of orange, pink, and yellow with matching hats, shawls, and gloves. They must have started getting ready yesterday.

I hand over my top hat and enter a small opulent room with columns and arches, painted to look like marble. The room glows a creamy gold, lit by gaslight chandeliers. It fills with the sound of excited chatter. Gabrielle and I find a corner and do our best to blend in.

"What's my name again?"

"Charles H. Taylor, publisher of the *Boston Globe*. I had to focus on you because the idea of a woman journalist hasn't gone mainstream yet. Just be businessy and confident and let me do most of the talking."

A woman engages Gabrielle in conversation. "My husband is here for the opera," she confides, leaning in with a conspiratorial smile, "but I'm here to see Monsieur Chevalier." Her eyes glitter, like an excited teenager. Gabrielle and the woman chat for a while before the husband appears and reclaims his wife.

I notice a familiar face, a ferocious elderly woman dressed in black. "I recognize her from the restaurant," I say, subtly pointing her out. We watch as the woman insists to one of the staff that she will be keeping her cane—thank you very much. She looks as though she might like to beat someone with it.

The assembled people discuss the new production. I overhear one couple mention the Phantom, how they hope to catch a glimpse of him. It makes me think of Nils and how hopeless this feels. It's all very well agreeing to try and find him, but now I'm here, on the ground, it's a different story. How am I supposed to connect with him?

The opera manager interrupts my thoughts with an announcement in a deep authoritative voice. "Ladies and gentlemen, may I please have your attention?" The room settles into silence. "Thank you all for coming today. I am delighted to announce that for you, our most valuable benefactors, we will be previewing a scene from our new opera, *Le Prophète*." A happy murmur ripples through the crowd. "Now, if you will all please follow me, we will pass through the Hallway of Mirrors and into the auditorium."

En masse, the excited crowd follows him into a cavernous golden corridor, as tall as a house. On both sides, golden pillars intersperse with grand gilt mirrors, thirty of them at least. Impressive chandeliers float above, lit with ornate gaslights shaped like candles. In the center is another huge circular chandelier, its multitude of crystals glistening like ice in sunlight. Our group is reflected on all sides as we head toward the auditorium, our footfalls echoing loudly on the polished stone tiles. I recall that on the night of the fire, after the main auditorium collapsed, there was another colossal sound, as though the world was made of glass and had suddenly exploded, and I wonder if it was here, the Hallway of Mirrors caving in on itself.

We emerge from the corridor into a colossal space. Tall arches and numerous balconies connect via a marble staircase that snakes up from the center of the opera house like the roots of an ancient tree. At the base is a dark bronze statue of swirling figures holding clusters of glowing orbs.

The opera manager claps his hands, the sound echoing around us. "Ladies and gentlemen, please follow me up to the auditorium, where we shall watch the finale of *Le Prophète*!" He is quite the showman, adept at generating anticipation, perfect in his role. He walks ahead, and the benefactors drift behind him on a sea of perfume.

Gabrielle pauses at the foot of the staircase and places her hand on the statue, her gaze unfocused.

"You're listening to the building, aren't you," I say, recognizing her expression.

"You should try it," she suggests. "You'll be completely useless at first, but you might learn something." I place my hand on the statue, the bronze cold to the touch. "Now listen," Gabrielle says. "Open your mind to the story. Try to feel it."

I try and tune in to the feeling I get from objects, but nothing happens. Then, colors flicker into existence, revealing themselves pixel by pixel, as though my mind is developing a photo in real time. I see the opera house, only partially constructed. Sketches. Plans. At the bottom of my mind's eye, a staircase appears, curving upward a step at a time. It coagulates and sharpens. The buzz of construction! I feel the passion and energy that went into this impressive building.

A loud voice breaks the spell. "Ah, there you are!" Dominic Monier calls down to us from the mezzanine level of the staircase, a bemused expression on his face. "You are admiring the details, I see."

Gabrielle presses her hands to her chest. "I'm so sorry we got left behind. We're quite overcome with this wonderful building. Such exquisite craftsmanship."

He glows with pride. "Exquisite is the word. If these walls could talk, they would be full of stories."

"I'm sure," she giggles airily, a picture of innocence.

He playfully ticks a finger. "Now, I must insist you keep up, as we are on a tight schedule, and I want to ensure that I have plenty of time with you after the performance."

"Of course." Gabrielle bows her head. "I apologize. Please lead the way."

We rejoin the group and ascend the staircase, beckoned to the heavens by a painted ceiling depicting robed angels luxuriating on clouds in a cobalt sky.

"I saw something," I whisper to Gabrielle. "Construction, blueprints."

"Me too. I think the staircase is where the inspiration began."

I'm struck again by the painful knowledge that this place will soon be a pile of rubble and ash. I imagine the foyer packed full of people, the fire raging. It looks as though there's so much stone that it's hard to imagine it burning, but a lot of this is a facade. What on the surface appears to be gold, stone, and marble is actually fabric, wood, and plaster, all of it ready to go up in smoke, as impermanent and illusory as the creations that play out on its stage.

We reach the top of the staircase, pass through a heavy curtain, and emerge onto the first floor of the opera house, above the stalls. The auditorium is one of the most impressive, opulent spaces I've ever seen, a gleaming golden ribcage of boxed seating, four tiers high, interspersed by circular stone pillars. It's lit by numerous wall-mounted gaslights, all burning hungrily, lending the dark-burgundy seating and curtains a luxurious glow. I survey the space in awe, drawn to an impressive chandelier that illuminates the stage, as well as a beautifully painted, domed ceiling. A fresco of power-ful godlike men, alluring women, and cherubic angels looks down onto the stage, which is fringed with gold and guarded by four gilded eagles, each as tall as a man. I shudder to think what they will soon witness.

The orchestra waits silently in the pit. We are shown to our seats, huge velvet armchairs offering an impressive view of the stage, which is currently shrouded by a ruffled curtain. The air is musty, with hints of stale perfume, sweat, and age.

Once we are all comfortably seated, the opera manager stands before us, just in front of the stage. "It is my humble opinion that Meyerbeer's masterpiece, *Le Prophète*, will go down in history as one of the greatest operas of all time." He pauses for effect, and we all clap politely. "Today, I must remind you that this is a rehearsal. We shall be presenting act five, scene two—the finale, which takes place in the great hall of the Munster Palace. What you are about to see is a preview of what I feel is one of our finest productions. No expense has been spared." His gaze passes slowly over us, checking that we're listening and suitably impressed. "Prepare to be transported." The orchestra tunes their instruments, eventually coalescing into a single, pleasing note before fading into anticipatory silence.

A lone figure walks onto the stage. Our group bursts into a sponta-neous round of enthusiastic applause. All around me there are gasps and the flickering sound of fans against the overheated faces of the gathered women. It's Philippe Chevalier, dressed in a pale-blue suit, a shade that complements his natural good looks. He bows slowly, nods in our direction, and then again to the orchestra before assuming his position as conductor. He is handsome, charismatic, and effortlessly cool, and I can see why the women are swooning. Philippe is the beau of his opera, a true celebrity.

Gabrielle leans over. "He's come straight from teaching a secret lesson with a bunch of street kids, to this."

It's true. Shifting from such a humble scene to all this pomp and cere-mony, Philippe is an interesting character, a chameleon apparently spanning two worlds with ease. I could easily become lost in the drama and excite-ment of the performance, but I'm constantly on the lookout for any hint of Nils, to make my attendance on this jump worthwhile.

The house lights dim and unseen hands draw the curtain apart. People gasp, and I'm one of them. The set is a masterful illusion of stone columns, arches, and drapes that give the impression of a full-sized cathedral reaching far back into the distance. The sky is the deep dark-blue of night, pricked with shimmering stars. In the center, a mirror, ingeniously lit, gives the impression of a glowing moon. There must be hundreds of concealed gas burners feeding this impressive display. It must have cost a fortune, and it's a complete safety nightmare. No wonder this place burns to the ground.

Philippe raises his right hand, and the music begins.

The smooth resonant tone of a cello accompanies plucked violins. An oboe eases in over the top with a playful, mysterious melody. A banquet table, laden with food, rises from an unseen platform in the middle of the stage. Actors flood in from the wings, wearing heavy and elaborate costumes.

A man and a woman in thick makeup step forward, their expressions filled with dramatic intensity. It's almost comedic, but then they sing and I'm blown away, not only because their voices are incredible, but also because previously incomprehensible sounds have become words full of meaning, phrases rich with emotion. I'm totally fluent in French without any of the endless studying, exams, and exasperated locals. I've finally twigged that my implant isn't translating what I'm hearing into English, it's somehow rewired my brain so that I now understand French. I always wondered how it would feel to be bilingual. Now I know, and it's glorious.

The company's impressive voices meld with resplendent French horns and reverberating timpani in an explosion of sound, soaring in intensity. The performers bear their souls under the hot lights, over the crescendo of the orchestra, without any amplification. The acoustics are sublime.

For the next twenty minutes, I am transported. The stage fills with even more people, who sing while they feast at the table. Philippe conducts his orchestra, their faces tilted up toward him, watching his every move. He is animated, passionate. This is clearly a performance for him too.

Everyone is transfixed.

Then, suddenly, an aching silence.

Smooth, soft strings ease back in with a solo voice, sorrowful and majestic. With a dramatic strike of violins and drums, a man and woman join in a soaring harmony of power and vulnerability. The prima donna transforms into a screaming banshee, but still, she reins in the lightning of her vocals with full and impressive control. The auditorium sounds like a giant finger rotating around a wine glass the size of the Grand Canyon. I feel as though my head and chest might explode.

I've always thought of opera as an impenetrable fortress, but actually, it's pure raw emotion, an expression of life. The pain and fire in the voice brings tears. I can't help it. Her sorrowful moan is power and knowledge. Laughing, I wipe my eyes and take a moment to soak in what I'm witnessing, what an amazing opportunity this is.

The scene reaches a crescendo when a battalion of soldiers appears. They lock the doors of the palace and demand the false prophet be executed without delay. A fight breaks out, and a fire starts. They use pyrotechnics. There are flames, and they are real.

"Gabrielle," I whisper, leaning over, "this is insane."

"I know, right?"

We both watch as the set of the palace collapses around them in some kind of complex stage trickery. I was not expecting this. There is no green screen, no projections, and yet this appears real. I'm painfully aware that there is no fire crew waiting in the wings, no extinguishers or complicated sprinkler system. These people are literally playing with fire for the sake of spectacle. I can't believe this place doesn't go up in smoke right now.

The two main singers throw themselves into each other's arms for a last farewell, while everyone else tries in vain to escape. Ribbons of red and yellow flash high from the floor and wings of the stage. It's an ingenious, impressive sight, but also a sad, dark prediction. A week from now, they'll get to see the real thing. The palace finally caves in, consumed in smoke and flames, basically killing all of the characters, as far as I can tell.

The music comes to a rousing crescendo, then a definitive close, and the lights come up. The benefactors around us rise to their feet with loud applause and cries of "Bravo!" The actors return to the stage and, along with Philippe, take a bow. Everyone seems pleased with the performance, none more than Dominic Monier, who soaks it up, his waving arms dispersing whisps of blue smoke that have made their way to the balcony already.

I turn to Gabrielle. "That was absolute madness."

She nods. "I think we might have just solved the mystery of how the fire started. These guys had it coming."

"Now!" Monsieur Monier shouts over the applause, "A rare opportunity, ladies and gentlemen, to witness the finest view in the house. Will you please join me for a glass of champagne on the stage?"

His guests jostle to be the first to take him up on his offer.

Gabrielle jumps up and turns to me. "Are you getting anything on Nils?"

"Sorry. Nothing. I've been thinking that my best bet might be to find Marguerite, the seamstress I met on our last trip who told me she'd seen him. If I can find her again, I can talk to her about what she saw, and maybe get backstage and see him for myself."

She considers this and checks her watch. "Sounds like a plan. We still have an hour here. Plenty of time for a sighting."

"Should we split up?" I ask.

"Maybe in a while, but for now, stick with me. The waypoint suggests we need to interact with Philippe. Let's get down there, try and get some time alone with him, then see about finding the seamstress."

We make our way to the stage. Champagne flows as the benefactors discuss the performance. A group of cooing women surrounds Philippe Chevalier, plying him with drinks, touching his arm. He looks uncomfortable.

Gabrielle suggests we wait a few minutes before we approach him. We walk to the edge of the stage, soaking in a unique view of the fabulous auditorium. I can only imagine what it must feel like to have all those eyes on you. What was it Gabrielle said? There is a power in observation. It's tangible, and standing here, I can feel it, a tingling on my skin, so subtle it could easily be missed.

My attention is drawn to the old lady I saw in the restaurant the night of our first jump. She's scowling at me. I smile and incline my head in acknowledgment, but her face remains stone-cold. She turns to the opera house manager and in a loud, angry voice says, "It's quite evident where our money is going, all of this trickery and expensive set design. Surely, the opera itself and the wonderful performances should be enough."

Monier rubs his hands together in supplication. "Madame Delacroix, we must keep up with the times, give people something they haven't seen before. We must compete, or we will not survive."

"At what cost?" She walks toward him, cane tapping on the wooden boards. "It seems to me this place is a chimney, a fire waiting to be lit . . . I hope you know what you're doing."

As some of the cast mingle with the crowd, Monier asks the group if they feel the expense is worth it. His timing is perfect. Madame Delacroix is outnumbered by her peers, and talk shifts toward the new opera and what many believe will soon be the talk of Paris.

They aren't wrong.

One of the benefactors, a young woman dressed in an elegant, pale-blue dress, peers out from the stage. "After such a performance, with all this drama, I wonder if the Phantom will be seen today."

The manager glows. "Madame! Be careful what you wish for, the Phantom may be listening." He announces this loudly, with all the theatrics of a pantomime villain.

"Poppycock!" cries Madame Delacroix, but again she's outnumbered by the other guests, who are desperate for gossip.

The crowd of benefactors, buzzing at the idea of a sighting and fueled by their second glass of champagne, sinks into excited chatter. They peer out from the stage, nervous with anticipation. Dominic Monier is in his element, busily describing the various sightings of the Phantom to a gaggle of entranced women.

We spot Philippe standing alone at the edge of the stage, as though he's about to take flight. It's clear that he enjoys this kind of pointless mingling as much as I do. Gabrielle suggest we try and talk to him, but as we approach, he flicks a nervous glance around the group and then slips backstage.

Gabrielle whispers, "Let's follow him, see what he's up to."

We weave our way through the fake debris of the collapsed palace and, while no one is looking, sneak behind the scenery into the wings and the darkness beyond.

21

Backstage is stuffy and dark, and I stifle a cough as we encounter the last traces of smoke from the finale. Narrow stairwells wind through the building like rabbit warrens. We rush up a short flight of steps to a polished brown door. I try the handle, but it's locked.

"He must have gone another way."

"Or locked it behind him," Gabrielle replies.

We try another door, which is unlocked, and find ourselves in a narrow dimly lit corridor with dark wood paneling on the walls. The hairs on the back of my neck lift, and I'm suddenly aware that we're being watched. Creeped out, and recalling Vinny's belief in the occult, I ask, "Do you think there's anything behind this ghost story?"

"Come on!" Gabrielle laughs, striding ahead. "Don't be an idiot. We need to think of a smart way to get inside Philippe's head. See if we can find out what draws him back into the building."

"Could we just ask him?"

"Maybe, but resistance might not let us. I like to plan around that." I think back to my throat constricting outside the opera house and wince. Gabrielle continues, "And anyway, it's kind of a strange question, isn't it? 'Hi, can you tell me why, if this place was on fire, you might run back inside?'"

"Fire?" booms a deep baritone voice behind us. We both turn, startled. It's Dominic Monier, his brow so heavily furrowed that his eyes are like a dark mask. "Please do not talk of fire. We don't want to go tempting fate now, do we? What are you doing back here, unaccompanied?"

Without missing a beat, Gabrielle picks up her skirt and sidles up to him, eyelashes flickering. "I'm so glad we ran into you. Allow me to explain. Mr. Taylor is pioneering a new, experimental form of news story. Something we are calling an 'insider piece'—an attempt to really get behind the scenes of the Salle Le Peletier opera house."

"Exactly," I tell him. "I want to write a piece that shows how modern and dynamic your company is."

"Modern and dynamic, you say?"

Gabrielle steps closer to him. "Yes, and if you would allow us full access, we will be able to evoke the most wonderful scenes for our readers and make your opera house internationally famous. I'm still looking forward to our . . . private interview," she adds, with lascivious undertones.

Monier looks deep into Gabrielle's eyes, his lips moving slowly as he thinks. "I'll give you full access, and in return, you will join me for dinner tonight." He takes her hand and kisses it, gazing at her as though she will be dessert. To her credit, Gabrielle doesn't even flinch. She drops a little curtsey and flushes rosy-pink. "I would be honored."

"My pleasure, I'm sure." He glances at me, clearly hoping I'm not going to tag along.

Gabrielle touches his arm. "Meanwhile, there is one person we would like to talk to, if possible."

"Aha!" Monier says knowingly, gesturing to a small stairwell, off to our right. "Follow your nose to the top. You will find Philippe there. If anyone asks what you're doing, just tell them you have the full permission of Monsieur Dominic Matthias Monier." He announces his name with pomp and splendor, like the master of ceremonies introducing the guest of honor at a ball.

We follow the stairs upward, passing through a latched door. I lead the way up another narrow, rickety staircase. I've slightly lost track of our position relative to the stage, but as we pass rigging and scenery, I catch a glimpse of the auditorium. It seems we are making our way up a tower block with a central stairwell. Gantries reach out over the stage, and we pass numerous storage areas. My knees wobble and my thighs cramp when I realize how high we are. I grab a thin handrail and focus on the steps. Faint violin music swirls from somewhere above, growing louder as we climb.

At the top of the staircase is a rough fabric curtain. Not wanting to interrupt the majestic violin playing, I peer around the curtain and see Philippe, eyes closed, lost inside the musical tapestry he's weaving with his fingers. The haunting melody starts low and fulsome, then slowly builds until the music soars like a bird. I'm not generally a classical music fan, but like the girl on the night of the fire, a lone violin has the ability to bypass my brain and go straight for my heart.

Philippe stops playing midphrase and puts the violin down on the table beside him, breaking the spell. "Good, good," he mutters. "B-flat minor . . . unexpected, wonderful." He scribbles furiously on the manuscript in front of him, and I understand that he's composing this incredible music, live. He picks up the violin, and the music spills from him again, his left hand exploring the fingerboard with the precision of a watchmaker, his bow arm moving gracefully.

I'm in awe of his skill but also overcome with the pain of knowing that in less than a week, those remarkable, gifted hands will be ruined, and his playing days will be over. I badly want to save this man from his fate. Amy crosses my mind. No wonder her "gift" is so hard to handle. Knowledge of the past is one thing, but seeing someone's future and being powerless to change it is a heavy weight to carry.

Philippe collapses back into his chair, his face smooth and relaxed, his soul's music captured safely. "Claude?" he calls suddenly. "Where are you? Have you found another naughty mouse?"

Something brushes my leg. Looking down I see a little gray cat with unusually clear blue eyes winding sinuously around my ankles. He lets out a little mew. I reach down to scratch his head, and he pushes against my hand, purring loudly.

"Claude says you may enter," Philippe announces playfully.

Gabrielle shoves me out of the way and strides into the room. "Please forgive us, monsieur," she says. "We didn't mean to interrupt you."

Philippe gives a slight nod of the head. "You understand the creative arts perfectly, mademoiselle. My muse, she is very coy."

Judging by the exposed beams and the structure of the roof, this appears to be the highest point of the opera house, one of many storage spaces situated above the backstage area. It's been cleared out and furnished with a random collection of interesting pieces. There is a small walnut table and single chair, and pieces of porcelain, mirrors, and clothes are strewn about. The only natural light comes from a single window that offers a limited but impressive view of the Paris skyline. In the corner is a washbasin next to a cramped bed. This appears not only to be Philippe's writing room, but also his home. Candles offer just enough light for Philippe's desk, which is covered in parchments filled with musical notation. Beside that is an oak-frame umbrella stand crammed with what appear to be more rolls of handwritten music.

Gabrielle gestures toward me. "Allow me to introduce Mr. Charles H. Taylor, publisher of the *Boston Globe*." I stare blankly at her before remembering that she's referring to me, and I smile confidently at Philippe. "And I'm Gabrielle Green," she says, adding through gritted teeth, "Mr. Taylor's assistant."

"Philippe Chevalier, a pleasure to meet you." He bows his head but keeps his eyes on us. "I noticed you onstage earlier. How may I be of assistance?" His tone is friendly, but guarded. He's clearly a celebrity of his time, and so I'm not surprised that he's wary of unsolicited attention.

"We're writing an article for our newspaper on the opera house, and we wondered if we could interview you," Gabrielle says in a breathy rush. I glance at her; she's actually blushing. It seems that being up close to Philippe, now we've seen him in action, has knocked some of the brash confidence out of her. Claude mews again and pushes against her ankle; she leans down and strokes along the length of his back. "And we'd like to interview you too, Mr. Cat," she says playfully.

Philippe's countenance softens. "I'm happy to talk to you, but I must insist that you don't feature me in your article."

"Of course." Gabrielle puts away her notepad. "May I ask why?"

"People have a picture of me in their heads, of who I am and what I am. I prefer it to remain that way. In my experience, if people know too much about you, that causes trouble. All I have to offer—my public persona—is given freely on the stage. Everything else—my personal life—that is not for sale."

"Fair enough," Gabrielle says, and I wonder if she's thinking the same as me, that many of the famous people in the present could do a lot worse than following his approach.

Philippe continues, almost apologetically. "Fame isn't for me. If it were not for the need to earn a living, I would happily play to no one." He picks Claude up and strokes him gently. The cat purrs and licks his hand. "Well, perhaps just to you, my little companion." He kisses the cat's head and then gently eases him to the floor. "Perhaps you could talk to some of the other performers? I'm sure they would be delighted to share their stories with you."

"We completely respect your wishes," Gabrielle says brightly. "How about we just talk, but we don't use your name or quote anything you say? We're really just trying to show our readers a little of how the opera house runs. Would that be all right?"

He studies her, his dark eyes and unblemished cocoa skin glowing in the candlelight. "I have your assurance that this conversation will not be published?"

"Absolutely," she says with calm conviction. "We're just interested in you."

Philippe sighs. "You mean, you want to know if I've seen the Phantom?"

That feels like my cue. "Er, yes. If you have any information, that would be very helpful."

Philippe turns, eyebrows raised. "Aha, so Mr. Taylor has a voice! I was beginning to wonder if your assistant did all of your talking for you."

"No, no, not at all. It's just . . . Paris is new to me, so I'm just finding my way."

Gabrielle glares at me. Philippe quizzes me playfully. "You say Paris is new to you, and yet your French is impeccable?"

"Thank you," I tell him, my ears ringing with English, yet aware that I must have said, *Merci*. I feel like such a fraud as I tell him, "I had a very good French teacher. Years of practice, you know. But anyway, you mentioned the Phantom—have you seen him?"

Philippe lays a hand on the wall beside him. "This building is full of ghosts. I feel them, I hear them in the creaks and the moans of the wood."

His eyes widen in mock fear for a second, then he chuckles. "I am toying with you. Although I do believe it is possible to be haunted, it's not by the souls of the departed. Our own memories and failures do a perfectly good job." He stares out of the window, reflecting. "In my opinion, ghosts are the constructs of our own minds. But of course, talk of a phantom is exceedingly good for business. This sideshow is a distraction, but one I can ignore. My focus remains on my music and *Le Prophète*."

"That is fair enough, monsieur," I tell him. "Thank you for your honesty." It doesn't sound as though Philippe is going to give us a lead on Nils, so I cast my eyes around the room for anything that might cause him to come back into the building during the fire. "Your violin," I venture, "it's beautiful. Is it very valuable?"

"I wouldn't know, but to me, it has great sentimental value. My father gave it to me. Do you play?"

"No, but I'm a collector of objects of interest and importance," I say, trying to tread the line of half-truth without undoing my publisher cover story. "May I hold your violin? If I'm careful?"

"Of course." He picks it up and offers it to me gently, as though passing a baby. Holding it, I imagine Philippe as a young man, his father proudly watching him play, and I feel the tingle of history, of psychometric energy. I would need more time to trigger a viewing, but I decide that the violin should definitely go on the list of reasons to reenter the building, along with Claude the cat and the scrolls of unpublished work. I hand the violin back.

"What did you do before you came to Paris?" Gabrielle asks.

"I conducted an orchestra in Marseille," he replies. "I taught music too. But it was always my dream to work in Paris, to be at the heart of French opera. So when this opportunity arose, I took it. Seized it." He clenches his fist, and the thought of his impending injuries makes me shiver.

Gabrielle scans the room. "And you live up here?"

"For now, yes. Monsieur Monier allows me to stay here. Moving to Paris and taking this position was a wonderful opportunity, but this city does not come cheap. I don't know how some people afford to live here at all. We must remember that there are many who live in poverty. I am one of the fortunate ones."

I consider pressing him on his secret teaching activities but decide better of it. Gabrielle seems to sense this and glares at me, tipping her head toward Philippe, her expression telling me to keep him talking.

I walk over to his desk and study the score he was working on when we arrived. "The music you were composing, it was amazing," I tell him honestly.

Philippe waves the compliment away. "You are too kind."

"You looked like you were really in the zone."

"The zone? That is a very interesting way of putting it."

I wonder again what actually came out of my mouth. How does my little translator deliver my words and understanding so smoothly?

"The music comes through me, through my muse. I really have nothing to do with it. I am merely a conduit. My role is to get out of the way." He indicates the rolls of notated music. "When the inspiration comes, you don't ask it to wait. You run as fast as you can and capture it before it slips out of the window and is gone." He turns to me, eyes alight. "Being here is a dream for me, but it is not my only dream. Perhaps that is greedy of me."

"Greedy?"

"I believe a man should not be restricted to just one dream. I believe he should be allowed to have many. What do you think, monsieur?"

I find myself warming to this fearless, openhearted man. "Why not? Dreams are free, after all."

"I like your attitude. It is unusual and, dare I say it, progressive."

I've been called various things that end with "-essive," but never that.

Gabrielle clears her throat. "Monsieur Chevalier, I have a question to ask you."

"Please, call me Philippe."

"Philippe. This is purely hypothetical, but suppose you were stranded on a deserted island, and could only take one item from this room with you . . . what would it be? Your violin? Your compositions?"

A slight frown flickers over his face, and he works his gaze slowly between us both. "This is by far the most unusual conversation I have had in some time."

"Good," Gabrielle says with confidence. "I think that in order to understand a person, you first need to know what matters to them. It tells you a lot."

"I agree." He surveys the room, considering his possessions. "Now, let me see. Music is endless, I could simply write more. My violin is precious to me, it would bring me pleasure on this island you describe, but we are not supposed to be alone. Therefore, I would bring Claude for company."

Claude's fur suddenly puffs up, and his tail swishes against the floor like a windshield wiper, his eyes fixed on the corner of the room.

"What is it, Claude?" asks Philippe with a grin. "Is it the Phantom again?"

Urgent footsteps clatter up the staircase, and a young woman bursts into the room. It's Marguerite, the seamstress I talked to in the restaurant. I stop myself from acknowledging her, because she hasn't met me yet. "Messieurs, madame, the Phantom has struck again!" she says breathlessly. "Monsieur Monier is requesting your presence onstage. Come quickly, please!"

"Lead the way," Philippe says calmly. He turns back and smiles at Gabrielle. "I was enjoying our conversation, but it appears we are required for the show's unofficial finale."

We follow Philippe and Marguerite down the stairs. Quietly, I ask Gabrielle, "Do you think the phantom they're seeing could be Nils?"

"Either way," she says, "we're about to find out."

We arrive on the stage. Dominic Monier spots us and looks pleased. He has the *Boston Globe* reporters and his popular conductor all present. There must be a dozen people on the stage, all standing alert as meerkats. I recognize most of them as benefactors from the tour. The men support the women, who fan their faces excitedly, peering out from the stage into the dark seats and shadowed balconies with expressions of excitement and trepidation. All except Madame Delacroix, the old lady we saw at the restaurant. Her black marble-like eyes are boring into the opera house manager, and her jaw is locked in an obstinate scowl. Her job, it seems, is to render his life a misery, and by his expression, she's very good at it.

He does his best to ignore her by talking to a woman in a pale-yellow dress. "Tell me again," he says, "exactly what you saw."

She wipes her nose with a handkerchief. "I saw a ghostly figure in a long dark cloak moving quickly through the shadows."

"Did you see his face?" Monier asks, with all the panache of a stage magician.

"No, it was covered," she says, her voice trembling. "I think he must be disfigured."

Gasps and excited mumbling ripple through the crowd. Gabrielle and I share a look. This is all very dramatic and all too familiar, but I guess it's new to the assembled group, and everyone soaks up the drama, chattering in excited tones. Monier is thrilled. "Please, remain calm," he says with thinly veiled delight. "And if you catch sight of the Phantom, do not be afraid."

"Afraid?" booms Madame Delacroix. "There are many reasons to be afraid, some of them are even real. Disease. Famine. War." She walks toward Monier, her cane tapping. "You, monsieur, are turning this beautiful opera house into a farce, whilst ignoring the very thing you should be the most afraid of: this place burning to the ground."

Monier tuts impatiently. "Must everyone keep talking about fire?"

"It's a better subject than your ridiculous phantom." She works her cool gaze around the group. "Let me be categorically, unequivocally clear: there is no such thing as ghosts."

As if on cue, a man yells, making us all jump. "There!" he shouts, pointing to the first floor. "The Phantom! There he is!"

Collectively, we peer out into the gloom, where a dark figure leans over the edge of the balcony, close enough to see his features. The Phantom flicks his cape over his shoulder and leers ominously down at us, his face pale partially covered by a mask. He runs along the edge of the balcony, gaslights flickering and illuminating the satin sheen of his cape as it flaps behind him. This is more like it. The production values have just leaped, like the Phantom himself, who is darting over chairs with ease. He is a talented gymnast and apparently, a natural showman. There are more gasps and cries.

Gabrielle leans over to me. "It's not Nils. Time travelers don't tend to be quite so dramatic. Ideally, they don't want to be seen at all. This is clearly a publicity stunt."

"Agreed."

The Phantom laughs, a deep, pantomime-villain laugh. It's supposed to be chilling, but I can't help but giggle. Then, with a sudden flash, the ominous figure disappears in a cloud of smoke. I stop grinning and wonder how on earth the production team pulled off that trick. The woman in the yellow dress promptly faints, her husband exclaiming that it's all true, that the opera house is haunted.

A crackle of light, followed by a snapping sound, draws our attention to a balcony on the third floor. It's the Phantom again, this time on the opposite side of the opera house.

Gabrielle frowns. "How the hell did he get there so fast?"

"Are there two of them?"

"Maybe." She turns to me, her voice low. "Listen, we're seeing this for a reason. I wonder if it's connected to Philippe in some way." Her mind is clearly working quickly. "If I can catch this phantom, it might give us leverage with Monier. I'm going to follow him. You see if you can find Nils." Before I can respond, Gabrielle is off, running to the side of the stage. Some of the crowd follow her with excited talk of seeing the Phantom again. Monier and Philippe are distracted, helping the woman who fainted.

Some of the scenery at the back of the stage appears to be glowing brightly. In fact, when I look in that general direction, everything seems a little more saturated. I remember this sensation from when Vinny and I were in London, following Frankie Shaw's car. At one point we lost sight of him and arrived at a crossroads with a seemingly random choice to make, and yet I knew instinctively which road was the right one. Gabrielle talked about resistance and also described the opposite; time wanting to help us and guide us. As I slip away into the dark belly of the opera house, I feel time's power, as though drawn by an invisible magnet.

Nils is here. I know it.

PART 5

22

"Excuse me!" A young woman scoots behind me and pulls a tin of buttons off a shelf, rummaging through it noisily and tutting to herself. She pulls out a large jet-black button and waves it at an older woman at the other end of the room. "Found one!" she calls and scuttles away. I'm in the costume workshop, and with just a week to go until the opera opens to the public, it's a hive of activity: mannequins with half-finished costumes draped over them, dressmakers busy with shears and mouths full of pins, a trestle table the length of the room piled at one end with rolls of different fabrics, some plain and drab, others thick and opulent with threads of gold.

Everyone is rushing, and no one seems to have paid the slightest notice to the ruckus and the screaming coming from the auditorium. The industry in this room makes me feel exhausted, and I'm obviously in the way, so I push through into a long corridor lined with endless linen cupboards. My watch tingles against my chest. I pull it out and see an alert that Nils's signal has been triggered. The needle spins wildly for a few moments, as though I've just wandered into the Bermuda Triangle, then settles very suddenly and decisively on a door that lies ajar at the other end of the corridor. As quietly as possible, I creep along the hallway. As I approach the door, I hear voices inside: two people are arguing—one is a woman but the other has a very odd-sounding voice, strained and whispery, as though the speaker might have a speech impediment.

Cautiously, holding my breath, I push the door open a little farther and slip through. I still can't see much—the room is dimly lit, hazy sunlight struggling in through a single, dusty window high in the opposite wall—but I can tell it's a kind of storage space. The air is charged with the fresh sting of ozone, like a storm has just passed. Just to the left of the door, pushed close to the wall, is a long, free-standing clothing rack with soldier costumes, scores of black tailored trousers and bright-red woolen jackets studded with gold buttons. I duck down, crawl behind the rack, and flatten myself against the wall, hardly breathing. Slowly, I part the jackets in front of me until I can see through a tiny gap.

A woman stands with her back to me, but I can see her face in the mirror she's staring into. I thought that voice was familiar. It's Scarlett.

She has her hands on her hips, facing the huge gilt-framed mirror leaning against the wall under the window. She's dressed in a contemporary outfit, just like me and Gabrielle, her light-green silk dress gathered into a fulsome bustle at the back, tiers of mint-green interspersed with layers of pink satin, and turn-backs of the same pink at her wrists. Her blond hair is pinned up and held in place by a hat tumbling with mint-green velvet ribbons and punctuated here and there with a bright-white fabric daisy. Her face is covered with a veil, partially obscuring her features. Was she at the presentation earlier? Was she watching me and Gabrielle on the stage?

At first I wonder if she's talking to herself, admiring her reflection—despite myself, I can't help thinking she looks very appealing in her costume—but I heard another voice in here too. Didn't I?

"You have to believe me," she says. "I'm truly sorry about what happened. It wasn't meant to be this way. I've come here to get you home."

She almost turns, but a voice snaps at her. "I've already told you, do not look at me!" The voice is thin and rasping, yet full of effort. It's so painful to listen to, it makes my eyes water.

I can't see anything in the mirror. Scarlett's in the way, so I shift very slightly a few inches to my left, hoping the dust I'm stirring up doesn't make me sneeze. Then, I see him, and at the same instant, my watch vibrates silently against my chest. A spectral figure—tall and statuesque, but translucent and shimmering iridescent—stands a few feet behind Scarlett. His shoulder-length hair hangs in damp strands around his square face. He's wearing a loose shirt and pants that stop near his ankles, but the clothes are torn and stained, just as they were when I saw him in my viewing. It's Nils.

I look over to the right, trying to see where he's standing, but my view is blocked by a partition of shelves stacked with metal helmets, so I return my gaze to the mirror. My heart flares with excitement at finding my quarry, but the feeling dissipates almost immediately. Nils's reflection exudes a sense of weary desperation, his cheeks gaunt, his shoulders stooped with the weight of unknown horrors. Scarlett got to him first. And what the hell has she done to him?

"Nils," she hisses urgently, "I don't know how much time we have, but you need to listen to me. You were going to fail your mission in Macau. I tried to give you another chance, but something went wrong. It wasn't supposed to happen. I need to undo what I did. I need your watch so I can put it back to how it was and get you home to Oslo."

"You must think me very naive." A shadow passes over his face, and he flickers, then his material presence settles again. "What do you want from me?"

"I was in Macau to help you escape, as you well know, but we don't have time to waste on pointless conversation. Give me your watch."

He shakes his head. "Even if I chose to trust you, it wouldn't matter. Thanks to you, I have not fully manifested here in Paris, and nor, therefore, has my watch. How did you think we were going to do this?" His face darkens. "Shall I drag you back with me?"

He takes a step closer to her, and she blanches. "I'm going to find a way to fix it," she says. She thinks for a second. "If I turn and look at you now, where will you go?"

"Back to the void, an eternal space with no limits, no form, no sensory inputs other than sight." The strain in his voice is evident and his jaw clenches as he tries to control his panic. "I lose all track of time and space. I don't know how long I spend there each time. It could be seconds or hours or centuries."

"You said this was your fourth landing here in the opera house?"

Nils nods.

"So when you come back here each time, what determines where you will land? Do you know?"

Nils laughs, but it sounds like the screeching of brakes. "Oh yes, I know! I find myself before a spinning wheel of doorways. Each one leads into a part of the opera house at a certain point of this mission. I have tried four of them, passed through the doorways and half landed. Each time I have been seen by someone and immediately returned into the void. There is only one doorway remaining. The others are now impassable."

"Where will the final doorway put you?" Scarlett asks. "Tell me, and when you come through, I will be there. I will bring you fully into being, and I will get you home."

I'm distracted by a tapping sound coming from the corridor. It's getting louder. I turn carefully toward the door and through the gap I see Madame Delacroix approaching, leaning heavily on her stick, her cheeks flushed and her lips pursed. Damn. As I turn back to the mirror, my shoulder inadvertently knocks against one of the jackets, causing it to jut out from the rack. The sudden movement attracts Nils's attention and he glances over toward me. The space where the jacket was reveals my hiding place and leaves a direct line of view from me to him, and for a split second our eyes meet in the mirror.

Nils stiffens, grimaces for an instant, and disappears.

Scarlett spins on her heels and sees Madame Delacroix. The elderly spinster has surprised us all.

"What in heaven's name do you think you are doing, young lady?" she says haughtily. "This is the opera's costume store. It is private property. I do not recognize you, and I wish to know your business. Answer me!"

Scarlett quickly scans the room, then pushes roughly past Madame Delacroix and runs down the corridor.

"Stop! Stop this instant!" the old lady commands, but the sound of Scarlett's footsteps fades, and we hear distant cries as she passes back through the costume workshop.

"Oh dear. Oh my goodness me," Madame Delacroix says, her voice wavering, and she leans heavily on her stick.

I clamber my way out through the military uniforms and hope that my sudden appearance doesn't cause her heart to give up. "Madame, can I help you? Are you all right?"

"Oh!" She presses the back of a hand to her forehead. "What in the name of the good Lord were you doing hiding there in the shadows, Monsieur Taylor?" she admonishes. "And who was that girl?"

"I . . . I don't know who she is." With the lie, my eyes flicker away from hers for a second, and she spots it.

She stamps her cane on the ground. "Do not take me for a fool, young man! Initially, I thought that she was talking to herself, but then I saw him. I saw that man standing behind her. He was there for an instant, but the moment our eyes met, he simply disappeared. A trick of the light perhaps, just a trick of the light." She shakes her head in disbelief. "You saw him?" she asks gruffly. It's not so much a question as a demand for acknowledgment.

Briefly, I toy with the idea of denying it, but this woman is sharp as a pin, and I can feel she's involved in Philippe's story—although I don't yet know how—so perhaps she's important to Nils's too. "Yes," I admit. "I saw him too."

"But where is he now? People do not disappear into thin air."

"I don't know," I say truthfully. "He was definitely here, sort of, but now he isn't." I cast my eyes around the room and shrug helplessly.

"Don't talk in riddles, young man!" Delacroix says, stamping her cane again. "You're talking as though he was a ghost, but ghosts are not real." She looks up toward the window and the beams of light streaming down into the store. "Ghosts are not real . . ." she says less certainly. She takes a few steps toward the mirror, peering deeply into it as though searching for Nils, then stands upright again. "I may be a woman of a certain age, but I am of good health and sound mind, and I know what I saw. He was very striking. You know, at first, I thought it was the ghost of my father, come to fetch me. I was a young woman when he died, and I always thought if I ever saw him again, it would be a comfort . . . But no. I felt judged."

"Try not to worry, Madame Delacroix," I say, trying my best to reassure her. "I really don't think that man was your father."

She peers at me through a pair of lorgnettes she pulls from her coat. "If you are so convinced that that man was not my father, then who, I pray, do you think it was?" She glares, daring me not to tell her the truth.

I hesitate, not entirely sure quite where to start.

She lowers the eyepiece. "I implore you to be honest with me, monsieur, because I am now of two minds. I am both a happy skeptic and"—she points at the mirror—"a reluctant believer. If you can enlighten me, I should be most grateful."

"Why did you think it might be your father?" I ask, trying to buy some time. "Do you have unfinished business with him? You said you felt judged . . ."

She wipes her nose neatly with a handkerchief that she pulls from her sleeve, then tucks it away again. "Sometimes, wealth is a burden. A heavy weight to bear. I fear my father may have come to tell me that I have not yet done enough with the inheritance he left me. I do try, I suppose, but I could do more. I *must* do more."

There's a knock on the door, and a muscular, ruddy-faced man in a tight waistcoat, his sleeves pushed up to his elbows, sticks his head in. "Monsieur Taylor? Your assistant has requested that you join her in Monsieur Monier's office. Will you come this way?"

What does Gabrielle want now? "Would you excuse me, Madame Delacroix?" I say politely, silently thanking the burly bloke for saving me from a tricky conversation.

"Good day, monsieur," she says and wanders away, trancelike, toward the mirror.

The man walks quickly, and I almost have to jog to keep up with him at times. The seamstresses eye me with concern, whispering behind their hands and standing out of our way as I trail him back through the costume workshop.

When we get to the door of Monier's office, there's an even heftier fellow standing outside the room. He's the size of a pro wrestler, and he has his hands clasped behind his back, which only emphasizes the gargantuan width of his shoulders. Wordlessly, he turns to open the office door, grabs me by the collar, and all but flings me into the room. I stumble into a very solid wooden sideboard, but I stop myself from falling.

"Ah, Monsieur Taylor, thank you for joining us," croons Monier.

I grimace and rub my elbow where it banged against the chest. Gabrielle sits very upright and very still at the desk, and Monier stands behind it, rolling back and forth on the balls of his feet, his hands in his pockets. I notice a half-empty bottle of champagne on the desk and two glasses, one of which still holds a splash of drink.

"I had a message that Mademoiselle had requested my presence," I say, glancing at Gabrielle. Her face is unreadable.

Monier strokes his beard and studies me. "Your accent, sir," he says with a flicker of amusement. "I can't quite place it. Where did you say you're from?"

"A long way from here," I say. Then, remembering our cover story, "Boston."

"Fascinating. And yet you speak perfect French?"

"My mother was French, sir," I say, trying to sound convincing. "She brought me up bilingual."

"And Mademoiselle Green, your mother was French too?" Gabrielle opens her mouth to speak, but Monier holds up his hand to silence her, then walks over to a cumbersome machine on a sturdy table near the door. "Do you know what this is?" It's about the size of a standard microwave, and it looks like a cross between a piano and a steam-powered meat mincer. He glides his fingers softly over the keys, tapping his signet ring on the top of the device.

"No, sir," I reply.

"This, Monsieur Taylor, is a breakthrough. The cutting edge of modern technology. It allows me to send messages to people thousands of miles away in a matter of minutes, and to receive a response just a few minutes after that."

"It's a telegraph machine," Gabrielle says, with an air of resignation.

"Yes, it is. And I have been making excellent use of it today." He pulls a long strip of paper from one of his desk drawers. "This is a length of ticker tape, a message from an old friend of mine. You'll know him, of course— Mr. Edwin Bacon?"

"Of course," Gabrielle shoots back without hesitation. "He just joined us at the paper earlier this year. How is he doing?" She has not one hair out of place. I have to admire her professionalism and the extent of her research, not to mention her memory.

"He is quite well," Monier says, "but a trifle confused. I asked him to confirm that you work at the paper, Monsieur Taylor, and he was able to confirm that Mr. Charles Taylor is indeed the Globe's acting business manager."

"I'm glad to hear he could put your mind at rest," I say.

"Not exactly," Monier continues. "He also explained that Mr. Taylor was standing next to him as he sent this message. I am, as you know, a man of the arts, not the sciences, but even I know that it is not possible to be in two places at the same time." Actually, it is, but now is not the time to argue. "You, sir, are an imposter! And you, mademoiselle—whoever you are—you're nothing but a hornswoggler."

Neither Gabrielle nor I look at the other, as this would be tantamount to admitting our guilt. I couldn't feel more like I was back at school, being accused of some prankish misdemeanor.

Gabrielle tries again. "Dominic, I can assure you, nothing is amiss. We are genuinely interested in finding out more about your opera company. What you've achieved here is nothing short of spectacular, and we want our readers to know about it."

Monier seems conflicted, preening himself at Gabrielle's words, and yet visibly deflated too. "And to think, I was quite taken in by you." He sighs and downs the rest of his champagne, turning to me. "Perhaps you could tell me the truth—Monsieur Bridgeman, is it?" He sniggers at the flash of alarm that crosses my face. "Oh yes, I know your name. I was suspicious from the start, but backstage when I found you doing whatever it is you were doing, your assistant here called you 'Bridgeman.'"

Gabrielle seems annoyed and shakes her head. "Wouldn't have happened if I'd been working alone," she mutters.

"And what line of work would that be, as it's most certainly not journalism?"

Gabrielle doesn't reply.

"I don't know what your game is, but I'm going to make a success of this place, a name for myself on the international opera scene, and the likes of you two are not going to stand in my way." He reaches into his desk and pulls out a small revolver with a mother-of-pearl grip. Hand trembling, he points it at me, then at Gabrielle, then back to me again. He looks terrified, and I'm worried he's going to kill one of us accidentally.

"Does that gun have a safety?" I ask, channeling every movie I've ever seen.

Monier ignores me. "You leave me no option but to call for the police." Keeping the gun trained on us, he sidles around the edge of the room, then knocks on the door. "Pichon? It's me. Let me out."

Pichon, the wrestler-type, unlocks the door, and Monier hands him the gun. "Keep a close eye on these two. I'm going to fetch the police. If they try to escape, do not hesitate to use maximum force."

"Understood," grunts the brute.

Monier glares at the two of us. "Lock them in," he says. The door slams shut, and I hear the rough metallic sound of the key turning in the lock.

Gabrielle jumps up. "Jesus, that was close."

"I saw Nils and Scarlett," I tell her quickly. "She was in the costume store, and he appeared to her in the mirror."

"Cool. You can fill me in when we get back." She checks her watch. "We have four minutes. Let's see what we can find." She begins examining the books and journals in a bookcase next to the desk.

"What if Monier gets back and we disappear in front of him?"

"That's the least of our worries." She finishes searching the bookshelves and rummages urgently through the contents of Monier's in tray.

"What are you trying to find?"

"A clue, a motive—anything that's not completely aboveboard."

"Are you thinking arson?"

"Maybe." She sifts through a sheaf of papers. "Hey, check these out. A ton of unpaid invoices from"—she rifles through the pages—"all from the last couple of months. Man. You can see why they're putting so much effort into drumming up business for *Le Prophète*."

I pull a crumpled piece of cream paper from the floor and smooth it out. It's inscribed with blue ink. "This is a final demand letter from debt collectors, addressed personally to Monier, for twenty thousand francs."

Gabrielle whistles. "That's a ton of cash in the 1870s. What's the date?"

"Yesterday. I guess he's been borrowing money to keep the opera house afloat."

"Never throw good money after bad, that's what my grandpa taught me. Look through the rest of those, will you?" She indicates a stack of papers on Monier's desk. I leaf through them rapidly, mostly letters of appreciation for *Le Prophète* from the patrons of the opera, plus a few solicitations from singers and musicians hoping to be invited to the next talent-scouting event.

Gabrielle makes a beeline for an oil painting of a bucolic summer country scene, deep-blue skies stretched above scorched meadows, cows grazing lazily. Lifting it off the wall, she reveals an iron door. "And there she is," she says smugly. "Now all we need to do is find the key. Give me a hand."

I start pulling drawers out of the bureau, trying to find wherever Monier might have hidden the key to the safe.

"Bridgeman! We don't have time for that. Use your intuition." She crouches low to the ground, places her hands on the wooden floorboards, and closes her eyes. Without thinking, I do the same. I listen to the room, trying to coax it into revealing the hiding place of the key, and in my mind's eye a green-and-gold vase appears, spinning softly. Opening my eyes, I spot the vase on the side table to the right of the desk. In two strides I've crossed the room and tipped the vase onto its side. Against my hand, I feel the reassuring weight of an iron key land in the palm of my hand. Bingo.

"Good work. Throw it over," Gabrielle says. "We're running out of time."

I hand her the key and she hurriedly unlocks the safe. "More papers!" she says. "Here." She passes me half the pile, and we both flick rapidly through them.

"Court summons for Monsieur Monier, for failure to pay the gas company," I say.

"Final payment request from the company who redecorated the foyer," Gabrielle reads aloud.

Every document is a demand for payment or a threat of legal action.

"Monier's in the shit right up to his neck," she says.

"Are you thinking what I'm thinking? That the fire was an insurance scam?"

"Could be. He could have insured the opera house for an inflated sum, started the fire, cleared his debts . . . and blamed the Phantom?" There's a buzz, and Gabrielle shoves her papers back into the safe. "We're out of time. We leave in fifteen seconds."

A hint of brain freeze hits me. Gabrielle fixes me with a wide grin. It's a little disconcerting. I can see the blood rushing beneath her pale skin. As we leave 1873, I wonder what Dominic Monier will think when he returns with the police and finds his locked office empty.

23

We arrive back at my loft. It's dark outside, and I forgot to leave a lamp on before we traveled, so I cautiously feel my way to the wall and switch on the lights, blinking a few times as my eyes adjust. The rest of me is adjusting more quickly to this post-travel phase—I guess I'm getting used to it—and I feel my shoulder blades settle as I begin to relax. The feeling doesn't last, though. Wordlessly, Gabrielle places her watch on the wooden floor and fires up ICARUS. With the drama of the Paris opera reverberating in my head, and the dust of Monier's office still tickling my nostrils, the present swaps out for the future in an instant, and nausea and dizziness assail me as I scramble to adjust again.

Night becomes day. Gradually, my befuddled brain assembles yet another location. We're standing in the center of a huge oak-paneled study. Shafts of rich sunlight cut across us. Three of the walls are inset with tall paned windows flanked by bookshelves that stretch to the vaulted ceiling above.

Iris stands near a grand mahogany desk in the corner of the room, with Felix at her side. I hear distant birdsong and the pronounced bass tick of a large clock, and I note the familiar smell of antique furniture and leather. Today, the future feels positively retro.

Iris smiles. "Welcome back to you both."

"Where are we?" I ask.

"This is my study at Greystone House," Iris replies.

"She bagged this room before I had a chance," Felix says. "Now she's got one of the best views in the building."

Through the window I see an ornate walled garden framed by miles of tree canopy in a vast green landscape. Beyond that, huge expanses of water intersect rugged, rolling hills, and in the far distance I can just make out a hazy mountain range. No flying cars, no people in weird clothes, no extra sun in the sky. I'm surprised by how familiar it all appears. One of the hills in the distance doesn't look quite right, though, so assuming that it's a digital projection, I flick my eyes away and then quickly back to see if I can catch it in the middle of a refresh. The hill's still there, but it definitely looks a little glitchy.

"Is all of that real out there?" I ask, vaguely indicating outside, aware of the irony of the question.

Felix answers. "It is, but we're suppressing a few details. Don't want your head to blow a fuse just yet."

"Right."

The door to Iris's study opens, and an elderly woman enters. She's dressed in traditional Japanese clothing but with a modern twist, comfortable layers covered by a long silk kimono, printed with pale flowers of blue and pink and held in place with a grass-green obi pulled around her waist. She's small in stature and moves gracefully through the shafts of sunlight toward the desk. Her thinning gray hair is pulled tightly against her head and held in place at the nape of her neck by a carved, mother-of-pearl hair clip, and her skin, though wrinkled and flecked with age spots, looks soft as cotton. She wears no makeup or jewelry. She stops a few feet from Felix, bows slightly, then turns to face the room.

"Welcome, Kyoko-san," he says. "Joseph, may I introduce Kyoko Kojima. Among the many vital roles she fulfills, Kyoko-san is our watchmaker."

Kyoko's dark eyes flit around the room and land on me. I blush, feeling weirdly exposed. Her face betrays nothing. She bows formally. "It is good to see you all. Joseph-san, it is a pleasure to meet you." Her Japanese accent is strong, and even though I have no idea what invisible processing my silver pea implant might be doing, I can tell she's speaking English.

Iris leans back against her desk and folds her arms. "Gabrielle, would you like to kick things off? How did you get on with your mission?"

Gabrielle updates the ever-growing team on the details. She runs through the highlights: our opera house tour, meeting Philippe, the "ghost" that is nothing but a crowd-pulling marketing stunt, and our altercation with the manager. "Basically, it was business as usual. It'll all come together on the final jump for sure." She turns to me. "Do you want to fill them in on what you saw?"

I tell them everything I can remember. When I finish, Felix turns to Kyoko, eyes narrowed in thought. "Fascinating, isn't it? Direct observation sends Nils back into the void."

Kyoko nods gravely. "Reverse polarity of the observer effect," she states. "Unusual."

Iris says, "So Nils has only one more chance to land in the change event?"

"I think so," I tell her. "Scarlett and Nils were interrupted before I could find out where the final doorway might lead, and he disappeared. I guess he slipped back into the void."

"It's ridiculous," Gabrielle says impatiently. "The last time we talked, Felix, you said we might need to ground Nils in 1873 before dragging him home, but now it seems that we can't even look at him. How the hell are we supposed to drag a missing time traveler into reality if we can't see him, let alone touch him?"

Everyone regards Kyoko expectantly. She has her hands clasped at her chest, her head bowed, chin resting on the tips of her fingers. For a few seconds, she is motionless, and I instinctively hold my breath. Then, she looks up, and the faintest of smiles crosses her thin lips.

"Please tell me you have a plan," Gabrielle says, sounding tired.

Kyoko tilts her head slightly. "You are aware of triterbium lanterns?"

Gabrielle curls her lip. "That's old tech." Kyoko remains silent. Gabrielle continues, "You guys used to use them like a catcher's mitt, didn't you, before ICARUS? To grab hold of travelers for a chat when they were on their way home from a mission?"

"The lanterns served a purpose, and they might again," Kyoko replies. "Using the data from both sightings, we may be able to modify a lantern in order to transmit an inverse observation wave, one that could ground Nils in 1873."

"Cool, and then I drag him home, right?" Gabrielle suggests.

"No," Felix says. "We can't risk further destabilization. Nils must travel back to 1920 Oslo on his own, exactly as he should have done from Macau. That means we need to update his watch, and we need to do it physically, in the field. It's not possible to do it remotely."

"Update his watch in Paris?" Gabrielle says, pointedly. "Is that even possible?"

Felix glances at Kyoko. "We're working on the idea of a localized patch that you can apply rapidly."

"Right," Gabrielle says, "so we fire the lantern to ground him in Paris, then we update his watch, and then he travels home?"

"That's the plan," Felix says.

I'm struggling to understand just how this is going to work, and I'm beginning to feel responsible for Nils's safe return. "That all sounds great and everything," I say, "but we don't know where Nils's final doorway leads. I mean, how do we know if the doorway he steps through will sync up with our next jump?"

"We don't," Kyoko says.

"We're working on assumptions," Felix says, "but Nils is only in 1873 because he was drawn there, attracted by the energy of the live Paris mission. We *have* to presume that if he's going to come through that doorway, the timing will line up with the change event."

Kyoko remains impassive.

"Do you have the data on our next jump yet?" Gabrielle asks.

"Yep," Felix says. "We're still running the numbers, but I reckon the next jump will be the final one, and you'll be landing on the night of the fire again."

"And how long before we leave?"

"Four days, give or take. I can confirm later."

"All right." Gabrielle turns to me. "In that case, presuming you're going to join me, it sounds like we have Philippe *and* Nils to save . . . at the same time."

"Good job there will be two of us then," I say, realizing that I'm committing myself.

"One and a half at best," Gabrielle retorts. She turns to Kyoko. "I know you'll tell me how it is, Kyoko-san. Is this going to work?"

Kyoko looks at Gabrielle, her expression cool. "I have some confidence that the lantern will operate correctly. The patch, I am less certain of. It's unproven. Either way, this will be very difficult, although the technology is unlikely to be the failure point. Overall, I would say the chance of success is extremely low."

Felix shakes his head. "I know you're just saying things as you see them, Kyoko-san, which is what we want you to do, but I think it's all going to be fine."

Gabrielle laughs, exuding pure sarcasm. "Ha! Well, on that note, I'm definitely in! What could possibly go wrong?"

Iris leans back on her desk and studies me. "Are you sure you're happy to go on the final jump, Joseph?"

"I want to be sure Nils gets home," I say. "Gabrielle has her work cut out for her with the main mission, and she needs my help."

We talk about the plan a little more, but it's clear that despite Felix's positive words, it's going to be a long shot. It will ultimately be down to Gabrielle and me, but Felix and Kyoko have some midnight oil to burn first. We say our goodbyes, and our surroundings return to the wonderful and familiar normality of my loft. For a while I struggled to think of this as my home, but as a deep wave of relief washes through me, my heart takes another step toward loving the place.

Gabrielle yawns and stretches. "I need to get some fresh air," she says. "What's the weather doing?" She walks to the glass bifold doors and peers out onto the deck. "Jesus, Bridgeman!" she cries. "You've got a freakin' Jacuzzi out there."

"Yeah, I have. I kind of inherited it."

She laughs. "There's no point feeling guilty." Pulling bows from her hair, she slides the door open. "Come on, it's time for a dip."

I follow her outside, and without asking, she pulls back the Jacuzzi cover and then slips out of her dress. I can imagine her at a massive house party, crowd-surfing in a bikini over hundreds of people.

"Er, I'm not sure this is a good idea," I say, looking everywhere but at Gabrielle.

She takes a step toward me. "Being in The Continuum isn't like being in the military. We're allowed to have some fun, you know?"

I swallow and face her. Not counting my run-in with Chloe (one of Other Joe's booty calls), it's been much longer than I care to remember since I've been this close to a woman in underwear. Black frilly underwear with red tassels in key locations. At best, I find her mildly attractive in flattering light, and her steel-wool personality cancels even that out, but it's impossible not to notice how toned she is.

She grins, hops up onto the side of the Jacuzzi, and slides in. She presses buttons until the water jets and lights burst into action, then leans back against the side of the tub and regards me, her face reflected in blue LEDs. "Come on, Bridgeman, what are you afraid of?"

Sharks cross my mind. Yes, even in a Jacuzzi. What if Alexia turns up and finds me having a reluctant but relaxed dip with Gabrielle, both of us in our underpants? But let's be honest, that's not happening. I'm simply out of practice when it comes to spontaneous fun.

I strip to my boxer shorts and join her.

The water is wonderfully warm. The bubbles bounce and jostle my tired muscles. I close my eyes and sink low in the water.

"*See?*" Gabrielle drawls, annoyingly. "This is nice, isn't it?"

"Yeah," I admit. "It's not bad." And it isn't. It's good to have some company, and for a moment I forget that I just agreed to join the final jump to Paris, that Gabrielle and I might end up fighting for our lives inside a burning opera house.

When she speaks again, I can hear that she's nearer. "So the old you, the version before you saved your sister—you didn't have much money, then?"

I open one eye and change the subject. "How about you tell me what happened when you chased after the Phantom?"

She blinks a few times. "I followed him—I think it was a guy, anyway—and cornered him in one of the corridors. He dropped a smoke bomb or something and vanished into thin air, like a ninja. Then, he appeared again at the other end of the corridor."

"There must be two of them," I say. "I saw a film once about a pair of identical twins who were both magicians. They could pull off some unbelievable tricks because no one knew there were two of them, not even the wife."

"Yep, could be. Either way, it's a distraction, and good for business too. Although considering Monier's finances, it could all have come a bit late."

"What happened to him after the fire?" I ask her. "Do you know?"

"He went bankrupt, and there are no records of him after that, not even a date of death."

It's hard to imagine. He was so determined to make a name for himself, came across as one of those people who oozes confidence and seems destined for success. That said, I'm living proof that a major life-changing event can destroy your foundations and beliefs, and derail your potential forever. Philippe suffered physical wounds, but there are other ways to destroy a life.

"Tell me about Nils," I say. "Did you know him before he went missing?"

"Our paths crossed a few times. He's a good guy, completed a ton of successful missions. He has a family—a wife and four kids." We're both quiet for a minute. I send up a silent promise to Nils, whenever and wherever he is, to do what I can to get him home to them.

"And how about you?" I ask. "How long have you been a part of all this?"

"Feels like forever sometimes. I guess it's been ten years or so. My tethered mission was in Shanghai, helping some dude I knew see the error of his ways. I was totally freaked out by the traveling initially, but then I got hooked on the buzz of those jumps, determined to put things right. Know what I mean?"

"Yes, I think so."

She drifts off for a few seconds, her expression growing dark. I wait, and eventually, she continues. "After that, I lost my way. I was in a bad place when Bill found me, pretty angry. But he showed me what I could do with my gift, and explained the potential . . . I could see the opportunities to do good and, I mean, what the hell else was I going to do? Anyway, I haven't looked back since."

I move my arms slowly through the warm, soothing water. "You said *tethered jump*. What does that mean?"

"I was hoping teacher could have a night off." She squeezes her hands together, pumping jets of water in my direction.

I fire back. "Sorry. I'm being an askhole."

She laughs. "An *askhole*?"

"I can't take the credit," I tell her. "That's one of Vinny's sayings."

"Vinny. He's the guy who helped you with Romano?"

"Yeah, he's my best friend. Anyway, tethered jumps?"

"Your first jump is always connected to your own timeline. It's like the training wheels are still on. We call it *tethered*."

I raise my eyebrows in recognition. "Makes sense. I thought of it like an elastic band, because the farther back I went, the less time I spent in the past."

"Yeah, something like that. Once you complete that first mission, you're untethered, no longer a time-travel virgin. Your cherry is well and truly popped. You have the potential to go farther, travel on other timelines. You're basically free, but it's ironic really, 'cause the chances of ever traveling again are slim, when you think about it."

"How do you mean?"

She cocks an eyebrow. "Do you honestly think you would have come across a focus object all by yourself? Just randomly stumbled upon one on a shopping trip?" She laughs. "No, you wouldn't. You would probably have lived your life with a constant sense that you weren't doing what you were born to do."

"Like most people then."

She smirks. "It's where The Continuum comes in, connecting travelers to missions via focus objects."

"Iris compared The Continuum to an immune system."

"Yeah, missions are time's way of healing itself where it can, and people like us, we're the antibodies. But to be effective, we need to know what to do, what to focus on. That's where Felix comes in. Without him, none of this would have happened."

"What's the story with him?" I ask.

She considers this, her expression playful. "He wasn't what you were expecting, huh? The surfer look, I mean."

"Not exactly, no."

"All the founders have played a part, but without Felix, there would be no Continuum. Without Downstream, all the travelers in the world would just be wasted talent, fishing alone in the dark. He saw it all, joined the dots, and got us organized."

"Does he have a family?"

"Ha! No, he's married to Downstream. That system is his one true love. Don't get me wrong, he's a cool guy, smart and everything. When I found out that he basically discovered time travelers, change events, and focus objects by analyzing data, I was blown away. And you know, he scrubs up OK when he bothers to put on proper clothes. When I first joined The Continuum, I actually considered jumping him, but I'm not really cut out for long-distance relationships, and anyway, turns out he's completely emotionally unavailable."

We sit in silence for a while, my mind connecting dots, until I notice my fingers are like prunes. I get out to find us some towels, and we dry off. I put on a robe and Gabrielle gets dressed into her familiar ripped jeans, thick shirt, leather jacket, and boots—all black, of course.

"Listen," Gabrielle says. "Before we head back to Paris again . . . I know you've seen her in your viewings, but Scarlett is manipulative. She's good at getting people to believe what she wants them to believe. Bottom line, she's squandering her gift and putting Nils's life in danger. You can't trust anything she says. If we see her, we have to stop her. Don't wimp out on me."

"I won't," I assure her.

"Good. Now, get some sleep. You look tired."

"I am. Aren't you?"

"Bushed," she admits. "Much like your sideburns."

"Man, I keep forgetting those!" I pull them from my face, and they reconfigure themselves into soft, slug-like strips, ready for the next trip.

She packs her suitcase quickly, then carries it across the loft to the stairs, where she puts it down again. "We have a few days. Call me if you need to, but we'll have a full planning session with the team before we head off."

I look shocked and shake my head.

"What?" she says, folding her arms and kicking out a hip.

"It's just . . . that was helpful and inclusive. I'm not used to it."

She winces. "I know you're going to ask me a ton of annoying questions, I'm just trying to beat you to it." She grabs her suitcase and heads down the stairs. Just before she drops out of sight, she turns back. "Hey, Bridgeman?"

"Yeah?"

"For a beginner, with very little natural talent . . . you did OK." Her brow narrows, and she flashes me her best LA grin and shouts, "Later, askhole!"

24

I'm interrupted from a deep, dreamless, post-travel slumber by the incessant chirping of my mobile phone. Grumpily, I reach over to check the time and see that it's 10 a.m., which I begrudgingly admit is a reasonable time to be calling someone.

"Hi, Sue," I say, picking up. I'm more of a screener, usually. I tend to wait and see if the person calling leaves me a message and then listen to it, to see if I'm inclined to call them back. Sue is an extension of Amy in my mind, though, and when I see her name, I immediately feel a twinge of guilt that I haven't spoken to my sister enough recently. "Is everything OK?"

"If you can call two sick under-tens, a grumpy husband, and a dog with diarrhea 'OK,' then yes, everything's fine. I'm calling about Amy, though."

My guilt turns up a notch. "What's up? Is she all right?"

"She called me at three o'clock this morning and left me a message. Luckily, I had the phone on silent, so it didn't wake me up, although when I listened to her message this morning, I thought maybe it would've been better if I had answered . . . She sounded manic."

"Oh God, I feel terrible, Sue. I've hardly spoken to her since the quiz. And you told me to keep in touch . . ."

"Keep your hair on. Panicking isn't going to help," Sue says, with the calm assurance of a parent who's experienced one too many attacks of norovirus. "She wasn't in danger or anything. She sounded quite high, to be honest, but she was rattling on about how brilliant everything was and about a picture she'd been painting. I tried calling her back this morning, but she didn't answer. I was wondering if you could try and track her down—go and see her? I know you have a job and everything, but I was just thinking we should check on her . . . I'd do it myself, but I've got both kids off school with hacking coughs." On cue, I hear a snotty wail in the background, and then Sue's muffled voice offering comfort.

"Of course, I'll go over now," I say. "Molly can watch the shop." I catch myself thinking how often I say that sentence and make a mental note to give Molly a pay raise.

"You might want to try her at the flat first," Sue suggests. "Miles told me she's been getting a bit flaky at work again recently."

After Sue hangs up, I try calling Amy, but I don't get an answer, so I head straight to her flat. She doesn't answer the doorbell, and I'm just turning to leave when I change my mind. I need to ask her why she called Sue and not me—I've checked, and she didn't leave me a message—but in the meantime, based on the last lot of paintings I saw, I decide to check out the new batch myself, to see if they offer me any further insights, either into Nils's fate or the state of Amy's mind.

I turn my key in the lock and push into the hallway, clearing more mail off the doormat. There's an unpleasant, musty smell from the kitchen, and when I get there, I understand why. The place is like a bomb site. Piles of dirty dishes are balanced on the side, empty soup cans and milk cartons stand on the draining board. Stained mugs and sticky teaspoons cluster around the kettle, alongside an empty blister pack of medication. There are a dozen empty wine bottles on the floor, and another half-empty bottle of Chardonnay in the fridge, along with an out-of-date block of tofu and a solitary lemon. Amy isn't the tidiest person in the world, but this is bad, even for her.

Feeling a little nervous about what else I might find, I go into the lounge. The sofa is strewn with pillows, a sleeping bag, and discarded items of clothing, but the rest of the room is cluttered with canvases, two large wooden easels, and paintings and drawings stuck onto every spare patch of wall. There's also a string hung from the wall going from one side of the room to the other, with a series of sketches hanging off it, attached by paper clips.

Last time I was here, all Amy's artwork was confined to the spare room, but she's been painting in here now too. There are jam jars filled with dirty water and soaking brushes, ice cream tubs packed with tubes of acrylic, and even splashes of paint up the walls. It appears as though she's used the coffee table as an artist's palette, with paint in patches all over the surface: vibrant oranges and pinks, cool blues and greens, and deep reds, browns, and purples.

Moving a sweater and a pair of pink-and-white-striped pajamas, I slump down on the sofa, trying to take it all in. It reminds me of a documentary I watched about a manga artist who slept with his paints in bed, in case he was struck by inspiration in the middle of the night. I scan the room more slowly, looking at Amy's artwork and trying to make sense of it all. Most of the sketches on the walls are pretty abstract, some in pencil and others in black pen or another single color. Many of them are impossible to classify, just squiggles and lines, although a few appear to show a clockface, both hands high up near the 12. But the ones that Amy's pinned up on the string are more intriguing. The way she's displayed them, I'd say she was trying to pull a narrative out of what she was drawing, attempting to find a thread to link them, perhaps. Many depict at least one square or rectangle, sometimes more, and some also show figures running through the frame. If you created a flipbook from these, I don't think you'd get a coherent animation, but working from left to right, there's a definite impression of movement. I'm trying not to be too literal in my interpretation, but if Amy's putting these images down in such vivid colors and strong forms, then I imagine she's getting strong visions too.

I spot the painting of the opera house in flames, but Amy has made some changes since I was here last. The additions are not improvements; they are crude and hurried. Basically, she's ruined it. When she first showed me this painting, Philippe was standing outside. He's since been removed, using a thin layer of black paint, but underneath I can discern the outlines of two more people, three figures in total. It's as though Amy can't decide how many people should be in the doorway. She's also added the couple on the rooftop, being rescued by firemen—although if I hadn't been there on that night, I'm not sure I would know what I was looking at. Like the other alteration, this addition appears to be hurried. It's evident from the lack of detail and effort that Amy was frustrated, and the painting has an abandoned feel. I remember her describing her visions like this: sometimes she sees future events, but she feels that time hasn't yet made up its mind. I tilt the canvas this way and that, checking for hidden words or forms beneath the top layer of paint, but all I can sense is my sister's frustration as she tries to decode the images in her mind.

The door to the spare room is closed. It's normally ajar, providing a glimpse of Amy's extraneous belongings and older paintings. Curiosity gets the better of me. Gingerly, I turn the handle, uncertain what I might find. The smell of fresh paint is overpowering. Amy has cleared the room and piled canvases against the right wall. The entire left wall, which must be around nine feet tall and twelve feet across, has been adorned with a mystical, psychedelic painting that bleeds from floor to ceiling.

What the hell?

The expressive style is unlike any of Amy's other paintings. For this one, she's used a radiant palette of luminous colors, along with other media like layers of paper and fabric, which she's woven through the contrasting shapes. Toward the top left is a scarred hand, reaching out like Michelangelo's hand of God, and on the right-hand side is a majestic bird of prey, its wings held close against its body, its head turned haughtily toward the hand that reaches for it.

The aesthetic reminds me of a 1970s concept album, a kaleidoscope of strange geometric shapes, organic growths, and whorls, the kind of artwork the Flaming Lips might put out now. It's mad, but it's also genius, a dramatic and intense creation. I know Amy doesn't do any of this for material gain, and I would never suggest it to her, but I reckon she could sell paintings like this for thousands apiece.

I have no idea what any of this means, but given the state of the place, it's a bloody good thing Amy owns the flat. Wondering if I'm missing something, I reach out and touch the eagle, and a squidge of vivid scarlet smears across my finger. The thicker paint is still wet.

Amy's voice behind me sends my heart rate soaring. "What are you doing here?" she asks, her voice calm and oddly lackluster.

I turn, and I'm shocked again by her appearance. I was expecting her to be bouncing off the walls based on what Sue told me, but Amy seems smaller than usual. Her eye sockets appear sunken, she's hunched over, and she looks bone tired.

"I was worried about you," I tell her. "Sue called me, said you rang her in the middle of the night, all excited about your paintings."

Amy's expression is blank. "Did I? God, I don't remember that." She wipes a hand over her eyes. In her other hand is a paper bag from a pharmacy. She notices me trying to read the printed label. "Just something to take the edge off. It was a busy night, though." She stands next to me and surveys the wall, studying the image as though searching for answers. "I painted this one last night. What do you think?"

"About you painting the walls or the subject matter?"

She produces a thin smile. "Unlike Banksy, I don't think I'm adding value to my flat by using the walls, but for some reason, a canvas just wasn't enough. This one needed to be big. This is important, Joe."

"It's stunning," I tell her honestly, "but what does it mean?"

"I don't know, but it's connected to your Paris mission."

"In what way?"

"It's just . . . when I was painting this, I felt like I'd discovered a secret, and I knew you needed to see it. This—in fact, everything I've been painting—it's all about you." Her tone has very little emotion, and I wonder if the pills are doing more than just taking the edge off.

We stand in silence and study the painting, the inspired use of color, the hand and the bird almost touching. There's a real sense of latent energy between them, as though they're about to connect and complete a circuit.

"Tea?" Amy offers. I follow her into the kitchen, and she puts the kettle on. "I'm sorry about the mess," she says.

"Don't worry about it," I tell her, "we've got two clean mugs for tea. That's all we need."

"Thanks, Joe." Amy slumps down into one of the kitchen chairs and silently stares at her hands, picking spots of paint off them as I prepare our drinks.

"I was in the living room earlier, noticed you changed the opera house painting."

She curls her lip slowly, as though it's an effort. "Oh, yeah. I wouldn't read too much into that. Each time I see it, it's different. I just can't decide how many people are in the entrance. I've stopped trying now." She tails off, as though she's lost her train of thought, but then brightens a little. "I've finished the other one, though."

"Other one?"

"Yeah, I'm really pleased with it now. Come and see." I follow her into the living room. She grabs a large canvas and places it onto an easel. The painting is the semiabstract piece she showed me the last time I was here. It still features a melting watch and a sea of shining silver, but Amy has been busy, and unlike the opera house painting, her alterations have been applied with care and patience. In fact, they make the previous iteration feel positively unfinished. This version is brilliant, an accomplished piece of art, but also rather disconcerting. As I soak in the new details, I feel a ripple of gooseflesh pass over my neck and shoulders. Amy has added angry clouds to the skyline, and the metallic, angular lighthouse has been replaced by an ominous black tower. Weirdly devoid of detail, this sinister obelisk looms over the entire scene, a new and dominating focal point.

Amy sighs. "It's a bit weird, but I'm happy with it now. What do you think?"

"It's unsettling, but it's brilliant." I pause, unsure how to say what's on my mind. "Just wondering though, why did you change the lighthouse into that black tower thing?"

Amy moves to the side of the painting and studies it, as though seeing it for the first time. "I got it wrong before. This is right now. This is what it's supposed to look like."

Emblazoned at the top of the tower is a blood-red ball, glowing with heat like a setting sun. Its reflected warmth cuts a thousand tiny shapes over the watch and the silver sea.

"I have to be honest, it looks pretty scary," I say, feeling uneasy.

"I can see why you might think that, but when I saw it in my mind I felt an undeniable sense that it's a guiding force."

I point to the tower. "What is it?"

"I don't know exactly, but it's helpful. If you see this, then trust it; I think its job is to show you the way home."

I promise her I will, even though what she's describing sounds more like a lighthouse than this black monolith. I stare at the searing red sun, and it feels like a watchful eye, one that sees everything and doesn't feel particularly friendly. Amy is trying to help me, but how can such a dark and disturbing painting show me the way home? And how does this picture, or the trippy madness of the painting that fills the entire wall of her spare room, connect with my trips to Paris?

Amy leans back against the wall, picking a bit of dried paint from under one of her fingernails. "I'm glad you came over, but I'm sorry everything's in such a state. I don't want you to worry about me."

"That's not really an option."

She smiles. "I wanted to ask your forgiveness, Joe. I've been thinking, I was pretty short with you after Dad's party, and it was unnecessary. I could've been kinder . . . should've been."

"That's OK, there's nothing to forgive," I reassure her. "You'd had a really crappy day."

"I forgive you for all of this as well, my painting and visions. I know none of it's your fault, that you're just helping people, and I love you for that." And then, without skipping a beat, calmly and with absolute certainty, she adds, "I also wanted you to know that I'm going to be traveling again soon."

"Why do you think that?" I ask, feeling a surge of panic, and in a rush, I understand why Amy's been so upset about my own time traveling. I want to hold her close and beg her not to go yet. I don't know if she's on her path to The Continuum, or if this is part of the "difficult patch" that Amy's letter and Iris talked about. I try to pull myself together. "You said the other day that the visions weren't strong enough. And all the paintings you've done, you said they're connected with me, so why do you think you're going to start time traveling again?"

"Things are changing and soon, and it won't be up to me anymore. It's like the seasons, or the moon waxing and waning. There are periods of my life when I've traveled, and others when I haven't. The time is coming to travel again. It's natural. Fighting it would be futile, like trying to hold back the tide."

She wraps her arms around me, and I'm overwhelmed by the fragility of her body. I know that telling her not to travel is pointless, just as her asking me not to help The Continuum wouldn't change anything. Some things are inevitable, it seems, and in this moment I understand that Amy and I are connected by something bigger than ourselves—we always have been—and wherever it is that we're headed, we'll go there together.

25

Next day, I'm feeling good. Amy and I have cleared the air a bit, and she was relieved to share her paintings with me. I can't forget that I'm going back to Paris again soon, that this is the calm before the storm, but I have to try to find a way to live between jumps, and Bridgeman Antiques is a godsend. It keeps me busy, keeps my mind occupied, and stops me from worrying about things I just can't change. The morning flies by in the shop. We have a steady stream of customers, but Molly deals with them, leaving me to check through the boxes of old stock and sort through what I want to let go of.

Around midday, I feel the draw of the Daily Grind. My coffee machine might make the best latte in town, but occasionally I like to have someone else prepare it for me, sample a different bean, and do a bit of people watching. Not insignificantly, the Grinders also bake the best cinnamon buns in Cheltenham: fat, spicy, and buttery, with just a hint of crunch around the base. I tell Molly where I'm headed, and soon I'm at the counter of the Daily Grind, clutching a paper bag bearing two cinnamon buns and watching the slick barista pour me a three-shot latte. I love this place. It's how I would have done a coffee shop if my life had taken a different turn. There's a lot of natural wood, the lighting is bright but relaxing, and they usually play great music. Today, it's Michael Kiwanuka.

I'm just leaving the counter with my latte when I spot Alexia walking in. Pink-faced and slightly breathless, she scans the shop and clocks me immediately. I don't want to appear creepy, but I don't want to be rude either, so I give a hesitant shake of my bag of cinnamon buns. Instead of waving back, she heads straight for me.

"Hi, Joe," she says easily. I'm surprised by how warm she seems. "Molly said I'd find you here. Do you have a few minutes?"

Hang on, if she's been talking to Molly, does that mean she's actually been to Bridgeman Antiques? I make a show of checking my watch. "Yeah, I'm in no rush," I say nonchalantly. "Shall we sit?" I lead the way to a small table for two, away from the loudspeakers. Alexia's hair is down today, just brushing the shoulders of her navy jacket, and she's tucked her jeans into long brown leather boots. I still find her attractive—I can't help that—and I'm happy to be spending some time with her, but with relief, I notice that my desperate longing to resurrect what we once had has receded. "Can I get you anything?" I offer.

"No thanks, I had an early lunch." She sets her handbag on her lap and pushes her hair back behind her ears. "How are things with your sister, by the way? Were you able to catch up with her after your dad's party?"

I'm slightly taken aback by the question. I take a sip of coffee. "Yeah. You were right, it was definitely a good call to go after her. We talked. She's doing a lot better."

"I'm glad," Alexia says. "Even when things are difficult and people seem to not want contact, I've discovered it can be a good idea to lean in."

Her words remind me. "How's it going with your book, by the way?"

She looks at me oddly for a second, as though my question has caught her off guard. "I've sold quite a few copies, mostly to my clients. Colin and I are never going to hit the *New York Times* bestseller list, but it feels good to have captured everything we wanted to say. If it helps one person, it will have been worth doing."

"It will," I agree. "So. How can I help you?"

Alexia leans back in her seat. "My mum came into your shop the other day."

"Did she?" I scan back through recent customers in my mind. "I don't think she told me she was your mother. I would have remembered."

"She wouldn't have said anything. She doesn't know that we know each other."

"No, right, of course," I say hastily.

"She came to see you because you helped an acquaintance of hers a few weeks ago. He brought in an old Japanese puppet to show you, apparently." Immediately, I recall the man, tall and slim with a waxy complexion and an unusually slow way of talking. "You told him the puppet had been given to his great-grandmother as a wedding gift. When he got home, he researched what you'd said, and it turned out to be true. Do you remember him?"

"Yes, I do. He didn't realize it had been in the family that long."

"How do you do it?" she says, crossing her arms. "I so want to believe that what you do is a genuine gift, but I don't see how it's possible. Sorry, Joe, but it reminds me of those fake TV mediums who get their cronies to chat to audience members before the show so they can claim to pass on messages from the dead."

"I can see why you'd think that," I say, "but it's just something I can do. I don't know why. I don't use any tricks, I don't take advantage of people, and the last thing I'd ever want to do is make money out of it."

"You never mentioned it before," Alexia says, "you know, when we were seeing each other."

My heart gives a sad little flip, then I pull myself together. "I don't really like people knowing about it. A lot of the time they don't take it well because they don't understand it, and they think I'm making a fool of them. Sometimes they even get aggressive, so I have to be careful. But to be honest, I never used to sense much at all," I say, trying to smooth the connection between me and Other Joe. "It's been a lot stronger since I fell off my bike."

"OK," she says, her voice full of doubt. "So how does it work?"

"Officially, it's called psychometry," I say.

"Psychometry? I've never heard of it."

"It's a recognized phenomenon. Other people can do it too. I didn't invent it. The thinking is that objects can soak in and permanently record the emotions of their owners. I'm not sure how it actually works, scientifically speaking, but if you're able to sense these emotions like I can, then holding some objects gives you a feeling, a connection to their past."

"That's incredible," Alexia says. "But only some objects?"

"Yes, and only some of the time. There are no guarantees."

"Science doesn't trust things that aren't repeatable," she says.

"I think it's just a very complex process. There are a lot of factors that affect it," I explain. "It depends on me too, I've discovered. I have to be in the right frame of mind, and calm enough to focus. It's a bit like meditation, I suppose. It's different every time."

Alexia reaches into her handbag and pulls out a small cardboard box. Lifting the lid, she reveals a small silver fountain pen, engraved with the letters *SJF.*

I recognize it immediately, and everything falls into place. "So *that* was your mum?" I say. Alexia nods. That explains why the woman looked familiar. I immediately scan back over the conversation and hope I didn't say anything untoward.

"Joe, I hope you don't mind me doing this, but when you said you didn't see anything, Mum was really disappointed. She's gone home to Derbyshire now, but she just won't stop talking about it. She was convinced you'd seen something but didn't want to tell her." She pauses, searching my face. "Did you? See something?"

I feel awkward. "It's complicated, Alexia. It's a big responsibility. I never know what impact my viewings will have on people. Sometimes I see things they don't want to know. And like I said, not all objects have a story to tell."

"A story?" Alexia seems more interested than ever. I'm not doing a very good job of putting her off.

"Yes," I say reluctantly. I lean toward her and lower my voice. "Sometimes I get an insight into what happened to the object, and the role it played in its owner's—or someone else's—life. My job is just to listen, that's all. I get to hear secrets, unfinished business, skeletons in the family closet. It plays out like a movie in my head." I stop, aware I'm sounding more and more crazy.

She pushes the box toward me. "Will you try again? For me?"

"I don't know if it's a good idea. What if I see something upsetting?"

"Whatever you see, I won't hold it against you. Please?"

Hesitantly, I lift the pen out of its container and hold it between my hands. It feels a little more reticent this time, as though it knows I stopped partway before. I focus my mind on the story it has to tell, give myself to the past. The sounds and the smells of the café fade away, and once again I'm at the field, among the tents, then inside one of them, with the man using the pen to write a letter.

Making a silent promise to the pen not to abandon it this time, I open my eyes. "Alexia, I need to ask again. Are you sure you want me to do this?"

Her eyes shine, and she leans toward me. "I want to know, no matter what's in there. If you can see something, tell me. I know you're just the conduit. Please." She touches my hand, and her touch reignites the viewing.

Closing my eyes, I return to the letter writer. In a flourish he writes the final lines, periodically blowing on his hands to warm them. Signing off as Stanley, he seals the letter in an envelope and hurries to one of the nearby tents, where he hands it to the postal orderly. The scene switches, and Stanley's in a trench, shivering with his comrades. It's pitch-black and raining heavily, the ground a morass of mud and filthy water. The call comes to go up and over the top. Wordlessly, the men clamber up the duckboards and run hopelessly across the flatlands. The enemy fire is rapid and relentless, and Stanley falls lifeless to the earth.

Another day. The sun is beating down. I see a young soldier collecting a package of Stanley's possessions and putting them into his knapsack. Then, images flicker rapidly through my head: the soldier on a ship, a huge explosion, the soldier in icy water, in a rowboat with fishermen, a huge wooden building in Regent's Park, a horse-drawn cart, Paddington station, a steam train, a wheelbarrow. The package is finally delivered to a middle-aged woman, who collapses onto the doorstep and weeps.

The viewing of the complicated journey of Stanley's letter fades into the comforting sounds and aromas of the coffee shop. I open my eyes and soak in the safety of the present.

"You were gone for a while," Alexia says. "What did you see?"

As I ground myself back into the moment, I carefully consider how to begin. "This pen belonged to a man called Stanley."

"My great-grandfather," Alexia says quietly.

"He was killed in the war, shot after going up over a trench into battle."

"Did you see it happen?"

"I did. One of his fellow soldiers brought the package containing Stanley's belongings back from Belgium, across the sea, to London. The boat was sunk, but the young man managed to hold onto his bag. He was rescued by some fishermen and rowed to shore, and in the end, Stanley's stuff got back home to his wife."

"So we nearly didn't have this pen, then," Alexia says. "What a terrible thought. Apparently, Stanley was buried in an unmarked grave in Belgium. Just think if my great-grandmother had never received his belongings. She would have had nothing left but her memories."

"There's something else," I say. "Stanley was writing a letter with this pen not long before he died. I think that's what this pen wanted me to see. Do you know if any letters got back to your grandmother from those last days?"

"I don't know, to be honest, but we don't have any letters now," Alexia says. "I don't suppose . . . could you see what he was writing?"

"I think I could," I say. "I didn't focus on it, but I think if I connected again, I might be able to see. Would you like me to try?"

"I would." She sits quietly and waits as I connect again with Stanley's pen, this time focusing closely on the words he's scratching onto the damp piece of paper. Careful not to pull myself out of the viewing, I slowly read the words aloud as he writes them.

Dearest Florence,

I thank you for your latest letter, which I received via the post this morning. I am quite well, but I am glad to know that you are thinking of me. I have heard that we are moving to the front soon, and while I trust that you will pray for me, we must accept that I may not return. You make my life complete, my dear, and even in our short time together, I have been happier than I ever was before. I pray each night that the war will soon be over, but if the worst should happen, my darling, then know that my last thought will be of you. Kiss the girls and give Bobby a pat for me. I love you with all my heart and then some.

Yours forever, Stanley

When I open my eyes, Alexia is sitting stunned before me, a tear rolling down her cheek. "Oh, Joe," she whispers. "That's so sad."

I pass the pen back to her and leave my hands on the table, just a few millimeters from hers. "It is," I agree. "Your grandparents' time together was too short. I could feel how much love they shared, though. It was pouring out of him as he wrote to her, and I know she cherished this pen once it was returned to her too. Love like that doesn't go anywhere. It shoots from our hearts out into the universe and travels forever, like radio waves. It just keeps getting bigger."

Alexia sniffs. "I like to think that in a parallel universe somewhere, Stanley escaped the war unharmed and went home to Florence, and they had more kids . . . a small farm, maybe. Grew old and gray together."

"It's a nice thought."

"Do you believe in parallel universes?"

Yes, yes, a million times yes. "I do, Alexia. And sometimes I feel as though I'm stuck in the wrong one."

"Since your accident?"

"Yeah."

She nods thoughtfully. "Whatever the reason, whatever happened to you, you're not the same man I knew before. The question is whether you're going to stay like it."

"Like what?"

"Better."

26

The sign outside the Indian restaurant reads, All-You-Can-Eat Lunchtime Special! Just £9.99! The poor guys obviously hadn't met Vinny when they came up with that idea.

Inside, it's quiet, just a handful of tables occupied by businesspeople shoveling down their money's worth. I don't think the décor has changed in twenty years: purple walls, rows of silver mirrors surrounded by carved dancing elephants, and tall brown faux-leather chairs—all the better to disguise the curry spatters.

I explain to a nervous waiter that I'm looking for my friend. "You'll know him, he's bald and he's pretty hungry," I explain. The waiter sighs heavily and gestures toward the back of the room, explaining that Vinny is seated at his usual table, enunciating the word *usual* like it causes him physical pain.

I find Vinny at a tiny table wedged between the door to the kitchen and the buffet. He doesn't spot me straightaway. He's too busy considering his next plateful of food, fingers interlocked comfortably over his considerable tummy. His stubbly head is beaded with perspiration, glistening beneath the bright overhead lights.

"Hey, Vinny," I say.

He looks up at me, face glowing. "Cash! Pull up a pew." I sit opposite him and assess the war zone: three empty dinner plates, half a naan on a side plate, and the remains of a dish of mango chutney. Vinny's T-shirt, dotted with a variety of greasy orange circles, depicts a headless bodybuilder and reads, "My Other Body is Ripped." "Fancy a bite?" he says, indicating the buffet with a stately wave of the hand.

"I'm not hungry, thanks," I say politely. "But don't let me stop you."

I needn't have worried. "You know my motto, Cash: live for today and eat like there's no tomorrow. Just give me a sec." He steps to the buffet and loads up a plate with onion bhajis, two sorts of curry, and a pile of pilau rice. Sitting back down, he pushes one of three full pints of beer in my direction and dabs his forehead with a napkin. "How are things going with your . . . ?" He silently mouths the word *mission*.

I take a welcome draft of ale, then fill him in on my latest trip to Paris. "I found out that Nils disappears when people look at him, something to do with the observer effect, but reversed, I think. And he only has one more chance to land properly in Paris, otherwise he'll be lost forever in the void, which, from what I can gather, is like a black hole of nothingness."

"Holy cashmolee," Vinny says. "I'm sorry for this Nils bloke and everything, but that's brilliant you can disappear him just by looking. There are some people in my life I'd like to do that to." Dark Vinny rarely makes an appearance, so when he does, it always takes me by surprise.

"Like who?"

"Oh, you know, some of my old teachers, a couple of exes, the tax man." He takes a massive forkful of food and chews slowly. "So how are you going to rescue this chap then, if he pops the second you clap eyes on him? Blindfold?"

"That's not as daft as it sounds, but no. The Continuum is going to develop a patch for me to apply to his watch, so he can land properly in Paris. They think that once he lands there fully, he'll travel back naturally to his own time."

"That's so cool!" Vinny says, eyes shining. "Cash, I know I couldn't come with you on this mission, but if you ever travel again, promise me you'll take me with you?"

"If I can, mate, I will." Vinny loved our trip to London, and I felt much more confident with him at my side. Compared to traveling with Grumpy Green, it was about a million times more fun.

"How's it going with Gabrielle?" he asks as if reading my mind.

"Slightly better," I tell him. "She finally admitted she was originally lined up to do the Romano mission before I got dragged into it, which is why she's been such a sulk-merchant. It's cleared the air a bit."

"I hope she's not upset with me too," Vinny muses.

"Of course not. Anyway, she's over it now. Water under the bridge and all that."

"Did you say her surname was Green? As in Gabrielle Green? Isn't she a music journalist?"

"Not that I'm aware of." I think about it for a second. We haven't talked about our day jobs, but she's certainly audacious enough to pry stories out of her victims, and she took to her role in Paris like a duck to water. "She could be a journalist, I guess."

Vinny thumbs his phone for a few seconds and holds it up to me. Gabrielle's face glares out from the screen. "Is this her?"

"Yes!" I say. When you've experienced Gabrielle in real life, the shiny, airbrushed mug shot is slightly nauseating. "Where did you get that?"

"*Rolling Stone* website." Vinny whistles. "Well, I never did. Gabrielle Green's a time traveler!" He chortles to himself.

I wonder why she didn't tell me she's a journalist, although I suppose I didn't ask. I think I presumed time traveling was a full-time job, but The Continuum has never offered me any money, so . . . what is it, then? A vocation? A hobby?

"It's all making sense to me now," Vinny says. "People call her the Rott-weiler. She's famous in the biz, you know!" He puts down his phone. "You need to ask her about that interview she did with Keith Richards. She's got some stories, that one." He chuckles again.

I have no desire to ask Gabrielle anything that's going to inflate her ego. I decide to change the subject. "I went to see Amy earlier," I say. "Did I tell you she'd been painting her visions? She's done a load more. They're mad, crazy mind dumps. She said they were all about me."

"What are they of?"

"One's the opera house fire, although Amy keeps changing how many people have come out of the front door. The second one was a massive picture of the hand of God and an eagle."

"Sounds pretty random," Vinny says, reaching across to the next table for a clean napkin and mopping beads of sweat from his brow. "Any idea what it's about?"

"None, to be honest. Amy didn't know either. She just said it had to do with me. And the last one she showed me was—well, originally it was a lighthouse, but now she's turned the lighthouse into this black Lord-of-the-Rings-style tower-of-Sauron edifice."

"That sounds bad," Vinny says grimly.

"I know, and it looks bad too, kind of evil. If you spotted it on your way back from the pub, you'd run in the opposite direction, but she said she was painting my way home." I shudder. "I'm telling you, Vin, I'm properly spooked. I don't think I'm up to any of this. I feel well out of my depth."

"You're just scared, Cash, that's all. But you're doing it anyway, and that means you're my hero, whether it goes OK or not. Stick with it. I have faith in you. Amy's paintings will make sense once you're back in Paris, I bet you anything."

"Maybe you're right." I take a sip of beer and try to shake my growing sense of foreboding. "By the way, Vin, how's it going with Kassandra and Charlotte?"

His face softens. "We went to that posh pub I told you about. It was amazing. I had belly pork and she had grilled monkfish, and then we shared a chocolate cheesecake. Just a slice, not a whole one."

"How was the conversation?"

"I looked up some jokes so I had something to say, and she seemed to appreciate them," Vinny says proudly. "And she said she thought I was ready to meet Charlotte too."

"That's brilliant! Isn't it?"

"It is, but I'm getting nervous," he admits. "Kassandra's been briefing me on what to say to Charlotte, and I'm worried I'm going to get it wrong."

"You just need to be yourself, Vin," I reassure him. "Don't think too much about it; just say what you feel, and you'll be fine. Charlotte will love you. I know she will." I know teenagers can be tricky customers, but this is Vinny we're talking about. What's not to love?

Vinny looks awkward. "Kassandra said the opposite, actually." He scratches his head. "She told me not to say what's in my head without filtering it first. She said my thoughts are like lumpy soup, and I need to get the lumps out before I give the soup to anyone else. She said she hoped that if she used a food semaphore, I'd remember it better. At least, I think that's what she said." I'll bet that's not what she said. Vinny sometimes gets his words wrong, but I don't correct him, because I find it endearing, and besides, I usually know what he means.

He wipes around his plate with the last of the naan and lays his knife and fork in an X in the center. He sees me eyeing his cutlery in confusion. "Code," he explains. "My way of telling the guys here I'm ready for my main."

"So that"—I point at the four empty plates—"was all just . . ."

"Appetizers," Vinny confirms, rubbing his tummy. "Come on, boys, bring out the big guns!"

I adore Vinny. But I don't like the sound of this Kassandra. She's gone from bossy to outright controlling, but I'm not going to be the one to say it. He'll work it out for himself soon enough. "Listen, Vin, just see how it goes with Kassandra and fire up the bat signal if you need moral support."

"You're a lifesaver," he tells me, and the corners of his mouth turn upward. "Now listen up, Cash. I've been researching your spinster, Madame Delacroix. I found out that she died without a will. And did you know she had a brother?" I shake my head. "They were estranged. When she died, he got his hands on her estate and divvied up the money between himself and his four kids, which might not have been so bad, except that they basically burned the lot and ended up in the poor house."

"What a bloody waste," I say. "She would have been horrified. When I chatted to her in the costume store, she said she was afraid her father would be disappointed in her, that he would think she hadn't done enough with her inheritance. He must have been turning in his grave when the brother and his kids got their hands on the cash."

The head waiter arrives with sizzling beef curry, spitting and crackling in its balti dish, and lays it on the table alongside a double serving of mushroom rice. "Another drink, sir?" he asks.

"Drink, Cash?"

"I'm OK with this one, thanks."

"Just the two pints of Guinness then, please," Vinny says to the waiter, who gives a slight bow and heads back toward the bar.

I check my watch—quarter to 2. Most people have had lunch and are now back in their offices, digesting.

"You all right for time, Cash? Not heading back to France anytime soon?"

"No, I've got a few days. I sort of have to try to be mentally ready, but not too distracted in the present either. It's hard."

"It must be." Vinny piles a forkful of food into his mouth. "I'd be crapping myself if I were you. I mean, time travel is brilliant and everything, but I'm terrified of fire."

"Are you? You never told me that before."

"Yep. My biggest fear is being barbecued. Let's be frank, I've got some layers of fat on me. I'd burn for hours, like a ginormous man-candle. If I got caught by cannibals, they'd have quite a conundrum on their hands: 'Do we eat him, or do we use him as a light source?' How about you, Cash—what are you most afraid of?"

"You know it's sharks."

"Well yeah, obviously. But what else?"

"Heights."

"Really?"

"I hate being high up," I tell him, "scares the bejesus out of me. Plus, I have this strange, almost overwhelming compulsion to throw myself off whatever it is I'm standing on."

Vinny scratches his stubble. "But if you were standing on a rock, you could jump and land in water. That would be OK, wouldn't it?"

"Not if it's the sea."

"Damn. Sharks," he says with genuine empathy.

"Yeah, and since saving Amy in the lake, you can add drowning to the list too. I'm even afraid of drowning in the bath."

He nods sympathetically. "It's understandable, mate."

He takes the last mouthful of his meal just as the waiter arrives with our beers. "Cheers," Vinny says, and sucks down a good half pint in one go. Vinny once told me he has more than one stomach, like a cow. I used to think he was pulling my leg, but I'm not so sure anymore. "Now listen," he says, leaning back and wiping sweat from his brow. "I need you to keep calm, but I think it's always better to know these things in advance, especially if you're a little bit sensitive."

"What do you mean?" I ask, immediately worried.

"I came across a bit of information about the structure of the opera house that might be useful when you go back."

"OK," I say cautiously.

"When they were digging the foundations, the construction team accidentally tunneled straight into an arm of the river Seine. They tried to pump the water out, but it just kept coming back. So in the end they got a bit more zen about it, and rather than trying to get rid of the water, they worked around it, and the architect designed an artificial lake, nearly five floors beneath the stage. They planned to use it as a store of water in case of fire, although I guess it didn't help when the place actually burned down."

"Interesting." Deep water, deep underground. Presumably shark-free, but still. "Thanks for the warning, Vin, I appreciate it. But five floors down, I won't need to worry about it, hopefully."

"I hope so too, Cash, but just in case . . ." He grins. "I wasn't in the Boy Scouts for nothing." He pulls a small plastic bag from under his chair and hands me a waterproof headlight, like miners wear.

I take it and remove it from its packaging. It looks military grade and feels tough, and glancing at the price ticket, I see that it was expensive. "Thanks, mate. That's brilliant."

Vinny seems pleased with himself. "Don't mention it, Cash. I just thought, if I were going to drown, I wouldn't want to do it in the dark. Just don't leave it lying around—twenty-first-century tech in nineteenth-century France, know what I'm saying? I wanted to buy you some kind of flotation device too, but I could only find inflatable dolphins, so I gave it a miss."

"Good call on the dolphins, but the light is great," I say. "I'm sure it will be useful."

Vinny waves to the waiter, and the man who welcomed me when I arrived hurries over, looking worried. "Just a Punky to go, please, mate," Vinny says, "and my bill, if you would be so kind?"

"Absolutely, sir," the waiter replies with relief, and heads straight through the door behind Vinny into the kitchen.

"What's a Punky?" I ask.

"Penguin ice cream. Not a real penguin, of course, that would taste way too fishy. It's a plastic penguin with a Mohican haircut and ice cream inside. You can't have a curry and then not have a Punky." He drains the last of his beer. "Right, I need to go and walk the dog."

"Is that a euphemism?" I ask.

"No, Cash. An actual pooch. Neighbor's spaniel, Herbie. The doc said I needed to get fitter, so I've been taking Herbie for walks and racking up the steps." He pulls up his sleeve and flashes a sports watch at me. "I just attach this baby to Herbie's collar and let him off the lead. When the doc checks my uploads, he'll think I've run a marathon!"

Vinny giggles and that starts me off, and then we're both guffawing, tears running down our cheeks. I tell you, a good belly laugh with your best friend fixes pretty much anything.

27

I spend a quiet evening at home, listening to the Beatles, chewing over Amy's paintings and our recent conversation, and wondering if we're nearing the time when reality will dovetail with Iris's promise of Amy's future. I reread Amy's letter too and look forward to finally being able to talk openly with her. London changed everything: secrets have no place in my relationship with my sister now, and it can't come soon enough. I soak away the day in a long hot bath, and I'm in bed by 10:30 p.m., relatively early for me.

Slipping effortlessly into a dreamless sleep, I'm awakened by a police siren some time later. I shove my head under the pillow and drift back to sleep, but this time the darkness gives way to heavy golden ropes of light spilling through the weatherboards of the hut in Macau, where Nils is slumped in the corner. I float gently down, sinking through thick, humid air until I am hovering just above Nils's head, realizing I'm about to have a viewing from his point of view.

There's a deep ache in Nils's ribs, a throbbing in his left leg, and the pitiless bite of brain freeze at the base of his skull, although it's hard to distinguish that from the background pain. His mind is desperate, a jumble of fear, confusion, shame, and anger. After everything he's been through, he's failed this mission, and he knows he'll never return to Macau again.

Scarlett is talking, her words a garbled collection of syllables at first as Nils struggles to concentrate, but then they slowly coagulate into distinct units of meaning. "Nothing is forever. New evidence is always coming to light. That's how science works." Nils is about to travel, and he feels himself phasing in and out, each time a little less material. Scarlett's voice is now barely audible, the rustle of a leaf on the wind. "Good luck, Nils."

Nils is suddenly surrounded by infinite, lightless space. His thoughts are slow, stuttered, muffled by the nothingness, but he pulls an idea from somewhere: *This is the void.* He has no sense of the passage of time, although wisps of memories tug at him, telling him that he's been here before—in another life, perhaps, or another universe. He looks down at his hands in wonder, their silvery iridescence reminding him of the strange bioluminescent creatures of the ocean depths.

After a while—who knows how long—a flickering shard of light appears, blurred at first, giving meaning and perspective to the endless sea of black. Then others appear, like lanterns glowing to life. They take shape like distant billboards, five of them. Faded memories struggle to surface, and Nils recalls jumping into zoetrope scenes before, a long time ago, his first mission, before he joined The Continuum. Nils intends to approach, and they close in on him, each scene revealing a looping animation within. Then, like a slow funeral march, they begin to rotate, a spinning gallery, portals to another dimension.

Fighting the fog that invades his mind, winding itself around his thoughts like a snake and threatening to suffocate his reason, Nils strains to interpret the scenes as they move past. None of them are familiar, and he recognizes neither his mission in Macau nor his home in Oslo. One roars with brilliant orange flames, licking at the edges of the doorway as though trying to escape. The others are indiscernible: marble surfaces, flashes of gold, and patches of muted color suggesting locations within a building, perhaps. He picks one at random and jogs toward it, moving to the right to keep up with the doorway as it spins lazily away from him. As he approaches, the scene within broadens as though through a fish-eye lens, but all he can pick out in the darkness are swathes of fabric. He doesn't know where or what it is, but he has no choice, and he launches himself through the frame.

He lands in a disorientating labyrinth of dusty curtains and wooden structures, but the landing is light, and he can only just feel the weight of his body bearing down on his feet. He checks his watch, but it's just showing the time like a normal pocket watch. He notices with concern that his skin is shimmering, and he can see through his own hands. Something has gone terribly wrong. Where is he, when is this, and why is he here? He hears music and is drawn toward it. Slowing his breathing and trying to keep control of his thoughts, he sidles past a tall, painted board and is blinded by dazzling light. Shielding his face, he takes another couple of steps and just has time to turn and see a thousand astonished faces staring back at him before he is flung back into the void.

For a few moments, he crouches, bent at the waist, and catches his breath. Questions spin through his head. Why did he land in a theater? Who were all those people? And why did he not stay? He hauls himself to his feet and sees that the doorway he jumped through has turned monochromatic, black-and-white, and frozen still like a photograph. He knows without trying that he can no longer pass through it. One down, four to go.

He picks another doorway, through which he sees a light, spacious hallway laid with marble tiles. Stepping through, he arrives in a corridor— or perhaps, this is the foyer. He checks his watch again—still showing its standard watch face. His hands are still translucent. He walks toward the main doors in front of him, wanting to look outside and work out where he is, but a young boy with a mop and bucket comes around the corner and sees him, and he finds himself back in the darkness again.

Now, there are only three doorways left. His chances are running out, and it's clear that the minute someone sees him, he disappears and lands back here. He can't remember if anything in his training prepared him for this, but he doesn't think so. And why would it knock him back into the void when people see him? He was taught that observation locks events in place—that is why The Continuum can only change things in the shadows—but this seems to be the reverse. That woman in Macau, whatever she did to his watch, this was her doing. She said she was giving him another chance, but everyone knows that when you fail a mission, the game is over. Was she trying to kill him?

Indignation fires him up, and in a fit of rage, he flings himself at the next doorway, arriving in a moonlit room set with dark silhouettes. A young woman sits at a small table, sewing by the light of a candle.

"Hello?" He tries to speak, but his throat is dry, and his voice box feels rusty. He licks his lips and tries again. "Excuse me, where am I?"

The girl, hearing the voice, looks up and sees Nils's shimmering reflection in the mirror before her. Their eyes meet, but Nils doesn't disappear. His heart leaps. "Please, don't turn around, but can you help me?"

Her hand goes to her mouth, and she drops her sewing. She looks terrified, as though she's seen a ghost.

"Don't turn around . . ." he implores her, aware that his voice is rasping and wheezy.

She gives a little cry and whirls around to face him, and he is gone.

More time passes. Or perhaps, no time passes. It's impossible to say. Nils has two remaining doorways. He doesn't want to jump through the one that leads to the fire, so he chooses the other, a room packed from floor to rafters with costumes and accessories, hats and swords and suits of armor. He takes a few seconds to enjoy the reassuring sense of being in a solid, three-dimensional room with four walls, a floor, and a ceiling. His watch is still on its standard at-home setting, and his skin is still translucent. He wonders how solid he is and moves toward a rack of dresses and frock coats. As he gets close, he waits to feel the fabric brush against his body, but it passes through him, brushing him on the inside, which is so bizarre and disorientating that he pulls back and crouches low for a while, recovering. When he rises again, he discovers that he is standing before a large ornate mirror, and the woman who tampered with his watch and sent him here is staring straight back at him.

"You!" he wheezes furiously, wishing his voice had more power. "How dare you show your face! What did you do to me? Where am I? Why have I not fully landed?"

"I didn't mean for this to happen. You're in an opera house in Paris in 1873, somehow connected to the change event of a live mission here. This was all a mistake. I've come to get you home."

Nils is conflicted. He cannot believe the gall of this woman offering to get him home when it's her fault he's stuck like this, but he does need help, and she's the only one who understands what's happened to him, and, perhaps, the only one who knows. Their conversation is interrupted by the sound of Madame Delacroix tapping her way down the corridor. Nils turns in alarm when he spots a movement in the room near the door, and in the split second before he travels, he locks eyes with a man hiding behind a rack of costumes, his face clearly visible through a gap.

Nils stands before the rotating doorways, considering his final chance, his jaw locked, his hands bound in tight fists. That bitch did this to him. She says she is trying to save him, but why would he believe her? Isn't it more likely that she's here to finish what she started?

As he watches the wheel spin before him, Nils assesses the situation. Hope is failing him; he knows this is his last chance to get home. He moves toward the final doorway, and the scene beyond reveals itself: a hallway of mirrors, a clock on a mantelpiece above a marble fireplace, flanked by carved dragons. A man stares at the clock. The time is ten minutes past 10. Nils doesn't know the man, but he recognizes him as the one he saw hiding behind the clothes rack in the costume store. A burning piece of fabric flutters past the man's face, spinning like a sycamore seed. The man holds his head in his hands in a gesture of despair. The face of the glass clock on the mantel cracks right down the middle. And then the scene repeats itself, on a loop. Ten minutes past 10, a shred of burning fabric, the man's defeated gesture. The clock face cracking.

Flames lick at the edges of the final doorway, and the idea of jumping through feels like madness, but Nils has to try. He has family waiting for him back in Oslo. He has colleagues depending on him at The Continuum. If he fails, it's been a hell of a ride. At least he will never know the pain of losing his gift. That would be the worst of all.

28

The Hallway of Mirrors shatters as I'm wrenched from the depths of the viewing and back into reality. My phone is buzzing. It's Gabrielle.

"I just had a viewing from Nils's point of view," I tell her breathlessly before she can speak. "He saw me when I was hiding in the costume store, so that must've established a connection, and now I know when and where he's going to come through."

"Good," she replies, "because we leave in two hours. I'm on my way."

"Two hours?"

"Yep. We'll call the gang when I get there."

She hangs up.

The gang. I sometimes feel like I'm in an episode of *Scooby-Doo*, though I doubt we're going to unmask anyone with a name like Old Man Withers, and from what I remember, the lives of the Mystery Inc. members were never truly in danger. Sometimes, I wish I could be more like Vinny and see this all as a big adventure.

I head out onto my balcony. Spending some time out here is becoming part of my prejump routine. Letting go of the present, perhaps, taking stock. Looking out over Cheltenham is a form of meditation, I think, a constant in a world that seems to be forever changing. Inhaling the cool air, I work back over my viewing. It was unnerving seeing myself in the Hallway of Mirrors, a moment in time that hasn't happened for me yet.

It's a gift, though: we now have a specific time and place for Nils's arrival, reassuring me that I have a chance of saving him, at least.

I find myself thinking back over my life, the one only I truly know. All through school, the bullying years—I didn't do the bullying—I've been searching for who I was going to become. Never in a million lifetimes could I have imagined this: a time traveler, with missions and lives to change. Intricate knowledge of the past and future, mysteries to solve. Gabrielle talked about time travelers feeling lost without purpose. I get that, because that was me for so long. But now, for perhaps the first time in my life, I feel part of something. I can imagine growing quite proud of it, actually. I often wondered what my ideal career might be. Have I found it now?

I complete my ritual by writing a few goodbye letters to my parents and other people who matter in my life, the kind that should be found and read "only in the event of my disappearance." I keep them short and simple, explaining what happened and how much I appreciate them. I guess Vinny and Amy would find a way to explain my fate to my parents. Writing death letters might sound dark, but it's good for the soul and ensures I leave my emotional baggage at home. That's reassuring when heading into battle, and that's what this is, I've realized. A battle across the centuries, fought against resistance, hope hidden in shadow. The last thing I do is send Amy a text, telling her I'm going on the final jump to Paris and assuring her that I will see her when I get back. She won't reply, but at least it's done.

With my letters done, it's time to let go of my feelings and focus on the practical details of my upcoming trip. The opera house blueprints aren't difficult to get hold of online. I've studied them, committing them to memory, but I give them one last look now. The layout is labyrinthine, and I can imagine that, under pressure, the numerous corridors and flights of stairs might get confusing.

Gabrielle arrives, wheeling her suitcase of nineteenth-century fancy-dress delights. She also has a leather satchel over her shoulder.

"What's in there?" I ask her.

"Whiskey."

"Cool."

She tuts, loudly. "Has anyone ever told you how horribly gullible you are? It's the lantern, and it's got enough radioactive triterbium inside to light up half the planet."

I stare in alarm at the innocent-looking bag and swallow with an audible click. We head to the loft. I pull the blinds. Gabrielle fiddles with her watch, firing up ICARUS. A white, windowless meeting room builds itself around us, its smooth walls and a low ceiling reminding me of the room in which I first met Felix, except this one is a little bigger. Felix appears at the side of the room, manipulating holographic controls at a small console table. He's dressed in jeans, a checked shirt, and boots. The cut and style seem odd to me, but he could walk into the present and pass as a hipster of sorts. In the center of the room are a tall table and a projection of what appears to be a three-dimensional night sky, pricked with stars and strings of glowing blue-and-red orbs that flicker like thoughts in a neural network. Iris and Kyoko stand beside it, studying it closely. They couldn't look more like they were from a different era if they tried. Iris wears a pale-blue angular-cut suit, her platinum hair swept neatly into a sharp wave. Kyoko's outfit is more futuristic, layers of flowing mustard-colored garments that should only really work on a catwalk.

Felix welcomes us first. He taps silently into a complex network of light in front of him. It disappears, along with the glowing display above the table. "Hey! Good to see you," he says. He claps his hands and rubs them briskly.

Iris asks, "All set? Did everything go OK with the lantern?"

"Yeah, I think so," Gabrielle shrugs. "First things first, though. Joe has some news on Nils."

Felix's brow wrinkles in consternation. "Is he OK?"

"I had a viewing," I tell him. "I saw Nils's journey, all the times he tried to escape the void, and I saw the final doorway. I know when and where he's going to land. You were right, it's on the night of the fire. At ten minutes past ten, Nils will arrive in a hallway filled with mirrors that Gabrielle and I saw on our last jump. But that's not all. I saw myself there too."

Felix blinks rapidly. "You saw yourself at his landing location? You sure?" I nod. He studies me as though he wants to believe but is finding it hard to make the leap. "Then that means we have a good chance of bringing him home."

Kyoko steps forward. "And you are certain of the time?"

"Yes," I tell her. "There was a clock. The time was right there in front of me."

"It's fantastic news, Joseph," Iris says, the relief in her voice palpable. "It's good to know that when Nils comes through, you will be there waiting for him."

"So what do we need to do?" Gabrielle asks.

Felix glances at Kyoko, who takes a step toward the table where the projection was a few moments ago. Iris holds up a hand and says, "Before we discuss bringing Nils home, I would like to say a few words." Kyoko bows her head and waits. Iris turns to me. "Joseph, your viewings and your presence on this mission have made a huge difference already, and we thank you for that." She turns to Gabrielle. "I've become very aware that saving Nils has been our focus, and your mission has in some ways been overshadowed by this."

Gabrielle looks awkward. "It's OK, boss, I get it. Nils is one of our own. We have to save him."

"True, but I want to be sure that you know the work you are doing to help Philippe Chevalier is valued. It's important to me, to all of us."

"It's fine," Gabrielle says, sounding almost surprised now. "Honestly, my eye has been on the ball the whole time. Joe has taken the brunt of the Nils situation. My focus is Philippe, all the way."

"Good to hear. The Future Change Index shows massive potential for Philippe. I didn't want that to get lost in the mix. You're prepared for the final jump, then?"

"Sure am," Gabrielle replies, overly positive and yet still all business. "I still don't know why Philippe goes back inside, but I know the players and understand the dynamics, and the layout of the building is burned into my brain." She winces, curling her lip at me. "Maybe not the best way of putting it."

Kyoko clears her throat. "You have the lantern?"

"Right here." Gabrielle slips the satchel off her shoulder. She pulls out an object with the shape and size of one of those foam rockets I've seen kids throwing in the park, except this is metal and looks heavy and dangerous.

A circular crystal the size of a tennis ball sits on top, surrounded by a thick, metal cage. It has a definite military-edition vibe. At its base are four hinged feet, currently bent up like a clawed hand, and it reminds me of a camping stove. Then it hits me: I've seen this before.

"That's so weird," I say.

"What is?" Iris asks.

I tell them all about Amy's paintings, how they seem to predict certain details of future events. The members of The Continuum don't seem surprised by this. I guess they know about Amy's gifts. "She included a light-house in one of her more abstract paintings, at least that's what I thought it was, but now it's obvious she was painting this lantern."

"I view that as a positive sign," Gabrielle says. "It means we're destined to travel with it, right?"

My brow furrows. "The thing is, Amy changed the painting recently. She completely replaced the lantern."

"With what?" Felix asks.

"I don't know exactly, some kind of black tower with a glowing red circle at the top. Does that mean anything to you?"

"Nothing," he says. "Kyoko?" She shakes her head. My heart sinks. I hadn't admitted it to myself, but I was convinced Kyoko would know what it meant.

Iris speaks softly, her tone masking her accent. "Are you sure you don't have any idea what this change to Amy's painting might mean? You haven't seen anything in your viewings?"

I take my time to think it through, but it's no good. "I've thought about it a lot. I'm sorry, but I don't have a clue."

Gabrielle bounces the lantern in her hand, as though weighing it. "Amy's visions can be helpful, but wondering what the painting means doesn't do us any good this late in the game."

She addresses Felix. "Why don't you tell us what we need to do?"

Felix folds his arms. "In short, you need to find Nils, use the lantern to manifest him in 1873, make physical contact to complete the grounding process, and then update his watch to ensure he returns home correctly."

"Sounds simple enough," Gabrielle says, without a hint of irony.

Felix smiles. "Let's go through it one step at a time. Kyoko?"

She moves silently to the console at the side of the room, and Felix steps aside. The smooth white surface glows, and Kyoko interacts with a panel of light, or perhaps it's the other way around. It's hard to tell. A triterbium lantern appears in the middle of the room above the table, twice as big as the real thing. The projection rotates slowly, the legs unfold, and I notice a covered button on the middle section, the sort you might find on the flight stick of a fighter jet. It's clearly the do-not-press-this-accidentally button.

Kyoko walks to the projection, close enough for her face to take on a bluish hue. Her tone is factual, her accent rising and falling around the words. "To activate the lantern, you lift the safety cover and press the button three times. The lantern is powerful but has a limited radius. When activated, Nils must be within twenty meters. This will drag him from the void back into reality and tether him to the present, in this case: 1873." As Kyoko talks, she works her gaze between Gabrielle and me. "However, this is a temporary state for Nils. To complete the grounding process, you must make physical contact with him before the lantern powers down."

"How long do we have to ground him?" I ask.

"Less than a second," Kyoko replies.

"A second?" Gabrielle lets out an exasperated laugh. "Are you kidding?"

Kyoko eyes her with an expression so glacial, it gives me goosebumps. "We had to balance power with portability. The lantern has been heavily modified, with a power boost of more than a thousand percent. The burst of energy required to draw Nils from the void will also cause a certain amount of time dilation. This will be useful."

"Time dilation," Gabrielle raises an eyebrow. "How much?"

"It will seem as though time has stopped," Kyoko replies. "One second will last approximately one minute, enough time to pull him through."

"But we will be able to move in real time?" Gabrielle asks.

Kyoko nods. "Anything within the radius will be affected. To an outside observer, you will appear to be moving at superhuman speed."

It's a lot to take in. I'm just glad we aren't going to spend sixty seconds in slow motion, like some John Woo movie.

Kyoko says, "You must have grounded him physically before the time dilation ends."

Felix adds, "You should also be aware that in the simulations we've run, it's amazing how quickly you adjust to time being paused. When it resumes . . . let's just say, it can be a hell of a shock."

Gabrielle bobs her head. "Like the ground rush in skydiving."

"Exactly."

Not a huge surprise to discover that Gabrielle enjoys throwing herself out of a perfectly functioning aircraft.

Kyoko raises her arm and gently rotates the projected lantern. On the opposite side of the activation switch, I notice an indented circular section. "Once Nils is fully manifested in 1873, there is one more step. You must place his timepiece here. This will update and rebalance the triterbium within its chamber. This must be completed to ensure that Nils-san returns to Oslo in 1920."

Kyoko's no-nonsense briefing is refreshing, but even with my limited experience I know that in the field, things can get a little hairy.

"Do you want to go through it again?" Felix asks.

I'm about to say yes when Gabrielle cuts in. "Nah, I've got it. Fire the lantern, grab Nils, update his watch, get out of Dodge."

I swallow my concern, hoping her confidence is justified.

"Cool," says Felix. "But listen, I'm going to be honest with you both . . . we don't know for certain that this will work. All we have is the data and our experience of the rules as we currently understand them. We've never used a lantern in this way before. We've never had a situation like this, so we've had to extrapolate some of our data."

"A leap of faith, then?" I suggest.

"You could say," he replies.

Kyoko swipes her hand through the air and the projected lantern disappears. As she moves, I notice the fine mesh of hexagonal shapes that make up her projected form. She looks at Gabrielle, her dark eyes shining, connecting across time. "The fundamentals are sound. Get close enough to Nils-san and there is a good chance that he will come back, but I would be remiss if I didn't warn you of the dangers. We are on the edge here, pushing the boundaries. If you fire the lantern and you aren't close enough to Nils, you will cause an imbalance."

"What happens then?" Gabrielle asks.

"Anyone within the radius could themselves be pulled into the void. Also, once you pull him through, it's imperative that you update his watch."

Gabrielle lets out a short laugh. "Let me guess: otherwise, we'll end up in the void?" Kyoko doesn't reply, which says it all. Gabrielle sighs. "Well, that's all the scary stuff out of the way. Shall we talk about how we're going to celebrate when we get back?" Her sarcastic optimism lightens the mood, and I'm grateful.

Kyoko turns her attention to me. I think this might be the first time she's acknowledged me. She bows. "Thank you, Joseph-san, for your service and bravery."

I offer her a respectful smile. "I will do my best."

"What about Scarlett?" Gabrielle asks. "Any sign of her popping up again?"

"Nothing," Iris says. "I wish we knew what she wanted. Then perhaps we could persuade her to stop."

"If I see her," Gabrielle replies gruffly, "I will persuade her."

"If I could go on this mission, I would," Felix says heavily. "You know that, Gabrielle."

"I know that if I had a dollar for every time you've said that . . ." Gabrielle replies. "Anyway, you can't, and we need you here. Don't worry, we'll save them both."

There's a moment of silence as we all send up a silent prayer for success. "I miss Bill," Felix says, breaking the silence. "He would know exactly what to say now."

"We all miss him," Iris says, and I detect a slight tremor in her voice.

"You know, in the very early days, Bill and I used to wonder if all the effort, all the years we spent trying and failing, would ever amount to anything," Felix continues. "We didn't even know if the travelers we found would want to join us, or understand what we were trying to do." He looks across at me and Gabrielle. "He would be very proud to see you both today, working together like this."

Gabrielle shifts on her feet. I bob my head respectfully, wishing again that I had known Bill for longer. I'm craving more understanding of The Continuum. They exist in the future, but they have a long history, their own story of trials and tribulations, victories and failures. Iris gave me the brochure version, but now I want to know everything about them: what they stand for, why they do all of this. But I understand that for now, we have our work cut out.

Iris says, "It's nearly time."

Gabrielle stretches and yawns loudly. "And this is the part where you say, 'Don't take unnecessary risks.'"

Iris laughs gently through her nose. "You know me too well." She turns to me, her expression stern. "We have asked much of you, Joseph, but there is a limit. All you can do is your best, but do not risk your own life. Mistakes happen, and sometimes we fail. The most important thing is that you come back to fight another day." She pierces me with her blue eyes that seem to glow through our connection across time. "You don't take any unnecessary risks. You understand what I am saying?"

"Yes," I tell her.

"Good," she replies, seemingly content. "Safe travels. See you when you get back."

Felix and Kyoko echo her words, and then the future fades away, leaving Gabrielle and me in my loft with our heads buzzing.

Gabrielle checks her watch and asks for mine. She taps them together and hands my silver hunter back. The fascia has updated with the final jump indicator, a tiny red jewel shining brightly. The readout shows we are due to leave in twenty minutes and will land on the night of the fire at 9 p.m.

"We need a plan," Gabrielle announces.

"Didn't we just do all that?"

"I know we just talked through the technical side of things, but you and I need to know what we're doing when we go through that entrance, right?"

"Right."

Gabrielle wanders the loft, speaking her plan aloud. "First off, all that fight-another-day stuff? Iris is right. You're not there to sacrifice your life, so don't do anything stupid, got it?"

I think she has me confused with someone heroic. "Got it," I reply.

"Good, but just so you know, it doesn't apply to me. I'm saving Philippe and bringing Nils home, no matter what. Clear?"

"Er, not really." If I had known Gabrielle at school, I would have spent way more time in detention.

She continues pacing. "One of us has to be in the Hallway of Mirrors with the lantern at 10:10."

"Probably me," I say. "In the viewing, I saw myself there."

"Yeah, but I could have been there too, right? You might not have seen me."

"To be fair, my line of sight was tightly focused." I shrug. "It's possible, I suppose."

"I say we stick together as long as we can," she says. "Is that OK with you?"

"Yeah, although that feels weird."

"What does?"

"You asking my opinion. I can't get used to it."

"Good, don't," she snaps and then pauses, staring unseeing at the photos of Other Joe on the wall. Her thoughts pour out in a calm stream of consciousness. "I did consider bringing a breathing apparatus, but when the roof collapsed, it created a chimney effect, so I'm pretty sure the smoke won't kill us. But the fire will, if we overstay our welcome." She looks at me. "We do our best to find Philippe and get him out. If we can't find him immediately, we go to his room, grab the violin, his precious scrolls, the kitchen sink, and the cat too, if we can find it. That way, if we bump into him, he has no excuse."

"You still think that's why he goes back inside?"

"I don't know, man. I wish we could have found out more, but it's so often the way. Resistance . . . it all comes together on the final jump. It's how we roll, but I gotta be honest here, just saying this plan out loud, it's more vague than usual."

"Vague, hmm," I say, almost matching Gabrielle for sarcasm. "And we also have to find a time-traveling ghost, caught between dimensions using an untested time-distorting lantern."

We both laugh. It feels good, though it also feels a bit like we're facing a firing squad and joking to take our minds off the inevitable. What we're about to do scares the hell out of me. There have been plenty of opportunities for me to back out, but I didn't. I committed, and yet I can't help but feel a bit swept along. My mind just keeps thinking up all the ways this could go wrong. I wonder if everyone who's ever been brave feels this.

Luckily, Gabrielle gets us back on track. "Next, timing. Philippe came out of the entrance at 10:40 p.m. The fire was raging by then, but the handful of reliable accounts we have claim that it started in the auditorium and took a while to take hold. That said, once it did, the opera house went up fast. So we do not want to get stuck in there. By 10:40 p.m., I want us standing on the street outside with Philippe."

A thought crosses my mind. "We'll already be there, won't we? I mean, the versions of us from our first jump."

"Yeah, we can just avoid ourselves, though," she says, in a pedestrian tone.

"Right," I murmur, imagining the four of us in Paris. Two Gabrielles. Ugh.

She scowls at me. "It's not difficult. We know exactly what we did and where we were." She pauses, thinking. "Is there anything else we need to talk through?"

"There is actually," I say. "You remember the house where Philippe taught those street kids?"

"Yeah."

"Guess who owns it?"

"Blanche Delacroix," she says. "I do my research."

"OK, but did you know that when she died, her entire estate was squandered by her brother and his family?"

She arches an eyebrow. "No, I didn't."

"She's loaded," I continue, "and she's helping Philippe, allowing him to teach children from her home."

"Yeah, and?"

"And she said to me that she knows she needs to do more. Maybe she's connected to Philippe's potential destiny. Maybe she's the money?"

"Maybe," Gabrielle agrees. "Good work."

"Actually, it wasn't me. Vinny's the researcher."

"Who?"

"Vinny, the record shop guy who helped me on the Romano mission." Another thought crosses my mind. "I can't help but wonder if Philippe invited the kids we saw him teaching to the opera, you know, snuck them in, and it was them he was going back in for."

"All possible." She studies me with amusement.

"What?"

"You're almost getting the hang of this." She checks the lantern over and puts it back into the satchel. "Anyway. We should get dressed."

I stare at the satchel. "Hang on. Felix and Kyoko created and modified the lantern in the future, but now you have it here?"

"You've heard of 3D printers, right?"

"Yeah, but this is . . . "

"And you know how people share data via the internet and email and stuff?"

"Obviously, but that still doesn't—"

She holds up a finger. "Just add over a hundred years of progress to all those things, pepper in some time crystals—which exist outside of time, by the way—pour in some triterbium and stir. Does that answer your question?"

"Kind of." I wonder if the magic printer is another subject that would have been covered in my orientation.

"And don't get your knickers in a twist about the fact that we print money. Doesn't every government these days? All I can say is, it's a good thing I have strong morals." Gabrielle grabs her suitcase and opens it. "In truth, getting hold of triterbium was more complicated, but all you need to know is that we have the lantern. Let's just hope it works."

She selects our clothing. It has the style of the era, but the cut and composition have been altered. The material of my suit is a fabric that feels slightly spongy, like Neoprene. Same with my shoes; they look like polished leather, but they feel like sports shoes, padded and soft. Gabrielle chooses a tight-fitting dress, dark blue and less fancy than before, with a small button-up jacket and hat. It feels a bit more practical than the last time. She reaches for my jacket and clips a tiny magnetic dot to my lapel.

"What's that?" I ask.

"A light. You tap it twice to turn it on, same to turn it off. If you're fond of your retinas, do not look directly into the beam. Bright as the sun. Clear?"

I feel instantly guilty. I was just about to go and get Vinny's light, but it looks like I've been given an upgrade. I can see his expression, a big sad puppy, but then I imagine telling him about my new tech, and I see his face brighten. I don't need his gift. Vinny is always with me in spirit.

Gabrielle undoes a thumb-sized container with a screw-top, dabs her finger into it, and then applies its contents to her nostrils, almost sneezing a couple of times. "It's a kind of gel, helps block out some of the smoke. It can't do it all, but it should certainly help." She hands one to me. "Apply it and then keep it safe. Depending on what happens, we might need to give it to Nils and Philippe."

I remove the lid. The gel is light blue and unexpectedly powdery to the touch. I smear it around the inside of my nostrils. It crackles and burns like raw chili for a couple of seconds, and then the sensation is gone. I smell the faint odor of rubber.

Gabrielle slips the satchel over her shoulder, looks me up and down, and winks. "Right, I think we're all set." She wanders over to the wall-mounted iPad. "OK if I put some music on before we leave?"

"Help yourself," I tell her. "I have vinyl too, depending on what you had in mind."

"Vinyl for sure, and you'd better have this one." As she works her way through my stack of records, I try to imagine what she might pick. Van Halen's "Jump"? House of Pain's "Jump Around"?

When I hear the needle drop and the percussion and guitar riff fade up and fill the room, it's a surprise, and yet somehow, the perfect song and mood for the occasion.

The Rolling Stones' "Gimme Shelter."

Gabrielle begins to flicker, and a light-blue aura dances over her skin. I feel the present sliding away, the promise of the past close now. Gabrielle takes my hand as Mick Jagger whines and snarls about needing shelter, about burning fire sweeping down streets, about fading away.

Gabrielle's eyes are closed, her head bobbing to the music.

"It's a cool track," I tell her.

She opens her eyes and shouts over the music. "Good thing you had this on vinyl, I would have strung you up otherwise. I actually chose this song for Bill. The Stones were his favorite." She shrugs. "I'm more of a Beatles fan myself."

PART 6

29

We arrive in a quiet Parisian courtyard. Small, dank, and empty, its high stone walls glisten in the moonlight. As my vision adjusts, I see a wrought iron gate. Gabrielle eases it open, and we step onto a street buzzing with people and talk of the fire. I catch the first bitter scent of wood smoke. We check our watches. My silver hunter has been set to alert me the second it picks up Nils's signal, but for now, it acts exactly the same as Gabrielle's. The word *Calibrating* is replaced with jump data, and at the bottom of the display, separated by a curved band, it reads *Time Remaining: 4 hours, 2 minutes*. Left of the dial, the date shows 29 October 1873. On the right, the local time: 9 p.m. The top quadrant of the display is blank.

"No waypoint yet," Gabrielle says, "but we've landed earlier than we did on our first jump. That's good news. We need all the time we can get."

I check the time remaining. "We have four hours to get this done."

"Let's make it enough," she says, holding the satchel close. "Come on."

Above us a brilliant swarm of white embers floats by, carried on the cool evening breeze with the distant cries of anguished people and the unmistakable cracking and popping of the fire. Nearby buildings illuminate our path in a warm orange glow, and Gabrielle and I break into a run, knowing that every second counts. As we pass through the streets, I berate my lack of fitness and decide I really must do more exercise.

As we approach the opera house, shadows of the busy crowd are projected onto the walls of the buildings around us, jerking like huge stop-motion animations as the flames behind them flicker. Compared to the last time we were here, the streets are noticeably missing survivors. The stream of people, horses, and carriages seems to be heading in one mass *toward* the opera house; the grim spectacle is drawing them like moths. I feel it too, an undeniable, morbid fascination.

We round a corner and join the Rue Le Peletier, where we soak in a familiar scene, albeit a little earlier in the evening. The opera house stands defiantly. Its center is already a glowing ball of ferocious heat, but the fire hasn't yet tightened its grip on the building. Swirling clouds of smoke obscure the night sky. A million glowing embers flutter and dance like agitated fireflies, raining down on a teeming mass of people. I see an occasional flurry of panic and activity as someone's clothing catches alight and people gather around them, beating the flames away with their bare hands, and someone else tries to calm a horse as it rears up and neighs in terror.

Men with determined expressions carry items from the opera house: cloth sacks, wooden chests, chairs and tables, whatever they can save from the fire. Women help too, dragging children beside them, holding them close as their little faces stare in awe and wonder at the burning building. I hadn't noticed this before, but they're not all wealthy patrons of the arts. The crowd consists largely of normal Parisians dressed in plain, everyday clothes. They may never have been to the opera, but they have come together now.

Gabrielle and I push our way through the crowd, easing between an organized row of people passing buckets of water down a line with calm efficiency. They shout encouragement. They believe the fire can be beaten.

From the first floor, people throw anything precious or flammable down to the street, where it is sorted and dragged away by the crowd below. We work our way around a pile of furniture, paintings, and curtains stacked a safe distance from the fire. Scattered among them is an incongruous collection of valuables: a clock inside a glass jar, a velvet cloak, a silver teapot.

To my left, firemen scramble up ladders propped against the adjacent buildings. Some of the men are already perched on ledges, supported by colleagues. Their hoses hang below them, lashing like snakes. Water plumes out in arcs from multiple angles, soaking the building. It's impressive, like it could almost succeed in fighting back the flames now working their way out of the roof, but knowing how ineffectual their efforts will be against the relentless fire weighs heavily on me.

Gabrielle and I are jostled and shoved as we work our way toward the entrance to the opera house. I don't want to go inside, but knowledge of the past is a double-edged sword. Although injured, Philippe was able to walk through the foyer and out of the entrance at 10:40 p.m. That's almost an hour and a half from now. We need to remain vigilant, but we know we have time on our side.

Flames that have been busily licking the windows of the first-floor balcony burst through in a shattering crash of fierce heat. The crowd gasps in unison. Gabrielle and I use their momentary stillness for a final sprint toward the entrance. Finely dressed men and women pour from the wide doorway, like water from a failing dam. They jostle for position, shoving and arguing as they stumble onto the cobbled street. Some fall and are trampled.

Gabrielle turns to me, ignoring the panic, and I realize I'm witnessing her journalistic ability to remain detached from her surroundings. "OK, timing is good," she says, her voice confident. "Let's get inside, see if we can find Philippe." I stay close as we head for the door, working our way around the seething mass of people coming at us.

A fireman stops us, his wide eyes accentuated by his blackened cheeks and forehead. Like most of the men, he has a broad mustache, and at first I think it's the chief who picked us up and brought us here, but then I remember that on our first jump, we hadn't arrived at the opera house yet. He yells, "What are you doing? Where are you going?"

"We need to get inside!" Gabrielle shouts back.

"Absolutely not!" he roars. "Until we get the fire under control, no one goes inside."

"My friend is in there!" she cries. "I have to help him."

"If he's in there, we will get him out, not you." The fireman is distracted by a group of men carrying a limp body out of the opera house. He runs over to assist them, and we seize our chance.

Inside the foyer, the air is surprisingly cool and smoke-free, but the sense of panic is palpable. Desperate cries echo through the hallways, and footsteps hammer the stone floor.

Gabrielle checks her watch. "I don't have a waypoint yet." She looks up at me. "I'm thinking we stick together for now, OK?"

"There's no point splitting up unless we have to. Do you think Philippe is still in here?"

"I think we should presume that he is. Luckily, the place is emptying out pretty fast. If he's here, he won't be hard to spot." She checks her watch again. "We've got time to reach Philippe's room."

As we stand here, it would be easy to allow this grand, beautiful, solid opera house to lull us into a calm certainty that the fire will be contained. It feels too big, too permanent. The passengers on the *Titanic* must have felt the same way. Could Philippe have believed he had plenty of time to reach his room, gather his belongings, perhaps even his cat, and make it to safety?

A group of people passes, so focused on the lure of the cold night air that they pay us no attention. The foyer is thinning out now. Gabrielle says, "I know a quicker way than the route we took on the tour. Follow me."

We run along numerous corridors and then through a tall room with a vaulted ceiling, a sort of museum and library combined. It's stacked with thousands of books, elaborate costumes, props, drawings, and scale models of stage sets in glass cabinets, all of it destined to burn.

Gabrielle's shortcut works, and we bypass the Hallway of Mirrors—my destination for part two of tonight's little adventure—reaching the grand staircase, which leads from the street-level entrance hall up to the auditorium. Only a few people remain now, and Gabrielle was right, the fire actually spread quite slowly at first. Even now, this deep into the opera house, I could convince myself that the fire was a false alarm, if it weren't for the black smoke that begins pouring from the numerous doorways and balconies above. They all lead to the main auditorium, and I decide that whatever the history books say, it looks as though the fire started in there, probably by the pyrotechnics for the big finale. Madame Delacroix was right.

As we climb the wide marble staircase, I hear the fire crackling and snapping, followed by a low growl that rattles up into a roar. I see the first signs of it since we entered the building, a single fire on the right-hand side of the second floor. Just one curtain alight, a gentle yellow flame climbing, like a fireman up a ladder. The smoke begins to thicken, rendering the frescoes above difficult to see. Even with the clever gel that I put up my nose, I'm beginning to think the smoke is going to be a problem.

"Gabrielle," I gasp, jogging up the steps behind her. "You said that gel would only do so much. Pretty soon we won't be able to breathe, let alone see."

"Don't worry," she says. "The gel was a precaution. Part of the roof collapses, allowing the fire to breathe and releasing most of the smoke. The top of the building acts like a chimney."

"Are you sure?"

"There were plenty of eyewitness accounts. Smoke wasn't the problem."

A terrible crash booms through the grand hallway like thunder. Paintings rattle against the walls, and plaster dust crumbles down over us. In one giant inhalation, the smoke clears, drawn back through the doorways as though time itself is rewinding the last sixty seconds.

Gabrielle turns back to me, grinning. "See?"

I am about to scold her for needing to be right all the time when I see a man staggering down the stairs above us. He holds a red cravat over his mouth with one hand, steadying himself with the other. When he sees us, he stumbles and almost falls, then collapses back onto the steps. As he removes his cravat from his face, I realize it's Dominic Monier. His eyes widen in terror. "You!" he says, voice trembling. "You vanished, and now here you are again. Where did you go?"

I try to imagine what it must have been like for him. We disappeared from his locked office a week ago. He's had plenty of time to think about it.

Gabrielle crouches down and reaches for his hand.

He flinches and pulls away. "No! It's too late," he wails, voice cracking as he blinks up at her, green eyes searching desperately for understanding. "What have I done?"

"What do you mean?" she asks.

He grimaces. "I was so desperate for success. I didn't mean for any of this to happen."

Gabrielle leans closer. "What are you talking about?"

His expression flattens, and he lowers his head. "I tried to get him out, but the fire has taken hold. Henri is trapped. I couldn't reach him."

"Who's Henri?" Gabrielle asks, echoing my own confusion.

"There's a trap door under the stage! It was all planned so perfectly. He was going to wait until after the performance, before he—"

"Henri is the Phantom?" Gabrielle interjects.

"Yes. He's just a poor street kid. He needed work, said he would do anything. I'm a miserable coward, mademoiselle. I left him in order to save myself." He stares at Gabrielle as though she just slapped him. "I told Philippe it was too late, but he went back for Henri. He said he couldn't just leave him."

Gabrielle grabs Monier's jacket. "Listen to me, we're going to save them both, but you need to get out of here!"

His face cracks as though he's about to cry. "Are you insane? It's too late; the opera house is lost, and Philippe and Henri with it!"

I haul him up. "You heard her, get out of here."

Gabrielle runs, and I follow, leaving Monier and his words of regret in our wake.

"So now we know why Philippe came back inside!" I shout to Gabrielle, as we scale the final flight of stairs at speed.

"Yes, but I don't remember anyone talking about Henri—there was nothing in my research. I just hope we're not too late."

As we reach the top of the stairs, I catch up with Gabrielle's thinking. Pieces of a puzzle fall into place. The Phantom—a street kid. What was it the man outside the restaurant said to me, when we were listening to the girl play the violin? *She is one of the invisible.* When the news reports claimed there were no deaths, they may have meant none that warranted reporting. What a tragic thought.

"Henri never made it out, did he?" I say.

Gabrielle shoots a quick glance my way. "If I have anything to do with it, he's getting out tonight."

We pass through a doorway and enter the main auditorium. The heat smacks my face, the air dry and sharp. The right-hand side of the auditorium is already consumed by a dancing wall of fire. The ceiling swims with searing heat, dripping luminous molten threads onto the seats below, each one bursting into life upon contact. The roof has partially collapsed, creating the chimney effect that Gabrielle mentioned, allowing the smoke to escape but also enabling the cool night air to feed the fire.

The stage is an island, surrounded by an encroaching sea of tangerine flame. I see Philippe, shimmering like a mirage, clambering over scenery. He appears to be working his way toward the center, where I presume Henri is trapped. An enormous length of glowing timber surrounded by smoldering debris covers that area of the stage.

There is a clear path to him, straight down an aisle currently untouched by fire. With no time left to doubt or wonder or plan, we just run. This is it, the mystery of why Philippe is here: Henri, trapped beneath the stage, his fate unthinkable. Only Gabrielle and I can make this right.

"Philippe!" Gabrielle shouts.

We cry his name repeatedly as we run. Finally, he hears us over the roar of the fire, desperate fear on his face. "Help me! There's a man trapped down there!"

"We know!" I shout back. "We'll get him out."

As we reach the edge of the stage and climb the wooden stairs toward Philippe, I hear Henri's desperate cries. Everything is happening too quickly now. The thick curtains on both sides of the stage ignite as another huge piece of glowing timber crashes down onto the front of the stage, bursting in fresh, crackling flame. Philippe cries out, covering his face. It was close, but he's OK. Henri is screaming now. Philippe reaches center stage before we do, busily wrapping his hands in rags. I can see what's about to happen.

"Philippe, no!" I scream at the top of my lungs. "You'll hurt yourself!"

"We can't just leave him," he shouts back.

Gabrielle and I beg him not to, but Philippe grabs the glowing piece of timber and lifts, hauling it aside. The rags covering his hands burst into flame. He cries out, but he doesn't stop or let go. He can't do it alone. Gabrielle and I grab a sizable oak banquet table and manage to push it against the edge of the timber blocking the trapdoor. The force of all three of us is just enough to move it aside. A blackened hatch is revealed, but as fresh oxygen hits its surface, it ignites. Philippe staggers back, howling in pain. The trapdoor lifts and Henri emerges coughing, his jacket alight.

"Help me!" he begs. He's a scruffy young lad, can't be any more than fourteen or fifteen, and his entire body is trembling. I remove my coat and beat the flames from Henri's clothing. Gabrielle rushes to Philippe, who is hunched over, examining his ruined hands. He's trembling in pain and shock, and disturbing flashes of red show through the charred material.

The speed of our failure is shocking. After all our planning and effort, Philippe is still injured. But when I look into Henri's eyes, that sense of failure is temporarily banished. "Thank you," he gasps, his voice choppy with fear and adrenaline. "I thought I was a goner."

"You're all right," I tell him, tears of relief welling in my eyes. "You're going to be OK."

"But what about Monsieur Chevalier?"

Gabrielle looks up at me and shakes her head. Philippe grits his teeth and stands. "I will live, but we need to go."

I check my watch. It's nearly 10 p.m. In all this madness, I almost forgot about Nils. We need to get to the Hallway of Mirrors in ten minutes. Above us, a flash of gold draws my attention, and I notice that one of the four golden eagle statues perched above the stage is leaning forward at a dangerous angle. I remember Amy's abstract painting—a scarred hand, a carved eagle.

"Get off the stage!" I yell. "NOW!"

No one argues. As we scramble our way along the edge of the auditorium, the huge eagle breaks free with an ominous, whining groan. It crashes onto the stage, its head cutting straight through the floorboards, exactly where Henri would still have been trapped without our intervention. Henri glances at me as we run. He's limping badly. Gabrielle supports him. When we finally reach the doorway leading to the staircase, a huge section of the auditorium's domed ceiling collapses. The sound is deafening, and the heat pushes us through the doorway. We take refuge on either side as searing air rushes past, setting fire to the curtains and showering angry sparks everywhere.

I remember the awful sound of the ceiling caving in from our first jump. It means that the other versions of Gabrielle and me are now outside.

Painstakingly slowly, we descend the staircase as waxy droplets of glowing fire rain down on us, periodically patting each other's clothes down as we support the injured men. The isolated fires are now joining. Soon the staircase will collapse, and this whole place will begin to boil. My silver hunter vibrates.

I check my watch. "Five minutes past ten," I tell Gabrielle. "We can still reach Nils."

"Who's Nils?" Henri asks.

"Someone else we have to save," Gabrielle says.

We reach the foot of the grand staircase. Smoke rolls at our feet. We move as quickly as we can toward a corridor that leads to the main entrance. Gabrielle doesn't know it yet, but we're about to part ways.

She turns back to Philippe. "Can you get Henri out of the building from here?"

Philippe grits his teeth in determination. "I can get him out."

"Go now," she says. "I'm right behind you."

Philippe takes Henri's weight as the young man leans against his uninjured side, and they make their way painfully toward the main door.

As I watch them go, my mind churns with all the changes we've made. "Gabrielle, you need to go with them."

She looks confused. "But we need to save Nils."

"We've changed a lot here," I tell her. "Philippe only just managed to escape the last time, and he was alone. This time, he's supporting Henri too. We could risk losing them both. They need your help."

"No way. We stick together." Gabrielle fixes me with a determined stare. "I can't ask you to do this."

"You aren't. You have your mission. Nils is mine."

She thinks about this for a second. "Why don't you guide those two out, and I'll get Nils."

"Gabrielle, I told you. It's me in the Hallway of Mirrors. I'm the one who brings Nils through, not you."

"But you admitted yourself that I *could* be there."

Frustration rises in my chest. Now is not the time to be stubborn. "Gabrielle! I thought it was possible when I had the viewing, but looking at what's just happened, you can't have been. You need to help Philippe and Henri get out, or it's all been for nothing. Please!"

Gabrielle's face settles on an expression I haven't seen before. I think it might be admiration. She hands me the leather satchel, and a spark of mutual respect passes between us. "The lantern looks fragile, but it's actually pretty tough. You get out, Joe, no matter what, OK?"

I lift the satchel over my head. "You think I want to be in here?"

She smacks my arm, hard. "I mean it. We're here until one a.m. Do not get stuck in this building. You fire up the lantern, do your best, but whatever happens, promise me you'll get out."

"To fight another day," I say with fake confidence.

"Exactly. And listen to the building like I showed you. Tune in. Time will help you." She turns to go, then solemnly, she adds, "Thanks, Joe."

I smile, but I don't want her gratitude, not yet. There is too much to do, and I'm running out of time.

30

Gabrielle, Henri, and Philippe disappear into one of the many corridors that run through the building like capillaries. I've studied the available blueprints, and they are basic but good enough for me to plan my route. Gabrielle is heading toward the foyer on the ground floor. The Hallway of Mirrors is situated directly above that, but the best way to get there is to continue down the main staircase to the second floor and head across from there. I descend the remainder of the steps, the sound of the fire drowning out the echo of my footfalls on the stone floor.

Our attempt to stop Philippe from getting hurt may have gone sideways, but we saved a man's life tonight, and there's still time to rescue Nils. I'm going to find him, drag him into this hellish reality, and then get us both out of here. A wheedling voice somewhere in the back of my mind asks if I really believe that. I tell it to shut up.

It's 10:07. Nils will arrive in three minutes. In the original version of events, we watched Philippe stagger out of the building at 10:40. We know the opera house was consumed by that point. So that is my deadline—which isn't my favorite turn of phrase. Let's call it a cut-off point. Something to aim for.

At the base of the staircase is a long corridor. I jog it, focused on the far end. It's a little cooler here, the sound of the fire muffled. That's one of the reasons I cry out in shock when a searing ball of flame smashes onto the floor just a few feet to my right. A cushion of heat and sparks pushes me off course, and I stagger, only just keeping my footing. Above me the decorated ceiling writhes and bubbles into foaming brown patches, like butter in a pan. The fire isn't devouring the opera house like some ravenous beast—it's more like a snake, slithering through hallways and cavities, igniting everything it touches. Judging by the appearance of the ceiling, it's made its way to the floor above.

Gabrielle's disembodied voice barks into my ear. "Hey, Bridgeman!"

"Jesus Christ!" I cry out in shock.

"Afraid not!" she bawls. "And you don't need to shout!"

"We can communicate?"

"Well duh, of course we can communicate. What did you think that implant was for? Contraception?"

Another section of the ceiling peels away, dripping and oozing. "I'm going to have to dodge some fireballs to get to Nils," I tell Gabrielle. I take one more step, and the domed hall at the far end of the corridor bursts into brilliant white flame. A broad section of wrought iron railings and stone collapses in on itself. Smoke and debris plume through an arch, heading in my direction. I back up, keeping one eye on the ceiling. "Scratch that," I say. "I'm going to need to find a different route."

"Stay focused," she replies. "We're nearly out. I'm right here if you need help."

I backtrack my way through corridors and passageways. The air is thick with heat now. Gabrielle's voice isn't the only one in my head; the primal part of me is screaming now too, insisting that I don't have to do this. I do my best to answer calmly. *Yes, I do.*

And I mean it, because what Philippe said when he was rescuing Henri is true. If there's a chance to save someone, you *have* to try, not only for their sake, but also because you have to live with yourself after the dust settles. I can't just abandon Nils when I'm so close. If the boot were on the other foot and I was the time traveler lost in the void, I hope someone would do the same for me.

My shoes were sticking to the floor earlier, but now I find myself slipping across smooth stone. I career around a corner and go barreling into a marble pillar. My ribs bend painfully close to their breaking point as the wind is knocked out of me. "Oof!"

"Are you OK?" Gabrielle asks.

"Yeah, I think so," I grunt, dusting myself off. I check the lantern, which seems fine—it *is* a tough bit of kit—and then inspect my new ice skates. "The soles of my shoes have melted. It's making running a little tricky. How are you doing?"

"Hang on!" She barks orders to Philippe. "Like you, we got cut off, but I think we have a route now. We'll be OK."

"I'm nearly there. Talk to you in a bit." I continue, adjusting to my lack of traction. By the time I reach the Hallway of Mirrors, my limbs are taut with adrenaline.

At first glance, the hallway looks serene, untouched by the fire and just as impressive as I remember it. The stone floor and marble columns appear strong and unaffected by the heat. The twenty or so huge mirrors that line either side are all intact. Golden statues hold clusters of lights above their heads, raised as though saluting the row of huge chandeliers that spans the full length of the hallway. But evidence that the fire is close is everywhere. A gentle heat haze forces the golden statues to sway in a sickening fashion. There are glowing patches in the plastered walls. The ceiling frescoes swim in places, like an angry sea. Innocent whisps of blue smoke swirl through the heavy air. At the far end of the hallway, I see the fireplace from my viewing, and on the mantelpiece above it, the clock.

Gabrielle buzzes in my ear. "Joe, have you seen the time?"

I check my watch. It's 10:21.

"Damn it!" I growl. "I'm too late, I think I might have missed him."

A terrible thought crosses my mind. Nils has been here for eleven minutes already, and here I am looking at the hallway. What if I just accidentally observed him, sending him back into the void without another way of getting out again? How could I have been so *stupid*?

"Are you picking up his signal?" Gabrielle asks.

"No." I rotate the dial on my watch. "Why isn't he here? My viewing was very specific, it showed him coming through at exactly ten minutes past the hour. Something must have gone wrong." I keep my head low and work my way down the hallway, moving my gaze cautiously from mirror to mirror, ensuring I don't look directly at anything.

As I near the clock, I call out, "Nils! Are you here?"

Nothing. No sign of him at all.

Gabrielle says, "As soon as you pick up his signal, you fire the lantern and get out of there, OK?"

"Right." As I reach the last mirror in the hallway, I close my eyes, walk to the fireplace, and open them again. The clock says ten minutes past 10. I check my watch: 10:22 p.m.

"What the hell?" I murmur.

"What is it?" Gabrielle asks.

"I think the clock stopped. At ten past ten."

"It must have been the heat."

"Which means that if I haven't already missed him . . ." I trail off, a dark realization hitting me sideways. "If the clock is stuck, then Nils could come through at any time. I have no way of knowing when."

A warm gust of air pushes into the room. I hear the fire now, crackling and popping, a grumbling moan threatening to roar. The ceiling glows with a sickening bluish-green mist that pops from the center and explodes into a sea of orange flame. This isn't going to work. It's too hot, there isn't enough time.

I wipe sweat from my brow and run my fingers through my hair, which is hot and wet with perspiration. I notice a mesmerizing strand of material spiraling down through the air, aflame.

I've seen this before.

The gesture I just made, my hands through my hair, the burning piece of material—I've seen this moment. I watch the clock, and right on cue, the glass bulges, then splits cleanly down the middle, as though sliced by the sharpest of blades. It all comes together in my mind at once.

The time doesn't matter.

Nils comes through when the clockface cracks, when I'm standing here watching.

"yes!" I cry out.

"What?" Gabrielle asks me.

"He's coming through now!"

I dive out of the way and feel the presence of another body rush past me. I override my natural instinct to look and force myself to peer into the massive mirror on the wall next to me. There, reflected in the mirror just a few feet from me, is the ghostly figure of Nils Petersen. His outline has a silvery sheen, his body translucent. He pushes his hair back and gazes around the hallway, his expression fearful but determined. When he sees me in the mirror looking back at him, his eyes widen, and he holds up his hands in a defensive gesture.

"No! Don't turn around!" he implores. "Please, you mustn't look at me!"

"It's OK, Nils," I assure him, my heart pounding in my ears. "I won't. I know what happened. I'm from The Continuum. I'm here to get you home."

"Who are you?" he says, his voice strained and distorted, just as it was when I overheard him talking to Scarlett.

"My name is Joseph Bridgeman."

"Bridgeman?" He says my name as though he recognizes it but remains focused on the immediate problem. "OK. What do I need to do?"

I slip the leather satchel over my head, and I'm about to explain the plan when the mirror I'm using to see Nils shatters into a thousand pieces and collapses.

"Nils?" I call out, staring at the floor. Nothing . . . just the roar of the fire moving ever closer. I notice cuts and abrasions on my forearms, and a deeper slice over the top of my right hand. I pull a thin fragment of glass from the cut and impatiently wipe the blood away. It congeals and dries quickly in the heat.

"Talk to me," Gabrielle says, panting.

"He was here, but the mirror I was using to see him smashed, and now he's gone."

"Fire the goddamn lantern!" she shouts. "Do it now!"

"But we only have one shot. I don't want to risk firing the lantern unless I can see and hear him." Another mirror on the opposite side of the hall explodes, then another, showering the floor with shards of glass. A terrible, thunderous boom makes the ground shudder. I remember this: a section of the auditorium's roof caving in. I keep my eyes down and head back the way I came, toward the biggest mirror I can see. When I arrive at the mirror, Nils is waiting. I pull the lantern's metal legs apart and place it on the floor. The bulbous head appears intact; all I can do now is hope it works.

I lift the security cover and press the red button three times, just like Kyoko told me to. Nothing happens.

"What is it?" Nils shouts, his voice sounding more distant.

I stare at the lantern in panic and wonder if I need to try again, but then a deep throbbing pulse passes through me. My teeth rattle. The crystal at the top of the lantern begins to glow, and the cage surrounding it begins to rotate, spinning faster with each revolution. A kaleidoscope of colors streams out in all directions like clashing swords on a hallucinogenic battlefield.

Gabrielle's voice crackles and sounds like it's being squeezed through a long, narrow pipe. At the far end of the corridor, a silent cloud of smoke rolls in and then suddenly stops. I look up. The chandeliers stop swaying. Orange goo dripping from the ceiling pauses in midair. Golden sparks of flame hover silently. The roar of the fire fades.

Time dilation.

I don't have long.

Keeping my focus on the mirror, I inch backward toward Nils. "Take my hand!" His hand locks around my forearm, and his skin is icy cold. A buzz of pure energy ignites my bones, and Nils cries, "You did it! Thank God! Thank you!" His voice sounds wonderfully normal. I look at him in the mirror first, not wanting to risk anything.

Standing behind me is a tall, *solid* man in torn, dirty clothing, his skin beaded with sweat. I turn cautiously, and when our eyes meet, nothing happens. I smile, and he grins back at me, but the exchange is brief. Both of us know this is far from over.

"How have you stopped time?" he asks, his Nordic accent discernible now.

"With the lantern," I tell him. "It's only temporary, though. It'll stop working any second now, and then we need to be ready to run."

The spinning cage of the lantern is a blur, but the warm glow of the crystal is fading. The air around us begins to move again, almost imperceptibly at first, just the odd flicker of light in the floating embers. That's when I feel the floor shift beneath me. A crack appears, right under the lantern. In slow motion it travels across the width of the hallway in a crooked grin, cutting it in two.

The floor yawns open slowly like a dark, toothless mouth. The lantern leans in, about to fall. I reach for it, but Nils pulls me back as the hole belches up an impossibly slow cloud of boiling steam. I can only assume that it's water from the basement rising up under some kind of pressure.

Suddenly, like a hand-cranked film being wound way too fast, time catches up with us.

The ferocity is shocking. The floor cracks apart in a deafening groan and sinks a few feet. I maintain my balance but watch in horror as the stone around me begins to crumble away. Large pieces slide and disappear, crashing into the foyer below. Flames lick at the floor's open wounds. The ground tilts, and for one horrible moment, it feels as though Nils and I are going to fall into the oven below. His strong hand grips my shoulder and pulls me back as the floor under my feet collapses and drops away, the lantern with it. After a loud crash, an excited shower of sparks coughs up from the newly formed hole, which is the size of a small truck.

"Are you hurt?" Nils asks.

"I'm fine, but we needed the lantern."

"Why? I'm out. I'm all right."

"No," I tell him, "we needed it to update your watch."

"What happens if we don't?" The question sits between us. I don't know what to tell him. "Never mind, let's worry about that when we get out of here."

Then, a blanket of smoke disperses around us, revealing the shape of a hooded figure, eyes sparkling red. The figure drifts toward us, its long cloak caressed by layers of smoke, and stops just a few feet away. Its features are shrouded in shadow, but I know it's Scarlett even before she pulls back her hood. Her bleached blond hair is plaited close to her scalp. Her skin is pale, her lips painted blood red. Her dark, unblinking eyes move from me to Nils, and the corner of her mouth twitches.

Nils steps forward. "What are you doing here?"

She nods in my direction. "Same as him. I'm here to get you out."

"What?" I growl back at her. "But you did this to him!"

"We're wasting time," she snaps. "In case you hadn't noticed, this place is burning to the ground, and your lantern is gone. You need my help."

"Not a chance." Nils turns to me. "Come on, let's go. Now."

Scarlett says urgently, "Listen, Nils! You may be fully manifested now, but you're attached to the change event. Once the mission ends, you will never leave here. You will never get home."

"And that's your fault!" he shouts. "Why did you do this to me? What was all that crap about second chances?"

She ignores him. "If you want to see your wife and kids again, then I am your only chance." She pulls a dark object from inside her cloak. I recognize it immediately. It's the black tower from Amy's painting, except it's not a tower, it's a device no bigger than a TV remote—a black slab with a glowing red circle at the top. "I need to reset your watch," Scarlett shouts. "Give it to me. Now."

It all comes down to this moment: a choice that I must make. Amy's painting finally makes sense of the connection between Scarlett, Nils, and his watch. In the original version of the painting, the lighthouse was like the lantern, but Amy changed it and replaced it with what I now know is Scarlett's device. Amy told me she felt it was a guiding force, told me that this was my way home, and despite everything that Scarlett has done, I have to trust my sister's intuition.

"Do it!" Scarlett shrieks, holding up the device. "Before it's too late!"

Part of the nearest wall crumbles away, revealing tendrils of flame and sending fresh heat sizzling through the air. My lungs and eyes burn. I cross my fingers behind my back. "We have to do what she says, Nils. We have no choice."

Grimacing, Nils lifts his watch from around his neck and throws it to her. Scarlett crouches down and places it onto the glowing red circle at the top of the device. It clicks and lets out a sharp whine. She sneers at us. "See, that wasn't so hard, was it?" She throws the watch back to him.

A piercing crack makes us all look up. A huge section of the fresco-covered ceiling peels away and falls. Three chandeliers come with it. Scarlett scrambles back. I pull Nils back as hard as I can, and we go tumbling to the floor. The ceiling debris crashes to the ground, sending plumes of dust and hungry sparks swirling through the air. The already weakened floor gives way, and the entire middle portion of the hallway disappears. This time the heat is a wall that knocks the air out of my lungs. Operating on pure instinct, Nils and I crawl back toward the fireplace at the far end of the room. The hole in the center is huge now, like the mouth of a volcano. Flames lick hungrily at its edges. Statues on the other side shimmer.

"Scarlett?" I shout as loud as I can.

My heart leaps and steadies when I see her stagger to her feet and raise a hand on the far side. She backs away from the heat. "I'm OK!" she shouts. "Are you both all right?"

"What does she care?" Nils snarls.

Scarlett jogs to the edge of the gaping hole. "You can cross here. I will catch you!"

There is no way. What's left of the hallway floor is perilously thin and it seems ready to collapse. Our most direct exit is blocked. Scarlett begins edging forward, her hands pressed against the wall.

"No!" I shout. "There's no way that's going to work. We'll find another way."

The ground crumbles. She pulls away. "But I can't leave you!"

"No choice," I shout back.

Scarlett checks the device. "The update worked. When the mission is over, you should go back to 1920. I'm sorry, Nils, about all of this. I didn't mean for it to happen this way."

Nils shakes his head, and then shouts, "Just get out of here, before it's too late."

Through the shimmering heat, she turns and runs back toward the entrance of the opera house, toward the safety of the cool night air.

No such escape for me and Nils. We are cut off. Fire climbs the walls, rapidly devouring the hallway. I hand Nils some of the smoke-proof gel, which he applies to his nose with relief, then I check my watch: 10:29. We're running out of time.

"Gabrielle, are you there?"

Nothing.

"Gabrielle Green?" Nils asks. "She's here too?"

"Yes, but I can't hear her anymore. She might be in trouble."

"More likely the lantern has messed with your gear." Nils's eyes glisten in the stinging heat. "I don't know if Scarlett fixed my watch, but let's find a way out of here, shall we?"

31

We choose a corridor, the atmosphere thick with heat, but as we turn the corner, we're faced with a wall of flaming rubble. We turn back and try another, but it's the same. Back at the foot of the grand staircase, which is now almost fully engulfed by the fire, the flames draw the oxygen from the air. Each breath scalds my lungs. Blinking is scratchy and painful, and my skin feels like baked leather. Nils and I don't talk. Our minds and bodies are in an instinctive mode now, our singular aim the avoidance of heat and the need for air.

Staggering through an arched doorway into the refuge of a narrow corridor, I hear Nils's ragged breathing behind me. As we run up a cramped staircase, my heart sinks. We're heading back into the auditorium, the heart of the fire; there's nowhere else left to go. Pushing through a wooden door into the auditorium is like opening an oven door and climbing inside. The inferno has gutted most of the seating, the stage has completely gone, and the tiered balconies above are a raging storm of crimson fire and billowing smoke.

The right-hand side of the ceiling has gone, and I can see the night sky. It looks cool and inviting and impossibly far away. The left-hand side of the ceiling remains, but it's sagging. I can see three floors above, compressed by the weight of a massive chandelier that somehow still hangs from the ceiling, like a rotten tooth.

On the far side of the theater, I spot a small area that is still untouched by the fire. It's our only option, but I can't see a way to reach it. What remains of the ceiling finally collapses, and the floors above go with it, followed by a tremendous golden explosion of brilliant, noxious flame. Glass, debris, and embers shower outward. In one of the numerous gaping wounds in the roof, I see a huge metal container, about the size of a bus, tipping forward, nudged along by a river of molten lead. It falls and lands near us, jolting the ground so hard my teeth rattle. The impact splits the container. Water pours out and sprays up in an arc with a screeching hiss and clouds of boiling steam. The water douses the flames directly in front of us, creating a slim path to safety on the other side of the auditorium. We run along the steaming stretch of soaked floor to a plush, upholstered section of seating on the far left of the auditorium, taking refuge beneath a first-floor overhang.

The respite doesn't last. The air heats again, wood hissing and whining as the water evaporates. We are now cut off on all sides, and I can't see any escape route. The heat batters us. My lungs feel like they're being cooked from the inside. My head throbs and I smell burning hair. Until this point, I don't think I'd allowed myself to imagine dying here, but I begin to feel the hope drain out of me now. Desperate panic rises in my chest, and I fight the urge to scream.

"I'm sorry, Nils," I tell him, my voice cracking.

"I'm sorry too. Thank you . . . for trying." He grits his teeth and closes his eyes against the heat. I see my family, Vinny, Alexia. Faces I won't see again. That's when I notice the lines of the carvings on a nearby section of wall. They begin to glow, not with heat but with the sense of attraction that time sometimes offers me.

That gets my attention. I study the wall, its numerous squares each containing intricate carvings, all of them depicting animals.

Wait. Amy's painting. The hand reaching to touch the eagle.

I study my right hand. The cut across the top has dried fully now. The blood has darkened, exactly the way Amy painted it. I work my way along the wall, and my heart leaps with joy when I find what I'm looking for: a majestic eagle carved into the wood, its wings tucked against its body. I pull

Nils to his feet and press my hand against the bird's chest, emulating the composition of Amy's vision. As I push I feel something give, and a small section of the wall clicks open, revealing a passageway. It's big enough for us to squeeze through but the warm air rushes in first, the flames drawn toward a new source of oxygen.

"Quickly!" I shout, squeezing through the doorway and dragging Nils behind me.

Once inside, he pulls the panel closed, blocking the sound, the heat, and the light. The narrow passageway is wonderfully cool, and I take my first proper breath in what feels like hours. We stumble along in the darkness, feeling our way, until I remember the flashlight Gabrielle gave me. I double-tap my chest, and a super bright beam of blue-white light shines, illuminating the passage, which is crossed with wooden beams.

"How did you know about this passageway?" Nils says.

"It's a long story."

As we hurry along the corridor, it occurs to me that this must be how Henri, dressed as the Phantom, was vanishing and reappearing in the opera house at such unlikely speed. Gabrielle said that however Henri was doing it, he couldn't travel through walls, but it turns out that's exactly what he was doing, traversing entire sections of the opera house using these hidden passages that weave and burrow through the building.

We reach a fork in the passageway. I smell smoke drifting from the left, so we head right, but that leads to a bricked-up section of the tunnel. We head back, the smoke thickening now. We aren't out of the woods yet. We follow the left fork until we find a sort of hub with six options: four tunnels and a rickety-looking staircase that leads both down and up.

Nils says, "Which way do we go? I would normally have a sense, but I'm wrecked. I can't feel anything."

"I'm not sure," I tell him, willing the feeling of magnetism and saturation, but it doesn't come. "I don't feel anything either." I wipe away the sweat stinging my eyes and survey the blind tunnels, trying to decide which one looks most promising. Then, I remember Gabrielle telling me to tune in to the building. Closing my eyes, I place my hands against a wood-paneled wall. One by one, my senses drop offline: smell first, the acrid stench of wood smoke; followed by sound, the distant crackling of the fire; then the heat. All of it fades, and I am left with the relief of nothingness. Keeping my eyes closed, I work my hand along the wood, and the subtle damp smell of a forest hits my nostrils. I become aware of great, towering oaks around me. I feel their last breath, see them transform and become the bones of this magnificent building. "Please," I whisper to myself, "show me a safe way out of here. Let me see how this all connects."

In my mind, I see shapes flickering into life, blurred at first, but then sharpening into carved labyrinthine corridors. A complete three-dimensional map of the building fills my mind. One tunnel glows the vibrant green of forest bracken, and I follow that line all the way to the roof of the opera house. It won't be easy, but our escape route is clear, glowing bright as day.

A rush of adrenaline brings me back to reality. My eyes flash open, and I finally feel that reassuring and undeniable attraction. I've felt this a few times now, back in London with Vinny, and again when I was drawn to see Nils talking to Scarlett. It's like an internal compass, but now with another dimension that combines intuition and knowledge into absolute certainty.

I turn to Nils, feeling strangely euphoric. "We need to go down the stairs."

"Down?" he says, incredulous, his angular features sharp in the beam of light shining from my chest. "Really?"

I glance at the stairs, their outline now flickering with latent energy. "I'm absolutely certain. This way."

As we work our way down to the third sublevel floor, I can feel Nils's reluctance building. We reach the bottom of the stairwell and find ourselves in a large cellar. It smells of wet earth, and the brick walls glisten with cool moisture. Huge wooden crates are stacked in rough piles, next to oak barrels and racks of wine.

"Can we stay down here and wait the fire out?" Nils asks.

"I'm afraid not," I say, searching the room. "I've read the news reports, seen the illustrations. All of this is going to collapse. We don't have long."

"What are you looking for?"

"There's another level, below this one. A reservoir."

"Water?"

I swallow, suppressing my innermost fears. "It isn't deep. We can work our way along it and then follow a route back up to the roof. We can be rescued there."

Because Nils is a time traveler, he accepts my impossible knowledge of events with apparent ease. We find the entrance to the subterranean chamber behind a stack of crates: a wooden hatch, three feet square, with a circular metal handle. The wood has swollen in the dampness, and it takes our combined strength to break the seal. As it releases, air hisses from its edges. It smells like pond water, but even down here, there's a hint of charred wood. I lean over, and my chest light illuminates an old iron ladder dropping down into still black water.

There's another distant boom and above us, the earth convulses. Dust filters down from between the bricks overhead, and a few come loose from the low ceiling.

"That didn't sound good," Nils says. "We need to get out of here."

"I'll go first. I can light the way."

I ease down the ladder, the rusting metal ice-cold against my skin. As my feet enter the water, I have to work hard to banish my demons. My fear of sharks is hardwired into my brain, has been since I was a kid, and it's powerful enough to make my teeth chatter. The cold, dark water evokes my fear of drowning too, and packaged up with the possibility of being eaten or burned alive, it's a once-in-a-lifetime three-for-one offer.

Luckily, the water is so stingingly cold, it soon takes my mind off of everything except my breathing. I groan as my waist sinks into the frigid water. The shock of it makes me gasp. My entire body clenches, shot through with fresh adrenaline, my breath arriving in sharp bursts. I let go of the ladder, and my feet find the bottom. I'm chest-deep. I hold my hands above the water, clenching and unclenching them to keep my fingers from seizing up.

As Nils climbs down the ladder, I direct the light toward him and check out our surroundings in the reflected glow. The tunnel is about fifteen feet wide, its silent walls built from massive, hand-hewn stone blocks. Water drips from the arched ceiling. In the distance I can just make out another hatch. Faint light illuminates another wall-mounted ladder underneath it, glimmering on the surface of the water.

"We need to reach that hatch," I tell Nils, my stomach tight like a fist against the cold. "It's our best chance to escape."

He lets go of the ladder and drops into the water with a gasp. We wade briskly, the freezing water robbing the heat from my core with merciless speed. My body cramps, locking the muscles in my thighs. My teeth begin to chatter.

I glance over my shoulder to see Nils leaning as he pushes his way along. "You doing OK?"

"Yeah," he grunts. "My legs are so weak. Feels like I haven't used them in months."

"Not long now; we'll be at the next hatch before you know it."

He stops. "Wait, Joe. What's that sound?"

We both hold still, and I hear a cacophony of thin, busy screeches in the tunnel ahead. They're getting louder. I focus the beam of light ahead and see the reflected scatter of orange unblinking eyes about fifty feet away, moving steadily along the top of the water toward us. Rats. I'm watching in horrified disgust at the thought of them scurrying over my body, when they suddenly veer to the right like a flotilla of tiny boats and disappear through an archway in the wall. I wade forward to see where they've gone and find an alcove that leads into a narrow channel off from the main watercourse. It's blocked by a lattice of metal bars, but the rats squirm and contort their bodies through the small gaps.

"Hey, Joe!" Nils yells at me. "We've got a problem!"

Nils points down the tunnel where the rats came from. Pushing inexorably toward us is a massive wall of black water, tumbling with unidentifiable debris and gaining on us with terrifying speed. There's no way Nils is going to get to the ladder in time, and I can't see any other alcoves or inlets.

"In here!" I shout above the boom of the encroaching water.

Nils wades toward me in what feels like slow motion. Fear rises into my throat. I don't think we're going to make it, but if this is the end, then I'm going to die trying. I half jog, half swim toward him and reach for his arm, pulling him back, frustratingly slowly, as though we're in a nightmare. He says something, but the water is loud as thunder now, so I just keep moving as fast as I can, my attention fixed on the alcove ahead.

Just as we reach it, the water hits us. It drags at my feet like a riptide, and as I stumble forward, I take a deep breath, squeeze my eyes shut, and shove Nils into the alcove. He grabs my arm and pulls me in after him. I just have time to draw another quick breath and brace myself against the metal bars before the mass of water fills the entire chamber and lifts us to the ceiling with ferocious speed. The water rushes past us down the main tunnel, scraping debris along and ripping chunks from the tunnel wall. I grip the cage, my lungs burning and cramping, as the water swells and spins, pushing harder and harder against us.

I can't see, I can't breathe. I'm running out of oxygen.

And then I get a flashback of Amy, drowning in the lake, her hands slipping from mine, her body falling away into the depths, and then I'm spinning down with her, surrendering to the weight of the dark water . . .

I'm just about out of breath when I feel the pressure of the water recede, and hear a distant, watery voice calling my name. "Joe! JOE!" I feel air against my face again, and I draw in the deepest breath I've ever taken. I wipe the water from my face with trembling hands, and opening my eyes, I come face-to-face with Nils.

"I'm still here," he says with a weak grin. "That was some ride."

"No kidding," I say, with a shuddering release of adrenaline. "Come on, let's get out of here."

I feel as though I've lost all feeling and strength in my body, but the ladder and hatch aren't far, maybe thirty feet, and so I force myself along the tunnel, supporting myself against the wall. I'm finally starting to believe we're going to get out of here when a thundering explosion shakes the tunnel. Nils and I grab hold of each other, steadying ourselves against the vibrations that travel through the walls and into our bones. Above us part of the opera house must have collapsed. I hear it crashing down, bringing down pieces of the ceiling above us. Bricks splash into the water as aftershocks grumble and echo down the weakened tunnel, followed by a dust-filled cloud of warm smoke. When it finally clears, I can't see the hatch anymore.

"This way!" Nils shouts. Fighting the tide, I follow in his wake, pumping my arms and legs manically. My whole body shudders, and my adrenaline-filled muscles are cramping again.

"Shine the light over here," Nils says.

I aim my chest at the wall, and there's the ladder, leading out of this watery mausoleum.

Nils goes first, then hauls me up, and we both cough and sputter, filling our lungs with wonderful, life-giving air. But our celebration is short-lived. Even through my soaked clothing, I can feel the heat, and I hear the sharp, crackling pops of an active fire nearby.

Shivering, our clothes heavy with water, we run down a narrow hall-way and find a staircase alive with fresh flame. Though alight, it appears intact. Nils and I exchange a look. Knowing that we have no choice, we run up the stairs. Flames swirl around us, the heat transforming the water in our clothes into steam. My feet pound the wooden steps, some of them brittle and weak. I hear an aching moan, and part of the staircase bends and breaks below us, but we finally reach the floor above, patting embers from our clothes. The narrow staircase is filling with dark noxious smoke, and the weight of my wet clothes drains my energy. I am acutely aware that my life is at risk, but my blood feels reluctant and sludgy in my veins.

Blindly, we climb the staircase, covering numerous steps with each stride, the fire biting at our heels like a creature, chasing and snarling. I lose all sense of place and time. Each inhalation provides less oxygen, and just when I think I can't go on, I see orange splashes of light through the thick smoke ahead.

Instincts take over again and somehow, we make it to the top. We emerge into a large domed room. I rub my eyes, blinking until I can focus. We've made it all the way up to the rehearsal room at the back of the opera house. Flames lap the edges of the room, and part of the dome and floor have collapsed, dragged down by the chandelier into the audito-rium below. I can see the night sky and feel its welcome breath. Nils and I squeeze through a gap in the dome and finally breathe the fresh night air.

I turn to Nils. "We need a way to get down to street level, and I know where to find one." I point to the front of the building, a section of the roof still untouched by the fire. The route is clear, but a thin mist of rain has slicked the lead tiles. We move slowly, inching our way over the flat central ridgeline. If we slip now, we will slide for a few seconds and then drop into the fire below. It howls up at us, along with shouts and screams from the streets below. People. A good sound.

The air whips around us. My fear of heights kicks in now, vertigo threatening to buckle my knees. I focus dead ahead and finally see what I've been looking for.

"We're not too late!" I shout to Nils, close behind me. "We're getting out of here."

I point to a tall stack of stone and brickwork, all that remains of the front left-hand corner of the opera house. Cowering beneath the last remaining statue, a couple shelters from the terrible maelstrom swirling around them. The woman is kneeling, head low, her hands folded in prayer. The man covers her, his face buried in her dress.

I saw them on my first jump with Gabrielle. I was convinced there was no escape for them, but I know they made it out, and that means we can too.

The wind changes direction, fanning flames toward the stranded couple. A thick column of stone falls away from its wooden buttresses, forcing the couple out onto a ledge, evoking desperate cries from the streets below.

"There's no way they're going to survive!" Nils shouts, his voice harsh and thin. "We need another plan."

"Stay close!" I shout back. We close in on the couple as the sea of fire cuts off our route behind us. Dizziness frazzles my brain, and I nearly go tumbling over the edge, but we make it at last, clinging to the statue.

The man looks up at me, his dark eyes pleading. "There's no way down," he says, his voice wavering, horribly close to madness. "We're trapped. Either we jump or . . ." His voice tails off. His wife weeps.

"It's OK," I tell them. "The wind is about to change, and when it does, we will be rescued."

The man shakes his head and prepares for the end.

Instead, a gust of cool air whips around us, pulling the fire back, and a few seconds later, a ladder smacks against the ledge, and a fireman appears.

"It's a miracle!" the young woman cries. "A miracle!"

And that feels about right.

32

"Hold on tight, sir! We don't want anyone falling!"

The fireman holds the top of the ladder still while I climb nervously onto it, holding the top rung as tightly as possible while I get a foothold on one of the rungs lower down. Heights are not my cup of tea, but they win over fire every time.

"Go as quickly as you can," he calls as I make my way down.

I look back up at him. Smoke billows above his head, and flames roar about thirty yards away. "Thank you," I call up.

Nils mounts the ladder above me and, followed by the couple, trails me down a step at a time. As we descend, I have the distinct impression of crossing worlds, from a land of searing heat and choking smoke through a protective canopy of trees into a nirvana of fresh and cool air, rain, and green grass. I get a nauseating wave of déjà vu and wonder if the original versions of me and Gabrielle, down there in the crowd, are now watching four people being rescued from the rooftop. And if so, won't they recognize me and Nils? Will that change anything? My brain clenches with the impossible logic of rewritten time, and I decide the best course of action is avoidance. I tell Nils to keep his head down, and I turn my face to the wall.

One by one, we reach the bottom of the ladder and the cool safety of the cobbled streets below. Two firemen holding the base of the ladder welcome us warmly and offer water. Nils and the couple look frazzled, streaks of soot across their faces, clothes ripped and stained. I'm sure I don't look any better. The couple wanders off, and Nils and I move quickly away from the building to the other side of the boulevard, where we can rest and catch our breath.

We made it. My body shudders, releasing some of the tension and fear of our adventure, and my thoughts turn to Gabrielle. We can see the front of the opera house from here, but there's no one outside, and no movement inside that we can see.

I pull out my watch and check the time: 10:47. Nils and I barely made it out alive. What if Gabrielle didn't?

"I thought we'd have seen Gabrielle by now," I tell Nils. "The first time we came here, Philippe was out by this time."

"I expect she's on her way," Nils says hoarsely. He leans forward, hands on his knees, and coughs painfully. He wipes his mouth on his sleeve. "Gabrielle has changed things. It means the timing won't be exactly the same. Be patient."

There's a swell of cries in the crowd, and I look up to see three figures staggering from the main entrance of the opera house: Gabrielle, with an arm around Philippe's waist, and Henri at his side. The outline is familiar. Three people in the doorway, a detail from Amy's painting that she simply couldn't reconcile and tried to paint over. I finally understand why she might have struggled to make sense of this sliver of time. Philippe's initial escape was earlier. Our interactions add so many variables. All that matters now, though, is that this is the final version of events.

Written. Permanent. Forever.

Relief sweeps through me like a rush of cool air. "Thank God. Come on, Nils!"

I jog toward the three, who are now surrounded by a gaggle of onlookers, and push my way through to the front.

"Gabrielle! I was so worried!" I fling my arms around her.

She emits a little retching sound and pushes me away. I look at her, concerned she's about to throw up, but she grins. "It's good to see you too, Golden Boy, but I have a strict no-hugging policy, OK?"

"Whatever."

"Nils," she continues, "good to see you, man. Welcome back to dry land." She gives him a resounding clap on the back.

"It's been a long time, Gabrielle," he says. "It's good to see you again. I don't know how to thank you."

"You can thank me by getting home safe to your family," she says. She pulls me aside and lowers her voice. "I checked my watch. Saving Philippe and Henri wasn't enough. This mission isn't done yet."

"Make way!" a voice behind me booms. Two stout men pick up Philippe and load him onto a stretcher.

"Where are you taking him?" Gabrielle asks.

One of the men jerks his head to indicate their intended direction. "Medical station on the boulevard."

"I need to go with Philippe," Gabrielle tells me. "You look after Nils till he travels. Catch up with me later."

"But the comms aren't working!" I tap my ear again. Luckily, the translation function is still operational, but I haven't been able to use my implant to contact Gabrielle since I fired the lantern.

"I think the watches are OK," she tells me. "Use your hunter. Oh, and stay out of sight of the other versions of us. I just saw us wandering around somewhere . . . over there." She points to her left, and in the distance, I see myself and Gabrielle walking along the street, deep in conversation. I shudder. I've met another version of myself before, but I'll never get used to it. "Anyway. Catch ya later. Safe travels, Nils."

Gabrielle jogs after Philippe, her outfit a little worse for wear—and her hat lost at some point since I last saw her—but still looking remarkably pulled together.

"She's one of our finest," Nils says. He shows me his watch. "I'm going to travel soon. Did Felix tell you what happens now, where I'll go?"

"Presuming that Scarlett updated your watch correctly, you're going home, back to Oslo."

He winces and passes his hand briefly across his forehead. "Listen to me, if I don't get back there, will you tell my family—"

"If you don't make it home this time," I insist, "then we'll just come and find you again." And I mean it. It's impossible to stand by and watch people suffer if you're in a position to do something about it.

"Thank you, Joe, for bringing me back," Nils says. "I always hoped to meet you."

We almost go to hug, but then both of us flinch and pull away. The side of his mouth curls into a grin. God only knows what would happen if we were touching when he travels. Neither of us wants to find out.

Nils looks around calmly, taking it all in, his skin rippling in the light. I follow his gaze, watching the people as they gawk at the fire, tend to the wounded, or clear debris.

When I turn back, Nils Petersen is gone.

My watch informs me that Gabrielle and I still have a couple of hours left, so I decide to try and find her. She was blasé about the ability of my watch to track her down, but I'm doubtful. I adjust the dial and, with astonishing quickness, it locates her signal. Five minutes later I'm pushing my way into a makeshift tarpaulin tent, which shelters stretchers on the ground and at least thirty nurses tending the injured.

"Joe! Over here!" Gabrielle waves to me from halfway across the tent, and I pick my way around the edge, trying not to stare at the wounded all around me. As I approach Gabrielle, her lips press into a thin line. Henri, crouching beside a stretcher on the floor, is in tears. Philippe is in a bad way, holding his bandaged hands before him in disbelief, his expression tormented. Life as he knew it is over; the promising future that was ahead of him is gone.

"It's going to be all right," Gabrielle tells him, speaking more tenderly than I've ever heard her speak to anyone. "I'm going to do everything I can to make this OK." Philippe doesn't respond.

Gabrielle tells Henri to look after Philippe, and she beckons me out through a loose flap in the tent. I follow her to the street.

"There's nothing we can do about his injuries. He's getting the best available care, and trying to talk to him now about an alternative future is just wrong. He has a period of grieving to go through first, and he needs time to heal. Nothing I could say would work." Her wrist buzzes, and as she checks her watch, her face drops. "*Calibrating*. Jeez, come on!"

"We didn't stop Philippe from getting burned," I say. "Doesn't that mean we failed?"

"Not yet. *Calibrating* means time's working to find us another waypoint, another way to change the story. If there is any hope, it will be in connections we aren't seeing . . . Dammit! There must be something!"

There's a loud rumble and screams, as a large part of the front of the opera house comes tumbling to the ground, leaving just the foundations.

"Foundations . . ." Gabrielle murmurs. "Support . . ."

"Are you thinking maybe this isn't just about Philippe, but about the people around him? You're thinking about the people supporting him?" I keep building on the idea. "You said Philippe needs time, but maybe there are others around him who we can talk to tonight."

Gabrielle's eyes shine. "Yes! Behind every great man or woman, there is always a story, always a team . . . If we still have a chance to make this work, it isn't about talking to Philippe . . . it's about building long-lasting foundations that will carry him . . . as he recovers and finds a new path." Her mouth spreads into a grin. She shows me her watch. "I think we're onto something, look."

Calibrating
New Waypoint

She checks the time. "Eleven fifteen, and it's pointing toward . . . yes! Look, there we are!"

We see ourselves from our first jump, a few hundred yards away, following Dominic Monier along the street.

Gabrielle frowns.

"What's the matter?" I ask.

She sighs. "I just hate working with paradoxes . . ." Before I can ask her what she means, she shakes her head. "It's OK. I know what to do. Come on, let's follow them; I can tell you the plan on the way."

33

I take a final look back at the opera house, a blackened, burned, and tangled mass of charred wood, smashed stones, and twisted iron engulfed in bright-orange flames. The building may be lost, but no one died. I can still hear the woman's voice echoing in my head: *It's a miracle.*

As we leave the main drag and turn down one of the side streets, the crowds thin out, and Paris becomes much more peaceful.

"What are you thinking?" I prompt Gabrielle.

"We need to set up a support network for Philippe that begins now and continues on in the future, an emotional and practical foundation for him to build his school on. I'm convinced that Dominic Monier and Blanche Delacroix have been woven into this mission for a reason. Philippe will need them. What we need to do is set them all on their path. Although, like I said, we have a paradox to deal with first."

"What do you mean?"

She stops walking and turns to face me. I brace myself for an acerbic remark, but there's no need. "Those two—let's call them Joe One and Gabrielle One—are supposed to get information from people in the brasserie tonight, information that's going to shape the mission." She waits patiently, letting the pieces fall into place. "On our first jump, Marguerite and Delacroix shared information that shaped our approach to the whole mission, as well as Nils's rescue. With me so far?"

"Yes," I tell her, surprised by the fact that I genuinely am.

"Thing is, if Joe One and Gabrielle One visit that brasserie tonight, things are going to go very differently. People will know them. The conversations will be different. For example, Madame Delacroix is likely to ask Joe One if he's seen the ghost again, but he won't have any idea what she's talking about. Still with me?"

"I think so."

"Good. We need to stop Joe One and Gabrielle One from going into the brasserie, but we must tell them everything they found out the first time around, so that they go home with the same knowledge and complete the loop with The Continuum. It doesn't matter if their experience here isn't the same; what matters is that they return with the same knowledge."

My gut clenches. "Wait. You mean we need to talk to them? Er, I mean, us?" It feels wrong on every level.

She shrugs. "I don't like it either. It makes me want to turn myself inside out, but needs must. Don't worry, let me do the talking."

She emits a loud whistle in the direction of our alter egos, and Gabrielle One and Joe One turn around. Gabrielle One waves and strides toward us. Joe One, his eyes like saucers, follows her at a distance. His face is a reflection of how I feel, an expression of horrified fascination.

I am struck by the eerie reality of seeing myself not in the flat, reversed reflection of a mirror, but just as others see me, in all my three-dimensional glory. I suppose it's how it might feel to be an identical twin, except that I know *exactly* what's going on in Joe One's head. He's having the same thoughts I am. And we both know we're not going to talk to each other. No bloody way.

Gabrielle One asks breezily, "So how did we do?"

"Overall? We rocked," Gabrielle answers, "but we aren't done." She glances at the brasserie. "We just wanted to let you know you don't need to go in there now."

Gabrielle One doesn't question this. "OK. What do I need to know?"

Gabrielle briefs her all about our first-jump interactions in the brasserie, what she found out about Dominic Monier and my conversation with Marguerite that revealed the first sighting of Nils. "You guys can just go and relax. We'll take it from here."

Gabrielle One nods. "Got it." She turns to look at Joe One, who, like me, is fighting the urge to stick his fingers in his ears and pretend this isn't happening. "Come on, Golden Boy, stop sniveling and pull yourself together. We just bought ourselves a bit of nineteenth-century downtime." She walks off toward the river, and poor Joe One, browbeaten and forlorn, trails behind her, and I'm forced to acknowledge how far Gabrielle and I have come as a team.

As I watch them go, I think of M. C. Escher's *Drawing Hands*, its impossible loop as each hand draws the other into being. "Hang on, Gabrielle," I say, "hasn't this all happened already? Why didn't we meet ourselves on the first jump? I mean, like we just did?"

"This is a reinsertion," she explains. "On a mission, time isn't written once. We keep changing it, and each time we overwrite what was there before." She pats my arm. "I know it's confusing. It's not that often we have to travel back twice to the same time and cope with multiple versions of ourselves. We call them recursive missions, and thankfully, they're pretty rare."

"OK, but why didn't we tell them about Henri? If they knew, couldn't they work faster, avoid some of the problems we had?"

"No." She sighs. "Look. I know it's tempting. It feels like we could make our lives so easy, but if we change too much, the ripple effect can be huge. I've seen it happen, and I've seen it go wrong. I'm not going into details now—we don't have time—but you need to remember that continuity is a foundational principle of recursive travel, and we try and stick to it. If we gave the previous versions of ourselves information that we didn't have the first time around, it would change our approach, create new forks and then, well, who knows? You, me, Nils, Philippe, Henri, we all made it out of the opera house, and we can't risk changing that. It's just not worth it." She picks up her skirts. "Come on. I want to get this mission nailed."

When we get to the brasserie, the young girl in the red dress is outside, playing a melancholy little tune on her violin. She looks up at us, hoping for a coin or two, but Gabrielle instead whispers in her ear. The girl stops playing, listening intently, and when Gabrielle pulls away again, she nods and slips away into the shadows.

"What did you say?" I ask.

"Doesn't matter now. Stay here, I'm going to get Monier and Delacroix."

"Is this going to work?"

"I don't know, but it's our last shot."

Gabrielle heads inside, and a couple of minutes later, she emerges with Blanche Delacroix and Dominic Monier. Delacroix greets me with suspicion. Monier's suit is scuffed and charred, his face reddened. He glances at me but doesn't hold my gaze. He looks ragged with guilt, and this time I understand why. When we saw him escaping the opera house, he knew he was leaving Henri trapped under the stage. It would be easy to judge him, but I don't think he's a bad person; a coward perhaps, but that doesn't make him evil. I don't think any of us knows how we would act in a high-stress situation. One thing I do know is that when faced with horrific choices and very little time, we can be driven by fear and instinct alone.

Monier pulls a kerchief from his pocket and wipes sweat and ash from his brow. "You wanted to tell us something?"

Gabrielle doesn't torture him. She gets straight to the point. "After we saw you, we found Henri beneath the stage. We rescued him and made it out of the opera house."

Monier's face contorts in disbelief. "Henri is alive?"

"Yes," Gabrielle says. "He's safe and well."

"Thank God, thank you both." Monier shudders and begins to cry. Whatever happens now, he no longer has to live with the crushing guilt of abandoning Henri. He's clearly unburdened by our news, his tears filled with relief.

"However, I'm afraid Philippe Chevalier was seriously injured," Gabrielle says.

Delacroix bows her head. "Poor Philippe."

Monier sniffs. "I am so sorry about the opera house, about what happened to Philippe."

Gabrielle fixes him with a stern expression. "It's done, and there is nothing we can do now to change that. All that matters is what happens next, what gets decided tonight."

Monier studies her. "What do you mean?"

"Please, both of you, listen to me now." Gabrielle turns to Delacroix. "You, madame, are a patron of Philippe's, are you not?"

"Excuse me?" The old lady looks uncharacteristically shocked.

"I know you helped him, gave him a space to teach at your house."

Monier looks surprised. Delacroix raises her chin. "My little secret is no longer of any consequence. Sadly, I suspect Philippe's teaching days are over."

"With respect, madame, you're wrong," Gabrielle speaks confidently. "He won't recover in a way that allows him to continue conducting, but his injuries will not stop him from teaching. It's not too late for him."

Delacroix looks pensive. "What are you suggesting?"

Gabrielle allows the question to hang. When she speaks, her tone is wistful, brimming with hope. "Imagine investing in future generations, an academy of music, run by Philippe. You've seen for yourself what a gifted teacher he is, how the children love him. A seat of musical learning would be a wonderful gift to posterity, and you could take an active part in it."

"Think of it as a kind of living legacy," I add.

"A living legacy . . ." Delacroix repeats this, trying on the idea and seemingly finding that it suits her.

Gabrielle continues. "Invest your wealth now, in something you can still enjoy, that you've chosen and believe in."

Delacroix appears close to agreeing, but then her expression fades. "It's a charming idea, but there are no guarantees with this kind of endeavor. Plus, I'm an old woman. I don't have the energy to start a new project of this magnitude."

Gabrielle turns to Monier. "That's where you come in, monsieur."

"Me?" he says. "What does this have to do with me?"

"I know you crave success, that you want to make something of yourself. Let me ask you this: When you are lying on your deathbed, do you want to be able to say, 'I made lots of money'? Or would you rather say that you changed the lives of thousands, perhaps millions of people? Henri lived; your conscience is clear. You can now live a comfortable, guilt-free life, managing this prestigious academy, working alongside Madame Delacroix."

"I don't know about this. I need time to think." Monier begins to pace slowly.

Delacroix regards me calmly. "Whatever's happening here, it's connected to the ghost I saw in the mirror, isn't it?"

"Yes, in a way," I tell her. She nods slowly.

"Ghost in a mirror?" Monier says weakly. "I fear the smoke had more of an impact on you than I first thought."

There are many ways to change the world, and they all begin like this. In any human story, everything starts with a single thought, which can either build or destroy. I feel energy in the air, the weight of potential change, but these two critical players remain undecided. Gabrielle beckons forward a shadowy figure, and the young girl emerges from the darkness and begins to play. The divine aria soars into the night sky, lifting our souls with it. I watch Monier and Delacroix, their faces transfixed, watching this child, this protegee of Philippe's, work magic with her violin.

Gabrielle has become the conductor of Philippe's fate, and this is a masterful orchestration. She listens for a few minutes, then addresses Delacroix and Monier again, more softly now. "The two of you will build a school that gives children skills and a future, as well as a home. Philippe will find new purpose by teaching there. And the impact of that school will be your legacy, all three of you, a chance to redefine who you are and how you will be remembered."

Delacroix and Monier look at each other. The foundations of Philippe's future are solidifying before our eyes. Something wonderful just happened. A seed has been planted. Monier takes Madame Delacroix's hand and kisses it. "Like a phoenix from the ashes, we will emerge," he says.

She smiles, then looks at me. I feel barriers of time, language, and culture melt away. In reality, we are separated by more than one hundred and fifty years, yet here in this moment, we are connected by a shared purpose. I think Delacroix feels this too, and she exhales loudly as a single tear rolls down her cheek. "So shall it be."

Gabrielle emits a muted sound, somewhere between a yelp and a whoop, and winks at me. "We did it," she mouths. I can't see her watch beneath her sleeve, but I guess she's just felt it vibrate to indicate that the mission is complete.

We're about to say our goodbyes when I spot the seamstress inside the brasserie. "I just want to have a quick word with Marguerite," I tell Gabrielle. "Tie up loose ends, you know?"

"No problem," Gabrielle says. "We've got time."

I pass through the crowd of people drinking wine and swapping stories. Marguerite sits at a table on her own. I want to put her mind at rest about seeing Nils in the mirror, but how?

"Hello," she says, recognizing my face from when she interrupted our meeting with Philippe in his quarters. "How are you, monsieur?"

"I'm fine, thank you. It's good to see you again," I say. "Listen, I've heard a few people talking about seeing a ghost and, in case you saw anything, I wanted to explain." She studies me nervously, but I know she's intrigued. "He was actually a friend of mine, and I know this might sound crazy, but he was trapped in a kind of limbo. I wanted you to know that I managed to help him. He's gone home now. You won't see him again."

"I see," she says, hesitantly. "I'm going to be honest with you. I saw him, and I've been worried. Thank you for letting me know that he's all right." She sighs and her shoulders drop.

"What's your name?" I ask, recalling that our original meeting in the restaurant no longer happened.

She blushes. "Marguerite. Marguerite Lenormand."

"Good luck, Mademoiselle Lenormand. The new opera house will be looking for a talented seamstress like you, I'm sure. I wish you well."

When I get back outside, Gabrielle is leaning peacefully against the brasserie window, watching the young girl as her performance draws to a close. Together, we bid goodbye to the opera manager and the heiress and leave them talking to the young girl about her dreams for the future.

"Feels good, doesn't it," Gabrielle says, taking my arm for a couple of strides, "wrapping up a mission like that, especially when it's not obvious how we're going to land the plane."

"It does," I agree. Connections that were tenuous and fragile now feel solid, hardened and fixed, and I feel instinctively that this stretch of time won't open up again. It's reassuring to know that it can't be meddled with. It's written. Done. "You were amazing, Gabrielle. I watched them melt under your powers of persuasion."

Much to my astonishment, she blushes, apparently unused to having anyone remark on her work but seeming to appreciate the validation.

"Cheers, Bridgeman. And thanks for your help too. You were a small part of it." She looks at her watch. "We still have a while before we go back. Fancy a bit of a look around?"

"Can we?"

"I keep telling you, we're allowed to enjoy ourselves occasionally."

We wander silently along streets now eerily peaceful, soaking up Paris for the last time. The distant fire is a dirty streak of glowing amber on the clouds above us.

"They were already building the new opera house, you know," Gabrielle tells me.

"Yeah, I think I knew that."

"The Palais Garnier," she says. As we round a corner, we see the huge building, its stonework shrouded in sheets. "It opens two years from now, and at the time, it was the world's largest theater and opera house. It's still standing—in our present, I mean."

"I can already see that it's going to be magnificent." I'm struck by the pattern of life, the cycle of death and birth in everything.

"Sure is," Gabrielle says. "Right, come on, we only have twenty minutes left. There's one more place I want to go before we leave. Here, carry this, would you? It's weighing me down." She rummages underneath her skirts, peering between swathes of fabric, and I avert my gaze until she waves a bottle of champagne in front of my face.

"Where did you get that?" I ask, examining the flamboyant, hand-scripted label.

"The brasserie," she grins. "I kid you not, we could make a fortune selling vintage champagne if we could carry enough back with us." She lifts her chin and, putting on her British accent, says, "But that just wouldn't be cricket, would it, Bridgeman?"

A few minutes later, we arrive at the Pont Neuf again, and I follow Gabrielle to the center of the bridge. She pops open the champagne, takes a drink while it's still foaming, then offers me the bottle. I take a hefty swig, and the deliciously dry effervescence of the alcohol makes my mouth fizz. "You deserve it," she says. "You did well for someone so . . . I don't know, *normal*."

I ignore her jibe and take another drink. "Monier and Delacroix seemed convinced back there, but how can we be sure they won't forget about the music academy in the days to come—you know, just change their minds?"

"Listen, dude, you have to trust the watches. They won't tell us a mission is complete if it's not. They report back on the actual future impact of the events we're witnessing, so I can tell you with absolute certainty that it's done. That conversation set them on their path. Sometimes that's all it takes. An intervention."

We stand in companionable silence, watching the rowboats moored at the side of the river bobbing in the gentle night breeze.

"Do you think Nils will be OK?" I ask.

"I hope so. We'll find out for sure when we get back."

I draw in a long breath. "I lost the lantern."

"You did what?"

"That's not all. Scarlett turned up."

Gabrielle scowls. "You're telling me this now?"

"We haven't exactly had a chance to talk about it."

She capitulates. "Yeah, fair enough. I don't know why I'm surprised. That bitch is always one step ahead. What happened?"

I talk her through losing the lantern, and how Scarlett arrived with a device I recognized, and updated Nils's watch. "I didn't have a choice. I had to let her do it."

Gabrielle takes a long slug of champagne. "I understand. All we can do is hope she didn't send him off somewhere else. Look, you did everything you could. Whatever happens now, it isn't your fault."

"Thanks."

Gabrielle is a complex bundle of feisty contradictions, but sometimes, I almost like her. She smiles, a genuine grin, and we hold each other's gaze for a few seconds too long. Her face contorts inward. "Hey, don't get any ideas."

"Oh Christ, you and me? No way!" Gabrielle looks slightly offended by my fervent denial. "No offense, but that just wouldn't work."

She looks as though she's discovered a bad taste in her mouth. "You're too skinny for me, anyway." She chugs some more champagne and winces. "Do you have someone? Special, I mean?"

I raise my eyebrows. "Kind of. Maybe. I hope so."

"Ah. Work in progress, huh?"

"You could say. How about you?"

She laughs. "Nah. Divorced. Twice. Time travel makes it tough to keep a life in the present. People get suspicious."

"How do you cope with all of this?" I ask. "I mean, this has been one crazy trip. I thought we were going to be lost in the fire, and then I nearly drowned. It's going to take me weeks to get over this. And a fortune in therapy."

She smirks. "Tell me about it. At one point earlier this evening, I had to use a piece of furniture to redirect a stream of molten lead so that me and the boys could get out of the opera house. But I've gotta say, not all missions are like this. You've been unlucky, Bridgeman. Frankie Shaw, and now this . . . It's been a baptism by fire for you, pun intended. Give yourself a break, Golden Boy. It takes time to process things, but I think you'll be fine."

She offers me more champagne. I decline, so she downs the rest of the bottle. "Time travel is amazing, isn't it?" she says, slurring slightly.

"It is."

She turns to me. "I mean it. It's special. You never know when all this will be over."

"That's pretty morbid. Aren't we supposed to be basking in our success?"

"No, no, no!" she grumbles, sounding like she hates me again. She's like a coin, happy on one side, then she flips herself. "I don't mean *dying*. I mean, you never know when it might be your last jump, when your gift might leave you . . . *whoooooosh*." She looks to the sky, like she's let go of a helium balloon and is watching it float away.

"What do you mean, your gift leaves you?"

She sighs. "Oh, my little Golden Fool. I forget you don't know anything." She stares out over the Seine. "We all have a certain number of jumps in us, but no one knows how many. One day you wake up, and you just can't travel anymore. No more psychometry, no objects calling to you, no people to save. It all just stops, like an old clock, and you're done."

"That sounds . . . terrible," I say, wondering how I'd feel if I couldn't read objects anymore, never had another viewing, couldn't go back and set someone's timeline straight. "Don't you get any warning? Doesn't The Continuum know when it's going to happen?"

"Nope." Gabrielle lifts the champagne bottle for a few final drips, but it's empty. "Time travel gives you purpose and fulfillment. It's a drug, straight to the vein. At first you resist, then you get hooked, then suddenly it stops. Make the most of it, man. Enjoy the view." She waves a drunken hand at the scene before us.

I gaze out, marveling at a thousand cuts of reflected fire dancing over the Seine, orange clouds scudding across the burning sky, flutters of ash drifting down like tarnished snow, and I do as I'm told. I enjoy the view.

34

When I wake up the next morning back in Cheltenham, back in the present, my face is creased and crusted with smoky drool, and my head is thick and foggy. I wonder why I'm awake, and then I realize that the annoying whine I can hear isn't tinnitus, it's my mobile phone.

I bring it to my ear without lifting my head from the pillow, growling a croaky "Hello?" It's Gabrielle. She's heard from Iris that the Paris mission was successful, and Nils landed safely home in Oslo. "Anyway, I just wanted you to know, we did good. All is well. I'll love ya and leave ya, Bridgeman. The Continuum will give us a proper debrief in a couple of days. Now, go back to sleep, Golden Boy." She hangs up, and my face cracks into a grin. When you get used to her, she's not so bad.

After texting Amy and Vinny to let them know I'm back safe, and telling Molly I've been afflicted with a bad head cold and won't be at work for a while, I spend the next two days lounging around. Nothing I have experienced can compare to the adrenaline crash and subsequent exhaustion after a mission. The mental, physical, and emotional toll, combined with a sort of jet lag, is unavoidable.

I get up only to feed myself some effortless basics (soup, bananas, herbal tea) and answer the call of nature. Otherwise, I sleep, and when I can't sleep—because of the flashbacks that periodically race through my mind without warning—I rest, drifting in and out of consciousness, reliving the fire, the heat, the confusion, and the key moments that changed everything. I still feel like there's an elephant on my chest, and I don't think any of my nostril hairs survived, but all in all, I'm grateful to have escaped one of the scariest adventures of my life.

On the afternoon of the third day, Amy comes around with a load of oranges and grapes. I tell her that a basket of fruit makes me feel like an invalid from a crappy 1970s TV show, but she says not to be ungrateful and insists the vitamins will do me good. I fill her in on my final trip to Paris. When I tell her that her painting of the eagle and the hand saved not only my life but Nils's too, she gives me a massive hug, and I don't mind saying that we both have a bit of a cry.

Amy is better than the last time I saw her. Miles is in Spain for a few weeks on a climbing trip, but she doesn't seem worried, and it sounds as though Sue's keeping close tabs on her. She tells me she's still painting, but less frantically, and the subject matter is more run-of-the-mill: landscapes, beach scenes, that kind of stuff. I'm still hoping that at some point she'll take the plunge and try to sell some of her work.

After she leaves, I take out the letter from future Amy and read it again.

The younger me, the one that's living in your time, is entering a difficult period in her life. She's going to need your help, although she's not always very good at asking for it. All you need to do is be there for her, for me, like you always have been. But please, don't mention this letter to her. Not yet. She isn't ready, and the effect on the future could be catastrophic. Be patient and try not to worry. She will eventually catch up with her destiny and find light in the darkness.

Iris told me it won't be long now. She couldn't tell me exactly what Amy's destiny holds, but some kind of change has got to be better than these cycles of ups and downs my sister's been through. All the great masters say that pain leads to growth, and I hope that it won't be too long before Amy and I can both look back and understand the purpose of all this turmoil.

Feeling much better after one of Amy's oranges—maybe she's right about the vitamins—I give Vinny a call and invite him over for a drink after work. He's so excited to hear about the mission, he closes his shop immediately, and twenty minutes later he's on the sofa in my study with a beer in one hand and a bunch of grapes in the other, pulling them off the stalk one by one with his lips like a monkey, and looking at me expectantly.

"Come on then, Cash!" he says. "Spill the beans! Fill me in! Tell your Uncle Vin all about it!"

I tell him the whole story from beginning to end, with as much color and flourish as I can muster, and by the end of the tale, his face is rapt.

"I can hardly believe you did all that, mate," he says reverentially. "Man, you were so brave. Were you scared?"

"I didn't really have time to be," I tell him. "There were split seconds, I suppose, when I was terrified, but things were moving so fast, I just had to make snap decisions and get on with the job." I take a sip of my beer. "To be honest, I've felt worse since I got back. I keep reliving the craziest bits and getting palpitations."

"Completely normal, mate," Vinny reassures me. "Your brain's just processing stuff now because it didn't have time to while you were there. It's like when you eat your third pizza when you're already full, and you know your stomach is going to have to deal with it later, you know?"

"I think so."

"It'll get better, but if it doesn't, promise me you'll see someone about it, yeah?"

"OK," I tell him, though I'm not sure that talking to someone would help much, with the added strain of trying to remember which bits not to say. I wonder if The Continuum offers a counseling service.

My doorbell rings.

"I'll go, stay there." Vinny jumps up and leaves the study. I hear voices in the hallway, then Vinny returns. "You've got a visitor, Cash," he says, face flushed. "A VIP." He's followed into the room by Gabrielle, wheeling a large suitcase. She's in her black leather jacket and jeans, with a neckerchief knotted around her throat in a black-and-white skull-and-crossbones pattern.

"Bridgeman!" she says. "Woah, you're not looking too hot. Really knocked the stuffing out of you, didn't we?" She grins, pulls a packet of cigarettes out of her handbag, and sticks one in her mouth. "Hope you don't mind." She offers one to Vinny, who takes it, looking starstruck. I've never seen him speechless before.

"Actually, I do mind," I say, wondering what on earth would possess someone who's just escaped a burning building to smoke. "You can do it on the balcony."

Gabrielle scowls and turns to Vinny, holding out her hand. "Sorry, we haven't been properly introduced."

He blushes. "I'm Vincent Fry—er, Vinny."

"Vinny? As in the guy who helped out with the Romano mission? Who didn't do too shabby a job on the Paris research either?"

Vinny blushes deeper. "Er, yeah, that's me. It wasn't a big deal, really." He shrugs nonchalantly, but I can tell he's ecstatic.

"Well, Vincent-Fry-Er-Vinny, thanks for all the amazing work you did. You really helped us out. Cute shirt, by the way." Vinny looks down at his chest. The print features a small Vinny's Vinyl logo above an illustration of the evolution of man, from knuckle-grazing ape through three stages to *Homo sapiens*. The final stage is the outline of a rock guitarist shredding.

"Glad you like it," Vinny says. "I sell them in my shop. I can get you one, if you like."

"I'd love one!" Gabrielle enthuses. "Send it to me care of *Rolling Stone* magazine in New York, OK? Don't forget to include your email address so I can arrange to pay you back." I've never seen Gabrielle be this nice to anyone.

"You don't need to pay me," Vinny says. "It's a gift. I'd be honored just to know you're wearing one of my shirts."

"Ain't he the cutest?" Gabrielle says to me, winking. Her wristwatch buzzes, and she suddenly snaps back to attention. "Right, Bridgeman, time for our wash up with Iris and the gang. Hey, Vinny, you were a part of this mission too. Wanna join us? I know you'd be welcome for the debrief."

Vinny looks genuinely conflicted. "I would love to, but I've got an appointment." He looks at me. "I'm going to meet Charlotte."

"That's fantastic, Vinny!" I say.

"Charlotte's my daughter," Vinny explains bashfully to Gabrielle. "I've never met her before—long story—but she's the only thing in the world that could keep me from joining a conference call with the future." He looks really disappointed. "D'you think there'll be another chance to join you all?"

"For sure," Gabrielle says. "No worries, man. Good luck with the offspring. Hope she's nicely disobedient."

"Good luck, Vin," I say. "Let me know how you get on."

"OK," he says. "Miss Green, it was an honor to meet you. I love your work. That piece you did on Keith Richards blew me away. I hope to see you again."

He backs out of the study, half bowing like a servant exiting a throne room.

"Later, Vinny," Gabrielle calls after him. We hear the door to the fire escape slam shut, then Gabrielle turns to me. "Surprisingly good taste in friends, Bridgeman."

"You're right. He's awesome. Shall we?"

I lead the way up the backlit stairway to the loft. Gabrielle takes off her watch, twists the back, and sets it down on the coffee table. The tiny green lights take off and scan the room, taking their places in the far corners and mapping our positions. Then, two forms appear: first Iris, then Kyoko. Kyoko bows slightly, arms crossed at the waist, her hands hidden inside long, loose sleeves.

"We're in the gardens," Iris says. "It's a beautiful day here. Would you like to join us?"

Gabrielle turns to me. "So, Bridgeman? Think you can handle it?"

"Let's do it."

The lights in the corners of the room flash, cycling through the colors of the rainbow more and more rapidly until they are shining bright white light into every crevice of the loft. Gradually, I find myself standing outside, in the sun, on a lush and neatly manicured lawn. A nearby fountain splashes and gurgles, and a low hedge surrounds a formal garden that leads to a three-story stone house. Its facade is stern and imposing, softened only by a flight of stone steps that rise from the garden toward a dais adorned with statues and small potted trees.

"The hedge demarcates the edges of the physical space in which you and Gabrielle are standing," Iris explains. "As long as you don't try to go outside of it, you will be fine."

It was dark when I visited Felix inside, and our other meetings were in small rooms. Being outside is a whole new experience. I look around in wonder. The ground feels hard under my feet, not spongy like grass, and there's no air moving on my face, but the illusion is nearly complete.

"Wow," I manage to say.

"Eloquent," Gabrielle fires back.

Felix comes trotting down the steps from the house and joins us. "Gabi, Joseph," he greets us. "It's good to see you safely back. Nils is on his way. He'll be arriving any minute now."

"Check it out, by the fountain," Gabrielle murmurs to me. I look to my left and see Nils's form take shape. He's had a shave and haircut and a few good meals since I saw him last, and he's dressed in a three-piece suit with his tie loosened.

"Greetings to you all," Nils says, beaming at Iris, Felix, and Kyoko in turn. "I know everyone here was involved in bringing me back, and I will be forever in your debt." He turns toward me and Gabrielle. "I am so happy to see you both under more auspicious circumstances. I do not know how to thank you. You encouraged me when I thought all was lost, you kept trying when things got difficult, and you saved my life."

I'm not sure what to say. "Don't mention it, Nils. I'm just glad you're OK."

He shakes his head. "If you ever need anything, you will ask me to help, and if I can, I will. Agreed?"

I'm a bit taken aback by the ferocity of his insistence. "Agreed," I say.

"Good." He folds his arms and turns to Iris. "Now, I need to know. What is the plan? Scarlett messed with my watch and sent me into the void, but then she came to Paris, reset it, and sent me home. She could have left me lost in the void forever, but she didn't. I have racked my brain, but I cannot for the life of me understand what she is trying to do. Do we have any further intelligence?"

"We do not," Iris confirms. "However, Kyoko, you said you have an update on Nils's watch?"

Kyoko addresses Nils. "Scarlett reset your watch, which enabled you to return home, but she also wiped it. We have no data from your trip after Macau."

I'm struggling to follow this. "How does this data thing work, then?"

"Observation directly impacts time," Kyoko says, "but a traveler's whereabouts, timing, and resistance are all measured directly by the watches, to be analyzed later."

Felix says, "The fact that Scarlett wiped Nils's watch means that when Nils got home, there was nothing for us to download. Makes life pretty difficult." He rubs his forehead. "Still, I want to recognize Kyoko's excellent work on the watch updates and the lantern. Kyoko-san, you had no reason to doubt yourself."

"The facts please, Felix-san," she says. "I knew my work was sound, I merely doubted the chances of success."

Gabrielle harrumphs. "You can say that again. We got through it by the skin of our damn teeth. I just wish I understood what Scarlett wants. It's been keeping me awake at night. I keep running through everything that's happened, trying to work out what her game is."

"I'm working on a way to establish her whereabouts," Kyoko announces. "You and Joseph-san were near enough to Scarlett, for long enough, to provide powerful data, and the lantern has also given me interesting readings."

"That's fantastic news," Felix says. "Please keep me posted."

Kyoko bows. "If I may go and continue my work?"

"Of course," Felix replies. "Thank you, Kyoko-san."

She bows to the rest of us and walks back toward the house.

"I would like to share with you the impact of your mission, Gabrielle," Iris says, "which is one of my favorite jobs."

"Go for it, boss," Gabrielle says, nudging my elbow. "I love this bit."

"This was an exceptionally impactful mission," Iris says. "With the financial support of Madame Delacroix and the business acumen of Dominic Monier, Philippe went on to set up a school, the Chevalier Academy of Music, along with a trust fund supporting annual scholarships, allowing children from poor backgrounds to attend the academy at no cost. They called it the Phoenix Scholarship."

"Great name," Gabrielle says approvingly.

"Philippe's students spread music like a benevolent virus, a positive tsunami that rolled forward through time and touched millions of lives."

"What happened to Madame Delacroix?" I ask.

"She was heavily involved in running the school," Iris says. "Numerous reports and diary entries showed that the students loved her. She lived another fourteen years, to what was a very good age in those days. Dominic Monier married and had children of his own. He wrote a memoir in his later years, illustrating how his values had changed. He cited the night of the opera house fire as the first day of his new life. The book explained that at one time he had been driven by money and notoriety, but as he witnessed the impact of the school, how many lives had been influenced for the better, he realized how much more fulfillment he garnered from his work with the academy than he ever had with the opera."

Gabrielle beams, and it suits her. "That's got me pumped," she says. "I love it when we help people grow like that. There's no better feeling."

"You did a great job, Gabrielle," Iris says. "Your hard work and dedication in the face of severe adversity set Philippe on his rightful path."

"More than once I thought we were done for," Gabrielle says. "Obviously, it pains me to say this, but Bridgeman helped piece it all together. I couldn't have done it without him." She turns to me. "Fair play, Golden Boy."

Hiding my shock, I say, "It was good to be a part of it. But I'm still wondering about Henri. Presumably, the first time around he was trapped under the stage and died in the fire, and he wasn't the focus of our mission. How come we were allowed to save him?"

Gabrielle bobs her head. "What we can and can't change is rarely straightforward, but it's often the small stories with low observation. Philippe's original injuries happened when he went back inside to save Henri. Their fates were inextricably linked. By getting involved in that part of Philippe's story, we ended up saving Henri too. Sometimes, we just get lucky and resistance doesn't stop us."

"Right." I grapple with the fact that we really aren't in control of what we can change. This time it worked out for us and for Henri, but I imagine there will be times in the future when we're not going to be so lucky. I hope I can handle it.

Felix steps toward me. "Joe, I want to reiterate my offer. Assuming all of this hasn't put you off time travel for good, I'd like to give you the tour of Greystone House and show you Downstream."

"And I'd like to tell you more about how we work," Iris adds. "If you'd like to know."

I'm not sure what to think. The echoes of Paris are still reverberating through me, and the thought of more adventure right now is about as welcome as a root canal.

Gabrielle nudges me. "He'd love to, wouldn't you, Golden Boy?"

"Don't push him, Gabi," Felix says. "Take your time, Joe. No need to decide now. Just think about it." He smiles his slow surfer's grin and puts his hands in his pockets. I'm not sure I've ever come across such a laid-back genius. I decide there and then that I like him.

"Meanwhile, what's coming up next?" Gabrielle asks Iris, rubbing her hands together.

Iris's expression is calm, but there is a hint of concern. "I think we might give you a short break before we send you off on your next adventure."

"I'm fine, I don't need time off!" Gabrielle retorts. "Things are quiet at work, so knock yourself out if you've got a mission that fits my profile. The thought of being stuck at home with nothing to do . . ." She shivers. "Come on Iris, empty your pockets. What've you got?"

"It's time for a break, Gabrielle," Iris says again. She turns to me. "Joe, before we wrap up, tell me: How does it feel to have saved Nils and helped set Philippe on his path?"

I'm not sure how to answer that because my feelings are complicated. I'm proud of what we achieved, of course, but the last few weeks have been such a roller coaster, I still don't feel like I've had a chance to process what's happened. I'm starting to realize that what I'm involved in isn't just about time travel, it's about people and their stories, and what feels like a much bigger picture than I could have imagined when I traveled for the first time.

Iris waits patiently. I offer her an apologetic smile. "It's hard to take it all in," I say. "But you're an amazing team, and it was good to be part of it."

"You used your skills well. And adjustment after traveling always takes a little while," she says kindly. "Give it time."

"What about Scarlett?" I ask.

"As soon as Kyoko learns more about how to track her, we will let you know. Meanwhile, keep your wits about you. I doubt Scarlett will approach you again, but use your intuition and do not let down your guard. And if you have any more viewings . . ."

"I'll be sure to let you know," I finish.

"Excellent. I'll be in touch in the next few days. Meanwhile, take a break. Be present. Spend time with your friends and family, people you love."

Iris warns me to prepare myself for another adjustment, then she presses a button on her watch, and the garden, Iris, Felix, and Nils dissolve into my home in Cheltenham.

"Woah," I say, grabbing onto the bar just behind me.

"You'll get used to switching out, like everything else," Gabrielle says. She pats my arm. "D'you remember what Felix said before the final jump, that Bill would be proud? He would, you know. And so am I. You did good, Bridgeman. You were brave. You'll make one hell of a time traveler if you stick with this."

"Maybe, but I have a life at home to consider too," I say. "Like you. Vinny told me you're a music journalist?"

"When I'm not being an active part of nature's immune system." She winks. "I'm a freelance music journo, but I do a fair bit for *Rolling Stone* in New York. The great thing about my job is I can do it anywhere. And people don't worry when I go 'missing.' In fact they expect it. Young, single, and freelance. OK, maybe not that young, but free and single for sure. The best way, man, the best way."

Listening to Gabrielle, I feel sad. That's not what I want out of life. I've spent too much of my life with no one to miss me.

"Hey!" She punches me on the arm. "You're feeling sorry for me. Don't."

"Actually, I'm feeling sorry for *me*."

"You should. Anyway, Bridgeman, on that note, I take my leave. My duty is done, and now, it's time to get back to what I was supposed to be doing before I started wiping your ass all day."

She clatters down the stairs to the shop, and I follow, noticing her signature scent of old smoke, tired leather, and floral shampoo.

As we push through the door into Bridgeman Antiques, Gabrielle says,

"Oh, I just remembered." She undoes her case and pulls out the metronome. "I thought you could put it in your shop, see if it sells, or keep it. Up to you." She hands it to me.

I look at the metronome, remembering the burst of energy that sent us to Paris, the mantel of Madame Delacroix's mansion, watching Philippe teach. "So you don't keep them, then, the focus objects? Store them in a museum or anything?"

"Nah. Once their job is done, we let them go. Like life, man. Don't collect, travel light."

"Thanks, I might keep hold of it for a while and see if I can find it a home."

She taps a cigarette out of a battered pack, pops it in her mouth, and lights up. "You have my number?"

"I do."

"Good, don't call. Unless it's something exciting"—she takes a drag—"that benefits me in some way."

"Got it."

"Just one last thing," she says. "I'm not one for fancy speeches like Iris, but you now have two major missions under your belt. Time has pushed you out of your . . ." She glances around the shop, exhales, and gesticulates. "Your extremely boring nest . . . for a *reason*. You're a time traveler, with a genuine gift. Think it over, man. It's a hell of a life."

"I will."

"And whatever you decide, we'll always have Paris." She winks, her tough exterior melts for an instant, and I see a glimpse of the elusive and vulnerable woman inside. We often see vulnerability as a weakness, but the truth is that strength is about being honest, authentic, and brave enough to show people who we are. I'm learning. Slowly.

I unlock the shop door and hold it open. "I guess I'll see you around then."

"Not if I see you first." And then Gabrielle Green—"temporarily at your service"—stalks off down the street, holding up her middle finger.

EPILOGUE

After a good night's sleep, I wake up feeling much more like my old self. Molly has the morning off, so I wash and dress, prepare a double latte, and enjoy the gentle buzz of my first proper coffee since I got home. I nip down to the shop at about 8 o'clock and find a huge apricot-and-almond fruit-cake on the desk. Molly's been looking after the shop while I recover from my "man flu," and she texted me last night to say she'd baked me something to help me rebuild my strength. She really is the salt of the earth. I drop Martin a note and ask him to increase Molly's pay by 10 percent.

I breathe in the reassuringly familiar scent of leather and polish, the happy, high-pitched percussion of the wall clocks ticking in perfect discord. A dark-haired girl passes outside with a toddler, presumably on the way to the nursery, and she reminds me of the seamstress, Marguerite. I wonder what happened to her.

I could probably ask The Continuum, but I decide to go old-school and see what I can find out for myself. Pulling out the iPad, I do a bit of browsing and discover that Marguerite Lenormand got married a year after the fire and had three children who survived into adulthood. I learn on one of the census sites that she died at fifty-three, an average life expectancy at the time. I hope at the end she was able to say that she had lived her time well.

I have to get used to the fact that we time travelers can only change a very few, isolated events, and that we don't choose them. I don't know why we were asked to change Philippe's life and not Marguerite's. I can only assume, for now, that there's a bigger picture, and that on some scale, all of this makes perfect sense. It's what I'm telling myself, anyway.

The morning whizzes past in a blur. The shop's really busy, and I make several sales, as well as taking in a wooden box of antique hunting and fishing gear from an elderly gentleman who looks like he's spent most of his life outside.

At precisely midday, Molly enters wearing a smart red trench coat, slim black trousers, and black suede pumps.

"How are you feeling?" she asks. "You still look a little flushed. Are you sure you're well enough to be here?"

"I'm fine," I assure her, thinking I should invest in some concealer. "Thank you for the cake. It looks delicious."

"You're most welcome." She hangs up her coat and bag. "Oh, by the way, a gentleman dropped this off for you yesterday afternoon." She pulls a paper bag out of her coat pocket and hands it to me. "A very tall man. Friendly. Charming, in fact."

Reaching inside, I pull out a copy of Alexia and Colin John's book. Inside the front cover, on the first blank page, Colin has scrawled a handwritten note:

She might forget what you said, might even forget what you did, but she'll never forget how you made her feel. Keep the faith and give her a call! CJ

I close the book and smile to myself. It starts at my mouth but ripples through me, inside and out. The message couldn't be clearer if he'd written it in the sky with a vapor trail. There may still be a chance for us.

Me and Alexia.

Molly seems to tune in to the change in my demeanor, and she disappears into the kitchenette. I sit back in my desk chair and watch a couple of sullen teenagers walking past, an empty takeaway carton blowing down the street, jackdaws on the fence arguing over a piece of stale bread. Mundane. Normal. Yet, never has the world seemed more luminous, more promise-filled. I think about Gabrielle, so insistent on working alone, apparently happy to keep her own counsel and company. We're fundamentally different people. I want someone special to share my life with, to eat toast with, watch TV with, climb mountains, put the world to rights, to laugh and cry with. If that were Alexia, it would feel like all my Christmases come at once.

But it's out of my control. Like her book says, love is an output. I can't make Alexia love me. Some things cannot be changed. And yet, as I think back on that fateful evening in Paris, particularly our last-minute chance to persuade Monier and Delacroix to help Philippe, I wonder. Gabrielle's determination, at just the right moment, altered the course of time. Her impassioned speech molded the future, set wheels in motion. It's a reminder that I mustn't give up on the dream that Alexia and I could have a chance. All fires begin with a spark. I just have to look out for opportunities, and when they arrive, I must be brave. I need to shape my own destiny, in the moment, before it's set in stone.

Molly and I have tea and cake, and then I tell her I need to get some air. I stride into the fresh air toward Leckhampton Hill. After a few days holed up, my legs are desperate for some action, and I need to get some oxygen into my smoke-weary lungs.

The hill has played an important role in my life, a marker of emotional milestones. We used to come up here on family walks when I was small, and then after I lost Amy, I would spend hours up here alone, looking down over the town, scanning the tiny houses and miniature vehicles, feeling sure that someone, somewhere, must know where she was and what had happened to her. Much later, when I discovered I could time travel, I jumped several times from the hill, with Alexia by my side. And just before the last jump, the one that worked, this is where we kissed.

I pull my scarf closer around my neck and take a seat on a bench perched on the northwest flank of the hill. Down below, the sprawl of Cheltenham extends out into the valley. Major roads finger their way through the green landscape toward Gloucester, Hereford, and the Malvern Hills, which undulate softly against the distant horizon. Up here I feel huge, and my life seems simple and manageable in contrast.

I remember what Bill said about the sacrifice we make as time travelers, and his words remind me of the strain that my traveling has put on my family and friends. I'm painfully aware of the cost to Amy's mental health since I landed in Other Joe's life. I hope, on balance, it's all worth it.

"Hey! Joe!" A woman's voice calls out, and I look up to see two horseback riders trotting along the path in my direction. From this distance, I can't make out their faces, so I stand up and shield my eyes.

"It's me, Jess," the first rider calls, slowing down to a walk. "From the quiz team!"

"Oh! Hi, Jess! Sorry, I didn't recognize you in all your gear."

She brings her horse to a standstill. She's dressed in a muddy riding kit, long brown boots, and one of those garish skull caps that jockeys wear, in pink and green. Her horse is very big and very twitchy. Horses are regal animals, but I have a policy of not trusting any living being that's bigger than me.

"Just taking in the view?" Jess asks.

"Yes, I love it up here."

The other rider approaches and pulls her horse up a few feet behind Jess. "This is Alexia. Alexia, this is Joe, from my pub quiz team."

"Alexia?"

"Hi, Joe," she says, looking as surprised as me.

"You two know each other? I didn't realize! How come?"

Alexia's wearing jodhpurs, long black leather boots, a black riding coat, and a classic black velvet riding hat with a brown chinstrap. You can keep your horses, but the gear is another thing entirely. She looks gorgeous.

"Joe used to be my landlord," Alexia says.

"Right." Jess obviously senses something because she kicks her horse. "Look, Nutmeg's getting fidgety, so I'll go on ahead and you can catch me up by the farm, Alexia. OK? See you soon, Joe." Jess trots up the hill, leaving me and Alexia alone—apart from the horse.

"How are you?" I ask at the same instant she asks, "Where've you been?"

We laugh awkwardly and fall into silence.

"Do you come here often?" I ask, acknowledging the cliché with a wince.

She laughs. "You look like you've been away, like you've caught the sun?"

"I've been to Paris," I tell her. "It was exceptionally warm for the time of year. I was checking out some antiques, hunting down some missing . . . items."

"Did you have to do that psychometry thing again?" she asks, sounding genuinely curious.

"I did actually. Turns out it works on buildings too."

"Really? That's interesting."

I've become so accustomed to Gabrielle's sarcasm that I wait for a punchline, but I think Alexia really means it.

"So how are you?" I ask her.

She looks out over the valley, distant for a moment or two. She turns back to me. "I'm fine, actually," she says. "Gordon and I split up."

"I'm sorry to hear that," I say, trying to sound genuine.

"It's fine"—that word again—"it's for the best. Although it's a bit awkward, seeing as I'm working in the office next to his. I need to find somewhere else."

"I can probably help out with that," I suggest, with a hint of irony.

"That could be good." She pushes a strand of hair out of her eyes and looks over Cheltenham again. "I've been thinking about what you said about parallel universes."

I can't recall the conversation in detail, so I just wait. I listen.

"I do believe in them, but they don't really matter," Alexia says. "The only one that matters is the one you're in."

"Well, that's true." More than she could possibly know.

"I'll give you a call sometime," Alexia says. She moves her feet against her horse's sides, and they walk past me and head up the hill after Jess. She calls back, "Maybe we could go for a coffee and talk offices and things."

"That sounds good," I say. "I'd like that."

I've spent so much time recently, in the past and in the future, knowing people's destinies. Now, I'm back in the present, and I haven't got a clue what's going to happen next.

And it feels wonderful.

ACKNOWLEDGMENTS

Thanks as always to the team at Blackstone, a thoroughly decent bunch of people to work with. Thank you to my agent, David Fugate, for his continued guidance and support. To my editor, Jason Kirk—@brass-wax—thank you for taking the time to teach me how to fish.

A long overdue thanks to Kate Jewson at Oxfordshire Hypnotherapy, an amazing hypnotherapist and inspiration for all things Alexia. To the team at Jubilee Hall Antiques and Interiors: I popped in to see if you could help me with my research, and three hours later, I left with tons of anecdotes, story gems, and character ideas. To Mum: Remember when I would spend hours playing with my action figures and making up stories? I do that for a living now! Love you with all my heart and then some. To Claire and Dan: your unwavering enthusiasm and support mean a lot to me.

To Microsoft: I appreciate you delaying the console release of *Flight Simulator*—it really helped my word count. To the person who eventually hands one of my books to Stephen King: thanks in advance, you have made my life complete. Bonus points if he likes it—that means I can die happy.

And finally, thanks to you, my readers and listeners, for continuing Joe's journey with me. I read somewhere that a series only really gets going after book three. So buckle up. Joe has a long way to go yet.

AUTHOR'S NOTE

Every time I start a new book, I attempt to reassure myself with a simple truth. I've written a few. I know how to do it now. Right? Wrong. Apparently, it doesn't work that way, for me at least. As I begin to plan, I'm humbly reminded that the process of writing a novel is not something you know. It's something you must learn anew, every single time. Of course, hard-earned fundamentals of the craft remain, but each book is a unique expression of life and, therefore, so is the journey. I appreciate that sounds like a cliché, inspirational poster, but it's true.

In the very early stages, while things are up in the air, I'm searching for familiar signs, something to tell me I'm on the right track. Just like the first three books in the series, I had flashes and ideas, feelings that sloshed around, equal parts fizz, confidence, fear, and doubt.

Let's start with the fizz. I knew, as far back as when I was writing *And Then She Vanished* that Joe was going to end up in an opera house fire. I saw it, clear as day, and I was excited.

All the Joseph Bridgeman books use real events, albeit with a good dollop of creative license. The Salle Le Peletier opera house really did burn down in October 1873, and unusually for the era, no one died. That was the spark of inspiration I needed. What if the miracles we hear about on the news are because a time traveler intervened? It was enough to get the story going. Details like how Joe got there and what needed doing could come later. I just knew it would work, and I was confident it would make a great story. I also knew that it was going to require more research than anything I had attempted before.

That's where the fear and doubt creeps in. Like Joe, I'm not exactly what you would call academic. I can spell F.U.D.G.E. with my exam results and the U (it stands for unclassified) was for history! And yet, here I was, about to embark on a book set in Paris in the late nineteenth century. What was I thinking?! Well, I surprised myself with how much I enjoyed researching the past. I discovered the key to bringing it to life was to allow Joe to be like me, totally out of his depth. If I could lean into that and then populate the past with real people and just focus on what I love the most—telling a good story—then I knew I would be okay.

I don't plan on writing hyper-accurate, historical fiction any time soon. If that's your thing, all good, there are plenty of authors knocking it out of the park. For me, I just want to explore the nooks and crannies and entertain you. I hope this story feels authentic *enough* and transported you back to the era.

Another, most welcome, surprise is how much my partner, Kay, has become an intrinsic part of my creative life. Over the years, with each conversation, tingly idea, meltdown, or creative dilemma, (often discussed over coffee or dinner) we formed a collaborative working relationship that has enhanced this writing life exponentially for me. I feel that this book in particular galvanized our shared vision of what the Joseph Bridgeman novels should really be about. I'm proud of what we achieved here. We worked hard, put in the extra hours, and made something cool.

And so, this book is dedicated to Kay Renfrew. Kay, your name may not appear on the cover, but your energy, words, and wisdom are woven throughout.

Why are we doing this? Because you said yes.

I like to keep in touch with my readers, so if you're interested, please sign up for my mailing list at http://nickjonesauthor.com/signup.

Subscribers receive emails about my writing life and stuff I find inspiring.

You can also follow me in the usual places:

Website: http://nickjonesauthor.com/
Facebook: https://www.facebook.com/authornickjones/
Twitter: https://twitter.com/authornickjones
Instagram: https://instagram.com/authornickjones
Goodreads: https://goodreads.com/authornickjones
BookBub: https://www.bookbub.com/authors/nick-jones

If you like, you can email me at nick@nickjonesauthor.com. I read everything I get.